A Pitch
In Crime

By Raymond F. Quinton

FTNPress
PORTLAND OREGON
© Copyright 2018 Raymond F. Quinton

FTNPress
Publishers Since 1981
2000 NE 42nd, Suite #194
Portland, Oregon 97213
503-933-0120
www.raymondquinton.com
ISBN: 9781981078486

Copyright © 2018 Raymond F. Quinton
All Rights Reserved

OTHER BOOKS BY RAYMOND QUINTON

Afternoon Lunch Guide to San Francisco's Financial District (Guide)

The Layperson's Uncensored Relationship Handbook (Self-help)

A Pitch in Time: Newspaper Carrier Handbook (Guide)

Best Ride Ever! Featuring Oaks Amusement Park (Children's Book)

Change the WorkGame (Business How-To / Editor)

Stop Stuffin' Your Pie Hold: And Lose Weight Today (Self-Help / Editor)

Writing By the Seat of My Pants (Memoir / How-To / Media / Business)

Chapter 1

Chico pumped the bicycle pedals with a focused determination as he cruised through the barely lit residential neighborhood. He smiled as he recalled his latest triumph, an unsuspecting stray Persian cat. He assassinated it an hour earlier. Chico lured the charcoal gray and white feline to his waiting hands with a piece of dried, rotting Bologna and sprung his trap.

He smiled as he replayed the scene over and over in his head; relishing the moment he grabbed the cat by the neck, wrapped his fingers tightly around its neck; tightening his grip, choking the cat as it fought desperately to get free. It scratched, clawed and hissed; finally giving in, and giving up; it's paws falling limp to its side like a furry rag doll, staring at a grinning Chico with blank, dead turquoise eyes. Satisfied, Chico threw the dead cat into the bushes.

It was four a.m. Thrilled by his kill and amped on coke, Chico was cocky and confident. He sniffed and rubbed his nose intermittently as the crisp night air bit at his face and eyes.

Chico froze as he saw the outline of Trixie's dilapidated van nestled in the shadows of the tree-lined street. It sat under a sprawling Oak tree that swayed in the delicate September breeze and partially reflected the yellowish glow of a lone street light. A faint light shone through the curtain-covered windows of the Van. Trixie was there.

Chico approached quietly, cautiously, and slid off his bike with barely a sound. He eased the kickstand down and gently leaned the weight of the bike on it. He crouched, keeping a close watch on the small windows of the van, looking for any type of movement. There was none. He tiptoed to the side of the van, reached out a closed fist and pounded as hard as he could on the door.

"Trixie! Wake up bitch! I need to talk to you!" he yelled as he pounded repeatedly on the door, not caring if the sleeping residents heard the noise.

There was rustling inside the darkened van. Then a blurred face appeared in the sliding door window as the lock disengaged and the aging door rattled open.

Trixie's pale, angelic face appeared in the door. Chico stopped yelling and stared at first, intimidated by her beauty and hesitant because of the uncertainty of his own intentions. It was not Chico's way, after all, to think everything through; to consider the consequences of his actions, or to even think at all. As he stared, he could tell she had been crying. Her cheeks and eyes were red and the tears glistened on her pale cheeks.

Chico swallowed hard, then nervously said, "Trixie, how come you diss me like you done?"

Trixie's intense blue eyes focused on Chico standing in front of her; defiant, hands shoved deep in his baggy khakis. She was apprehensive and still shaking off the night's event. She had never seen Chico this wound up before.

"I know Chico. We have a problem, and I need to talk to you about that."

She stepped down from the van and into the cold night air. She hugged herself and rubbed her shoulders and stood facing Chico, her pigtails flowing over her shoulders and the stud in her navel glistening under the single yellow fluorescent light.

"You know, Chico, I can't do this anymore. I thought there was something I could do to help you, but I was wrong."

"There is something you can do to help me, bitch," Chico said, defiantly.

"Chico I told you not to call me that."

"Shut up bitch!" I followed you today and I—"

"You what?" She interrupted.

"Thas right, bitch, I followed you to that fucking SP fuckin' CA."

Trixie's eyes widened as she yelled, "Chico, you are a fucking asshole. How could you?"

"How could you, bitch," he shot back.

Trixie placed her hands on her hips, and leaned towards Chico. "Chico, what I do with my time is none of your God damn business. You have no right following me you little prick."

Stepping back, Chico yelled, "Look, bitch, I can do what I want. Second, you and the fucking SPCA can kiss my ass, and last, I don't have a little prick."

Trixie almost laughed, but could see that Chico was serious. He took one hand out of his pocket and pointed it accusingly into her face.

"All you got to do is give me my fuckin' money."

"I have my money Chico and you've got nothing!" Trixie yelled. Their voices rose steadily, echoing into the dark night, bouncing off uncaring trees and ghostly houses, with owners sleeping, dreaming as the Trixie lost control.

"Chico, you are a worthless piece of shit. I should have ditched your ass six months ago. If you weren't so pathetic, I would not have wasted my time on you, but I made the mistake of feeling sorry for you and thinking there was hope for you, and now I regret it. You're an idiot, a loser, a prick and, yes, you have a small dick. Fuck off and have a nice life Chico!"

She turned and raised her foot to step back into the van when Chico demanded again, "Give me my mother fuckin' money or I'm going to kill your skinny ass bitch!"

Trixie recognized the sound of a hammer being cocked on a revolver, so she froze and turned her head slowly towards Chico. The small pistol pointed at her head. Trixie stared, not sure what to say, her mind now working on overdrive, careful what to say next.

Nervously, she placed her foot back on the gravel and turned fully towards Chico and said softly, "Look Chico, this is not you. You're not a violent person and I'm the only friend you've got, and—"

"Shut up!" Chico shouted, his legs shivering as he nervously gripped the gun and shifted his weight from side to side.

"Chico, think about what you're doing. Your life is hard now. If you pull that trigger, you can't take it back. If you kill me, you can't just fix it or talk about it or walk away from it. You will have taken my life. And you'll have to live with that. This is not what you're all about Chico."

"Shut the fuck up God damn it," Chico demanded again, "I'm tired of everybody fucking with me. I don't need to be psychoanalyzated by some ho."

Chico gripped the pistol harder in both hands as he tried to steady his arms, but they were visibly shaking and the muscles in his arms flexed and ached with tension as he tried to rationalize what he was doing.

"Chico, I'm sorry about the SPCA," Trixie said, thinking that might calm him. "If you need money that badly, I'll give you some money. But I can't help you when you've got a gun pointed at my face."

Tears appeared in Chico's angry eyes. He didn't blink. She was getting to him and he knew it but tried to hide it. More tears streamed down his cheeks and he shivered as the cooled air washed over him like a shroud of despair. There he stood; tough and ridiculous; intimidated by a girl again.

"Why is everybody always fucking with me," he blurted between sobs, "Why come nobody loves me. Am I so fucked up that I don't deserve love?"

"Chico I love you."

"Bullshit," Chico spat, offended.

Trixie quickly responded, "Chico, I do. But I don't mean it the way you think. You are a human being Chico and in spite of your faults, you have a soul, a conscious, and you deserve love. I love all people, including you."

"Trixie, don't bullshit me. I've had a hard mother fucking day. Mother fuckin' cats all over the place. Spyin' on me. Wrecked my bike fuckin' followin' you bitch and got a bunch of prickers in my ass too. Don't you fuckin' fuck with me no more!"

"I mean what I say Chico," she said, straining to sound sincere, "When have you ever known me to not be honest with you?"

Snot streamed down Chico's nose as he wept openly. Through his tears, Trixie appeared as a diffused watercolor ghost, outline barely visible, and the features of her face hardly discernable, but her presence was overwhelming for him, more powerful than the cheap crack he snorted daily. He knew he probably wasn't strong enough to make good on his threat. But he could scare her as much as he could. This was his only advantage. This was all the power he had.

When the flash hit Chico's eyes, it lasted only milliseconds. But those were the milliseconds between reality and unreality, and seemed to last forever. The sound arrived seconds later, a thunderous clap that stabbed at his ears and made him flinch.

Trixie blinked. A reflex. A single thought. Scream. No time. The bullet entered Trixie's forehead between her delicate brows. A dark, red hole appeared. It exited out the back, splitting her head open and spraying the red and white goo that was her brains, hair, and blood throughout the interior of the van.

Her body went limp and she dropped to the ground like a puppet that lost its puppeteer. She lay there, face upright, legs and arms contorted in unnatural positions; her eyes frozen open, staring up to the stars, up at nothing.

Chico's eyes bulged in horror as he looked down at Trixie's lifeless body. The night air became solid. He could not breathe it. He felt as if he were under fifty feet of water, his body wanting to suck in oxygen, but fearing his lungs would be flooded with wet, salty death.

His stomach convulsed and he covered his mouth instinctively. He fell to his knees as putrid vomit leaked between his fingers. Someone just dropped an anvil on his gut then jumped on it for good measure. He thought his insides would rupture and he would die right thereon the spot.

What have I done? What have I done? The question screamed in his head as he wiped his hands on his pants and focused again on Trixie's body. Her blank eyes still stared up at him. His only friend was dead. This was not supposed to happen. *What do I do? Money. Get it. Got to hide. Get it. Got to Run!*

Chico stood quickly and stepped over Trixie's body then into the van. He covered his nose with his sleeve trying to avoid the coppery smell of blood and his own vomit. He avoided looking at the remnants of what were Trixie's head and brains scattered inside of the van and focused on finding any money she may have hidden.

He lifted the small mattress that sat on a diminutive fold-up bed and found what he was looking for, several crumpled hundred dollar bills. As he grabbed the bills, he saw a book lying next to them. He picked up the book and crammed it in his pants, thinking there might be bills stashed in it. He frantically shoved the money into his pocket and jumped out of the van, stepped over Trixie's body again, then ran around to the front of the van, and darted into the street.

As he entered the street, he was blinded by two bright, white lights as a vehicle screeched to a halt inches away from him, nearly pulverizing his small, stocky frame.

Panicked, Chico stood in front of the vehicle and stared, paralyzed by fear. There he stood, as if on stage at Carnegie Hall in the headlights, gun in one hand, hundred dollar bills in the other, running away from the dead body lying at the side of the van with a bullet in its head. This is fucked up he thought and he instinctively pointed the gun where he thought the driver's head would be and pressed the trigger.

No sound. No shot. Gun jammed or misfired. Nothing came out. No time to think about that. Chico turned and ran towards the opposite side of the street, and disappeared into the darkness.

Chapter 2

The alarm went off at 2:30 a.m. sharp, jolting Rich out of a deep, short-lived sleep. He forced his eyes, which had been sealed shut by three hours of restless sleep and corner crust, open and slowly focused in on the angry green glow of his combination alarm-CD-clock radio. Andre Previn's version of *Ain't Misbehavin'* played softly through the small speakers, which was the only thing that kept Rich from hammering the evil apparatus into a thousand pieces.

He reached over and slammed his hand down hard on the snooze button; almost knocking it and the ten-deep stack of murder mystery novels that cluttered the top of the night stand to the ground. He retreated under the covers and drifted back to sleep, only to be jolted into half-consciousness again by a bony elbow in his ribs.

"Wake up, Rich," a familiar voice said softly, "or you'll be late again."

Rich sat up slowly, forced his eyes open and looked around at the darkness, unable to see anything recognizable except the neighbor's bright, obnoxious, yellow safety light beaming into his bedroom window.

Next to him, he could hear the rhythmic breathing of the voice that prevented him from slipping back into a comfortable slumber, the voice of his alter-ego, his wife of ten years, April, an efficient, pretty brunette with emerald green eyes and a practical streak that far exceeded his.

April automatically woke up when his alarm went off, and if Rich drifted back to sleep, she was there to remind that it was time to wake up with a jab or a polite "honey time to get up."

April would not allow him to slip again, as he had done so many times before. She could not afford to. They needed the money from this job. Even though it wasn't the job she imagined him having, it was better than nothing.

Chapter 3

Chico de la Toro Espinoza Hector Juan Carlos Garcia hated his name. It reminded him of all the, aunts, uncles, parents and grandparents in his life he despised.

Chico's day started at midnight to the minute in a roach-infested studio apartment on 42nd Avenue and Alberta Street, across from the Tidy-Didy diaper plant that often flooded the neighborhood with the acrid smell of rotting diapers and chlorine.

Chico rarely noticed the smell though. The years of cocaine snorting had killed every nerve in his nostrils and the smell from the diaper laundry only complimented the incessant smell of rotting food and moldy cloths.

Chico sat up in bed and eased his legs over the side, tapping the ground gently, feeling for his slippers with his big toes. Not too quickly.

Chico walked carefully to the switch on the far wall. He could hear the popping sounds as he squashed the fat roaches under foot. He could also hear the barely audible tick-tick of tiny feet as thousands more crawled over every surface in the room.

As he reached the entrance to the bathroom, he flicked on the light. Behind him, the small brownish dots scurried under the bed, behind the kitchen counter, under the piles of dirty dishes in the sink. There were so many, he could actually hear them shuffling behind and inside the cabinet and walls.

"What the fuck!? Little son of bitches," he said, with a slight Spanish accent, an accent he'd struggled to lose most of his life, with no success.

Chico was born in south central Los Angeles to Mexican immigrant parents. He spoke fluent Spanish and English, but lacked the vocabulary to use either effectively. He had been in Portland, Oregon, for close to a year, to find a better life he convinced himself. Anywhere Chico went would be a better life than where he was. He had screwed every person he knew; his fellow gang members, his family, his friends, and even his pets. The IRS, the DEA, the FBI, civil courts, the DMV, and the SPCA all had open files on him.

To add insult to injury, Chico was even being sought by PBS, the malevolent public television station network for making outrageous pledges to get gifts then refusing to pay.

Chico was sure no one would ever think to look for him in Portland, Oregon. As far as he was concerned, everyone in south central Los Angeles thought there were no drugs in Oregon, only pale, sickly-looking white people and hippie nature girls with hairy arm pits and granola for brains.

Chico walked into the small closet-sized bathroom, pulled his underwear down and peed into the bowl, making sure not to miss the unfortunate cockroaches hiding there.

He glanced at his reflection in a mirror over the toilet. The hair net he wore every night held his slicked back, jet-black hair in place. His rounded Aztec face was a constant annoyance to him. He thought Mexicans were stupid for letting the Spanish steal all their shit and fucking up the Mayan worrier gene pool.

Chico grinned and leaned his head back slightly. He admired the stocky frame that supported his rounded, flat head, particularly the muscular upper-body with defined tattoo-covered arms and a thick wrestler's neck.

Chico considered himself intimidating, so he kept his muscles permanently flexed and furrowed his forehead incessantly, bringing his thick black eyebrows closer together over his beady, angry brown eyes, like the pictures of Mayan worriers he'd seen. That worked for some. But for most, however, he was just too short to be intimidating, barely exceeding five feet in height.

That pissed him off too.

"Little fucking assholes. How could you be so fucking stupid to hide in the pisser? I got you little son of bitches," he said with a sneer.

He finished peeing, then smirked and puffed up his chest like a boxer who'd just won the world title. Chico was on top of his game. He had killed fifty roaches and he'd only been awake for fifteen minutes.

He walked to the refrigerator and opened it. Lining the three small shelves were cans of Coors Lite, about fifty in all. He took one out, pulled the metal tab, and, feeling a rush of anticipation that first drink caused, he quickly brought the cold can to his lips and began gulping the contents, grunting as he forced each mouthful down.

Some of the beer overflowed from his mouth and ran down his cheeks, down his chest, tickling him slightly and making his nipples and his penis erect. He finished the last of the beer, exhaling loudly as he placed the can on the counter.

Chico sucked in his stomach and let out a belch that was loud and long.

"God damn piss water taste good in the morning," he said. "Where's my fucking blow?"

He couldn't remember where he had put it and looked around the room nervously, like a groundhog on a mound, scouting for predators. He spotted the little glass cylinder with the black top and the silver linked chain on the coffee table, along with 15 razor blades, some crumpled 10-dollar bills, and a stack of big tit magazines.

He walked quickly over to the table, sat on the smelly, second-hand sofa. He unscrewed the small container and tapped a small amount onto a mirror, then meticulously arranged the powder into three short strips. He rolled up a 10-dollar bill, shoved it in his nose, plugged one nostril, and sucked up the cocaine through the other. One after the other, the lines of cocaine disappeared up his nose.

Chico sat erect and tense, eyes blinking like a chicken in a slaughterhouse. "Son of God damn bitches!" He spit out loudly as the pain shot through his nose and into his brain. "Son of God damn mother fucking bitches!" He screamed.

He stood up and paced the room, slapping himself on the sides of the head with both hands until the pain subsided. Within minutes, Chico was on top of the world, surging with power, sexually aroused and ready for something, anything.

He reclined on the couch, pushing aside dirty underwear with exposed skid marks, and smelly, tattered muscle shirts to make room. He opened one of the magazines, *Latin D-cup Babes*, turned to the centerfold, and begins fondling himself.

"Goddamn fucking bitch. Mother fucking goddamn big fucking tits. Suck my mother fucking cock you bitch. Make me shoot my mother fucking wad bitch," he growled, gripped and massaged his erect penis. He flipped the pages faster and cursed louder and jerked his penis until it erupted on the magazine.

"Son of bitches," he groaned, dropping the magazine on the floor as his entire body went limp. He closed his eyes and absorbed the power.

This was Chico's morning ritual, and he was very meticulous about it, performing this routine almost exactly the same way every morning of the year, with few variations.

After he recovered and wiped the spunk off of his underwear, he dressed for work, not bothering to shower, only stopping in the bathroom long enough to splash several large handfuls of Brute onto his face and chest.

Chico was oblivious to the sweat, cologne, sex and beer stink that wafted from his body. It didn't matter. He was pretty. He was a pimp. He had an important work to do and he was going to do it. And he was going get paid. He had expenses.

He slipped on a pair of baggy khaki pants, his Nike high-top sneakers with the pump ball, sneakers that had cost him two hundred dollars. He pulled on a white muscle shirt and his gold chain with the crucifix dangling on the end. He grabbed his oversized, hooded coat, slipped on a stocking hat with a Raiders patch, and he was ready for work.

When he opened the door, the cool September morning air hit him like a cold shower. "Son of bitch," he mumbled to himself as he fumbled in his coat pocket for the keys to his transportation. He closed the door behind him and walked down the concrete stairs that led to the parking lot of the apartment building. His footsteps echoed in the empty night.

From a distance, his transportation reflected the light from the single lamp that stood sentry. He admired it; dew glistening off its chrome bumpers and white wall tires cleaned to perfection.

He walked up to it, stood next to it and stared. His transportation was a 20-year-old Schwynn 15-speed bike with a kryptonite lock holding it secured to a light post. This was Chico's pride and joy, his coupe de ville. He made it a point to tell everyone it had 15 speeds, not 10. And he waxed it every weekend and sprayed Armorall on the tires.

He carefully unlocked the bike, shoved the lock into his pocket, climbed on and pushed himself into the parking lot. He shifted gears, pressed on the peddles and glided into the street, off to find the key to his enterprise and his fortune, Trixie, a young, innocent runaway, one of those hippie girl with hairy armpits he had claimed to have turned out at age 16.

Chico was not happy with her. She wasn't giving him as much money as she used to and he was convinced she was holding out on him, maybe doing too many drugs.

"She needs to leave that shit alone," he said as he considered what to do when he found her. He had to teach her a lesson.

He rode into the night, cocky and confident, as if he was driving a Rolls Royce Silver Shadow. Pimping, petty theft and drug dealing, he thought, are honorable professions, only undertaken by real men, no putas. And he knew that if anyone fucked with him he had back up. The last item he retrieved before leaving his apartment was ten-inch custom made Al Mar retractable switchblade with pearl handle and inlaid tortoise shell pattern that said Chico's Peacemaker.

Fuck everybody, he thought, as he glided onto 42nd avenue and began casing the neighborhood. Chico was the big cock of the Cully neighborhood, one bad ass mother fucker.

Chapter 4

After Rich's eyes fully adjusted to the dark, he stepped out of bed and walked to the bathroom. When he flipped on the switch, his eyes squinted at the brightness as he leaned over the wash bowl and focused in on his face.

Still a Negro after all these years, he thought, not disappointed, not impressed, just simply observing. His beard was cut in a goatee, and his thick, slightly grayed mustache was balanced above two full lips; thick "African" lips he liked to call them. His eyebrows were heavy like Bob Marley; family trademarks from his mother's Jamaican side, and he, of all his seven older brothers, was the only one who, at 40, still had a full head of hair on his head.

He examined his hair more closely, using his index finders to make a small part so he could see the roots. It was still jet black with hints of grey scattered throughout, hardly noticeable from a distance. Not bad looking, he thought.

As he stared into his almost black pupils, he thought about the contrast of what he saw and how he envisioned himself. He pictured himself as a Woody Allenesque, nerdy hypochondriac. But every morning he looked into the mirror he saw someone who looked more like a cross between a short Denzel Washington, a not so black Wesley Snipes and a not as skinny Tommy Davidson.

That's probably why, he thought, his wife had fallen for him. They had met in San Francisco ten years ago. He was a social chameleon and successful book and magazine editor. It wasn't love at first sight or anything close. He was far too preoccupied to think about love and marriage seriously. But they fell in love and married.

As far as Rich knew, they were still in love two kids and 10 years later. But that fact didn't qualm his insecurities. Though a perfectionist and a dynamo at every job he's ever had, his publishing missteps sometimes gave him the impression that she thought he was kind of a fuck up. And sometimes, he thought he was too.

But what great men, he thought, have not fucked up every now and then. He shook off that notion and focused on the stranger who stared back at him in the mirror.

He opened his mouth wide to examine his teeth, leaned closer into the mirror, and stared deep into his eyes again.

Coon he thought. Nigger, spear-chucker, jungle bunny, Uncle Tom, darkey. The words rolled through his mind like memories of familiar friends. He mentally shouted these words every morning. It helped him wake up, like a cold shower. As he did so, he thought of his Catholic grade school classmates and how they used to call him these words like they were doing him a favor. "You know Rich," they would say, "you're okay. You're not like the others. You're one of the good niggers."

He smiled. These comments came from perfectly normal kids, from perfectly normal Catholic families, in a perfectly normal small town in Kansas. The only problem was that these kids were all perfectly fucked up as far as Rich could tell.

He was almost awake now. He was still black. He was still alive. And he wasn't half bad looking. He could have coffee now. He turned and walked towards the stairs near the bathroom door, flicking off the light as he passed through the doorway.

It was pitch black again. Only a faint night light glowed from downstairs. Before he reached the first step, his toes collided with a Tonka rescue helicopter that had been strategically placed to end his life. Pain shot through his big toe as if someone had pounded it with a hammer and he angrily yelled under pursed lips, "God damn it! Little rascals! Trying to kill me again"

He ground his teeth, and growled a low guttural growl, thinking he'd deal with the children when they woke up.

Rich kicked the rescue helicopter aside and went down the stairs to the kitchen where he quickly made a thick, sludge-like, substance that resembled coffee in a single, Zen-like motion. Coffee secured, he walked to the den, a small bedroom towards the back of the house; his Sanctuary, and the only room in the house where the children were *not* allowed to touch anything.

He flicked on a small banker's lamp on the desk. The green glow filled the room immediately. Then he pressed the switch to turn on his computer. The light was like a welcomed friend. He was very particular about the lighting in this room. No overhead lights, only small incandescent bulbs in strategically placed lamps to cast shadows and color on every element in the room.

Rich opened the door to a small closet and took out his uniform, a pair of musty black sweats, thick hiking socks, two dark cotton shirts, a black slicker, his black Reel.com baseball cap with white sweat stains over the bill, and a pair of well-worn Sketcher ATS shoes. He called the shoes all terrain shoes because they were wide, flat, leather, and not Nike.

This is what he wore every morning of every day of every month to deliver the morning *Oregonian* newspaper. He'd been delivering for six months and the job suited his current situation.

The computer beeped, signifying that it was booting up. It was almost three a.m. And he only had a couple of minutes to get to the station before the newspapers were delivered. There was time to get dressed, have one more cup of sludge, and drive the seven blocks to station number nine. He wanted to check his e-mails before leaving, but decided to wait until he got back. He headed for the door.

Chapter 5

Trixie transported herself to somewhere else; anywhere but where she was. She didn't want to think about what she was doing. She didn't want to think about the reasons that she was doing what she was doing. She didn't want to answer any questions. A beach. That's a good place. A safe place. She could hear the rumbling of a newly forming tide in the distance and the splashing and gurgling of a spent wave gliding back out to sea and crashing into an incoming wall of green, foamy water.

She tried to maintain this vision as long as she could, but was pulled back. Pulled back. Back, back by grunting and creaking as the shock absorbers strained to stabilize the old van as a hulking, figure bore down harder and harder onto her delicate frame, trying to reach that point of ecstasy; oblivious to the sounds and the noise and the pathetic, desperate scene he was creating.

He was grunting and sweating on top of her, forcing his hairy stomach between her tiny legs. She opened her eyes just as a large bead of sweat fell from her nightmare's head into her eye, stinging like hell as if a needle had been stuck in her eye, causing her to flinch and squirm under the hulking body.

"Shit, Delbert," she screamed, bringing her hands to her eyes to block the dripping, "wipe the fucking sweat of your head before I go fucking blind!"

"Oh, I'm sorry Trixie," he said, tentatively and in between breaths; pausing to look at here face. "Are you okay, honey?"

There was no sincerity in his voice and just a hint of frustration. Trixie knew he just wanted to finish like all the others before him.

He grinned at Trixie and said, "Remember to call me daddy not Delbert." He shifted his body on top of hers. "I'd rather you not use my name."

"I'd rather not go blind you sick fuck," Trixie screamed, pissed that he was more concerned about his name than her eyes. "Get the fuck off of me you fat fuck!"

She pushed at his chest. Her fingers seemed to melt into his flabby breast like putty. He grunted more as he pushed his bulk up and rolled to the mattress beside her. He had been pounding away at her for an hour. She'd already earned her money, she thought, and done what he wanted and what she intended to do.

She stared at him under the dull, single, overhead light. She despised him. He was a regular customer and insisted on having his way with her multiple times, and spraying his cum all over everything; on here ass, beside her ass, in her hair, in her mouth, on here underwear, in here hand, in a wine glass. Then he expected her to lap it up like some kind of trained dog.

"How's daddy's little girl," Dilbert said, propping his head up on one hand and smiling through uneven teeth at her, almost proud of himself and his performance. His breath smelled like whisky and Banaca.

"Daddy's little girl has your sweat and cum all over me, God damn it. And I'm ready to get the fuck out of here."

"It's okay honey, daddy will take care of you."

"Okay Delbert—I mean daddy, I know you'll take care of me." she said "You'll take care of me by giving me my money so I can get the fuck out of here too?"

"Okay, honey," Dilbert said, still grinning, "Just let me get my cloths on and I'll pay you. You're so good to me. I love you honey."

Dilbert labored to pull his mass to an upright position and slide it towards the edge of the bed and to the floor, landing hard and causing the van to shake and rattle.

"You're a fucked up daddy," she said under her breath as she rolled her eyes, sure that he heard her but not really caring.

While Delbert collected his clothes and dressed himself, Trixie lay back on the mattress, naked and feeling violated. She looked up at the ceiling of the van. There was nothing to focus on except the air vent on the ceiling and a light and her unlikely home on wheels.

The van had been her home for almost nine months. She bought it neighborhood drug dealer and fencer named Barclay who lived two blocks away with two dogs, mountains of trash, beater cars, and car parts covering every corner of his yard. It was a piece of crap of a van, she thought, a 1978 GMC camper that had been fitted with a platform bed large enough for two people. It had a small propane stove, a fold-up table, a chair set made from cheap plywood, and it was paneled like a tacky basement cocktail lounge. The van barely ran, so, all Trixie had to do was move it a block every few days so it didn't get ticketed and towed as an abandoned vehicle. It wasn't much, but it was home.

As Delbert finished dressing, Trixie became even more aware of the stinking collage of sex, sweat, perfume, and expensive aftershave lotion.

She glance at Delbert. He was putting his shoes on. She could only think about how she hated everything about him; the shiny bald spot of his fat head, the white Van Husan t-shirts he wore under his white pressed button-down Tommy Halfiger shirts. Why do old white men wore those God damn stupid looking white v-neck t-shirts under their seventy-five dollar shirts. Was it to keep the pit shit off their expensive shirts? And she was disgusted that he even wore white boxer shorts, underwear that should have never been invented. If underwear was to protect men's balls, she thought, what's the point of boxer shorts?

Trixie had been seeing Dilbert once a week for three months. She had figured out that he was some kind of insurance company executive and this was the one thing he looked forward to every week of his seemingly normal but fucked up life. He called her his little girl and paid her a thousand dollars an hour for any kind of sex he wanted. The sick part, she thought, was the reasons why he did what he did. He had confided in her that he had to do this so he would not be tempted to appease the sick sexual attraction he had for his 14-year-old daughter. He didn't want to destroy his perfect family, tucked away in a five hundred thousand dollar house in Lake Oswego.

Dilbert's kinky streak even surprised Trixie at times. She thought she'd seen it all. Dilbert sometimes brought his daughter's cloths and asked her to dress up in them. Sometimes he videotaped their sex acts. And sometimes he got a little rougher then Trixie was comfortable with.

Dilbert slipped on his slacks. His, pale, bulbous stomach hung over his belt like a sack of potatoes, and he seemed not to notice or care. He pulled up his knee-high, black nylon socks and slipped on well-worn wing tip shoes, slightly sloped from supporting his 300 pound bulk. He was breathing loudly through thick, black hairs that protruded from his nostrils.

Dilbert was fully dressed. There was not enough room in the van to stand fully upright, so he leaned forward slightly as he moved around. He opened his wallet and pulled out ten hundred dollar bills and placed them on the mattress.

"Thank you Trixie," he said, smiling and reaching for the door latch. Trixie said nothing.

He turned towards Trixie and said, "I'll see you next week."

Trixie sat up quickly and spit at him, "Fuck you Delbert! Get the fuck out! You can go to hell!"

Delbert sheepishly opened the door and stepped out into the night air, closing the door timidly behind him. This was how they ended most sessions. This was their sick ritual. This is what turned Delbert on. This is what kept him coming back. Coming back for more.

It was after three a.m.; early for Trixie. She had time to go for a walk, maybe get something to eat. She had to get away from the stink and the memories of Delbert, let the night air cleanse her.

Trixie was five foot seven and very petite, with all the curves in the right places. She had long sandy, reddish blond hair that she wore hippie-girl free style. She looked like a freckle-faced teenager, pretty, with turquoise green eyes, pouting lips, and full rounded breast with perky, puffed, pink nipples that made men dream of sneaking a peak or squeezing them just to say they had the privilege.

Trixie had no problem finding high-paying regular clients. She'd done her homework. Johns loved the fact, too, that she never shaved her armpits or pubic area, and the light hairs that proliferated there attracted regulars who were turned off by the shaved, silicone enhanced, sickly, aging hookers who walked the streets.

Few of the street hookers had her natural schoolgirl looks. She felt she had another advantage too. Here fake ID said she was nineteen, but Trixie had only turned eighteen two weeks earlier. But who needed to know, she thought, as long as she could earn money to eat and support her habits, and continue her mission, she was fine.

Chapter 6

Rich walked out the front door to the green Toyota pick-up truck parked on a gravel driveway beside his house. For a loser, he thought, he'd done some things right over the years. Their Craftsman style home built in 1920 had an impressive wrap-around porch that ran the length of the front house. This was their second Portland home, each one purchased at a bargain price and sold at an respectable profit.

The only setback he could see was a tiny pumpkin orange colored ranch-style house, that, during daylight hours, seemed conspicuously out of place. It sheltered the Peasleys, a family Franklin considered Jerry Springer escapees. Their idea of landscaping was a 1978 rusted and brown Camaro with flat tires all around, no engine, and a spare transmission on the side. Next to it was another Camaro that had been converted to a NASCAR racer and sat on a trailer in the middle of the yard.

Axles, brake drums, oil pans, and 40 ounce beer bottles littered the yard, and the grass was almost as tall as a young boy.

In the house slept Jim Peasley and his delinquent son Jack, an eighteen-year-old idiot savant who had, he estimated, the IQ of a pea pod. Both, he concluded, had demented family values and a warped sense of place. Rich and April feuded constantly with the Peasleys about the trash, the beater cars, the engine tuning at all hours of the night, and—worst of all—the death rock Jack and friends listened to as loud as possible whenever the mood struck them.

Rich would not let thoughts of the neighbors spoil this moment. This was his time, the early morning time when everyone else was sleeping…the world was at peace right here and now.

Condensation covered everything, and the air was filled with the aroma of Great Americans, Gypsies and American Beauties, roses that grew prolifically around his yard without much pampering.

Rich wiped the condensation off the windshield, placed the keys in the ignition, turned the key, and the truck roared to life instantly. He pushed the gear in reverse, backed out of the driveway, and drove to the station.

Chapter 7

Chico cruised up Alberta street, pumping the bike pedals slowly, listening to tick, tick, tick of the chain and the sound of the night. He thought about all the things he had stolen from houses or cars he had burglarized in the past months along this street. He was proud of his accomplishments. He had stolen stereos, camcorders, rings, watches, diamonds, Gameboys, and even big tit magazines.

There was only one house in the neighborhood that Chico could find nothing of value to steal. The thought of it still made his blood boil. Chico neared the same house, which only made him think about vengeance. The house was a small, red and green bungalow. It was owned by an organic, athletic, Eddie Bauresk couple who loved to take frequent weekend jaunts to recreation spots around the northwest.

"Mail order catalog lookin' mother fuckers didn't have shit," he said out loud as he passed in front of their house. He coughed up a thick green loogie and spit it onto the window of the Honda Accord parked in front.

He broke into their bungalow a month earlier and, after an hour-long frantic search, couldn't find anything of value to pilfer. He was stunned by this revelation because the couple drove a new Honda Accord *and* a new Mitsubishi Isuzu Trooper. Chico didn't get it. No television. No jewelry. Nothing. All he found was wind surfing magazines, wind surfing gear, wind surfing posters, Hood River travel brochures, and Eddie Bauer mail-order catalogs. The only thing he could figure was that they spent all their money traveling and reading.

Educated mother fuckers, he thought.

Frustrated and wanting to leave the house with something, Chico settled for a package of condoms he found on the upstairs dresser. If he couldn't find any valuable shit to take, he figured he could always use some condoms.

This was Chico's logic. He was angry about investing his time scoping the house, studying their schedule, then breaking in when he was sure they were gone for the weekend. He found absolutely nothing he could fence or pawn.

In retaliation, on his way out of the house, he stopped in the dining room—which had no dining room table—to crudely scribbled a note on a piece of paper he fished out of the recycling bin. On it he scratched: *cheep son of bitches. Why don you buy some shit so I can steel it. If you were here id kick your mother fuking asses. I took you motherfucking condoms and I'm going to use them to fuck my girlfriend. Fuck you!"* He signed it *the theef.*

Chico smiled as he thought about the note, sure that no other mother fucker had ever done such a bold thing. He rode on, like John

Wayne on his trusted steed.

Alberta Street was one continuous street that took up seven full blocks. Most houses were 30 feet off the main street and were of varying styles and sizes, bungalows, shotguns, Portland's, Cape Cods, and some Craftsmen. There were no sidewalks, so front yards were filled with grass, shrubs, flower beds, or long unpaved driveways. Many had rusting beater cars for decorum.

It was quiet at one a.m., and, as Chico rode, he made mental notes of potential new victims. He had a talent for judging which houses to hit by casing car types, number of cars, toys in the yards, and types of bicycles.

Young, childless couples with expensive SUVs—stupid utility vehicles he called them—were his favorite. In Oregon, he observed, these people liked to go camping, hiking and fishing, shit he'd seen on television. He couldn't imagine himself out doing that shit. But he saw their follies as his opportunity.

The really stupid people, he thought, were the ones who left boats on the side of the house all God damn winter, then packed it on the SUV the night before they left for a week of fucking around in the woods. In fact, Chico was surprised burglars didn't line up in front of certain homes and draw lottery tickets to see who got to take shit.

Stupid mother fuckers were just inviting thieves to hit their homes. Chico smiled again. He was smart. He didn't need no college to figure shit out.

Stealthy shadows of feral cats criss-crossed the street in front of Chico; most scurrying under the shrubs as Chico approached. Then, one white cat stopped near the edge of the street as Chico passed and stared at him in defiance. Chico sneered when he saw it. He turned towards it and sped up, standing as he pumped the peddles, picking up speed quickly, thinking he might be able to run over the cat before it could dart back behind a stand of shrubs alongside the road.

But the cat's reflexes were too quick. It turned and dashed under the shrub, looking back only briefly as Chico bore down on it. Chico could see the glow of its eyes reflecting the street light, like a demon in the night, before it disappeared. He pressed hard on the hand brakes and the bike groaned to a stop just before he would have smashed into the thick rhododendron bush where the cat vanished.

Chico sucked in air deeply and blew out warm air that puffed like powder in the chilled air and disappeared not far from his face. He wheezed as he struggled to breathe. The short dash for the cat caused sweat to form and stream down his forehead. It had been a while since he exercised.

"God damn mother fucking cats," he said, spitting the words while struggling to suck in air, "I'll get all you son of bitches. You fuckers owe me some shit for what happened in LA. You fuckers owe me!"

He remounted his bicycle and continued casing the neighborhood. His legs burned and he was weak from exerting himself. His Nikes kept slipping off the pedals as he struggled to keep the bike balanced and moving in a straight line. He rode like a 4-year-old who'd just had his training wheels removed.

It took a full block for Chico to recover enough to refocus on his task of finding Trixie. He turned on 47th street and rode up to Going. As he turned onto Going, he saw Trixie's Van.

Chico stopped a half a block away from the van and scanned the area. Parked behind the van was a pristine new Jaguar. Chico had never seen this car before and didn't know Trixie had such high brow clients. He decided to keep his distance and watch for a while. He got off his bike and pulled it into a driveway. He used the tip of his shoe to release the kick stand, then took the kryptonite lock out of his coat pocket and locked the bike to a thick branch of a nearby shrub. Have to protect my shit from thieves, he thought.

Chapter 8

Rich drove the dark, deserted nine blocks between 42nd avenue and 51st avenue, turned left onto Prescott Street, and parked in front of the tattered one-story building with the faded, peeling sign that said OREGONIAN DISTRIBUTION STATION #9.

A late model BMW truck idled in front of the building. Clouds of white smoke puffed from a vibrating tailpipe, while a double-chinned, overweight man wearing well-worked Oshkosh overalls and checkered shirt wheeled stacks of newspapers down a clattering aluminum ramp and through the opened front door.

Two new mini-vans, a partially rusting Ford LTD, a pristine Lincoln Continental, and a ford Taurus with no hub caps, several pronounced dents and rust spots were parked in front of the building.

Rich turned off the engine, rolled down both his windows. As he did so, they squeaked like squeegees as small waves of water accumulated on the rubber and flowed down the corners of the window, some overflowing over the top of the glass as it disappeared into the door.

He stepped out of the truck into the cold night air after finishing the second window and walked towards the building. He stopped to grab an Albertsons shopping cart, observing the advertisement for a local realtor staring at him from the back of the basket's fold out child seat.

Not today, he thought. The cart bounced and shook as it rattled along over cracks and gravel in and on the sidewalk on the way to the front door.

He entered the propped-open front door of the building and was hit with the familiar, pungent, toxic smell of drying printer's ink.

Several carriers stood in front of an improvised plywood shelf that was hip-high and covered the full length of the square room. Each carrier was spread four feet apart. They carefully pulling newspapers from the four-foot high stack perched on the shelf. They folded them, shoved them into plastic bags, and tossed them into the shopping carts.

Rich's bagging station was to the left, inside of the front door. Three hundred papers were stacked there, ready for bagging. He walked to the shelf, glanced around, then took the first paper from the stack, folded it in half, then again, then into a perfect tube.

He knew that even though he started after all the other carriers, he would still finish before them. After all, he had perfected the folding *and* stuffing process.

The faint sound of a toilet flushing came from the back of the office. The door opened and Jimmy Davis, the station allocation manager, limped into the room and over to a desk near the front door. The pungent fumes from last nights dinner followed Davis to his desk.

Davis arrived at the station hours before everyone else. He opened the doors, checked the add/delete list, fielded complaints and parceled out papers to each carrier's station.

Davis, who looked every day his 64 years old, could play the roll of an African American grandpa in any commercials and movies. He had a well-trimmed graying afro and matching Cab Calloway mustache. His attitude, however, would kill his chances of winning any leading roles. The distinct limp that caused him to walk like the mummy from those old horror films didn't help either.

"Morning Jimmy," Rich said, glancing in Davis' direction quickly, than back to his papers.

"Mornin'," Davis said, not bothering to look up, "paper came early this morning. No inserts, pretty light."

"Just the way I like them," Rich said, "Seen Ted this morning?" Rich asked.

"No, I ain't seen Ted yet," Davis responded, "but he's on his way. Roger called in sick this morning, so Ted got to come in and do his route. When you're the boss and people don't show up, ain't nobody else to throw the route. I talked to him earlier and he ain't happy 'bout that."

"Didn't last long did he?" Rich asked, knowing that when a carrier called in sick that was pretty much the end of his career.

"Bout a week. Didn't think he would last that long. He was too pretty for this, probably likes to eat good, chase tail and sleep in late," Davis said, a bit of envy in his voice.

"Well, not everybody's like you Jimmy. You been at this for thirty-five years. This is your life. Most people who do this now have other lives."

"Yep. You right. Almost thirty-six years and never missed a day. I'd still be pitchin' if that car hadn't hit me. Crazy son of bitch."

Davis paused, contemplating his memories of the accident.

"But, you know these young people today can't handle pressure or risks, what with their other lives and all. They want everything easy. Not willing to work hard for it. When I was ten years old I had three jobs and had to feed my mother and seven brothers and sisters. And I never complained."

"I know Jimmy. We're too soft today, right?" Rich said, having heard Davis' story before. "People today just haven't suffered enough. In the words of the old Negro spiritual, 'nobody knows the trouble Jimmy seen.'"

Davis laughed with Rich. "Damn straight, chief. Nobody knows the trouble I seen; three wars, 10 kids, civil rights, and 100 million newspapers later—"

Davis paused again. "You know, most of you people ain't gon make it," he said, glancing quickly over his shoulder at the other carriers who silently stuffed newspapers into plastic bags and tossed them into shopping carts.

Rich knew Davis was right. Before he stuffed the next paper into the bag, he looked around at the other carriers. It was eerie how quiet it was; the only sound outside of their muted conversation was that of papers sliding off the stacks, crumpling folding, the crinkling sound of paper being forced into their tiny tubular baggies. The last sound was of the distinctive rattle of the paper landing in the shopping cards alternately.

Rich rarely spoke to the others, but he felt he imagined their lives and situations based on overhearing conversation and eavesdropping on cell phone conversations and judging them by their cars.

He mentally did a quick character sketch of the other carriers as he folded papers.

Peter Sharp, route 24, was a 68-year-old retired executive. Medical bills, a few bad investments and inflation forced him to get an extra job where age was not a factor. His Lincoln Continental, which was to be used to tour America with his now deceased wife of 40 years, was taking a beating but he kept it in tip-top condition for trips to the coast...alone now. He was one month into this and liked the physical activity.

Alice Friedlander, route 6, was a mother of four, unskilled but hard working. Her husband's alcoholism and drug abuse had tapped the family bank accounts and forced her to leave him, then leave her children with her grandparents in the mornings and take on a route. She waited on tables during the day and sold Avon to friends in the evenings. She kept to herself, preferred to toss her papers slowly, and the solitude allowed her time to think about her problems and try to figure out what to do about her ballooning size. Her 1988 Ford Taurus blew a gasket, had two flat tires and had a close call with a garbage truck during her route. The eight hundred dollars she made pitching papers wasn't much, but she was thrifty and since there were no taxes taken out, she could do far better at this than at most temporary jobs. She was determined to find her way back.

Roger, route 14, was done, a no show, and one other carrier was late. Rich called him Africa. Africa was Rich's favorite, a charcoal black Nigerian who spoke some kind of derivative of alien, African and American. In six months, his blue Hyundai Sonata had morphed from a new car to a demolition derby pace car. On some mornings, he strayed into other carrier's neighborhoods and nearly missed colliding with them because he got disoriented and strayed from his own route.

Where was Africa, he thought.

It was 3:15, and Rich had a half an hour to fold and bag 300 papers, load his truck and hit his route. Time to get serious.

He spread his feet wider apart for balance, he took a deep breath and picked up his pace.

Seconds later, he heard a loud muffler outside the station, then the sound disappeared as quickly as it came. A car door opened and slammed closed immediately.

Africa.

Africa stormed through the door of the station, stomped over to Davis and stood within inches of his face and started yelling, "I nno I you pepple cooono lee um spada infffrnna d guud dammmmdoo! Wadddis sheeeet mannn!"

Africa was fuming about something, but Davis could not understand what exactly he was saying. Africa's arms were flailing about in the air and his shoulders were hunching up and down in between waves, like some strange ancestral dance. He was a sight, this black, peeved shadow of a man screaming unintelligible gibberish.

"Im na goona keep put up wid dis sheet evy dooddamn mornnni man? Why is de people dem keep paakin dem auto inna front inna my spot." Africa said, leaning into Davis' face now, beads of spit danced with every word as they leaped from his mouth.

"What the hell you talkin' 'bout buddy," Davis said, "ain't nobody got no reserved spaces. Everybody got to fend for themselves."

Davis backed away, fanning his face, "and, man, when was the last time you brushed yo teeth?"

With that comment, Africa huffed and puffed like a grouse in full mating ritual, threw up his hands in disgust, then turned and walked quickly to his station while repeating, "I kant figga out you amerikan and why pepple wont leave a place to pak dem kar so dem kan do dem job,"

He continued to rant to himself, though not quite as loudly, but steadily as he started bagging papers.

Hot on the heels of Africa was the station manager, Ted Pimber, a tall skinny, balding man who looked like a younger version of Bob Newhart. When he entered the door, his eyes were blazing red from too little sleep and too much pot.

"Mornin' Jimmy. How's it lookin' this morning," he asked, stopping by Jimmy's station and checking the start, stop and call-in reports.

"Mornin' boss," Davis said, handing him the stack of white papers. "Not too bad. Roger's route needs somebody and Africa is at it again." Jimmy pointed a thumb at Africa and snickered. Pimber grinned as well. They both knew the drill. Africa was not perfect, but he showed up, finished the route every day and allowed them to bill the newspaper…everybody got paid.

"Mornin' Rich," Pimber said, walking over to Rich and handing him three sheets of paper. "Looks like you got another perfect run yesterday."

"Mornin' Ted," Rich said, trying not to breath too hard for fear he might get a contac high from Pimber's army field jacket. Pimber's jacket absorbed so much weed over the years it qualified as high grade weed.

"Did you expect anything less?" Rich asked?

"Nope," Pimber replied quickly. "You were trained by one of the best."

Pimber laughed as he said that, knowing full well that Pimber was one of the worst carriers that ever lived. Rich thought about his training, which consisted of two days of driving up onto people's lawns, dropping the papers out of the window and speeding away.

Pimber could do a route faster than anyone alive because he never got out of his van and could field all the complaints that came in. He didn't really care as long as the route was completed so he could bill the publisher.

"You're way ahead of your time, Rich," Pimber said, a God damn paper pitching prodigy, and I appreciate that."

"Right," Rich said, rolling his eyes as he took the list from Pimber and perused the sheets. Two new stops, one drop and no misses. He had reached newspaper carrier nirvana. He committed the new stops to memory, tossed the list aside and continued bagging as Pimber walked past him to Africa's station. Pimber attempted to calm Africa down. Rich could overhear a little bit of the conversation.

"How's everything going, Steve," Pimber asked, almost laughing as he said the name, which did not fit the man who stood before him.

Steve's real name was Mamello. When he applied for the carrier job he told Pimber he was a doctor and a prince and that his name meant "patience." But because he said he had little patience for arrogant Americans, he chose the name Steve to fit in.

Pimber didn't really care. He had seen doctors, lawyers, and smelter workers, everyone imaginable come through his doors. He knew if they were pitching papers, most were either unemployable, mentally unstable, or a little of both. Mamello (Steve), he concluded, was a little of both.

Steve launched into his tirade, "Ima gonna quit dis job if I kan fine a plaze to pak." He did not look up at Ted, and angrily stuffed papers into bags and slammed them into the cart as he spoke.

"Are you okay with doing your route this morning?" Ted asked," speaking slow as if speaking to a 4-year-old and trying to sound concerned, careful not to set Steve off any more than he already was. "Your car looks fine. But you're parked in the middle of the street. You might want to go move it."

Africa slammed another paper into the cart. "Das wut am talkin' aboudt. If I kan pak my auto in da spott out deer, how is I kan get de papas to de peeple out der? Hows dat?" he asked, acting as it every word was spoken in the King's English and showing Ted his back in defiance.

Pimber, not wanting to provoke Mamello any further, patted him on the back and said, "you're doing a great job, Steve. Keep up the good work. I'll see what I can do about getting you a parking spot in the mornings. Steve, I've got to do a route this morning, but I'll talk to you later."

Steve didn't respond. A prince did not need to.

Rich took the first batch of papers to his truck. He threw them through the open window into the back seat of his extended cab. The two small seats behind the passenger seat filled quickly. He went inside and bagged the remaining papers and repeated the process two more times until papers filled the back seats and the passenger seat.

It was 3:45, time for flight check.

As Rich sat in the driver's seat, he scanned the dashboard, then, after flicking on the overhead light, he pressed the button to turn on the emergency flashers. For show. He turned the ignition key and the 283 horsepower, six cylinder, Japanese built truck roared to life and began purring. He had 300 papers crammed in the cockpit, and all systems checked. It was showtime.

Rich removed an unlabeled disc from a black CD holder he kept in the truck. Scratched on the CD were the words PITCHER'S TRACKS. This was, he thought, the music that made him great, the rhythm of the night, and kept him on time and on track.

He placed the disc in the player and queued track one. The

familiar bow, bow, bow, bup-bup-bup, of Herbie Hancock's synthesized bass filled the cockpit. *Chameleon*, Rich thought, would set the pace.

He set the volume so it filled only the cab. The level indicators on the CD danced back and forth, looking like a futuristic, sophisticated data transceiver. Rich monitored the levels closely because he didn't want to disturb customers. He pulled the consul-mounted gearshift into hyperdrive, turned off the overhead lights, and turned the headlights on. Time for Rich's run.

Chapter 9

After Delbert closed the door, Trixie listened intently to his footsteps as he walked passed the side of the van to his car. She heard the muted whoop as he turned off the alarm, opened the door, slammed it shut and started the engine. Every muscle in her body went limp as the purr of the engine and crackling of rocks under the wheels diminished into the night.

She was alone again.

The dim light barely illuminated the interior of the van, and she thought about how miserable this existence was. Suddenly feeling dirty, she stood up, reached down to the floor near the bed platform and picked up a plastic container of water. She grabbed a roll of paper towels hung over the small inoperable sink, tore off five sections, took bar of soap from a shelf under the paper towels, then wet the towels and began to frantically clean herself.

She reached over and pressed the play switch on a small, silver boom box on the sink counter. The haunting sound of McKinley, a local singer she loved, filled the van, quickly changing Trixie's mood as she wiped her hairy armpits carefully and cleaned between her legs, throwing the paper towels away and methodically tearing new ones off. She wanted to wash every bit of Delbert's grotesque presence off her body.

The small cabinet that held her personal toiletries wasn't much bigger than a shoebox, crudely built of plywood, and was painted dirty brown to cover the years of smoke and grease stains from years of transients and campers who owned the van before her. Inside was her shampoo, combs, brushes, deodorant, and her most valuable possessions, her scented oils.

She removed a small two-inch tall, unlabeled glass cylinder with a black top. She opened it and held the opened area close to her nose and inhaled deeply. She closed her eyes and all her cares and worries melted away for an instant as the scent of China Rain flooded her nose like misty, sweet, ice water. When she opened her eyes seconds later, sadly, her worries were back.

She put some China Rain on the tip of her finger and lightly touched here neck in delicate, graceful strokes, making sure to slide her finger from the back of her ear to the tip of her chin.

The perfume's flowery scent reminds Trixie of her secret, late-night cleansing visits to Multnomah Falls where she bathed naked in shallow, misty, fresh-water pool at the base of the 300 foot tall waterfall. She would often hitch rides there during summer months and stay in the hotel for a night, than sneak out at night before the tourists woke up.

This is one of my many little secrets, she thought. *I may be a whore, but I have layers, deeper interest, and spirituality.*

McKinley's song *Could Be Cruel* brought her thoughts back to the van. She put on her pink paisley covered panties, a pair of hip-hugger Guess jeans with flared bell bottoms, a wide, white leather belt with a shiny round buckle, and a pastel blue halter-top that left her bare shoulders exposed and her midriff mostly uncovered.

A one karat diamond twinkled in her pierced navel as it dangled from a sterling silver chain and accentuated a tight, flat stomach. The last thing she put on was a string of mix-matched beads on a necklace she had made herself. They consisted of glass and wood beads of all types, including large African trade beads she thought held mystical powers and could help protect her from the evil that lurked all around her.

After brushing her hair and tying it in pony tails with bright colored tie-dyed scrunches, she climbed back into the platform bed. She reached behind the mattress and took out a hand-bound book. The book covers were made of pressed rice paper with multi-colored, oddly-shaped sections layered on top of each other. A gold and reddish colored Maple leaf protruded from the closed book.

Trixie criss-crossed her legs, brushed her pony tails behind her shoulders, opened the book, picked up a pen that lay on mattress near her disheveled fuzzy, pillow and began to write.

Delbert just left my van. He is a miserable wretched lost soul and I feel sorry for him, the fuck (pardon my French). I feel sorry for him and pity him. His appetite for me is a sick testimonial of the spiritual decay that exists all around. His body harbors a tainted soul and is a repository for evil. While he was pounding away at me, he kept saying things like, "come to daddy," and "this is the way you like it" and "feel how big I am" and "would you like daddy to cum in your mouth." I hate him so much. What disturbs me most about Delbert is that he says my breast look and feel like his daughter's. I asked if he was fucking her and he denied it. But he said what he meant was if he had sex with her, it would feel that way. Bullshit. He's up to something. And I need to find out what. I understand that he is a sick fuck. But men should not destroy the souls of their daughters. Sometimes I feel like a prostitute priestess. I feel as though I have a higher purpose. Maybe I am here to help this sick bastard or his poor daughter. I don't know. All I know is when he is inside of me, it is hard not to feel like throwing up.

Trixie stopped writing suddenly because she thought she heard something outside of the van. She glanced around nervously and listened intently. She heard some industrious crickets chattering amongst themselves, and a few early birds getting a jump on their day, chirping in brief, playful exchanges. The only other creatures, she thought, that were active this early were her spiritual protectors, the thousands of feral cats that hunted evil in the night and kept her spirit safe. She sat perfectly still, listening, tense, not wanting to exhale for fear it might make too much noise. When she was satisfied there was no one, she continued writing.

This is my first life and I accept that fact. In this life I must be the receptacle for evil to flow through. In this life, there must be bankers, there must be doctors, there must be lawyers, there must be paperboys, and there must be whores. Is the whore a bad person? Sometimes I think so. But so many Christian men, who consider themselves so high and mighty, worship whores and spend lots of money on them. Whores are not without virtue, or without redemption. We sometimes may not have shit to our names, but we are good people. And we are necessary. We keep sick fucks like Delbert from raping their children. We keep men from killing their co-workers and we absorb the evil of life. Society should not spurn us. Some of us are well read. We know the secrets that the souls of men harbor. There is much society can learn from whores if the dumb shits were willing to listen. They would learn that men are all frauds. They educate themselves and give glorious speeches, but in their hearts they lust after anything with a pussy. They will do anything to have an orgasm, including jerking off to big-tit magazines and videotapes of hairy hippie girls like me. I must love them or I will lose my hope. But I can also despise them, sick fucks. And maybe I can help some. Maybe.

Soon, I hope to have my annual soul cleansing. The Dalai Lama will be in town and I will go to see him and kiss his hand. He said judge yourself by what you give up to get it. I give up my body to save others. And maybe in my next life I will be a queen instead of a whore.

Trixie's attentions were drawn to the van's sliding door handle again. There was another sound, faint but sure. Hear heart started pounding like a jackhammer and almost as loud. The handle was turned. *Shit!* She'd forgotten to lock it. She sat, frozen, unable to move as if she an invisible force field was surrounded her body, holding all her limbs in place. *Jump! Run! Lock the door!* The right messages were there, but her body betrayed her. It would not move.

The handle kept moving, nearing the point where it would release the door and whoever was out there would come in and kill her, she thought.

Finally, she was released from her fear and reacted quickly. She threw her book under the mattress and removed a large, pearl-handled butcher knife. She clenched the knife with both hands and pointed it at the door, her eyes wide, darting back and forth to each side of the door, her breathing, quick and shallow. With a swift motion, she looked toward the back window of the van, thinking of how she might get out of this. It was too small. There was no way out except the sliding door or to cross the length of the van, jump in the drivers seat, open the door and run. By that time, she thought, the intruder would be at her back. She cursed under her breath for not locking the door right away.

"You better get the fuck out of here you mother fucker!" She screamed as loudly as she could, hoping to scare the intruder. "I've got a gun mother fucker and I'll blow your mother fucking head off!"

The handle stopped turning. She stared at it, squeezing the knife so tight, her knuckles started to ache. There was no sound outside, only silence, and a short grinding sound of gravel under the intruder's feet.

"Get the fuck out of here mother fucker or I'll kill your ass!" She repeated, knowing that her 90 pounds were barely enough to fend off even a small, skinny, determined adolescent.

Suddenly, in a swift, single motion, the handle moved down and the door rolled open so fast Trixie barely had time to react. A blast of cold air rushed into the van, followed by a dark, hooded figure that rushed towards her, knocking the knife aside as it's full weight landed on her, knocking her over onto the bed. She screamed.

Trixie tried to bring her legs up to block the figure, but she wasn't fast enough. She tried to force her knees up between the figures legs, hoping to connect with its groin and land a crippling blow. But the figure blocked her attempt and forced here legs and shoulders down against the bed as she squirmed to get free.

In a last show of strength and effort, she forced one hand free and reached up towards its face and grabbed where she thought its eyes would be and made contact. Her thumb sank into a warm, wet, shallow socket.

It screamed and its hands moved quickly from her body towards its eyes. That was Trixie's opening. She pushed hard with both hands and it fell backwards, hitting its head on the fold-up table with a muted smack. The intruder screamed again. She started kicking it as hard as she could and cursing at it. It screamed louder, giving out guttural whines and wails, sounding now like a coyote caught in a bear trap.

"My eye, my eye!" it screamed in between slobbering howls. "Bitch you almost put out my mother fucking eye!"

"You mother fucker! Get the fuck out!" She screamed.

It was on the ground, shielding itself with its arms. She spotted the knife lying on the ground next to the open door and lunged for it, picking it up quickly, turning and focusing on the dark figure's head. She lifted the knife, and, with both hands gripping the wooden handle, she aimed the point at its head, ready to thrust it as hard as she could.

"Don't fucking do it Trixie," it pleaded. "Don't fuckin' kill me God damn it. I'm blind! I'm blind! Don't mother fuckin' kill me. Some a bitch!"

Chapter 10

The sound of Herbie Hancock's *Headhunters* filled the truck cab as Rich accelerated away from the curb. The driving beat motivated him. He turned right at 52nd street. The first house on the corner was stop one, ground zero.

He stopped in front of the small ranch-style house, jammed the gear shift into park, opened the door with his left hand, grabbed a paper with his right, stepped out of the truck, and, with one quick step away from the truck, sent the paper flying. It landed perfectly on the porch. Bullseye.

Rich's had named all his techniques. This was the "patented" underhanded right-hand, left-side toss. Deadly. Accurate. It's propeller-like motion allowed it to cut through air and land in any space with uncanny accuracy up to 20 feet. He considered this a lethal toss and felt sorry for any sleeping pets that came between the porch and the paper.

As Rich rounded 48th street, he scooped up five papers with his right hand and performed an unusual left-hand shift into park, which required shifting across the steering column, gripping the gear shift and pulling it towards him and up at the same time.

Genius, he thought. He leaped out of the truck and sprinted to the next group of houses, which were all in a row, all with pristine, sculpted yards, and probably owned by retired government workers with yippy dogs.

He tossed the first paper and, without stopping, grabbed the next paper from his right hand and did a knife toss over a low porch railing.

Dead ahead was a five-foot shrub that extended from the house to the street. Bringing to bear all the skills he learned as a high school hurdler, he lead with his right foot extended straight in front, tucked his left foot up and behind and glided over the shrub.

As quickly as he landed, he filled his left hand again with a paper and, without stopping, lobbed it down a small walkway between an Oldsmobile and the porch. The customer preferred it there in the mornings.

As Rich tossed papers, he could only consider the most outlandish of ideas. At one point he imagined himself to be some kind of paper-tossing super hero, the black blur in the night, Mercury's blacker brother. These thoughts came and went as quickly. The weather was perfect for tossing, slightly chilly, no wind and no rain. It was him, the feral cats, Herbie Hancock, and the other odd characters that claimed the night.

He was a half-hour into his route. He was on target to meet his goal of delivering all his papers before 6 a.m. To do so, he had to employ every move he had developed. He might even use a secret toss he called the Muhammad Ali. He called it that because it was a mysterious toss that employed Zen techniques, including some meditation before tossing.

The music droned on. Brake. Shift. Right window Frisbee toss. Nailed it. Brake. Shift. Run. Sweat. Driveway slider between the camper and the house. Easy money!

As Rich tossed, he thought about new techniques he might develop and perfect and add to the book he was writing about pitching newspapers. He wondered whether he could find a publisher for it. Didn't matter. Thinking about the book made it easier to stay motivated about perfecting each move and staying on schedule.

He felt like he was pitching papers for a purpose…not just for the money. This was not his chosen vocation. This was not his destiny. This was an opportunity brought on by unfortunate financial circumstances that manifested themselves. The $1,000 he made every month from this would help pay down the $30,000 credit card bills he had accumulated during yet another failed attempt at magazine publishing.

No time to think too deeply about my problems.

At the next house, Rich threw a round-the-back triple-flick toss in full stride, like a gazelle with a newspaper. Pitch it fast. Pitch it quick. Preserve a perfect time and a perfect record. Financial problems were insignificant considerations compared to the paperboy quester for the perfect run.

After *Headhunters* played twice, Ramsey Lewis' *Sun Goddess* was next. The beat. The Rhythm. Almost done.

Rich was on the home stretch, heading towards Wygant, where his house was the last house on his route. He altered his official route slightly so his last pitch could be to his house and the safety of his home. He would not toss his neighbor's houses during daylight. He needed to remain anonymous to his neighbors. Noone ever saw Rich leave. If neighbors ever realized he was their paperboy, it would have disastrous ramifications. Whenever they saw them during daylight, non-delivery hours, they would have that "I'm the boss of *you* Paperboy" look in their eyes.

Rich was sweating profusely and his knees ached. He wasn't as young as he used to be and getting in and out of the truck was grueling on his body.

Chapter 11

Trixie recognized the nasally, accented voice and halted the descent of the knife only inches before the pointed blade would have sank into the soft tissue and slid as far as it could in to whatever got in its way. Fear quickly turned to anger as Trixie realized what had happened.

"Chico, you mother fucker! What the fuck do you think you're doing!" She screamed, still holding the knife tightly, inches above Chico's head, tense, angry, breathing heavily, and still deciding whether to plunge it into the back of his neck as he cowered on the floor or back off entirely.

"Don't mother fucking do it! I was just playing God damn it. I was just fuckin' with you bitch," Chico said, not realizing what he had done, his voice cracking as he pleaded and wept.

"Mother fucker, I should kill your ass right now," she screamed. "What the fuck are you doing sneaking around and bursting in here like that?"

"You're my bitch. I have the right to come in here, don't I?" Cowering and defiant now, Chico looked up at her and pushed his hood back. He stared at her, trying to look confident as he kneeled there, prostrate before her, pathetic, visibly afraid.

"The only right you have Chico, is the right to kiss my ass!" she yelled, not loosening her grip on the knife handle.

All Chico could think of was that fact that he was about to die at the hands of a sweet, pony-tailed, hairy hippie girl with a diamond navel ring and a butcher knife held over his head. His uncle La Toro Gomez, a notorious Crips gang leader who was gunned down years earlier, would be laughing in his grave at the sight.

"Today may be your lucky day, Chico," Trixie finally said, her voice less strained, and relaxing her grip on the knife. She lowered her arms slightly but kept the knife tip pointed at Chico. She backed up to the bed, sat and stared at him in amazement.

"What the fuck do you want?" She asked.

Chico struggled to his feet and stood straight up in the cramped space without hitting his head. His baggy pants hung low on his hips. His face glistened with tears, and red scratches lined his face under one blazing red eye.

"Like I said, I was just checking up on you, bitch," Chico said, showing the courage that had escaped him minutes earlier.

"Don't call me bitch, Chico. My name is Trixie, and I don't need checking up on. When I need something I can come get you."

"That's not how it supposed to work, bi—," he caught himself. "I'm the pimp, and I'm supposed to check up on you and keep you in line, bi—," he caught himself again.

Trixie sized Chico up, rolled her eyes slightly, then said, "Wrong Chico. I work. I make money. I call you when I want to give you some. And you leave me the fuck alone."

"That ain't how it works in the movies, Chico responded without hesitation, "Didn't you see the Mack and Superfly and shit like that?"

"That was before my time."

"Well, the bad ass mother fucker pimps kicked their bitches asses all the time and took their money."

"Chico, that's the movies."

"Movies like reality."

"Maybe some of it is, but not the part your talking about and not here."

"Look, bitch, I need some mother fuckin' money and I ain't got no time to debate finance and movie shit."

She ignored his last verbal indiscretion, hesitated before answering, thinking about the best way to get rid of Chico. "All right, Chico, because I know you need it, I'll give you some money. She reached in her pant hip pocket and pulled out two $20 dollar bills and handed them to Chico.

He took the bill, unfolded them, looked on both sides as if to verify their authenticity, then said, "Is that all you got, bitch?"

"That's all you get, Chico, and don't call me bitch or that's all you'll ever get from me again. I grew up in this area and I'll disappear faster than you can jerk off, which is pretty God damn fast."

"I don't jerk of, bitch. I get mo' pussy than Kareem."

"Thanks for sharing that, Chico, but you have to get the fuck out of here right now. I'm tired." She stood up, placed the knife on the bed behind her, now confident that she didn't need it. She had known Chico long enough to know what power she had over him. She walked to the open door, intending to escort Chico through it.

"You bed not be holding out on me, Trixie. I saw that mother fucking sweet ass ride that was parked out there. How much did you soak that mother fucker for?"

"None of your God damn business."

"It's my business 'cause I turned you out and made it possible for you to do this shit."

"Chico, I don't know where you get these ideas from. This was all my idea. I told you I would help you. I've been doing this for years before I met you. But I saw that you were so fucked up and desperate, I decided to help you. Now you've turned this whole thing around.

Chico, you need me. I don't fucking need you."

"That ain't right, bitch, I'm you're pimp. I protect you," he said, sneering and sounding agitated.

"From what, Chico? Feral cats?"

With that comment, Chico went into a fit of rage. "What do you mean mother fucking feral cats? What the fuck does feral mean? I will kill every God damn mother fucking cat I see when I get me some money!"

Chico paced the three feet of walking space between the front seat and the bed, turning quickly as he walked the two steps it took to cover the distance, brushing past Trixie but ignoring her.

Trixie was calm. She had been playing this game with Chico for over a year. Chico was one of her projects, a powerless piss ant who she felt deserved a shot at redemption, even if it meant putting up with his insults and his insecurities.

"Chico, your spirit is lost," she said, changing the subject. "Why don't you come see the Dalai Lama with me tonight. I think he can help you see the light of truth and enlightenment."

Chico stopped pacing and faced Trixie. "Fuck that," Chico responded. "Unless he can score me some good blow, he ain't got shit I need. Who the fuck is this dolly lamma anyway?"

"He's an enlightened Buddhist master, one of the greatest spiritual leaders of our time, and—"

"I ain't got no masters," Chico interrupted. "I am the master and the only thing that can enliken, or enlightening, or whatever the fuck that shit is is some pussy. How about it, Trixie?"

"I don't think so, Chico. I had sympathy sex with you one time and that was enough."

"What do you mean by sympathy?"

"It means that I think that buried deep inside that asshole you call your personality is potentially a good person, who, if he's not set free in this lifetime, may be set free in your next lifetime. Sex is a way of touching a person's soul, of seeing through them. I touched your soul, Chico. I saw the good person in you. He's buried deep, so it will take a lot to bring him out. That's why I decided to keep working with you."

"What the fuck are you talking about Trixie. There you go with that spiritual shit." Chico scoffed. "I thought you just loved some of this big dick." He cupped his groin, imitating his hip-hop heroes, and pointing down at his crotch at the same time.

"Chico, if I just wanted big dick, you would not be my first choice." She resisted the urge to smile, or it would have blossomed into a full-blown laugh.

"What's that supposed to mean? You makin' fun of my dick, bitch?"

"No, Chico, there is really not much to make fun of here," she said, internally applauding her knack for innuendo.

This one slipped past Chico. He pushed his head back and grimaced, looking like a dog waiting for his master to throw a stick, working hard to find the insult. "What do you mean there's nothing to make fun of? Is that some kind of dick crack?"

Trixie again resisted the intense urge to laugh. She tightened her stomach and chest, holding back the laugh as if trying to contain a sneeze, and the edges of her mouth twitched like the skin of a cow scaring away flies with quick movements of skin.

"Look Chico, your dick is fine for what little you need to do with it most of the time. I see all your magazines, and that's great for you, but I see lots of dicks and some of them are pretty God damn big. So, if I need a big dick, I don't wake up in the morning and scream your name."

"I think you're makin' fun of my dick." Chico said, still attempting to put the pieces together. Chico's forehead furrowed. Then he tried another tactic because his brain was betraying him by not being able to make any logical connections between what was said, what he heard and what he wanted to say. He raised his hands and with fingers outspread, like a gangster rapper wannabe, he leaned into Trixie's face and locked eyes with her.

"Listen close, bitch, all I need is money and you got some. Gimme all the fuckin' money you got and I'll get the fuck out."

Trixie met his stare without blinking, but could not lose the teasing twitches from suppressed laughter urges that pinged her gut and her face. Calmly she said, "I've stood up to scarier assholes than you Chico. You get what I give you. Now go fuckin' cool of with your magazines. Use that forty bucks to buy yourself a good breakfast and come see the Dalai Lama with me tonight. There's still hope for you."

Chico wrapped the raised fingers from one hand into a clenched fist and held it close to her face, pursed his lips and stared at her with angry, hate-filled eyes.

Trixie stood defiant with ponytails draped over her shoulders, lips tight, breathing stead, staring at Chico, holding back her smile and letting her fear work for her as she waited for him to make his next move.

Finally, Chico relented, put his arm down, opened his fist and looked down at the $40 dollars in his open hand, then closed his fingers around the bills, crumpling them again, and shoved them into his oversized pockets. He pulled up his pants, which had slipped down during the tussle and were hanging past his butt crack, turned and walked towards the sliding door.

Before he stepped out of the van, he glanced back at Trixie and said, "My momma told me to always respect bitches, especially her. Otherwise, I'd kick your ass. This ain't over bitch. You gon' gimme my mother fuckin' money and then I'm going to fuck you the way you like, in the ass with my big dick."

Chico didn't wait for a reply. He stepped out of the van, slammed the door shut behind him as hard as he could, Rocking the van and causing the curtains to all lift as if a wind cannon had shot a burst of wind through the van.

Trixie listened to the footsteps and Chico cursing in Spanish all the way to his bicycle. She could hear the kryptonite lock release, and listened as Chico began peddling away, still cursing and talking to himself. The tick-tick of the bicycle chain faded as he rounded the corner to 47th. It was quiet again.

When Trixie refocused her attention from Chico to herself, she was shivering, partly from anger, partly from disgust and partly from pent up fear. But it was not from the cold. In fact, if she were wearing more cloths, she would have been sweating and that might have given her away. The air got thicker and she found it difficult to breath. She had to get out. She grabbed her little lunch-box purse with the images of Power Puff Girls flying through the air from under her mattress, a black leather waist-length jacket that hung in a corner by the door, opened the sliding door, and stepped out into the night. She closed the door, locked it, and walked towards 48th street.

She began to cry as she walked. Here spirit was in pain. Tears flowed down here cheeks. Her head was down. Slowly, she looked up at clear night sky, at the twinkling stars surrounding a disappearing half moon, hoping to find an answer.

Was I meant to suffer? Is this my destiny? She thought. As her eyes returned to the street in front of her, she observed three feral cats crossing the street, their eyes glowing like yellow stars. They are absorbing evil, she thought, and she wept even harder. Her pain ran deep.

Chapter 12

When Rich turned the corner onto Going street, he was surprised to see a woman walking in the middle of the street. Her head was tilted back and her arms were outstretched as if she were praying to the dawn, swaying slightly as she meandered towards the intersection. Rich had to slow down because he could not easily get around her without the risk of hitting her.

As she walked in front of his truck, she suddenly stopped and turned. It was still dark enough to require headlights, so Rich could see her face clearly.

He could see that she was crying as she squinted in his headlights. Rich had seen her before. She looked young, almost too young to be doing what he thought she might be doing.

She stood staring into his headlights. She seemed like an illusion or an angel. She smiled.

Rich also noticed she was only a few feet away from a camper van he had seen parked in a different spots on different nights. Various times he had seen cars parked behind it and the light on. He paid little attention to it; simply made a mental note. Mental notes, he thought, would save his life in this line of work.

After a few seconds Rich realized his route time was dying as he gazed at the mysterious woman. He shifted the truck in reverse and slowly backed up so he could safely drive around her.

Her eyes never left him. As he passed her, she smiled and raised a hand in a tenuous wave. She could not see him but he could see her. She looked so innocent and vulnerable. She was a beautiful and haunting image at the same time. He wondered what her story was but didn't have the time to contemplate too much. She faded in his mirror and he focused on finishing his route.

Next stop. Brake. Shift. A revolving kite hanger to a house that was inset 50 feet off the road. Only the kite hangers would make that distance. It was tossed with an extreme vertical arch and an extra snap in the wrists. Prevailing westerly winds thirty feet up would catch the paper and send it forty feet to land near the front steps.

Chapter 13

The truck was nearly empty. Only two more streets left. The second to last street on Rich's route was Alberta street, a street that looked like it belonged in some rural mountain community instead on in northeast urban Portland.

It was a long, quiet street lined with bright, yellow, stick-mounted Oregonian tubes and postal boxes that lined the streets from one block to the next like one-headed, yellow sentries.

This was an easy street for Rich. He rarely had to leave his truck. He simply reached in from the driver's side and shoved the papers into the tubes, doing one side first, then doubling back and doing the second side.

Only one house did not have a tube, which he thought unusual. Tubes allowed a certain amount of privacy and were somewhat of a status symbol, allowing residents on this street to enjoy their morning routine of fixing a pot of coffee and strolling their minor estates to the tube to get their papers at 6 a.m.

These were finicky customers as well. Most were awake before the papers arrived and if papers were late by more than one minute past 6 a.m., some would call the station immediately and complain.

There was *that* one house, however, that Rich thought was different. It was the only house on the street that could be considered a mansion and was owned by a middle-aged African-American.

Rich had seen him jogging in the mornings. The other homes were modest, bungalows, old Portland style homes, a mish-mesh of 1970s experiments, or what some architects might consider mistakes. This *different* house was built during the last year on a vacant lot by a person who rich assumed had impeccable taste for architectural details.

To deliver papers to this house, Rich was required to park in the street and walk the papers up a lengthy driveway to the front porch and drop the papers in a custom newspaper/package chute. Fortunately, the porch light was always on, otherwise, in absolute darkness, it was creepy and lined with obstacles.

Rick parked in front of the house. Trimmed, 10-foot-tall laurels lined the front yard. They were tall enough to afford some privacy from casual passersby but not tall enough to hide the three-floored Craftsman structure, with exposed cedar singles, huge picture windows, expert masonry, bedrock smokestacks for multiple fireplaces.

Rich grabbed a paper, stepped out into the street. The Sun's beams created a bluish tint over the tall Douglas Furs and Alder trees that lined the street, promising a spectacular sunrise.

Rich walked past the laurels and approached the front door.

Four candle-shaped bulbs glowed yellow from the antique light fixture and illuminated a porch supported by two, massive hand-hewn posts. The oversized door was made of dark wood with maroon, yellow and blue stained glass windows. It had a chute large enough for the paper and small boxes.

Rich reached to open the chute. The bolt on the door clicked.

He panicked briefly. He hated encountering customers. Some paid him no attention, while others wanted to ask a lot of questions. He quickly opened the chute and dropped the paper in, turned and started running for the street when he heard, "Hey!" Come from the house behind him.

"Come here for a second," the deep, male voice said. Rich stopped as quickly as he started; frustrated that he hadn't gotten away.

As Rich turned, he said, "Yes, sir. It's just me. *Oregonian* delivery."

"I know," the voice said from a shadow in the partially opened door. "Step up here please, I'd like to talk to you."

Rich turned and advanced slowly back onto the porch and towards the partially open door. As he neared, it opened completely and he could see the owner of the house standing there in his multi-colored jogging suit.

"James Clarence Walker the third," the man said as he extended his large hands.

"Rich Franklin." Rich shook his hand.

"Say, you do a hell of a job delivering papers," Walker said as he smiled a toothy smile that emanated from a face that looked like it was custom crafted from a *GQ* mold. He was well over six feet tall, with a shiny shaved head and a gold earring in his left ear. His body fit snugly inside his flashy Adidas running suit, and he wore a thick gold watch with matching rings, one that visibly displayed a school letter that started with an "H." Walker's complexion was mahogany dark, and he winked a playful eye at Rich.

"Thanks," Rich replied, "didn't mean to disturb you."

"No problem at all," Walker said, "I just wanted to catch you before you left."

"Oh, are you going on vacation and need your papers stopped, 'cause I—"

"No, nothing like that," he interrupted. "I want to thank you for doing a great job. I also wanted to ask if you've been receiving the tips I include with the bills."

"I believe so. I get the tips from the station manager."

"I know, but I'm not sure you guys always get the full tips we put in our bills."

"I should be."

"If you don't mind my asking, how much in tips did you get last month."

"I don't mind you asking. I got a hundred bucks total."

"Then you got my tip," Walker said. "And no tips from any other customers?"

"That's not likely," Rich said, a little perturbed by this revelation. "Most of my customers tip according to the reports. And I work damn hard to make sure they feel good about the service and about tipping."

"What did the reports say I tipped?"

"Ten dollars, which is better than most."

"Then there's a problem," Walker said. "My tip is $100 a month."

"What!" Rich said, surprised. "There certainly is some kind of problem,"

"Well, it's not a problem you need to worry about. I'll take care of it," Walker said. "Don't even mention it to your station manager. I'll make sure you get every penny I've left for you. I used to deliver papers. That's how I got my start, so I know what it's like. One of my customers, back when I was a kid, used to give my $50 every month. She was retired and about 90 years old and living on a fixed income. But she appreciated how considerate I was and scraped together the tip every month until she passed away. I never forgot. So I always pay it forward."

"Thanks," Rich said. "You're a true gentleman. I appreciate it very much. I'm trying hard to make this work for me."

"I can tell," Walker replied. Rich and Walker made true eye contact instead of tentative eye contact for the first time. Rich could tell by the way Walker spoke that he was educated, sophisticated and appreciated drama. But he didn't have time to fully analyze his character.

"I gotta scoot now," Rich said. "I have promises to keep and miles to go before I sleep."

Walker laughed. "A student of the classics I see."

"A degree in journalism and English helps. They made us study all the white poets. The Caucasian indoctrination didn't end after Catholic high school."

"Harvard was no exception my man. You know Rich, I don't know you at all, but you all right. Keep up the great work. Maybe one of these days one of your magazines will make it or you'll get an agent for your book. If there's anything I can do to help. Be sure to let me know."

They shook hands Rich was too surprised to respond fully to what Walker had actually said before the door closed. How did he know about the book and the magazines?

He stood for a moment, thinking about the tips and what Walker had said when he noticed the red, purple and orange streaks across the sky.

The sun! Dawn was my reward for a route well done. Morning was my enemy. Sunshine will eat my flesh and dissolve my bones to dust.

Rich ran for the truck, pushed the lever in gear, and drove quickly towards his final street. He was in such a hurry, he barely noticed the pathetic shadow of a Mexican American on the side of the road strangling a feral cat and cursing at it in Spanish. His 15-speed bike was balanced against a light post a few feet away. In the rear-view mirror he also observed Walker emerge from his driveway and jog in the opposite direction. Walker took leaping strides like a black impala, and, as Rich considered him, he dubbed him customer #287 African-American Man of Mystery, and made a mental note to grill him about how he knew about his book.

Rich tossed the last house on Wygant street and, with a great sigh of relief, pulled into his driveway. He had survived. The world was still sleeping, his flesh was not burning from the direct rays of the Sun, and the last song he listened to after every route was playing.

The song was called *A House is not a Home*, a Luther Vandrose song that Rich loved. This was their song, one Rich and April listened to together hundreds of times. They listened to all the versions. Ones by Dusty Springfield, Dionne Warwick, all of them. He sat in the driveway, listening to the ticks of the hot motor cooling and Vandrose's silky, smooth voice working the words of the song. Tears formed in the corners of his eyes.

This is my life. What am I doing here? Is it good or is it bad?

As the song ended, and the air cooled in the cab, Rich noticed the sweat causing his shirt to stick to his body and causing a slight chill nip at his skin. He also smelt the familiar locker-room smell wafting up from his body and felt the familiar aches of his aging body asking him *Are you sure you should be doing this?*

The Sun. Times up. He went inside.

Chapter 14

Rich's den was the smallest room in the back of the house. His desk was a decrepit Queen Anne-style vanity he'd fished out of a neighborhood dumpster. He sanded and sealed the half-peeled top with a thick four coats of polyurethane.

His aging executive chair fit like a glove and squeaked like a frantic song bird as he pulled himself close to the desk. He clicked the button of his keyboard and the computer blinked on and he was instantly connected to the Internet.

The room was quiet except for the soft whir of the CPU fan and the occasional creaking of an 80-year-old house that had yet to settle. He sipped the too strong coffee from his favorite mug, a Chinese porcelain tea mug with hand-painted floral patterns spaced between metallic gold painted sections.

After he sipped the hot brew, he picked up the remote control for the CD player, and pressed start.

There were five CDs in the carriage. The first CD that queued up was Darryl Grant's *Smokin' Java*, a slick traditional set of jazz tracks. Grant, a friend of Rich's, was a local jazz intellectual who taught at Portland State University. Rich loved his persona and his precision.

Rich turned his attention to the computer screen. As he perused the new message list, he saw the usual 10 to 20 unsolicited messages, most of them spam from pornographic web sites with subject lines that read, *I want to suck you dry* or *Double your penis size today!* Rich laughed when he read that one. Doubt it, he thought.

As he methodically deleted messages, the instant message notice popped onto his screen.

The message was curt and rude: *"Dear Rich, Fuck you mother fucker! Signed, Kyle"*

Without hesitation, Rich typed a reply to this textual assault, *"Dear Kyle, kiss my ass! Love, Rich."*

He pressed the send button. A replay came back immediately, causing Rich to sit up.

"Nigga, you fucked up. What's happnin' black?"

Rich laughed out loud and clicked on the reply button and typed, *"Not much bro. Sup with you?"*

"I got yo last message and now I know you really fucked up. Nigga, you got to figure out what culla you is!"

Rich shot back, *"Mutha fucka kiss my ass. You know I'm right. O.J. fucked shit up for all bruthas."*

"What the fuck you talkin' 'bout nigga. I read what you said the first time. Now splain yo self."

"Bruthas like Sidney Portier and Quincy Jones and even Clarance Thomas, almost made it okay for a brutha to marry a white woman without a lot of bullshit attached. Then O.J. comes along and murders that beautiful blond model he is married to, a perfect specimen of white womanhood. White people get all fucked up about the shit again and start lookin' at niggas with white women all funny again. Therefore I must conclude that O.J. fucked up all the good shit Portier did in 'Guess Who's Coming to Dinner,' putting niggas back in the dark ages again"

Kyle responded, "Nigga, you been watching too much God damn TV. First of all, we don't know O.J. did that shit? Could have been some deranged white mother fucker who just wanted to fuck somebody up. Or maybe it was just somebody pissed at O.J. for fuckin' up a bet. Who the fuck knows?"

Rich wrote, "Maybe. All I know is if he didn't do it, he wouldn't have done that shit with the Bronco, drivin' all up and down the freeway talkin' on his cell phone and shit. If the mother fucker was innocent, he would have marched into the poleece station with 10 lawyers and proclaimed, 'I didn't do this shit, now all you mother fuckers been sittin' around on your asses for the last 25 years collecting my tax dollars better get the fuck out there and find the mother fucker who did this shit or I got $10 million dollars says that if you fuck this up I will have all your mother fuckin' J-O-B-ESSES!' And by the way, don't try to lay this shit on me. She was the mother of my children, the love of my life and my ass is made of Teflon.' Now that would have been some great shit."

Kyle wrote, "Life ain't like that mutha fucka. If you knew L.a. p.d. was after yo ass and you know how l.a. P.D. is, you da got in whatever the fuck you could find that runs and tried to drive yo black ass to Hawaii if you had to. Hell, everybody know L.A.P.D. worse than them backwoods Mississippi redneck mother fuckers. They would have shot O.J. on sight."

Rich wrote, "You can stick up for what O.J. did all you want. All I know is that since that O.J. side show and the verdict, white dudes been look at me differently. They see me with my fine ass white wife and I know only three words pop into their heads."

"What three words mother fucker?"

"Pimp, nigger, O.J." Rich wrote.

"What!!!!"

"Thas rite," Rich answered, "They be thinkin' 'O.J. nigger pimp gonna cut our white women up.'"

"Now I know you really fucked up. Those kinds of mutha fuckas only know two words: Dead and nigger and it ain't got nothin' to do with O.J."

Rich wrote, "Amen bro."

Kyle continued, "Black and white relationships have come a long way and there ain't no goin' back. Not even an O.J. can change that. Used to be a white man saw a black man with a fine ass white woman, and he'd call a brutha out in a crowded room if he had to and tell him straight up, 'I'm going to kill you, nigger.

You keep your nigger hands off our women.' But they can't do that shit no more. The tide has turned. Plus, nobody knows who's black any more. We got 400 years of racial inter-breeding. Who knows who's really black or white anymore. Some white people would be shocked to find out who they mamma is."

"I know what you sayin," Rich wrote. "You have a good point, but I still think there's some O.J backlash and when I think this shit through some more, I'm gonna lay down some really intellectual shit on you."

"Wishful thinking Mutha fucka."

Rich changed the subject. "On to bigger and better things. You know how I been working on my novel for years. I think I'm about done, and I got a great story."

Kyle wrote, "Congratulations, nigga. Only took you 25 years. Ever since we was kids back in Junction City, Kansas, we used to cut up about breakin' all the rules in film, in writing, in real life. And you was always talking about that book you was gonna write, and you finally done it."

"I know. We both had dreams. I'm kind of jealous 'cause you been living your dream. You actually broke Hollywood's black ceiling by making movies you want to make and managing to keep your roots in Kansas."

Kyle wrote, "Don't sell yourself short, bro. There are only a few mutha fuckas can publish shit and actually make any money at it, especially in a city like San Francisco. Mutha fucka, you was kicking ass. I read your shit."

Rich said, "All right. All right. We could keep suckin' each other's dicks like this all morning, but you know how I feel about that."

Kyle wrote, "Ait, was this book about?"

"It's about a vigilante paperboy, you know a Charles Bronson Death Wish thing, only with a Negro paperboy, O. J. and a ho," Rich replied.

"You crackin' me up. And I know you bullshittin' me. Listen, all I can say, bro, is your story got to be something that gets people to sit on the edge of their seats. They have to give a shit about what happens or you lost them. Then you have to make yourself interesting; have flaws, be deep in some shit that you can't get out of. Course, that won't be hard for you 'cause you already there, fucked up mother fucker."

Rich replied, "It is all that mutha fucka, now kiss my black ass. You keep doggin' me and I'm gonna write some shit about you that will embarrass the black off your rusty ass."

Kyle replied, "You don't scare me nigga. Just make sure I get a copy of that mother fucker before yo mamma."

Rich added, "Yeah, you and my dick will be the first to get a copy. Listen, I gotta go. Little munchkins will be up soon. I'll check in with you tomorrow."

Kyle replied, "Say, before you go, have you come clean with April about that financial shit you got into?"

Rich could feel his pulse quicken as he read the question. He hesitated before answering, knowing this was an issue he avoided thinking about, and definitely didn't want to write about. He slowly and carefully responded:

"No bro. You know the fucked up thing about life and marriage and shit is that men can go off and fight wars, shoot mother fuckers without thinking twice about it, rip pig guts out of live pigs and eat them raw, drink their own piss, and amputate both their own legs to save their own lives if they have to, but when it comes to telling their wives that they've fucked up and lost a shit load of money, they freeze up like chicken shits. We hide. We sneak. We avoid. We deny. It's just one of the hardest things in the world to sit down face-to-face and come clean about that shit."

Rich read the message several times before sending it. He pressed the enter button. A minute or two passed before the response came back.

Kyle wrote, *"I don't want you to think I'm unsympathetic. I am. My first movie was a disaster. I had Mafia looking mother fuckers chasing my ass, looking to jack me up. Everything went wrong. But I kept my wife in the loop and she helped me through that shit. I remember the day I had to tell her that the investors turned out to be shysters. I had promised her our family was not at financial risk. I felt about two inches tall telling her that we could lose everything we had worked so hard for all these years. She was great. She looked at me and said, "Kyle, you're a good man. We won't let this happen. What do we need to do to fix this." Rich, that shit was better than anything I ever wrote in a script. Let me tell you, man, I started crying and shit. Big, tough, war fighting, flesh eating, deer hunting black man ass mother fucker. Weeping like a baby."*

Rich suddenly found it difficult to swallow. He imagined Kyle at six foot three, the epitome of black militancy, curled up in his wife's bosom, blubbering, the black mystique, and macho running screaming out the front door.

"You are one bad brutha. I know one day I'm going to have to fess up. But I don't know if it's going to play out like that," Rich wrote.

Kyle replied, *"Only one way to find out. And by the way. White people must never know about this cryin' shit. It's one thing to have white society's blessing to marry white women and have children with them, but if they find out that we be cryin' and shit, they may try to use that against us somehow. You dig."*

Rich, now with tears swelling up under his eyelids, laughed and wrote, *"Your secret is safe with me brutha. Food for thought."*

Kyle wrote, *"I'm checkin' out. But I just want you to know that you still fucked up after all these years. But if you wasn't I probably wouldn't love the shit out of you bro."*

Rich smiled and typed, *"And fuck you too. Later. Bro Raymond."*

He clicked the send button for the last time, stopped typing and sat listening to the silence of the morning. The house creaked again and through the window he could see the half-naked branches of the plumb tree with twitching purple leaves, ready to fall off at the slightest breeze. It's branches brushed against the side of the house. The hazy blue of dawn was dissipating as the full sun highlighted more of the back yard landscape with each passing minute. Beyond the plumb tree, he could see the green, jagged leaves of the Oregon grape plant, and next to it was a mature grape vine bearing gold, rust, and green leaves and plump, hard grapes that would be ripe in another month.

Kyle had been Rich's best friend for 25 years, and the only person on earth who actually knew that Rich was a white man disguised as a black man so he could learn more about "their world." Rich told Kyle that once he learned what he needed to learn, he would turn white and surprise the shit out of everyone.

Rich smiled at the thought. He and Kyle talked about anything and everything. Nothing was sacred. And they often typed *black*, a carry over from childhood when they used to spend hours in Kyle's family basement listening to Richard Pryor on 8-track. Their combined imagination fueled a world of thought and they would go on for hours and hours, doing skits, imitating popular characters, talking about women, taking jabs at politicians.

Everything and anything went when they talked. He looked forward to their e-mail message exchanges. They inspired his creativity and allowed him to vent some of his frustrations about living in Portland having impersonate white people all day.

"Daddy!" A tiny voice said, interrupting the silence and wrenching Rich back into the here and now. He sat up quickly and swiveled around to see a diminutive form in Tonka pajamas with two big, alert eyes standing in the doorway with thumb in mouth, peering at him.

"Cold!" The little figure said, and walked over to Rich and pounced in his lap, forcing itself between Rich's arms, his lap and the desk.

"Hey big guy, how are you?"

Not looking up, the little head buried deeper under Rich's armpits, and Antonio, the younger of his two children, repeated, "cold."

Antonio was five, too cute to ever get mad at, with his short-cropped curly, sandy-brown hair, big green eyes and dazzling smile. He was so cute, older girls followed him around his elementary school and asked him to smile for them. This was cause for irritation and amusement by his older brother, Juan, who sometimes thought he got the short end of the looks stick. But he, too, was cute, borderline beautiful, with big bluish hazel eyes, loose curled Sandy, blond hair and both had even, very light brown complexions.

They were beautiful blended kids; the same kids that adults used to warn him about. The parish priest used to say, "mixed children have a difficult time with their identity, so races shouldn't mix." This used to anger Rich, who, around age 12 decided the Catholic church was a racist, sexist, homophobic institution that indoctrinated people to worship a boring white guy who didn't even write half the shit people said he did. He considered God and Jesus to be plagiarist and hypocrites, stealing great shit from the apostles and scaring people into submission with it.

Antonio squirmed and made baby kitten sound. Antonio's disposition most matched Rich's, which is why he often would not get as upset with his antics as his mother. Watching Antonio was too much like watching himself. And how could he ever get mad at himself.

Rich looked up as he heard the creaking of the ceiling. Someone larger was stirring upstairs. The sound of NPR radio could be heard, and that signaled start of the race to see how much could be done in a day before everyone rushed home, exhausted, ready to go to sleep.

"Come on tiger," he said as he stood with Antonio tightly curled in his arms, insisting on being carried like a basketball, "time to get this shoe on the road."

Chapter 15

Sam Enison worked for Associated Collection Services for nearly 10 years. He loved his job. Not because it was fun. Not because it was rewarding. But because it allowed him to wield a power over clients called his victims. Enison considered himself a warrior and a hunter and going to work was his chance to bag the financial vermin of the world. He considered this ironic, too, because 20 years earlier, he had been expelled from Yale because of excessive alcohol consumption, excessive spending and had, himself, been a target of his own industry, racking up thousands of dollars in credit card bills and other debt by the time he was 21.

Angry, frustrated, and hounded by creditors, he filed for bankruptcy, sent all the collection agencies a polite "fuck off" letter and vowed to never be the victim of what he called collection agency scum again.

So, it was with much hesitation that he accepted an offer from a college classmate to join a new collection agency in Oakland, California. But his friend offered him a piece of the business, a hefty salary plus commissions and told him he would have free reign to do things his way, knowing his flair for drama.

At first, he felt like a fraud rousting old ladies, young college students, and executives, apologizing at every turn and allowing himself to be pushed around. It took a full year for him to polish his approach, accept his fate and exercise the power he possessed.

As he sat in his high-back executive chair, surrounded by rare artifacts and scanning the view of downtown Oakland in the distance, he reflected on how he bagged his first high-rolling victim, a 21-year-old deadbeat woman named Susie who had amassed $100,000 worth of credit card bills and was slippery and clever and very sophisticated in her efforts to avoid paying back a penny.

Susie had been skating from low-paying jobs for four years, avoiding Enison's calls, slipping past him like a mouse in a cornfield. Frustrated, Enison decided to try something different. He bought a ticket to Sarasota, Florida, where Susie called home and after searching property records and corporation registrations, he located Susie's real address and discovered her real vocation.

He learned that the restaurant jobs were diversions. A search of local building and registered business records showed that Sweet Susie, as he fondly called her, had taken huge cash advances on her credit cards to invest in apartment complexes in Miami and Sarasota. As her investments prospered, her deliberately distanced corporations purchased sailboats, leased luxury cars and afforded Sweet Susie an envious lifestyle while she cried poor and used the waitress jobs to get laid every week.

A social security search by a well-placed friend also turned up several aliases. And, finally, a review of her tax records showed that sweet Susie's net worth was over two million dollars, as she had managed to turn her $100,000 investments into a burgeoning real estate empire.

When Enison finally broke through to Susie on her cell phone, she answered with here usual, perky, "Hi, Susie here."

"Susie, this is Sam Enison with ACS." Susie hung up immediately.

Enison called back without hesitation. He got her voice mail and left a very polite message that said, "Hi Susie. This is Sam. How are you? Susie, I've done little homework, and I would like to tell you how things are going to be from now on. I know about the limited partnerships, the boat, your aliases, and your other investments. We have a judgement against you, which exposes all of your assets. We have begun the paperwork to have all of your assets seized and sold and will inform your partners that their investments are in jeopardy. Now, Susie, you're probably a sweet girl and really want to do the right thing here. So, do both of us a favor and call me back and let's make a deal. You can end this cat and mouse game with one phone call."

Enison recalled how he hung up the telephone, folded his arms across his chest, leaned back in his chair, and stared at the telephone as if he hoped to bend it with his eyes. When it finally rang, he let it ring exactly 10 times before slowly picking it up and casually saying, "Sweet Susie, are you ready to make a deal?"

The girlish voice he had heard in past, brief conversations, was now all business. "What are your terms?" Sweet Susie asked curtly.

"$25,000 in two weeks and the balance 30 days from today plus $10,000 dollars in expenses," Enison answered. There was a silence. The first one to speak loses, he thought.

"$10,000 wired today. That's for you you prick. Go out and get yourself laid. $25,000 in thirty days and $50,000 in sixty days." She said without pausing.

Enison shot back. "Acceptable, but I need some guarantees and a contract to take back to my boss and my client."

"Fax me your terms. You can confirm the funds availability with my financial advisor. I'll give you his name and telephone number and he will also personally vouch for my credit. But if you mention your agency name or the fact that you're a collection agent, you son of a bitch, I'll sue your ass."

Bingo, Enison thought. The mouse was finally cornered.

"Save you threats Susie," Enison responded. "I'm not easily intimidated and I don't give up. Give me the information and we'll keep this between you and me. Keep your payment commitments and we can settle this matter and you can go back to building your empire. But if you slip this time, Susie, I won't stop until I personally have done everything humanly and legally possible to recover what is legally due and bury your ass. And you'll foot the bill for this effort."

"Fuck you," she replied. She gave him the phone number and the name and hung up without any other pleasantries.

Enison smiled, dialed the investment counselor's number, an executive named Jeff Bradley, who worked for Merrill Lynch in Miami. He vouched for the available funds and arranged a wire transfer of the first $10,000 payment. He was more pleasant than Sweet Susie.

Before Enison hung up, he asked Bradley, "So, between you and me, what is Susie really worth?"

The advisor did not answer immediately, but then replied, "Between you and me, perhaps she is worth more than you and me combined. She's doing better on her own than Trump did at her age." Enison could sense him smile. They were both cashing in on Sweet Susie. Enison said goodbye and hung up.

It was almost 10 o'clock and Enison's attentions focused back on his desk. He shuffled some papers, returned some phone calls, and then slid the next file in front of him.

He stared at the name before opening the file. He truly liked this guy. But business was business. The cat always had to get the mouse. He opened the file and read the brief profile he had written about Rich Franklin.

40-year-old African American named Rich Franklin. His credit record shows some minor blemishes over the years, but he has, for the most part, been fiscally responsible, the last year being the exception. He owes $50,000 in credit card debt to two card holders, debts from cash advances used to support his publishing business. The magazines he published have ceased operations. He has been somewhat responsive, but is looking for a job and bringing in what income he can as quickly as he can now. His wife, April, has a good job as a graphic designer and is currently the major income producer. Her paychecks allow them to meet all expenses. Not much more. My conversations with him indicate he has not told his wife about the extent of his debt. But I like this guy and will try to work with him. He is a writer, editor, publisher and jazz pianist. He intrigues me. Allow a little latitude for him to maneuver, but will tighten the rope if collections take more than 90 days. He's currently delivering newspapers in the mornings, doing writing and graphic *design freelance projects during the day and sitting in with the Albert Collins Trio in he evenings at Jazz de Opus. I have seen him play. Not bad. Will take another trip to Portland to learn more about full recover potential opportunities for him and see him play again. Particularly liked his rendition of Bill Evan's Waltz for Debbie. Plus, I think he is writing a book, but I'm no sure. Need to find out more about that.*

Enison smiled. He considered himself more than a collection agent. He was a *secret* collection agent and loved his roll. He studied his subjects. He went where they lived. He observed them. In some cases, he even made friends with them under assumed names, and became part of their lives. The cost of a plane ticket and a few days had made his firms millions in the last 10 years. Franklin was a special case. He needed to know more about him. Franklin had a lot of potential. He needed to talk to him. He dialed Franklin's cell phone number.

Chapter 16

Mornings at Rich's house were pure chaos. April, Juan and Antonio all had type A personalities, so conversation, tempers, and laughter could explode at any given time. Juan and Antonio acted like typical brothers, with the younger taunting the older and the older being too respectful to slug him one. April usually stayed upstairs and dressed for work before joining the trio at the breakfast table. Then she had about fifteen minutes to probe Rich for information—information he was reluctant to share—before leaving for work.

Rich made French toast for Antonio and Cheerios for Juan They focused on their plates, occasionally looking up to make faces at each other between mouthfuls. They had an hour to eat, get dressed and get to the bus stop.

April appeared at the base of the stairs. Herbal soap, conditioner, and China Rain scented oil followed her into the kitchen. Rich loved the way she smelled. She walked around to him and kissed him on the forehead.

"Good morning dear," she said, as she reached for part of the morning paper. "Paper was late this morning."

"It was here," Rich said, putting his paper down and focusing in on her.

"Oh," she said, "I thought you were going to deliver it to our bed. Don't I deserve a special delivery?"

Rich laughed. "'Course you do. How special did you want it?"

"Surprise me tomorrow," she said, blushing. "So how was our route this morning?"

"It was fine," Rich said. "A lot of feral cats out there. Plus, even though I try my best to avoid it, I met one of the customers this morning who said I should have gotten a hundred dollar tip from him last month."

April was confused. She asked, "Did you say a hundred dollar tip?"

"Yep," Rich answered.

"So what did he want from you?"

"It was nothing like that." Rich was irritated by her question.

"Don't you think that's a little unusual?"

"Not at all. He used to be a carrier himself and now he's fairly well off and wants to give something back."

"Well, that's awfully nice of him. Now if you could get the Oregonian to pay it back to you, we'll be doing great."

"He said for me not to worry about it. He'd take care of it."

"And you believed him?"

"Yes, I believed him," he said, his body getting tense as the conversation deteriorated.

April managed to put Rich on the defensive in their first 10 minutes awake together.

"I hope he comes through. Our insurance premiums come up this month and things will be tight. We need all the money we can get this month."

Rich did not respond. He knew where this conversation was leading. He instead picked up his paper and focused on the articles while Juan and Antonio crunched and slurped and occasionally burped or farted. Man and his boys eating, he thought.

After the boys finished eating, they required constant supervision to get dressed. They preferred to play and fight, anything but what they were supposed to do. Rich hustled them upstairs then went down stairs to say goodbye to April. She had her usual four bags in hand and was heading for the front door.

He looked in her eyes first, then looked down, avoiding prolonged, direct eye contact. He knew he loved her very much. *Tell her now*, he thought. No. She would have a bad day, cry, scream. Call me terrible names. He imagined a horrendous scenario.

"Do you have any more interviews today?"

"Not today," Rich answered, hesitantly, as his eyes met hers again. He continued, stumbling over his words as he spoke, "I signed up with two more agencies and they're looking. I think something will come through soon."

April gave him "that" look and along with the look came a slight rolling of her eyes. Having a master's degree and perhaps an ounce of respect left for him prevented her from doing a full eye roll. But a slight forehead furrow, a tilt of the mouth, and squint of the left eye were enough to say a sarcastic *right, I'll believe it when I see it*.

"Well, don't forget to pick up the kids today after school." She said and dashed for the front door.

Rich went inside, herded the kids into the truck, then hustled them to the bus stop. They scrambled onto the bus and blew kisses at him as the bus drove away.

He breathed a sigh of relief.

The kids were his pride and joy but they were like two tornadoes, spinning in opposite directions.

He returned to the house, gathered his folders, brief case, then drove to a small office he maintained downtown, a leftover from his publishing empire.

It was on the third floor of the Minnesota Hotel, a renovated former house of ill repute turned historic office space. His space was 300 square feet and was fully furnished with folding tables and small, swivel chairs.

It was around 9:30 when he got there. He had time to work on a guidebook for a friend, a design project he'd secured when it was clear the magazine was not going to make it. Then he would meet a friend for lunch later.

As he powered up the Macintosh, his cell phone rang.

Chapter 17

After the first phone call, Rich's morning went downhill quickly. The first was from Chuck Yeager, a bill collector with a likable manor and a southern drawl from Pensacola, Florida.

He wasn't as pushy as some collectors, but he was persistent and consistent. He called every morning at 10 a.m. He acknowledged the last payment Rich had sent and subtly pressed Rich for a new payment commitment.

"Mr. Franklin," he would lead with, "you do understand that you have a commitment to pay this debt? When can we expect the next payment? And can we expect a larger payment this time?"

After giving his usual litany of excuses, Rich committed to another payment on the first of the month, with a slightly larger payment after that.

The second call was from a bill collector who Rich thought was a little too personable. He seemed to ask too many personal questions, and Rich got the feeling he knew more than he was letting on.

In a bizarre prisoner-of-war-interrogator sort of way, Rich began to enjoy talking to Enison. If he weren't trying to pry money out of him, they might have been friends.

Sometimes their discussion went well beyond money and slid into topics such as jazz and literature. Rich new he was being manipulated, but that didn't matter. Enison was the only collector who didn't make him feel sub-human. He seemed to empathize with Rich and seemed to understand how someone smart could do something so dumb.

"Rich, you're probably a very talented, intelligent guy, and what happened to you can happen to anyone, even me," he would say. Then he'd follow up with, "if I owed this money to you, you'd want me to figure out a way to pay you back, right?"

If Rich didn't affirm his question, he would ask again. "Right?"

Rich would reluctantly replay, "yes, sir."

"So, let's you and I figure out a way for you to pay me back," he'd say, "now, you get paid from you paper gig on the first of the month. How much of that check can you send me."

He would go on to outline the income sources Rich had told him about and they would arrive at a payment amount. It was much like talking to a financial advisor.

Before Enison would hang up, he would ask, "have you had any more interviews?" Rich would immediately think of April and wanted to say *your not the boss of me.*

But not wanting to aggravate his collector, he gave a straight answer. "Yes, sir, I've had a few and have some good prospects with agencies."

That seemed to suffice. But after all was said and done, both collectors wanted the same thing; money Rich didn't have and a commitment to pay twice the amount he'd paid the month before.

He was confident non of the collection agencies would send goons to break his legs if he didn't pay, but the process always left him feeling shifty and untrustworthy; two characteristics he never really wanted to associate with his persona. Then, he'd have to go through this same process again in a few weeks.

Rich spent part of the morning thinking of ways he could get more money. His thoughts even drifted to illegal means like bank robbery, or drug dealing.

Crime, he concluded, was not an option for him. But there were days that he felt like a caged animal, trapped in his life, needing quick solutions to persistent financial demands that he could not resolve.

Last month he had such a day. On that day, he gathered up some gold necklaces and opals he collected at estate sales and, visited The Silver Lining pawnshop on Sandy Boulevard.

When he walked in the front door, the line, which was 20 deep, snaked around the front of the shop, and the characters in line looked like they were auditioning for scumbag number six in a Brian De Palma movie. This was the shop where every fence, crook, or alcoholic dealt merchandise.

He remembered how all heads turned towards him and sized him up after he walked in. They all seemed to be thinking the same thing. *You may look respectable but today you're one of us.* As they waited their turn, they scratched and fidgeted, some looking around nervously, and a few abandoning the line because, after 20 minutes, their biological clocks had ticked off too much time without a fix.

Rich edged forward in the line. He watched each person who walked to the window and listened intently to their pitch and what the net result was.

In most cases, the results were not good. Directly in front of him a man with unkempt hair wearing tattered jean jacket, and gray dress slacks stepped up to the window. He shoved his hand into his pant pocket and retrieved a ring with a fair sized diamond on it. Rich could see the glistening rock from where he stood.

The clerk was a stocky man with hairy arms exposed past rolled up sleeves. He examined the ring under a magnifier. He looked at the customer. He looked at the ring again. Neither spoke.

Then he looked at the customer again and, without asking for a name, finally said, "How much you want?"

The man answered quickly, nervously, "I don't know. I bought it for $10,000. I need at least a thousand."

The clerk smiled and said, "Hmm," sizing up the customer's situation, which he assumed was desperate. Men who bring in their wives rings were always desperate. The clerk examined the ring again. He finally said, "I can give you fifty bucks."

"Fifty bucks!?" The customer yelled, shocked. "It's a very expensive ring," he reminded the clerk. "I need a thousand!"

The clerk glanced over at a large, muscular man with a crew cut who stood to his right. The security guard wore a swat team jacket, camouflage pants and had the distinct bulge of a Glock under his jacket.

"You know, I'd like to give you more, but we get lots of diamond rings. Most people don't pick them up and we get stuck with them. Fifty buck and we got a deal?"

The customer, bright red from anger and shifting from one foot to the next, put his hand to his forehead, turned, not knowing what to do next, oblivious of the eyes peering at him, finally said, "all right."

He had no other choice. He had gone beyond the end of his rope and $50 dollars was better than nothing.

At that point, Rich had had enough. He turned and walked out. He felt bad for the customer and for himself. That, he thought, was too humiliating.

As he drove back to the office he told himself that part of being brilliant required getting into jams *and* figuring a way out. The solution to this situation, however, was a little more elusive then he'd figured, but he would not—could not concede defeat. Not yet anyway. He still had a few cards up his sleeve…if he could only find them.

Rich's thoughts drifted back to the work he was doing. Rich spent three frustrating hours picking fonts, writing headlines, selecting clip art and other graphical elements, and fighting off the nagging sense of futility and dread that threatened to sabotage his efforts.

The sense of impending doom was overwhelming. And by the time noon came around, his tiny office felt even tinier. It was suffocating. He had to get out.

When the clock hit 12, he practically ran out of the building, barely remembering whether his feet landed on the three flights of stairs or not on his descent. When he was outside and the bright autumn sun hit his face, the demons fled, back into the dark, into confined spaces, afraid off the warmth and optimism the sun brought. He was safe for now.

He walked up Fourth Street towards the restaurant where he would have lunch with Phil Goldberg. Perhaps lunch with his good friend Phil would cheer him up. The lunch had been scheduled for weeks, and even though he wasn't feeling particularly sociable, he couldn't miss this date. A lot depended on it.

When Rich reached Burnside street, he turned west and, with a steady, assured stride, walked past seedy restaurants, dingy bars and silenced night clubs with dark characters from every situation imaginable lining the sidewalk. It was like a parade of the destitute.

Business people hurried by, not wanting to pause or linger too long or be forced to acknowledge the suffering or their own fear. They had businesses to run and millions to make. There were sad, life-worn street people, sitting, lost in front of run down hotels, eyeballing everyone who walked, looking for sympathy or an answer to the riddle that is their life. There were also White gen-X kids in baggy pants huddled in groups with skateboards lying on the ground beside them

A few blocks took him past the Burger King that provided gourmet goods to the downtrodden of Old Town, past Powells book store where Portland's White literate regulars and elite spent hours perusing books and feeding their minds with ideas of the ages, most oblivious to the suffering only blocks away.

One block beyond Powells were the remnants of the former Henry Weinhardts brewery, now a condo complex for those who could afford a $900,000 views.

Downtown Portland was a contradiction in action. Most buildings were aging commercial structures built during the 1900s by lumber barons as testimonials of their incredible wealth.

Rich knew the truth behind their wealth, though. Early pioneer families made millions based on their ability to cut down trees and sell them to the highest bidder. More importantly, they had gotten here first and claimed the most amount of land, coincidentally, with the most trees and the most resources.

In the northwest territory, if you were White and arrived early enough, you could claim a 600 acres of land, or buy as many claims as you could for next to nothing. It was a hell of a deal, Rich thought, as he admired the buildings.

Some of the building were ornate with sculpted ironwork facades and terra cotta trimmings, while others were neo-classic Italianette structures, perfect examples of a city that had—and still has—illusions of grandeur. Early builders threw in a little Italy,

Germany, France and Southern into their building designs.

The sad truth, Rich though, was that Portland would always be an oversized cow town with more brewpubs and strip joints per capita than anywhere else in the country. In its effort to keep up with other popular cities, Portland had morphed into a pseudo-cosmopolitan barely-urban city with one good restaurant for every 100 bad ones. The lumber barons and the lumber were gone and Portland was left to find its way in the economic dark without a flashlight. Rich felt it was up to people like him and Phil to put Portland back on the map and make it a halfway interesting place to live.

Rich was meeting Phil at Jake's Famous Seafood Restaurant, one of his favorites. Phil would be there ahead of their scheduled time. There was a lot of preparation that went into their lunches; photographers, crews, even make-up, which Rich was not looking forward to. The idea of brown makeup 25 and lobster was not appealing to him. But it was necessary for what Phil had in mind.

Rich crossed Burnside and headed towards Ankeny Street. The block that housed Jake's was a living, throbbing cultural anomaly. On one corner was Jake's, which opened in 1898. It entertained such celebrities as Humphrey Bogart and Joan Crawford. It was an expensive restaurant by Portland standards.

Above the restaurant was a transient hotel, a low-rent hiding place for destitute souls and a first and last home for forgotten Portland residents who'd lived there for fifty years or more.

Each corner surrounding the restaurant had a different commuter hotel with names like the St. Francis, the Drake, the Knight's Inn, and the seediest of them all, the Empire.

Their names exuded upscale luxury, and, at one point housed the cultural and social elite of the city. Now, heavy bars covered the windows of the lobbies, and you could see the shadows of lonely, forgotten characters in open windows. Every third or fourth window, looked like the smokestack of a steam engine as cigarette smoke wafted out in regular intervals. Other rooms had sullen, pasty, or black wrinkled faces staring out, waiting for it to get dark so they could hit the liquor store on the corner and get juiced up for the night. Some faces, clearly said, "I'm waiting to die."

The blinking red and green neon lights on Jake's marquee flashed around a giant lobster and looked like an island in a sea of sleaze, a true beacon buoy in hell's harbor.

Rich walked quickly, confidant, so he was not accosted by any of the huddled groups outside the liquor store across from the restaurant. As Rich got closer to Jake's, he could see that the usual gaffer trucks had arrived, and inside was wild scrambling, preparations for his lunch with Phil. He took a deep breath and dashed across the street to the restaurant entrance.

Chapter 18

When Trixie woke at around noon that day her head hurt. It hurt with the kind of dull throbbing pain she often got from crying too much, sleeping too little and not eating enough. Her mouth was dry. Cottony. She let out a muffled cough and cleared her throat several times as her blurred surroundings came into focus. The bright sun could be seen through the edges of the van's dark, plaid curtains. The smell of China Rain was strong in the air.

It was warm and stuffy and light beads of sweat covered her forehead and her chest. Her clothes were drenched. Before falling asleep, she had closed all the windows and locked them, fearing that Chico might come back and try to break in.

She suddenly found it difficult to breathe. She panicked. She quickly reached across her bed, pushed the back curtain aside then shoved the glass open. The window clicked open.

Trixie's thin, white, silk T-shirt fluttered against her skin as the cool breeze came through the window. Goose bumps formed over her entire body. The breeze tickled her exposed skin and swirled under her blouse, instantly cooling her off.

Trixie enjoyed the sensation and leaned back in the bed and moaned as nature surrounded her body. She closed her eyes and imagined the wind as an icy cold tongue, licking her body, arousing her, teasing her, preparing her for something extraordinary. The China rain caressed her nostrils and she felt herself quickly getting aroused.

She breathed in deeply, and imagined the wind was her lover, sent by the sun to wake her and pleasure her. She sighed and moaned and ran her hand from her thigh, over her stomach, across her breast, up over her head and there she felt for the on button of her CD player.

She gently pressed the button and the first song queued and started slowly with acoustic guitars, followed by the sullen, sensual voice of Jill Cohn singing…

…*Some of us are not of this world*…

Trixie moaned again as the excitement began to build.

…*My pain is all I've known until now*…

Eyes still closed, she let the pleasure consume her as her fingers probed and rubbed and the wind surrounded her, lifting her beyond the van and into that place she longed to be, beyond earth, beyond space, beyond men, beyond women, to a place where there is only nature and pleasure and peace.

Her motions became more pronounced as she became more aroused. She tried hard to suppress her moans, but it was difficult.

…*I think I'm going to disappear and escape all the things that are haunting me all these years…*

She was too consumed with pleasure to sing along as she usually did, but she knew the songs Cohen sang were appropriate for her. She was lost in her passion and pleasure and she could feel the music inside of her, filling her, touching her. It was the music and the China Rain and the wind and the sun that caused her body to tremble and spasm

…Hey, I'm free, hey, I'm free and I'm no longer afraid to be…

She was free, she thought and no longer afraid. As she heard those words, her whole body tightened and spasmed. There was nothing and everything, no thought, no feelings, only pure emotion. Her spirit was whisked out of her body and sucked into a vortex with walls lined with everything good Trixie had ever seen or felt. She traveled at the speed of light, faster, faster. Then, as if a Rocket shooting into space that runs out of fuel, she quickly descended from that mysterious place, energy sapped. Her body went limp. She was cold and sweaty all over. Her breathing was deep and rapid, and her heart pounded like a bass drum. For a few minutes she was tragically happy.

Chapter 19

Jake's was bustling with activity when Rich arrived. Count Basie's *One O'clock Jump* blared over the loud speakers. He walked past the long, ornate, mahogany bar. An aging, discolored tin ceiling hung overhead, and antique pictures of pioneer scenes were positioned on the walls in the middle of each of the high-back, private wood booths. Each table was dressed with a pristine white tablecloth, impeccably buffed empty wine glasses, full cloth napkins and fancy polished silverware.

A few well-dressed patrons, waitresses and a slew of fashionably dressed arty types busied themselves with light meters, cameras and equipment. Rich recognized most in the bar as friends and members of Phil's posse of creative cronies. This was a lovable, affable bunch of mostly creative misfits who supported Phil because he was their landlord in the cheap artists lofts he owned, partly because he paid well, and partly because they thought he was a quirky, kind-hearted, creative genius. Rich thought the same and allowed Phil to sucked him into many of his crazy schemes. This was one of them. Fortunately, they had cooked this was one up together and had no idea where it would lead.

"Richie," a familiar voice yelled from across the room. "We're over here and we're almost ready."

Rich waved, smiled, took his jacket off and hung it on the brass hook by one of the booths. He walked over to Phil, who was dressed in khaki slacks and a conservative button-down blue Siskol & Ebert shirt. His bifocals hung just below his eyes and his graying short, thinning hair was pressed and starched, and a pretty make-up lady named Brenda Rapp was fusing over it as he walked towards Rich.

"I can't get these last hairs to stay down, Phil," Brenda said, frustrated. Brenda held up a mirror in front of Phil. He looked at himself, frowned, then said. "Let it stick up. It will give viewers something to laugh about. Brenda, can you work your magic on Rich."

"Sure Phil. Hi Richie. How are you?" She asked between chews of her gum.

"Fine, Brenda. You?"

"I'm peachy," she replied hugging Rich and extending her cheek for a kiss. "Are you ready for the shoot today?"

"Been looking forward to it all week," Rich said sarcastically.

"Rich," Phil said as he gave Rich a familiar bear hug, his six-foot frame swallowing Rich whole. "Got a great show today Rich. You and me. We're gonna put Martha Stewart out of business."

"Are you sure about that?" Rich asked.

"Sure I'm sure. Nothing like this has ever been done before.

And you and me make a great team," Phil said, "an Jamaican African American intellectual and an eccentric, Jewish former guru, talking restaurants and current affairs."

He laughed out loud and put his hands on Rich's shoulder, "Rich, it's perfect."

Rich smiled at the thought. "You're right, Phil, but some days I kick myself in the head for planting this idea in your head, knowing how you are."

"Well, Richie, my dear friend, as they say in the movies, it's just too God damn late, so enjoy the ride."

They exchanged raised eyebrows and familiar, friendly smiles as they walked over to a single table in the far corner of the restaurant by the large window that looked out onto the street. Inside, there was a frenzy of activity, lights, and cameras.

Outside, people stood around marveling at the activity. Brenda followed Rich to a table near the one that was the center of attention. Rich carefully navigated past the digital camera power cords, audio mixing boards, an electronic TelePrompTer, flood lights and reflectors and sat in one of the vacant chairs. Brenda sat next to him and opened her small tackle box that contained her makeup kit.

"Don't tell me, Brenda," Rich grinned, "Brown 25, right?"

She giggled. "Right Rich. Just for you so the cameras won't lose you in the dark wood background."

Brenda was by far one of Rich's favorite Phil cronies. She was a painter, dangerously pretty and completely selfless about it. The bright red lipstick she wore highlighted full lips, and, at five foot 10, she turned heads of men and women wherever she went. Brenda had an incomprehensible air about her that was part royalty, part artist, and part flake. Because of that, serious relationships eluded her. She preferred to spend her time painting, reading, or working on Phil's projects like these. She felt at home with the characters Phil attracted.

"You know," Rich said loud enough for Brenda and the camera man, Rock Teasdale to hear, "they could make a camera that is designed to balance out the skin color of black people. Then you'll have to put brown 25 on Phil. Don't you think that's fair? After years of oppression, we are still getting dissed by camera manufacturers. Brutha can't get a break!"

"Rich," Rock said, "it's nothing personal. We just need to set up more manufacturing in Africa so products will come back slightly different, adjusted so they're perfect for black people."

Rock smiled and added, "For example, stereo volume buttons will start at 10 and go to 20. You know how we like to listen to our shit loud."

Brenda, Rock and Rich all laughed in unison.

"See, Rock," Rich added, "you and me got to stick together. We can change some shit."

"We're doin' that right now," he replied, "so pile that brown 25 on like your life depends on it and let's make a film."

"When this is all over, I'm going to write a sitcom about a couple of black cops called Brown 25 where are you."

They laughed again and Brenda continued to brush on Rich's make up.

Rock was a likable soul with dreadlocks and thick Malcolm X glasses. He adjusted his cameras and the lighting. Rock was the director and a perfectionist. He graduated from NYU during the Spike Lee days. As one of the few black filmmakers in the school, he was expected to follow in Spike's footsteps and make films about black anger. Rock wasn't having any of that. He preferred instead to take on odd projects like this one, ones that bridge the gap, as he called it between black and white society in a non-threatening, non-confrontational way.

Rock grew up in the same project that Spike Lee grew up in, saw the same "niggas" get shot, didn't know his "daddy", spent plenty of time in jail, had the same black stigma as any other brutha, but he was not angry.

During their midnight chess and coffee sessions at McMenamins Pub, Rock would often say to Rich with conviction, "we still got it better then most mother fuckers in the world, so we need to stop bitchin' about our situation and find creative ways to get what we need and manipulate the system through art. Through literature. Through sound. After 400 years, White people get tired hearing about that same shit over and over and over. There are millions of White people who got it worse when many of us. What do we say about them? That they got it bad because of prejudice. No, they got it bad because they gave up. We, as a people have an opportunity here. And we can never give up."

Rich loved Rock. They could identify with each other. Rock confided in Rich that if this project involved two White guys, he would not have taken it. But because he considered Rich a "God damn genius without a fuckin' clue" he took it on. Rich's reply to that comment was, "I don't know whether to thank you or kick your ass right now. You choose."

Rock was incredible bright and sly. He smiled, sipped his Amstel Light and said, "use your talents brother, use your talents." This was Rock. Always turn anger and confrontation into positives.

"Snap out of it Rich," Phil said as he walked towards Rich. "I can tell you're drifting off to some literary, intellectual never, never land, probably doing some kind of character analysis on Rock or something. But there's no time for that now. I think we are ready. Here's today's script." He handed Rich a single sheet of paper.

"Phil!" Rich exclaimed, sitting up and turning the face of the paper towards Phil and pointing at it as he continued, "this is not a script!"

"Sure it is, Richie. It's—"

"It's one page, Phil." Rich said. "These are instructions."

"That's right, Rich." Phil responded, befuddled, "script instructions for this episode of *Two Guys Having Lunch*. But it's more than we had for our first shoot."

"True," Rich agreed, "but I'm not sure we're making progress with this. What are we supposed to say and when? What are we supposed to do?"

"That, Richie, is up to you and me."

"You remember the last shoot, Phil, there was more dead air at our table than at the local mortuary."

"I was a little nervous. I've never done anything like this before." Phil said, embarrassed. "I've been rehearsing. I think it will be better this time. I just have to think about all our regular lunches without the cameras and I'll be fine."

"And let me get this straight," Rich said, "you say here that today's topic is whatever comes to our heads."

Rich read the instructions again to be sure.

"Well, er, yes, but to tell you the truth, you can pick a subject. I'm okay with that."

Rich scratched his head. He wasn't angry. This was Phil's style. He just had to figure out a way to salvage this shoot so it wasn't a disaster like the first one.

"Okay, Phil," Rich conceded, "while my brown 25 dries into clay and makes my face stiff like a used pair of underwear, I'll be thinking of something."

"Thanks Rich. I knew you would come up with something. You're a God damn genius you know that?"

"Everybody keeps telling me that," Rich replied, "but I'm not buying today. *We* can make this work, not *me*. So let's take a deep breath and see where it goes."

Rich glanced at Rock. Rock winked. Rich smiled. Phil gave him another bear hug and as he walked over the maiter'd, he fussed with his hairs sticking up on top of his head with a big comb.

"A little more Afro sheen please, Brenda." Rich said. This time she laughed hysterically. She leaned over and planted a big kiss on Rich's cheek.

"Now," she said, "you're ready. Brown 25 applied to perfection and big ruby red lip marks on your cheek."

"Bring in the clowns," Rich said. They both laughed again as Brenda brushed out the red lip marks and balanced Rich's cheek bones so the cameras didn't make him look dead or severe.

Chapter 20

Trixie waited for the bus on 42nd Street. She was melancholy but not sad. She had a few hours during the day to do whatever she pleased. She had plenty of money, $5,000 stashed away in a thermos in her lunchbox purse, and she had lots of creative ways to spend it.

Trixie was a stunning sight to behold. She did not dress provocatively during her off-hours, but it was nearly impossible to hide her curvaceous features. She could attract attention simply standing at a bus stop. Men and women alike did double-takes to glimpse the pretty, Sandy-haired, girlish siren standing innocently by the sign.

Her black, skin-tight, leather bellbottoms flowed evenly over stylish, matching black platform shoes. Her hair was brushed free-style to perfection, partially covering the shoulders of her black, knee length leather jacket. The thin. white blouse she wore was designed to hover over her navel and fit tightly around her breast. She never wore a bra.

When the bus arrived, she boarded and took a seat towards the front, in full view of the bus driver's oversized interior mirror. There was nothing to do now except wait for her stop. She turned and stared out the window, thinking about her plans for the day, aware that a pair of eyes were, at that moment, undressing her.

The bus driver, Bud Guzman, was a pudgy, frustrated fifty year old with a failing marriage and kids who hated him. The best part of his job was eyeballing women who entered his domain. He felt he had a special privilege and a right to ogle as he pleased. He had seen Trixie before and, from the first time he had seen her, he was smitten. She was a real-life embodiment of the woman he conjured up during those rare private moments at home when he beat out his sexual frustration by himself in the bathroom.

Guzman sneaked peaks at Trixie in the wide mirror as he navigated the first few blocks. Trixie was aware of the attention. She took some pleasure in it but pretended not to notice. At one point, she fanned her chest with her hand as if too hot, then subtly unbuttoned her jacket and pushed it open.

Guzman could barely take his eyes off her. As he drove, he was like a chameleon, one eye was on the road, and the other was on Trixie. At every stop, he imagined he was at home, in his bed performing all sorts of repulsive acts on Trixie.

As Guzman indulged in his fantasies, he ignored his right rear-view mirror. If he had been watching closely after Trixie got on the bus, he would have seen the impish Mexican American frantically peddling his 15-speed bicycle after the bus as it pulled away from the curb. He would have seen the pathetic figure edge closer to the bus and grab the Thomason Auto Group advertisement frame and let the bus pull him along while he steered and braked with the other hand. The pathetic figure looked like he was going into cardiac arrest.

That pathetic figure was Chico hitching a tow from the bus. Chico was barely out of sight behind the bus as it pulled him along. He was desperate to find out where Trixie went during the daylight hours and what she did with her money. So today he broke his pattern and came out during the daylight hours to follow her.

Trixie was oblivious. The bus driver was oblivious. The only one who noticed Chico was a five-year-old standing in the back window looking at the flat headed Mexican American clinging to the bus.

The five-year-old boy laughed at Chico and stuck his tongue out at him. At the next stop, Chico glanced up and saw the kid laughing at him, sneered and flipped him off. The five-year-old, not knowing any better, turned to his mother and, showing her the gesture and asked, "What does this mean?" The mother slapped the boy hard on the head, grabbed his shoulder, and forced him to sit down. As he sobbed and sniffled, he attempted to say, "Bommby, a Mexican man made me do it." The mother slapped him again for his racial insensitivity and told him to shut up before he was given something to cry about.

Chico was sweating and afraid. Chico cursed at the driver. He was insane. He took extra time at stops. He speed up at speed bumps instead of slowing down, and he recklessly pulled away from the curves as if he were driving a Volkswagen beetle instead of a city bus.

The dust and fumes got into Chico's eyes, making them burn and itch. He felt nauseous and several times, he almost didn't grab on quick enough, so he would have to peddle to catch up or risk losing his hitch altogether.

The bus turned on Columbia Boulevard and Chico panicked. Should he abandon this crazy idea or hold on. Columbia Boulevard was a main thoroughfare, a road where drivers reached speeds up to 65 miles per hour. The bus began to pick up speed. Twenty. Thirty, forty. Fifty. Sixty. Fumes and dirt and gravel slammed Chico in the face like a Midwest bug storm.

Passers by attempted to flag the bus driver down to let him know that there was an uninvited Mexican American attached to his rear end. But Guzman just smiled and waved back. He was too busy eyeballing Trixie and trying not to get an erection at the wheel. But it was difficult. Trixie's breasts were partially exposed through her unbuttoned leather jacket and every bump was an adventure for

Guzman. The faster he went, the more the force of the bumps caused her breast to vibrate and giggle. The more they vibrated and giggled, the harder he got. Soon, he had a full woody and had to grab a rag on the dash to cover himself or be found out. An older women, about age 90 looked at him suspiciously. He smiled a guilty smile at her and turned his attention back to Trixie.

Trixie pulled the cord to request a stop. A bell sounded in the front of the bus. Guzman pulled over to the bus stop. Trixie stood up and walked slowly past him. She glanced over at his beet red face, then down at his crotch, now covered with a greasy rag. Bud was sweating and his bright red face was like a neon sigh screaming, *I just pitched a tent!*

"Thank you, sir. I enjoyed the ride. Did you?" Trixie asked. Guzman could say nothing.

Trixie stepped off the bus, smiling the entire way. She knew the power she wielded over men. Guzman reluctantly closed the doors and planned an unscheduled stop at a gas station a few blocks away. He had a mess to clean up in private.

Chico saw Trixie getting off the bus. He panicked and peddled quickly to the opposite side of the street, across the four lanes of the busy road. The bus offered a shield to keep him from being detected by Trixie, but it would soon pull away from the curve, so Chico had to hurry.

As he neared the center median a semi-tractor trailer blared its horn as it passed Chico, only inches away from ending his life. He was going too fast. He was too frazzled and exhausted to apply the brake properly and avoid a car blocking his path. He slammed into the side of the car and found himself airborne, screaming as he flew over the hood of the parked beater car and landed in a ditch filled with mature blackberry bushes with inch-long thorns.

Pain shot through every part of his body as the thorns pierced him from all directions like a thousand stinging bees. After he came to a stand still at the base of the ditch, he jumped up immediately and scrambled out of the ditch as quickly as he could, ran around to he opposite side of the beater car, grabbed his bike, inspected it quickly for damage and pushed it around to the side that shielded him from view of the bus. Chico's instincts and ability to run and hide were legendary in L.A.

The city bus drove away just as Chico found shelter behind the car. Trixie stood there, looking around, oblivious to Chico across the street. She saw the car and thought she detected movement, but could see nothing upon inspection. She then turned and walked towards the large, new building with an enormous sign that invited passers by to come in and participate.

After Trixie disappeared in the front door, Chico emerged from his hiding place and peered at the sign. As Chico read the sign, he clenched his fist and teeth so tightly, they started to ache. He was fuming with anger. He cussed loudly in Spanish and English, spitting his words and kicking at the abandoned car while screaming "Son of bitches! God damn mother fucking son of bitches!" He began slapping himself on the head and pacing in a circle. "I don't believe this fucking sheet!!"

The sign on the building read in simple San serif text SPCA. In smaller letter it said *Our New Facility is Now Open*.

Chico was furious. This was the insult she added to injury. He had confided his hatred of the SPCA to Trixie and explained that "anyone who is a friend of cats is my enemy."

This was personal. Other people were always fucking with him, he thought, and he didn't need no cock-tease hairy hippie bitch doing the same. He got on his battered bike and started riding back to his studio. His front tire wobbled slightly, bent from the impact with the car. He had tiny bloodstains on his pants, shirt, and face from his fall in the berry vines. Chico was a remarkable sight, riding alone on a busy street, the bike vibrating angrily as it picked up speed. Chico had been dissed. Chico was tired. He needed to go to bed. He had some shit to tend to that night.

Chapter 21

A pandemonium of activity now filled Jake's as Rock performed light checks, Phil busied himself with details and Brenda did her nails, while looking extremely lovely and extremely bored.

"Phil," Rich called as he stood and walked over to the register where Phil and Ben Stafford, the restaurant manager stood discussing the shoot.

"Yeah, Rich," Phil answered, "What's up?"

"Excuse me Ben," said Rich, exchanging handshakes with Ben, an impeccably dressed, square jawed, former fraternity captain with strong cologne, polished teeth and a perfect false Oregon tan. "I need a computer with a printer to hammer out some ideas."

Phil turned to Ben and said, "Ben, I appreciate all that you've done here, and I know the request keep coming, but—"

"Don't mention it Phil," Ben interrupted. "Whatever you need, I'll try to take care of it. You and Rich have more than paid for anything I could do for you in lunches over the past years. I have a small office in the back with a laptop and printer. I'll show you."

"Thank you Ben," Rich said. "I'll only need it for a few minutes."

"Got an idea, Rich," Phil probed.

"I think so. Rich replied as he walked with Ben towards the rear of the restaurant. "Can you stall everyone for about a half hour?"

"A half hour?" Phil asked, surprised. "Rich, I have to pay some of these people. What do I tell them?"

"I don't know Phil. Tell them we don't have a script and you're waiting for me to write it."

"Are you serious?"

"I'm sort of serious. Give me a half hour and I'll work this all out. I also have to make a few phone calls."

"All right Rich. I'll put in an order for our meal. Are we having Lobster for lunch today."

"Is it the most expensive meal on the menu?"

"Nothing quite compares."

"Then sign me up. I work best when I've had a really expensive meal."

"Rich," Phil said, "If I didn't know better, I'd swear we got mixed up at birth and that you grew up in the Connecticut suburbs with my family and I grew up in Junction City, Kansas, the son of first generation Caribbean islanders."

"Phil," Rich replied, with a hint of sarcasm, "When you were a guru, didn't they teach you that we are all part of a collective consciousness?"

"Of course. But I never bought into that."

"Believe it Phil. I am your brother," Rich said and paused, thinking about what he had said. He continued, "And your mother and your father and anyone you've ever know."

Phil laughed out loud. "Can we talk about this over lunch…mom?" Phil asked.

"Make sure you eat your spinach." Rich shot back, "I have to go to work now. I'll see you in a half hour."

"Okay, Rich. I'll keep the troops assembled."

Phil returned to the main restaurant area while Rich followed Ben to the office. The office was a tiny room beyond the bathrooms in the back of the restaurant. An ancient laptop sat on a small wood desk, almost obscured by bills and invoices and letters. Ben apologized for the mess and told Rich to make himself comfortable and call if he needed anything. Rich thanked him again and sat at the table, opened Microsoft Word, sat back in the chair and gave him self two minutes to collect his thoughts.

Rich knew how his brain worked. His talent was predictable and reliable to a certain extent, and most people who ever worked with him knew that. He either planted an idea in his head, slept on it and by morning had a complete picture. Or, he thought about the problem for two minutes, then turned on a switch in his head and ideas came flowing out. The only thing he required was something to write with. He flashed back for a second to his days as a reporter for the *Kansas City Star*. This scenario was typical; a half hour to produce a feature story from scratch. Being a reporter, he reflected, was the best training for creativity on the fly.

Chapter 22

When Trixie entered the offices of the SPCA, everyone recognized her and greeted her enthusiastically. The receptionist, a young, plain girl with long brown hair and forgettable features, talked with Trixie. Trixie told here she wanted to see the executive director and was escorted to his office, where she made a small donation to the organization and afterwards spent about an hour visiting with and playing with the animals and talking with the employees.

She was aware of all the bus schedules, so, noting that she was due for her next visit, she rushed out the front door after saying goodbye to everyone and reached the stop in front of the building just as the next bus was arriving. She waved the bus down and jumped on.

The bus took her through North Portland, over the expansive St. John's Bridge, which crossed the Willamette River just North of downtown Portland. The view was spectacular, and Trixie loved this route. She marveled at the expanse of the river and it's power as it meandered towards the ocean.

After the bus crossed the River, it turned south on Highway 30 and traveled through the industrial area, towards downtown, eventually turning on to Burnside Street and traveling west on Burnside to 4th Street. She got off the bus there and made two more stops at two more Non-profit organization offices, Central City Concerns and The Oregon Food Bank, making sizable donations at each office.

As she walked on Burnside, the cat calls came at every turn along with other obscene gestures and suggestions. Trixie ignored them. When she reached Powells, she crossed at the light. As she crossed, she could feel the eyes on her, undressing her, touching her, fondling here, wanting here. But she was unfazed. She walked towards Ankeny, stopped at the Empire Hotel front door and pressed a buzzer.

The attendant pressed a button to release the door. Before she opened it, she turned to see a handsome African American man walking quickly by. She was stricken by his intensity. Their eyes met for only a few seconds. She mapped his features. He seemed to map hers. She watched him as he walked by, holding the door open as she stared. He quickly crossed the street to a restaurant she'd eaten in many times before. She noticed that something unusual was going on at Jake's. There were trucks and people gathered who seemed to be doing everything but eating.

She walked into the hotel, went up to the third floor, fished for a key in her lunchbox purse, inserted it in the door and turned the key. As she opened the door, a familiar smell hit her nostrils. She knew what was waiting for her there.

Chapter 23

When Rich emerged from the small office in the back of Jake's, all eyes focused on him as he approached Phil with a handfuls of white, loose papers and handed them to him. Rich and Phil walked toward the front of the restaurant and huddled there, analyzing what was on the paper, nodding intermittently.

Eventually, they turned towards the crew, observing that all eyes watched them closely. As the crew saw the smiles on their faces, several, including Rock, breathed an internal sigh of relief. Rich walked over to Rock and handed him the 20 pages.

"Okay, Rock," Rich said reluctantly, "This is what I think we can use as a script for today's shoot. "If you don't think we can do this, we cancel the shoot for today and come up with something that makes sense for next time and I'm sorry we wasted yours and everyone's time."

Rock carefully perused the papers, expressionless, only occasionally glancing up at Rich, neither smiling or frowning, nor giving away his approval or disapproval.

When he finished reviewing the last sheet, he let his hands fall to his sides, still holding the script, looked at Rich and said, "God damn, Rich, you really expect us to do this?"

Rich, replied nervously, "Listen, Rock, I know it's ambitious, but I think—"

"Rich," Rock interrupted, "Don't get me wrong. This is fucking brilliant, I'm just asking if you think we can do this. Yes or no?"

Rich was tense, on guard, and it took a few seconds for Rock's question to sink in. "Rock, we can do this. Yes. Yes. I think we can do this."

Rock began nodding without saying anything, and looked Rich straight in the eyes, deciding what to say next.

Finally, he said, "Okay, Rich, let's make it happen. After that disastrous shoot last week, I figured you'd think of something else."

Rich could only smile and say, "Thank you Rock."

Rock turned to his crew, "All right people, here's what we need. I need these cameras moved and one additional camera over here. And bring the steady cam in and have it ready. Plus, I need someone to run down to the newsstand to get some cigars."

"I'll get the cigars," Brenda volunteered. "My work is done, so at least I can pick my favorites. I love cigars." Brenda walked towards the front door.

"I have a lot of work to do in 15 minutes," Rock said with a commanding, more serious tone. "Be ready for camera call gentlemen.

We roll tape for exactly one hour straight with no cuts and no breaks. One take does it. Rich, is everybody scheduled? And will they all be here?"

"Yes, sir, Mr. Rock sir. Everything's ready. Everyone's confirmed," Rich saluted Rock.

"Very funny, private. All right, Let's do this. You and Phil spend some time covering your discussion points and the queues. It doesn't have to be perfect, but we do have to have enough to edit."

"We'll be ready," Phil said. He and Rich retreated to the back office to review the script, confirming the schedule with Ben on the way. Ben barked a few instructions to his staff and everyone scrambled in a frenzy of activity.

Chapter 24

Trixie pushed the door to the apartment open and breathed in deeply. The air was rich with the fragrant smell of jasmine, herbal oils, rose petals, and China Rain. Mixed in with those scents were layers of other sweet scents, such as, lavender, strawberry and mango.

The main room of the apartment was small, and every wall was lined with at least one second-hand book shelf and photographs, paintings and illustrations of women and erotic art.

Some paintings were originals while others were pages torn from magazines and taped in cheap frames. There were pictures of Freda Kalo and Gertrude Stein, Cindy Crawford and Madonna, and prints of paintings by George O'Keefe and Edward Degas ballet dancers.

Trixie closed the door, set the deadbolt, took off her jacket and hung it on the hook behind the door. She walked slowly around the room, touching the books on the shelves and the potted plants as she passed them, smiling and breathing slowly and deeply.

Each shelf had hand written labels taped to the edges. Each shelf was categorized by subject and painted a different pastel color. The labels read *Earth, wind, sky, human nature, men, women, sex, history*.

This was her secret place. Her reading room, her escape. Her library. Her space. She perused the book titles. There were books about Native American culture and spirituality, about women and sexuality, about earth spirits and giaia and tantric love making.

One of the book shelves contained an incense holder and cinnamon Feng Shui incense blocks. She lit the block and walked over to a small couch near a window that looked out onto the street. She could clearly see Jake's across the street and hear the sounds of cars passing below.

A small CD player sat on a table next to her couch and CDs were scattered on the table next to it. She picked them up, shuffled through them, then selected a CD by Janice Skroggins, another local jazz singer she'd been admiring for years. She put the CD in and Janice's strong, deep, passionate voice eased into *Stormy Monday*. Akbar Depriest kept tempo on the drums, and legend Frank De La Rosa was smooth as silk on bass. Janice rounded out the trio on keyboards as she sang.

The cinnamon incense filled the room. The afternoon light danced through the sheer curtains that lined the single window. Trixie looked around and turned the movie cameras on in her head. The music, the light, the smells all created a scene she loved. Janice eased in to *You've Changed*, as if on queue and the sunlight adjusted to the scene.

Trixie drifted into a deep sleep. The music became part of the psychedelic canvas that swirled around in her head, a Peter Max painting with jazz and the scents were colors, the car horns were oils, and the sudden intrusion of yells in the hall all melded into the canvas. The moment was devoid of anger. Devoid of frustration. Her past was past. There was no here. There was no there. There was only this place.

In a distance there was a ringing that formed into rose hips and bright red Camellia flowers. Each ring was red or blue or chartreuse or magenta. They got louder and louder and louder. Scroggins sang *God Bless the Child*. The ringing got louder and louder and louder, and Trixie's eyes snapped open.

Her cell phone was ringing. It was in the bathroom. She walked into the small bathroom, picked up the phone and pressed the button to talk.

"Hello," she said. She listened intently then answered. "Okay. Same place? All Right. Bye."

She hung up the phone, sat on the toilet and began to sob softly and Scroggins sang, ...*thems that got shall have, so the Bible says*.

Trixie was frustrated that she could feel so much joy and feel so much pain at the same time. She needed a long hot bath with 50 candles burning so she could be absolved by the earth spirits that watched over her. She had an appointment at the Benson Hotel, then she would be blessed by the presence of the Delia Lama. Then she would return to her van to complete her mission.

Chapter 25

Sam Enison was 30,000 feet in the air and settling into his last-minute flight as two gin and tonics warmed his stomach. While the plane gained altitude, the pressure increased and the buttoned-down collar of Sam's white, pressed shirt and multi-colored paisley silk tie seemed to cut off his circulation like a boa constrictor tightening its death grip around his neck.

He loosened his tie, opened the first button and the relief was instantaneous. The plane vibrated slightly between occasional jolts as it settled into the jet stream. The bumps were fine, but the jolts made Sam nervous. He hated flying. Three Gin and tonics helped him relax. But they were rarely enough. The afternoon sun was so bright it caused Sam to squint as it blasted through his window. He pulled the shade down half-way, clenched the leather arm rest of his first-class seat as if preparing for impact, breathed in deeply, mumbled *here's looking at you, kid*, then took another sip of his drink as he thought about the events of that morning that led to him being on this flight in the first place.

The trip was the result of a last-minute brainstorm he had after talking with one of his targets. He was so excited he e-mailed the travel agency and had them book the first flight out. He had 10 hours to execute the next phase of his plan then catch a redeye back to Oakland and be at his desk by 9 a.m. the following morning, in time for a meeting with a new client.

This idea, he thought, was so brilliant, it was one he might even be able to retire off of afterwards. If he was lucky. The thought caused a sly smile to form on his face.

Clearing the last-minute flight at the office was not as easy as Sam had hoped. Sam rarely asked for permission to take trips, but recently, all of his trips were scrutinized by the CFO Chet Baker, a wound-up pencil pusher who's suits and glasses were too big for his body, and the bald spot on top of his head get bigger by hourly increments instead of years. He was Sam's nemesis, always looking for ways to discredit Sam by pouring over his expense reports, even intercepting his e-mails, trying to find a reason to get him fired.

For Sam, it was a game. But Baker was playing for keeps. He was a whiz at numbers. He held a Ph. D in Business and a law degree from Yale. He had rescued ACS from the brink of bankruptcy two years earlier because Sam and Jeremy were so busy closing accounts, they didn't have time to scrutinize an incompetent, embezzling accountant.

Baker, with his flawless knack for numbers and knowledge of tax law, cleaned up the paperwork and organized the books. Now, ACS was a model company, regularly hiring new agents, very profitable, and very much in demand with large corporate clients. Accounts like American Express. After Sam secured the account with Sweet Susie, American Express handed their firm hundreds of millions of dollars worth of delinquent *celebrity* accounts to collect on a silver platter.

Sam's position and success didn't matter to Baker. Baker considered Sam a has-been, an unnecessary expense, a general burden on the company and the ledger.

Baker's problems was he only looked at numbers and ignored history. He also severely lacked recognizable people skills. Sam treated Baker like the equivalent of a corporate performing monkey. Bring him to meetings, turn him lose, sit back and let him perform. But after the meeting was over, hustle him back to his corporate cage and feed him a healthy salary. Never, ever leave him alone with the clients.

Baker resented Sam's treatment and attitude. Baker thought he had a lot more to offer. But time and again he proved that office politics was not his forte and he ended up being the butt of many office jokes and stepping on many toes.

Baker intercepted Sam's e-mails to the travel agency that morning and minutes later barged into Sam's office, frothing at the mouth and sprinkling dandruff flakes everywhere as he huffed and puffed in front of Sam, berating him about the last-minute trip.

"What the hell is this Enison, another one of your Goddamn escapades?" Baker yelled. "You know, it was these trips that helped get the company into hot water in the first place. I worked my ass off to dig us out of the hole you helped put us in yet you still repeat the same patterns? What do I have to do to get you to follow procedure? All trips have to be approved two weeks in advance and we need to run the numbers on them to make sure we're not losing money."

Sam, leaned back in his chair after Baker's initial tirade, put both hands on top of his head, hooked his fingers behind his head and stared at Baker. He allowed him the pleasure of finishing, but not the benefit of a reaction. Baker, his dark suit dragging in the air that surrounded it because of its size, had worked up an angry sweat.

"Well,' Baker demanded, "what do you have to say for yourself?"

Sam stared at Baker as he rocked slowly in his chair. Silence, he thought, was the most intimidating response. Sam said nothing.

Air in the room seemed scarce and was heavy with Baker's cheap cologne and stifling disdain. Sam continued to stare. Baker attempted to return the stare but instead blinked uncontrollably as the pressure welled behind eyes that could only identify with Excel spread sheets and access databases.

"Chet," Sam finally said, "don't get yourself all worked up. You're only 48, and you're heading for a heart attack."

"Jesus Christ Enison!" Baker fired back, "This is not some kind of game. Your lack of respect for me is legendary and I've had it up to here with it!"

He held his hand up to his neck. "You're walking on thin ice around here."

Sam stood up, walked around his desk and sat on the edge, uncomfortably close to Baker, who backed up slightly.

Sam folded his arms across his chest and said, "You know Chet. Unlike everyone else around here, there are days where I actually like you. I know you're a whiz with numbers, and you're very good at what you do. Unfortunately, I have to remind you of some simple facts in spite of your Ph. D and your MBA. My methods may be unorthodox, but I'm the only agent with a 100 percent collection record."

Sam paused as these indisputable facts sunk in for Baker.

"As a result of my successful recovery rate, I have directly or indirectly been responsible for two thirds of the companies revenue,"

"Mr. Baker," Sam continued confidently, "My collections result in million of dollars in profits for this firm. Either way you cut it, that's a lot of money. So, let me tell *you* how it's going to be. In about 10 minutes I walk out of that door. I catch a flight this afternoon at 1 p.m. and I'm back in the office at my desk at 9 a.m. tomorrow. This trip will cost approximately $4,000, and we stand to recover $150,000 total. Our cut of the recovered amount is $50,000. You do the math."

"You make a great case Enison," Baker said sarcastically, "but that's $4,000 in revenue we won't have. Multiply that by all the little trips you take and the weird electronics gadgets you purchase, and it all adds up. And I suppose it's okay for you to make LESS profit than more because of your so called methods."

"Not at all Baker," Sam returned, "I work a certain way, just as you do. I can't be successful if I don't work a certain way. My techniques are my tools, just as your computer is your tool, or the telephone or even those five pen hanging out of your pocket. Without my tools, we would not have any profit to debate about and without the millions in revenue, you would not be standing here nit-picking with me."

Baker's brain was on overload. Anger and logic collided while he looked for an angle.

"Well, this trip is not authorized." Baker spit. With that

comment, Enison walked back around his desk, pressed the talk button on his speaker phone and dialed the president's extension number.

"Jeremy," Enison called out as the phone picked up, "are you napping in the executive tower again?"

"Sure Sammy," the hollow, electronic voice replied, "after my nap I'm going to play a couple of rounds of Golf in Monterey. You interested?"

"No thanks buddy. Say, listen, I've got Baker here and he says he needs authorization for a trip I want to take this afternoon. Can you help him?"

"Sure Sam. Baker, you there?"

"Yes, sir," Baker responded quickly, standing at attention and stepping closer to the phone.

"Listen, take care of Sam will you please. He's a Goddamn pain in the ass but I don't know what I'd do without him."

"Yes, sir. I'll take care of it right away sir."

"Okay, anything else I can do for you gentlemen," Jeremy asked, "because the fairway is waiting for me?"

"Nothing here," Sam said.

"No Sir," Baker said meekly, sounding defeated.

"I'll see you when I get back," Sam said. "Are we still going to check out Darryl Grant at Yoshi's tomorrow night?"

"Wouldn't miss it for anything. Guys a goddamn phenomenon at the keyboards. They must grow piano players up there in Oregon. See you tomorrow."

Sam pressed the button to end the call. He looked at Baker and said, "I think we're finished Baker. Thanks for stopping by."

The chief financial officer, after a bit more grousing, finally said, "All right Enison. This isn't over. They pay me to do a job around here and you can't stop me from doing it. Get me a full report by noon tomorrow about everything you did and a full accounting of expenses."

"Sure thing Baker," Sam said.

Baker, embarrassed and intimidated, quietly turned and walked out of Sam's office. Sam, feeling as though he'd already wasted too much time, grabbed his laptop, smart phone, a few files, trench coat and Humphrey Bogart brim, as he called it, and hurried out of his office.

As he passed the receptionist, a sexy short-skirted, immaculately dressed brunette named Amy, he stopped, leaned over and whispered in her ear, "Make sure Baker doesn't grow a set of balls while I'm gone and I'll make sure you have his job in five or six years."

She laughed and said, "Sam, you slay me. Have a safe flight."

Amy was Sam's eyes and ears. She made sure Sam knew everything about everyone, especially Baker. Sam knew things about Bakers personal life even Baker himself didn't know. Amy's was smart and confident. She was as smart as they come and perceptive. It was the perceptive part that Sam appreciated. He'd met too many smart stupid people like Baker. Sam committed to making sure she got everything she deserved while she worked a ACS. Sam hurried out the front door, hailed a cab and rushed to the airport, arriving in barely enough time to catch the flight.

Chapter 26

"Quiet on the set!" Rock yelled, as he prepared to count down five seconds before the camera went live. "We go live in five, four, three, two, one, and action."

He pointed a finger at Rich and Phil, who sat at the brightly lit table in the window corner of Jake's restaurant.

The red light flashed on. Rich smiled at the camera and launched into his introduction.

"Welcome to another edition of Two Guys Having Lunch and Talking Tough. I'm your host, Rich Franklin and this is my co-host Phil Goldberg."

Rock pointed at Jimmy, a freckled 20-year-old gaffer/camara man, who immediately switched on camera two. Phil's face filled the monitor screen.

"This is the show that is our answer to *The View*, where two guys get together and talk politics, food, and music from a uniquely Pacific Northwest point of view. Phil, tell our guest how this show came to be."

Phil panicked but quickly remembered the first taping and that prompted him to action. The first taping was a complete disaster. Phil panicked when he was introduced and every word that came out of his mouth sounded like gibberish. He wouldn't let that happen this time.

"Well, Rich," Phil started, "you and I have been friends for years and one of our favorite things to do is have lunch at new restaurants once a week and catch up on current events and talk about the food, music and politics."

Phil's face and muscles relaxed more as he spoke.

"It was during one of those lunches last year that you mentioned that our lunches were so interesting that it might be fun to do some kind of series based them. That's where I took over and we began collaborating to put together a pilot. And here we are."

"Right. This is our second series. The first was a disaster, Phil. Neither one of us has ever hosted a show so it was a little foreign. You were *very* nervous."

"We both were. We were the absolute worst host I've ever seen, Rich. It was a spectacular disaster," Phil said.

"Me! Are you kidding. At least you could understand what I was saying and I didn't choke on the Jambalaya on the first bite, sending me into gagging fit while the cameras were rolling."

"I was nervous."

"You were petrified," Rich added. "And I swore we'd never do another show. But I stand corrected on that matter. And we're back at it."

They both laughed.

"We both know this is a good thing we're doing here. So, Rich, What's on the menu to day."

"You mean the menu menu or the guest menu."

"Both," Phil answered.

"Well, first you and I have to let off a little steam, like we usually do. You know, talk about us. I want to ask you if Black men and White men can *truly* be friends."

"I don't think so—"

"Now hold on a second. Wait until we get to it. I know you're anxious to lash out at me. But you have to wait. We also have two wonderful dishes, put together by our host, Jake's owner Ben Miller and Chef Vitory Aspugio. After lunch, we'll be joined by Darryl Grant—the Professor—on Piano, then we'll move to the Maltese Falcon Room where we'll smoke cigars and talk with special guest Jeff Abrahamson and Isaac Washington, two Portland school board members who have been embroiled in controversy over comments made about Jews and Black. The question: who has suffered the most and deserves the most help, Jews or Blacks. Both men have agreed to be on our show today and we're going to pose the question and hope to get some fascinating responses."

Rich glanced at Rock, who was smiling and giving a thumbs up. Brenda occasionally reached in when the camera cut away to tap the sweat off of Phil or Rich's forehead without smudging the makeup.

Phil said, "Let's get started. We only have an hour for lunch. Then, like most people, it's back to work."

"All right. Let's dive into the black and white friendship issue. Phil. You've never held anything back over the years and I've learned a lot from you, but on issue we've never discussed is black and white male friendships."

"Never had a need to. We've always operated under a presumption of friendship even thought there are cultural, religious and economic bridges between us. I've never questions our ability to be friends."

"I have," Rich answered.

"What question is there?"

"I don't have a chip on my shoulder, but I am black."

"And I'm white. So what."

"In the deeper recesses of my subconscious, I can't help but think that you'd rather spend your time with a white person than a black person."

"That's outrageous," Phil said, looking slightly shocked.

"It's supposed to be," Rich shot back. "But it may also be true. Think about it Phil. We're all victims of social conditioning, from birth. That conditioning, in some cases is unconditional and it's perpetuated by magazines, newspapers, television, from the image of the all-American boy to the ideal friendship. Wouldn't you agree with that?"

Phil thought for a moment then replied, "I would agree with some of that. The conditioning part I agree with. The unconditional conditioning, I wouldn't. There are always exceptions. Or, we, as thinking adults have the opportunity to create exceptions."

"So, you think our friendship is one of those exceptions that you—I mean—we created?"

"Absolutely," Phil answered.

"Well, tell me about your conditioning. Where did black people fit into the picture in your childhood?" Rich asked.

"What black people?" Phil answered. "There were no black people in my neighborhood in Connecticut. As children we believed that all black people lived only in Harlem or on plantations in the south. I had no knowledge of black people as pioneers, cowboys, surgeons, dentist, things like that until after I graduate from high school in 1965. The civil right movement was always characterized in our household as uppity Negroes stirring the pot and we always asked why can't those people be satisfied with what they have? This question flowed effortlessly from the lips of my father, a prominent, well-respected lawyer."

"So, when did your reconditioning begin?" Rich asked.

"During college. That's when I met my first 'coloreds' as we called you people back then."

"Coloreds! You people!" Rich fired back. "That's what I'm talking about."

"That was the vernacular," Phil responded, "this is reality TV, right. Let's tell it like it is. Let's call a spade a spade."

"A spade!" Rich exclaimed. "You and me are going to have it out right now. I am not a 'you people.' Honkeys used—"

"Aha!" Phil said. "It's in there. Come on Rich. Let it out. Let that anti-white people conditioning flow. You'll feel better."

"Well, okay. I admit. It's there," Rich conceded, "My conditioning was obviously a little different from yours. But the result was the same. My conditioning was fueled by being around too many white people who hated me. They tolerated me because I went to a mostly white Catholic school. And, you know, the Catholics in America are convinced that all important Catholics are White and that Catholicism is a hierarchical structure based on ethnic origins and gender. White males run the show, with the Pope being the alpha male, women being breeders and homemakers and black and other ethnic groups are to be subjugated by the Pope and God. White men get to heaven first, White women second, and all other people of color wait in line at the BACK door to maybe get their souls saved."

"Whoa," Rich, "That's some pretty heavy shit," Phil said. "You want to put that into plain English?"

"Yeah," Rich said, "All those white Catholic assholes used to piss me off calling me nigger and shit and complaining about homosexuals, Jews and Mexicans. Is that plain enough for you?"

"That's better. Now, deep inside you hate me. You hate all white people?"

"Absolutely not!" Rich answered. "I hate what you represent. That's what African Americans have to deal with. We're motivated by hatred and anger, brought on by centuries of abuse. We know we did not create this paradigm. We were unwillingly forced into it. White people were not forced to come to America and be slaves. If the roles were reversed and Black people had brought White people here to work in the fields and treat them like animals even to this day, White people would be pissed off about that shit too. On the other hand, most white people hate black people because we survived all the shit they could throw at us. They hate us out of fear and ignorance. The only reason they want Black people to go back to Africa is because they now realize they're forefathers made a tactical error. I'll be the first to admit it. They got greedy and lazy and brought over too many Negroes. E.B. Dubois wrote extensively about this. If early settlers wanted to work the fields themselves, there would never have been what they called the Negro problem, and it would have been easy to selectively exclude people of color from America. What can I say? They fucked up. And we have been catching hell for it ever since. Now, people watch re-runs of *Leave it to Beaver* and watch *Gone with the Wind* over and over and get pissed off when they see a black person walking in their neighborhood. They're thinking, 'we fucked up. Shouldn't have been lazy bastards. Now we can NEVER EVER have a white nation.' That's powerful social medicine at work."

"I saw a little of that in our household, Rich," Phil said, "We were not necessarily taught to hate. We were simple not taught enough. I don't know which was worse. Because to us, black people were not really real. You were more of a color, an entity, this black thing, not to be discussed and not to be associated with. Black was an it, not a they.

Whenever my father heard news about black people on the radio, he always seemed to make sure we heard him say 'oh for God sake why can't those people ever be satisfied?' So, he never said hate those people, but he never said not to."

"When you went to college and actually met black people, how did he influence you?"

"You know Rich, I never wanted for anything in my life. We always had the best of everything. While I appreciated all that, I never settled into that as being all there was. You know, eat well, grow up, get married, create 'White' heirs to the family fortune. I never settled for that."

"But you never rejected it either," Rich stated.

"Hell no." Phil fired back. "You think I want to be poor? Not on your life. I enjoy being wealthy? I enjoy being White. I make the best of it. But I knew the struggle between blacks and whites was something important, something I needed to be involved in. So I got in my *new* Ford Mustang—a high school graduation present—and drove down to Mobile, Alabama to see if I could get involved in the Civil Rights Movement."

"Tell me, Phil, 'cause you're a little older than I am, was your initial perception of the Civil Rights Movement, that of an exclusive club for privileged White kids who just needed something interesting to do with their spare time. I mean, was it an adventure to you. Or was it sincere?"

"You dig deep, don't you?"

"Damn straight bro."

"I will admit. It was an adventure. I was so protected and safe. Our world was protected and safe. But it was only protected by artificial borders, a cultureless, social void. To thrive in my world, I had to ignore the rest of America and pretend that my world was the real America, the way it was supposed to be. I found it pretty boring. So In another year, I would have a law degree from Harvard, a place in my father's firm any time I wanted and the idea of poverty never occurred to me. Out of the blue I told my father I was going to the south for a few months to see if I could get some legal background on civil rights in case we needed to defend our way of life."

"You put it that way?"

"Not exactly. I told him I was going to take the summer off to vacation in the Padre Islands and visit with some of his Harvard cronies who had established practices in Texas, Alabama, Mississippi. While there, I would familiarize my self with practicing law in those states."

"What did you discover?"

"I discovered a deep seeded hatred of Negroes everywhere I went, like you said. The privileged class was extremely privileged and avoided Negroes by way of exclusion. The poor were extremely poor and hated Negroes for all the reasons you pointed out. Poor people, in the south, in fact, would rather invest all their time hating Negroes than pulling themselves out of poverty, educating themselves and providing a better life for their children. They were so pissed, they could not imagine having to lift a finger to better themselves. They still think black people should be slaves even to this day. If they remained slaves, they would not require any resources outside of food. And I didn't get it. So I sought out some of the black intellectuals to learn more."

"So, you were on some kind of southern Negro vision quester?" Rich asked.

"That's right. And I found out what I needed to know. The one liberal friend of my father's introduced me to a gentleman who he thought had something important to say. He arranged a lunch. We had to meet at an all-black restaurant called Smiddy's, in one of the poorest parts of Mobile. This lunch changed my life."

"Was it the abject poverty you were confronted with, or was it the soul food?" Rich asked.

"Both. I had chittlins for the first time. I wasn't told what it was. I was just told to try it. Jew or no Jew, I found that food is an important step in crossing the cultural divide. And what this gentleman had to say, took me the rest of the way. He spoke about equality of the races, something no one I knew of every spoke about. He spoke this historical relevance of the civil rights struggle and tied it back to my own Jewish heritage. He made sense of stories in the Bible, the Koran, the Tora, and Buddhist teaching, and he brought all of them together to present a common picture of common struggles amongst oppressed people. Our one hour turned into two, three, even four. We ate fatback, chittlins, cornbread, collard greens. And of the hundreds and hundreds of people who came through the restaurant that day, not one disparaging word was heard. Not one racial epitaph, only extreme respect and a willingness to allow us to exist."

"He must have been extremely respected and talking some powerful talk to take up four hours. Who was this gentleman?" Rich asked.

"You've heard of him, Rich. He's a prominent civil rights leader."

"There a lot of those, a lot of civil rights leaders who have done extraordinary things."

"Well, this Dr. is one of the best known of them all."

"You can't be serious?" Rich asked.

"That's right. Dr. Martin Luther King, Jr. We became friends that day. And I truly believe that he saw no colors when he spoke to me. He was singularly focused on his message and his mission. And black men and White men and children and women were all solders in this great civil rights struggle."

"Man, that's some heavy stuff. Is that what started the reconditioning process?"

"That's right, Rich. Now what about you?"

"My story is not as complicated. By the time I was a teenager I was smart, frustrated and angry. I spent all my years in Catholic schools, amongst White farmer and military family kids. I was convinced that they all hated me and only tolerated me because I had 7 older brothers and if anybody messed with me, they had to answer to them. There wasn't a week that went by where I wasn't called a nigger. All the other teenage boys were talking about girls and whenever it came to be my turn, everybody just kind of laughed and skipped over me. High school was stupid and a waste of time. One day, this young priest walks into our classroom. He's young, you know, kind of dorky looking, with huge glasses and a goofy, crooked smile. Sister Mary Theresa introduces him as the new parish priest. He gives this little speech about how he's happy to be at St. Xavier and looking forward to getting to know all of us."

"For those of you who don't know, you grew up in Junction City, Kansas, right?"

"That's right. Right next to Fort Riley. There were two schools, one Catholic and one public. My mother was a devout Catholic from Jamaica, so she made sure we went to St. Xavier."

"So, what happened with this Priest?"

"We met in the hall one day and got to talking. I'm thirteen mind you, and as far as I was concerned, every student in that school had the intelligence level of a Neanderthal. Every day in school was a painful reminder of how different I was and how much people hated me. It was terrible. Well, this priest, Fr. Frank, invited me over to the Parish after school one day. I guess he saw something in me. I remember it as clear as day. The parish house was an old sandstone block building, three stories high, enormous by any standards I knew. The interior walls were dark and mysterious with paneling everywhere; very regal, very intimidating and religious. Fr. Frank's office was on the second floor, a tiny space with religious figures, books covering every subject and cozy. Like your meeting with Dr. Martin Luther King Jr., a perfectly simple meeting turned into a lifelong friendship. Fr. Frank was the first real friend I ever had, and I mean an unconditional friendship. Because I spent 10 years of my life around white people who tolerated me, I became particularly keen at spotting the phonies. Fr. Frank was as real as rain. We talked for hours that day and became good friends. I couldn't wait for school to be over so I could get together with him every day if possible in his tiny office and talk about world politics, life, people, even love, and occasionally, the Eucharist. He was, after all, still a parish priest. But he opened up a world of possibilities for me, and may have even saved my life. I was also willing to overlook the fact that he was a honkey. I'd never been able to do that with my classmates. He even taught me to play racquetball."

"Are you healed, Rich? Are you fully re- or deconditioned?"

Rich thought for a moment before answering. "Yes. But I'm deconditioned conditionally."

"Rich, you're full of contradictions."

"Because life is a contradiction. White people still piss me off. I understand now that they are actually capable of achieving the same intellectual capacity as black people. They can read and write and invent things. They are not pale, white-skinned apes. Some of my best friends are White and they can be quite civilized.

Rich never cracked a smile as he spoke, which threw Phil off. Seconds later, he added, "And that's all the crap we both have had to throw out with the trash, right Phil."

Phil smiled, "Right Rich."

Rock typed into the teleprompter the instructions for the next segment. Phil read the text.

"Rich, I think it's time for lunch. Let's bring out our chef to tell us a little about this afternoons meal."

Chapter 27

Trixie emerged from the bath, refreshed. Steam rose from her body like translucent wings, swirling, dancing, then disappearing. Water dripped in the bath and onto the plush peach colored rug on the floor as she wrapped herself in the thick cashmere towel. Beads of condensation made it impossible for her to see her reflection in the small mirror that covered a medicine chest mounted on the wall over the sink. Her hair was wet and tangled and dripping water over her delicate shoulders. She methodically dried herself, careful dabbing with her towel instead of rub so she didn't damage the skin. Then she wrapped the long, tangled strands of her hair in the towel like a turban, leaving the rest of her body naked and covered in Goosebumps from a draft that blew in from the single open window.

Trixie walked out of the bathroom and into the main living room, over to the bookshelf at the far end of the room. She picked up a lighter and lit another incense pyramid. This time she chose Jasmine Nights. She walked over to her small closet, opened the door and scanned the collection of clothing that was crammed into the tiny space. What to wear for her special rendezvous.

The Benson Hotel, she reflected, was one of Portland's classiest historic hotels, so her hippie girl garb would not do. She needed something sophisticated. She retrieved a black, silk dress, that was simple, elegant, and she thought and would hug the contours of her body like a second skin. This would get their attention, she thought.

She quickly dressed, blow-dried her hair and brushed it like her mother used to, for almost an hour.

She didn't remember much about her mother. But she remembered her father. He also brushed her hair, but he only did so when he wanted something. It always started with her hair. Then he kissed the top of her head, then her shoulders, then touched her chest.

She was too young to have breast, but he touched there anyway. He had convinced her that that was what fathers did with their daughters. That fathers were teachers, lovers and could make their daughters feel things they had never felt before. But he only made her sick to her stomach. If she resisted, he threatened to beat her. The thought of this angered her. Over the years, Trixie had faced these memories and worked to transcended them. She read books about men like her father, about his motivations. She knew he would pay for his sins, either in this world, in this life or in the next world in the next life.

To heal from the abuse, Trixie read books about abused kids, especially girls who turned to lives of prostitution and personal abuse, drugs and alcohol, their self-esteem battered and irreparable damaged by the time they reach their teens.

Trixie would not settle into that mold. She knew what she was doing. She didn't need to do what she was doing. She liked what she was doing. She knew about extreme lifestyles, dangerous lifestyles. Compared to rock climbing and race car driving, she thought, her life was pretty tame. She was building layers to her life by day, giving everything she had, but she maintained a place for herself that no one could touch. And she convinced herself she was doing a cruel world a favor.

She glanced at the clock. It was getting late. Trixie wrapped her hair in a loose knot and put it up in a bun, securing it there with jewel encrusted hair needles. She lightly colored her cheeks with blush, put on a clear, glossy lipstick, and a hint of mascara. As she inspected herself in the now-cleared mirror in the bathroom, she looked like a debutante, perhaps even a contestant in a beauty pageant; simple, beautiful, and sexy, very hard for any man, married or single to resist.

She put on a conservative pair of black pumps. They looked great but she hoped they didn't cause blisters like they did the last time she wore them. She grabbed her leather coat from behind the door, dabbed her clothes and any exposed parts of her body with China Rain, held one nostril closed and the open bottle to the other and inhaled as if taking a hit of cocaine, closed her eyes and enjoyed the sensation.

The Benson Hotel was only four blocks from her hotel. She was very punctual and believed that tardiness was rude and inconsiderate.

Chapter 28

Rich was surprised at how smoothly the shoot was unfolding. They segued into the food segment. The chef personally delivering a broiled lobster with saffron rice and sautéed vegetables to Rich and grilled salmon with medallion potatoes to Phil.

After a brief interview with the chef, Phil and Rich talked about the meal and Rock, with steady cam in hand and perched on a ladder, showed close-ups of each dish. All was going like clockwork.

As they finished dessert, which consisted of English toffee pudding and chocolate cheese cake, the front door of the restaurant opened and in walked the entertainment, Darrell Grant. Realizing that the shoot was still in progress, Grant held up his hands in apology and grabbed the door so it wouldn't slam closed and interrupt shoot.

Rich, nodding to Grant to acknowledge his arrival, said "Once again, we're filming this episode of Two Guys having lunch and talking tough at Jake's Famous Seafood Restaurant, one of Portland's oldest, classiest restaurants. We're your host, Rich Franklin and Phil Goldberg, and we're pulling out all the stops breaking all the rules and having lunch."

Phil said. "Jake's is certainly on or top-10 favorite Portland restaurants list, and has wonderful atmosphere, and we got off on a pretty fascinating topic about white and black male friendships."

Phil paused, looked down at table then continued, "You know, Rich, I appreciate you're sharing your feelings about White men. I never knew you felt that way."

"That's okay Phil, most White men don't understand why Black men are angry about things and why we find it difficult to trust them."

"There's still a lot of suspicion between us," said Phil, "White men are angry about the end of slavery and Black men are angry that their ancestors were slaves to begin with. Plus, too many White men still live a lie that someday a giant Negro ship will come to take all Black people back to Africa and the "Negro" problem will go away. But the reality is that this country is actually more of your country than it is ours. Black people fought for everything they have. White people fought other White people because they had too much to begin with and somebody else wanted it. And even so, blacks helped White people keep what black people helped them build. Frederick Douglas wrote extensively about this in his treatise. He was, I think, one of the foremost intellectuals our country has seen."

Glancing at his watch and noting that they were running out of time, Rich quickly said, "Well put Phil. Now I have to ask the question so we can move on: Can black men and white men really be friends in the same way that two White men or two Black men can?"

"I don't know. I'm not so sure now," Phil admitted. "There's so much more to consider."

"I think all we can do is keep trying," Rich added. "We've been friends for almost eight years and my life has been enriched by our friendship. Whether it's perfect or not doesn't matter. You and Fr. Frank have a lot in common. And you're about the same age as Fr. Frank."

"Is that a compliment?"

"Sure it is. You're a good man."

"I think the feeling is mutual."

"At that, let's cut away to this afternoons musical guest. He's the professor, department head at Portland State University and a personal friend, Dr. Darryll Grant, piano player extraordinaire doing a cut called *Spring Skylight* from his latest CD called *Smoking Java*. We'll see you in the lounge later with our special guest, two school board members finally settle their ongoing feud concerning who has suffered most, Blacks or Jews."

While Grant played, Phil, Rich and the skinny gaffer relocated to the dark wood paneled meeting room in the back of the restaurant. Brenda was sent outside to intercept the two guest and escort them to the entrance on the side of the restaurant away from the piano.

Abrahmson showed up first. He and Rich had been friends and business associates for several years and he owed Rich a few favors, so he reluctantly agreed to participate in Rich's little experiment. Rich had to agree, however, to allow him to see the final cut. He had political aspirations beyond the school board. He was a lawyer and a bureaucrat to the core and he wore it in his camel overcoat, wing tips, pleated slacks, horned-rimed glasses and ivy league hair do that Ronald Reagan would have been proud of.

Washington arrived minutes later and although he and Abrahmson were cordial, there was obviously no love lost between them. Washington was born and raised in Portland and grow up on what could laughingly be called the mean streets of Northeast Portland. Washington often called it a ghetto, but could hardly muster any sympathy from anyone familiar with Portland. Even the toughest parts of Northeast Portland could not be considered dangerous by any stretch of the imagination, which is why Portland rappers got so little respect. Washington was a youth activist who worked with the House of Umoja, a home for troubled African American kids. He had worked wonders transforming the home from a rag-tag no-name Negro-based non-profit to one of the most recognized organizations in the city. He was a new school board member with nothing to lose and a chip on either shoulder.

Abrahamson and Washington had gotten into public debates about who deserved the most help, black kids or Jewish kids and it had caused a media firestorm that didn't seem close to being resolved. He was angry and not afraid to show it. He was the consummate African-American, wore a Kente cloth patterned dashikis, long, tight braids hung from his head, the tips surrounded by brightly colored beads. His forehead was permanently furrowed and the centerpiece of a permanent scowl that hovered over a broad, pimply nose, anthropologically perfect full, characteristically Negroid lips, and puffy cheeks, all blended into a coffee black face and supported by a chubby body with about 50 too many pounds.

Rich told both of them in separate phone calls that they could give their sides of the story and address the question as well as he and Phil would facilitate an exchange and perhaps come to a truce.

In truth, Rich didn't know what the hell was going to happen. But there they both were, in the same room, willing to talk. He had done something even the school superintendent couldn't do, and that was worth a few minutes of tape.

Chapter 29

Trixie blended in with the glamorous backdrop of the Benson hotel, an extravagant luxury hotel that was built in 1915 by lumber baron Simon Benson. Dark wood columns, carved with classical patterns filled the open spaces and the mahogany paneling absorbed the light and created a mysterious atmosphere in which to dream of exotic rendezvous and lavish costume balls.

Trixie sat on a plush stool in the Benson Lounge, located to the left of the huge, brass-lined revolving front doors, manned by a valet dressed like the Jack of Hearts with coat-of-arms bedecked red and black uniform with tasseled top hat, black knee-high boots and a whistle perched in one hand and a finger extended as he flagged down a cab for a gentile elderly couple who exited the hotel.

Trixie had not been at the bar long before the young, smitten bartender, Steve Dorsey, tried to pry information out of her and perhaps secure a phone number.

Dorsey was 25, cocky, divorced and happy to be free again. While married, his life as a bartender and his desire to not keep a job for more than two months conflicted to much with his wife, infant daughter and his in-laws. His only allegiance was to his Corvette, Tequila, a new beautiful woman every week. His passion for irresponsibility eventually led to a bitter divorce and hefty child support payments he conveniently forgot to pay every month.

After delivering the Chardonnay to Trixie, Steve asked, "Where you visiting from?"

Trixie, sized him up and answered, "I'm from here. Meeting someone." Hoping that would be his queue to leave her alone.

"Your husband's pretty lucky." Steve said, feeling no shame about having used this line hundreds of times before to fish for information about her marital status. He watched her reaction while juggling a tooth pick on the end of a silly smirk.

Trixie smiled, "How many girls have you used that on?"

Surprised, Steve, wasn't sure how to answer. He wasn't used to girls confronting him, especially the bimbos he usually encountered at pick-up bars. He thought they all loved playing the game.

"Er, well, some, er, a few. Um, not many," he said awkwardly, but determined not to skip a beat. "But a hot chick like you must be married, right."

"Don't worry," Trixie rescued him, "It's not the worst I've heard, but certainly shows a lack of imagination."

"But to show you I'm a good sport," Trixie said, extending her hand to him," My name is Trixie."

Not smiling, Steve hesitantly took her hand and gave it a tenuous shake.

"Steve, you look like in intelligent boy. What's a smart boy like you doing in a place like this?"

Steve was not used to being on the defensive with a beautiful woman, but he didn't have a choice. He was cornered. Trixie was the only other customer in the bar and he couldn't feign being busy. He had to talk about himself.

"Well, you know. A friend hooked me up with this gig a few months ago. I think it's great. The money is good. The hours are great."

He didn't know where to go so he meandered through his muddled life in short, choppy segments.

Noticing his floundering and discomfort with his own history, Trixie said, "Steve. Take a deep breath. Slow down. I don't want to sleep with you, I just want to know a little more about you. Now, I'll bet you went to either the University of Oregon or Harvard. Which one was it."

"U of O," Steve answered quickly, slightly more comfortable with the topical terrain.

"What was your degree in, Steve," Trixie asked.

"I majored in political science," Steve said, regaining some confidence. He, fumbled with the toothpick and smoothed back his cropped, brown hair and rubbed his clean shaven chin. He was sure Trixie was out of here element.

"If you studied political science, that means you either had in interest in public servitude, law, or international relations, right?"

Not wanting to back down, Steve said, "Sure. That's right."

"Something I've always been curious about. Are you familiar with Article 17 of the constitution?"

Steve, searching for words and information, looked up at the ceiling and unconsciously began digging for earwax with his pinky, a nervous habit he'd acquired from his father. He was unaware of the act and how disgusting it appeared. "

Well, if I recall—" he mumbled, "Well, it's been a long time. I—"

"It's okay Steve, let's not worry about that. Politics is so dull anyway. Could you please get me another Chardonnay. And it won't be necessary for you to make any more small talk with me. That doesn't seem to be a strong point for you. But you are cute."

Steve was in full shock now. He wasn't sure how to take what Trixie had said. The permanent grin on his face was melting into a scowl as the stark realization that a seemingly young but beautiful customer had not only insulted him but had squashed his advance in a way he'd never been squashed before. There was too much to process, so after he gave Trixie here drink, he retreated to the end of the bar, propped his foot up on the small sink under the bar and thought about his life as a failure and a drop-out.

Trixie, calmly nursed her drink, not bothering to give Steve a second thought, before she was joined at the bar by a dignified looking man who carried himself like a politician and dressed like he meant it.

They left after the man drank a shot of expensive malt Scotch—two hundred bucks a pop. Then left the bar. Steve collected the glass and the napkins. Underneath a napkin he found a hundred dollar bill and a note scribbled on a piece of paper that said, STEVE, YOU'RE STILL YOUNG. DON'T GIVE UP. THERE MAY STILL BE HOPE FOR YOU. LOSE THE COCKY ATTITUDE, GET A REAL JOB. DON'T SETTLE FOR BEING A DICK FOR THE REST OF YOUR LIFE OR YOU'LL DIE ALONE, HATED, MISERABLE AND BROKE. LOVE TRIXIE.

Steve sneered as he read the note and wondered who the hell she thought she was anyway. "Bitch," he muttered as he crumpled up the napkin and angrily tossed it into the trash. Thinking too much about his screwed up life was the last thing he wanted. He poured himself a shot of Quervo Gold. Then another. After the third shot burned at his stomach, everything was okay again for Steve.

Chapter 30

Around three fifteen, as everyone was exchanging congratulations for what seemed like a successful shoot, Rich glanced at his watch and, in a panic, said, "Oh, shit, I'm late. Phil, Rock, Brenda, this was great, but I've got to run to get my kids. They're going to kill me at the school."

He grabbed his hat and coat, shook hands with everyone on his way out, making sure to steal a hug from Brenda. He paused briefly when he got to Rock and said, "All right Rock, we put on a show for you today. You think you can carve this down to a half hour show."

Rock was grinning like a Cheshire cat by now. His second love was being behind a camera. His first was his video editing suite, which was more sophisticated than many major video production houses.

"You leave that to me Rich," Rock said. "Sometimes I have to spin wool into gold. That's hard. This time I have to spin gold into platinum. That's easy. You are one bad ass mother fucker. Stay Black bro."

Rock gave Rich a quick hug, not too much contact, fisted hand across the back. No hip touching, only shoulders colliding quickly, tight grip with one hand. Than a quick release. Very direct. Very macho. Very Black.

"You stay black too brother blood bleed. I'll be black in touch with you later bloodmeister soul shaftman."

Rich tried to suppress a laugh, but both he and Rock found that impossible.

Rich passed by Phil, who was standing at the front door. They hugged, a different kind of hug, a sensitive White man hug Rich liked to call it. Passionate, full shoulder contact. Really heart felt. Phil was for real, in a White man way.

"God damn great show Richey. God damn great show."

"You the man, Phil. We did it. Now let's see how it looks after Rock works his magic on it."

"Rich, it's exactly what we had in mind. Let's start thinking about next week's shoot and how we can sell this to PBS or the Networks or whoever?"

"All right Phil," Rich said, hedging towards the front door. "But right now I've got to get my kids and my car is in Old Town. Right now, my life is in jeopardy, so let's talk tomorrow, okay."

"You got it Rich. May the fleet be in your feet and the wind at your back. Catch you later."

With that cue, Rich ran out of the front door, across the street and didn't stop running until he got to his truck in a Park-and-Go Garage a block from his office. He didn't remember much about the

10 block run.

He was almost 20 minutes late by the time he got to his truck and no doubt the principle would have called April and the children would be in the office, confused and waiting for anybody to come pick them up.

As he rounded the tight turns in the garage, the eerie squealing of the tires echoed throughout the cavernous structure sounding like the wining of whales on wheels, rhythmic and haunting.

When he got to the gate, a dark faced man with straight hair, possibly of Indonesian or East Indian descent, took his ticket and his money and opened the gate. He lurched forward, quickly pressing on the brakes as the car in front of him stopped suddenly. In the rear view mirror, the attendant gave him an intense look of disapproval.

Rich hated being late when it came to the kids. He cursed to himself for not paying attention to the clock. He subconsciously knew the shoot was taking longer but he didn't want to acknowledge it until they were completely done. Everything was going so perfectly.

The last segment between Abrahamson and Washington could not have been staged any better by Ron Howard, Oliver Stone or Francis Ford Coppola put together. Even Stephen Soderburg would be envious of the footage they got when Abrahamson and Washington both forgot briefly they were being filmed. They let their guard down and were candid about their views. Each brilliantly called on quotes and historically relevant events to frame a debate that rivaled soliloquies Kevin Costner could have delivered.

Rich was looking forward to seeing the first cuts. Even Abrahamson and Washington were impressed with themselves and though what they said was controversial, they thanked him for a neutral forum to voice their opinions. The jury would be in when the edited proof was in and that was in Rock's hands. For now, he was biting his lip, anxious to get to the school.

Chapter 31

Rick raced across the Burnside Bridge but was stalled mid-span by early commuters hoping to beat the after-work rush from downtown. As he stared at the break lights of the car in front of him, he felt his jaw tighten. He wanted to stomp on the accelerator and ram the car in front of him or drive on the sidewalk or press a button to ignite the jets that would lift his truck up and over the bumper-to-bumper rows of cars.

As he daydreamed about being liberated from traffic by some fantastic event, the cars edged forward, finally reaching the intersection on the opposite side of the bridge as the light turned yellow. He speed through a yellow and hit the stretch that led directly to Baldwin Elementary School.

Parents were lingering in front of the school, most picking up children from after-school activities. Rich felt obvious and self-conscious as he got out of the truck.

He always felt that way when he went to the school. No matter how Rich tried, he could never quite feel like he was part of the "Baldwin" community. He found it difficult to get to know parents on any level beyond the superficial. He'd spent hours thinking about. Was it Oregon? Was it the air? What? In frustration he'd concluded that while Baldwin School was not a private school, most parents treated it as if it was because it was an private arts magnet school, a school for creative and gifted children.

It was an exceptional public school and very difficult to get into. And, coincidentally, most kids at the school were White. They were escorted to and from school by pasty-faced mothers with tired, makeupless, blank faces. These were mothers more worried about their children than anything else, and mothers who'd given up their individuality years ago and focused all of their attention on making sure their children were perfect, went to perfect schools and had perfect friends. Most were biding their time in marriages with men they didn't love, but they'd picked carefully to allow themselves enough time to have 2.5 children, time for their husbands to make a good income, then they planed for a divorce after 10 to 15 years and still be guaranteed a revenue stream. They'd long ago given up on being sexy or attractive, preferring instead to wear nondescript, frumpy, Lands End outfits, Birkenstocks and second-hand jeans from Good Will.

Rich secretly despised these parents because they were afraid of him and seemed to have that curious "What are you doing here" look in their eyes whenever he walked into the school. They treated him differently because he was Black. But they either didn't know it or ignored that fact. They would be friendly, but they would rarely go beyond that. They were, meek, safe and afraid.

Two parents came out of the front door as Rich reached for it. The looked at him, startled. *There's that look*, he thought. A constipated smile and the quick downward glance. *You're not one of us...coon!*

In the office, Juan and Antonio jumped up when they saw him and came running over to him and tried to download everything they'd seen or heard that day at one time.

He huddled them both around his waist and glanced at the principle, Irma Westfield. She was not smiling and threw him a disapproving glance before saying, "Mr. Franklin, may I see you in my office for a moment?"

Even though it was a question, Rich knew it was not an option.

Without answering her, Rich told the boys to wait and walked around the swinging gate towards a door Mrs. Westfield had already disappeared through. Rich felt like a kid who'd been caught smoking in the boy's room.

Westfield was already sitting behind her desk when Rich rounded the corner. She was impressive and intimidating. She was principle of the school, captain of the ship. Her gray hair sat balanced high on her head like sphinx, guarding the Pharaoh's tomb. Severe wrinkles raced in every direction on her face, a topographic marvel with convoluted valleys. She had dealt with fathers before. And to her, Rich was no different. She did not discriminate. Here rules applied to all equally.

"Mr. Franklin."

Uh, Oh, Rich thought.

"Your children were very afraid. They thought you had forgotten them." She paused, steely blue eyes that had seen a thousand years of wisdom stared at him, unblinking. She did not expect a response. Rich glanced down at his shoes and shifted uneasily from one foot to the next.

"We set certain standards here for the children, Mr. Franklin," She continued. "We also have certain standards and expectations for the parents. The most basic of them being to pick up your children on time."

One of them is for you to kiss my ass, Rich thought.

But he said humbly, "I agree with you one hundred percent mam."

"This is not the first time you have been late to pick up your children and I'm concerned that this is becoming a habit for you."

"No mam, I assure you it is not. I apologize, I—"

"You needn't make excuses," she interrupted, "You are not one of my students here, Mr. Franklin."

"I just wanted to—"

"I understand," she said. She walked around the desk to where Rich stood, "I phoned your wife and let her know that the children were here and that if you did not show up within 15 minutes, she would have to leave her work and come get her children. Needless to say, she was not happy about that."

"I imagine not." Rich tried to hide the panic in his voice. "I assure you, mam, this will not happen again."

She delicately gripped Rich's arm and, looking more grandmotherly now said, "Rich, I'm 60 years old. I've been a teacher and an administrator for 43 years. I didn't get this far by not being able to read my parents like books and by not doing my homework. You and April are two of the best parents in this school. Your children are kind, polite, well adjusted and smarter than most I've seen. Rich, no matter what you may think of the parents here at Baldwin, just know that I'm on your side."

In a matter of minutes, Rich had gone from a defensive position, to a humble position to a shocked position. He didn't know what to think. Perhaps he had underestimated Ms. Westfield. Maybe she was not an imposter like all the others, he thought.

"Your children love you and don't like to think they've been forgotten about no matter what the excuse is. Take them home."

She pointed a finger at Rich and with a stern face said, "If I have to have you back in my office again, you'll be sorry young man."

She was half kidding and half serious. Rich didn't dare a smile. "Yes, mam. You won't be seeing me again. Thank you mam." Rich turned towards the door.

"And Rich," Ms. Westfield say, "One more thing."

Rich turned, surprised. "I read some of your articles on the Internet. Not bad. That review you wrote of the Lichee Garden Restaurant in Chinatown was great. I actually ate there the last time I was in San Francisco. You know Mr. Franklin, this Internet thing really is making the world a smaller place."

She paused, smiled slightly, then turned while saying, "Good day Mr. Franklin."

She sat at here desk and busied herself with some lose papers.

Rich, dumbfounded, could only turn and walk out into the outer office, his head reeling at what he had just heard. He wasn't sure how to interpret it. He hated the idea that she may know more about him than he wanted her to. But he was also pleased to know that she was not one of *them*. She seemed to be the genuine article, an old White lady who may actually be hip and may not think that all black men will take advantage of any opportunity to rape and kill any White woman they can. Rich had seen Mandingo when he was a teenager, and he knew then that if any White people ever saw that movie, Black men would never be allowed to be alone in the company of White women again.

Rich hustled the kids past more zombie mothers who gave him hemorrhoid smiles then looked away immediately, afraid to make eye contact or risk being possessed by the Negro manspell and want to throw him to the ground and grip his pithy man rod and ram it inside of themselves, impregnating themselves and delivering a Negro baby to the shock of their family and friends.

Stop it! Stop it! Rich urged to himself. Focus on reality for a change.

Chapter 32

On the way home, Juan and Antonio were in usual character. Juan sang every song he could remember from the radio and improvised parts he couldn't remember. Antonio read his Legion super hero books, only glancing up if Rich pressed on the brakes too hard. He was a voracious reader and only came up to see what there was to eat, watch on TV or play on his Gameboy. When he wasn't reading, he was tormenting his brother and wondering when he would get to boss his parents around. Rich reminded him on a regular basis that he was the kid and his job was to do what he was told. The curse of having smart kids is that they can see right through any bluffs. His sarcastic reply was, "Dad, you're not going to beat us. You'd feel too bad about that. So, if I don't do what you ask, what can you do?" Rich's curt reply was "I will not stop thinking of creative ways to make your life a living hell while you live under our roof." That, at least, gave them something to think about, even if they weren't afraid.

Rich rounded the corner onto Wygant Street, and as he did, he felt a knot developing in the pit of his stomach. He could see blue smoke bellowing from the front yard of the dirt brown ranch style building that housed the Peasley parent and his brood. The hood of the 1978 Camero was propped open and Rich could see the blubbery asscrack that peeked over a pair of tattered jeans. It was Peasley senior tugging on the throttle. It sounded like a full-on NASCAR race taking place in the front yard.

Rich's pulse quickened as he prepared for a confrontation. He parked and herded the kids out of the car and to the front door. As he opened the front door to the house for the boys, they coughed and fanned away smoke that floated across their yard like a thick fog. Rich walked calmly over to where the Peasley's ass-crack was hanging out from under the hood of the car.

"Peasley!" he yelled. Peasley couldn't hear him. After repeating the call three times, Peasley finally glanced at him and stood up. Even idling, the mufflerless engine made it necessary for both men to yell.

"What the hell are you doing?"

"Just opening her up," Peasley said, offended that Rich would ask.

"Well, the smoke is chokin' us over here. Can't you do that somewhere else."

"It don't got no front axle," he said. "Wrecked it in a race a few weeks a go. Can't take it no wheres else."

"Well, Jesus Christ Peasley, why don't you take it to a garage or something so you can fix it up and drive it somewhere,"

"Why don't you just mind your own business?" Peasley replied, staring at Rich through dead, beady, black, bloodshot eyes. He picked up a Budweiser bottle that was balanced on the fender and tipped it straight up into the air and sucked the remaining liquid out of it. He propped one fist on his hip and said. "This is a free country Rich. Man ought to be able to do what he wants on his property without getting harassed fer it."

Rich could feel his blood boiling. He knew Peasley wanted him to take the bait. He also knew Peasley wasn't a violent man, just ignorant as hell. He'd been given the privilege of a body without the benefit of a brain. He had to reason with him somehow, make him feel as if he had some control, then at least he might be able to get Peasley to bend a little.

"You're right Peasley." Rich said. Peasley raised an eyebrow and smiled, happy to hear this news. "Can you do me this favor? Could you please just give us a chance to enjoy a few minutes of quiet while we have dinner?" Rich asked.

Peasley, pleased with himself now, smirked and said, "I'll see what I can do." He belched and Rich could see his protruding gut deflate, inflate, then giggle like a gigantic tit.

"By the way Rich, you know anything about a complaint I got about abandoned vehicles? Police came by today with a tow Truck and tried to haul my Camero off. Sons of bitches. Probably old lady Winslow over there."

"Could have been anybody on this block, Peasley. You've got more beater cars around here than anyone. "

"I need them all too. Never know when one might break down."

Rich rolled his eyes, frustrated. The storm door on Peasley house opened and Peasley junior appeared. He wore a white, wrinkled T-shirt with a picture of a Camero on the front. A Budweiser was held in a death grip in one hand while the other flopped at his side like a rubber arm. His hair stood straight up on his head as if he just woken up. His jeans were covered with oil stains and he wore black Army surplus combat boots.

"Pa, everything okay?" he asked then stood next to Peasley senior, staring at him like real live William Wegman photograph dogs. Both looked at Rich with empty, dark eyes. Clearly, there was nothing else going on behind them.

Rich shook his head. "I'll see you later Peasley. See what you can do." There was no response. Rich turned and as he walked toward his front door, he glanced around to confirm his suspicions. It was true. The pods had visited the Peasley house. He expected them to point at him and squeal a warning at any moment. Instead, they remained motionless, each with a Budweiser in one hand, thinking about absolutely NOTHING!

Before he reached the door, April drove up. She had that look on her face. The one he knew well. It said, I'M REALLY PISSED AT YOU AND I'M GOING TO LIGHT INTO YOUR ASS IN A MINUTE. Rich hated that look. It reminded him of his mother. And he never imagined he'd have to endure that kind of look as an adult. That was the cruel joke life played, he thought. You dream of love and romance and marriage and when you find it, you realize that there's no way to avoid becoming your parents because you're dealing with the same shit all over again, life's Boolean loop.

Chapter 33

Chico returned to his apartment, irritated and visibly injured. He stripped his cloths off to inspect his wounds from the blackberry bush ditch-dive he took while following Trixie. The sides of his legs were covered with crimson streaks, welts and specks of dried blood.

When he saw the wounds, he yelled, "God damn son of bitches. I don't believe this sheet. Somebody has to pay for this sheet."

Chico ran to the bathroom, crying and cursing the entire way. He turned on the shower, went back into the kitchen and took two beers out then walked back to the bathroom and stepped into the shower. With a beer in each hand, he sat down and let the water cover his head and drip into the open beer cans.

He drank alternately from each container for the next hour, while he drained every ounce of hot water in the complex tanks.

He contemplated who or what would feel his wrath next. Beast, man or object. He didn't care. Some suffering must take place. He deserved that satisfaction.

Chico picked up a bar of soap and washed himself quickly, as the warmth faded. He rubbed the soap in his pubic area, creating a mound of full lather. When he felt himself getting excited, he rubbed faster and harder until his penis peeked through the lather.

Once he was hard enough to grab a half fist full of himself and pumped his penis furiously until he spasmed and fell to the floor of tub, knocking over the cans of beer that were propped in the corners.

There he lay, twitching, and groaning like a newborn calf. Chico couldn't move. He was a mess. Chico mustered the energy to reach up and turn the shower off and immediately drifted into unconsciousness.

The long, black limousine seemed out of place as it glided towards Trixie's van. The tinted windows gave no hint of who might be behind them, staring, spying, or even performing obscene acts without fear of discovery. It stopped next to the battle-worn camper van. The driver stepped out on one side, walked around to the other and opened the door. Trixie stepped out as if she were attending a movie premier. The man sitting next to her, who was obscured by the shadows in the plush interior, did not get out. He did not give her money. Trixie, instead, slipped a piece of paper to the driver.

"Same account?" he asked.

"No, a different one," she replied as if talking to her financial advisor. "I like to diversify."

As she stood by the open door of the limousine, the man inside said, "Trixie, you're a wonderful girl, an amazing character, but I worry about you. Are you sure you know what you're doing?"

Trixie leaned into the car, and whispered into his ear, "Only a man who has something to fear is afraid to live. You don't need to worry about me Senator. If this life ends before I have completed my mission, I will return and finish it in the next life…and the next…and the next."

The senator knew she was serious. He had been seeing her off and on for nearly a year. He blew her a kiss and said, "I'll see you next time I'm in town."

"You have my number," she said, then turned and walked to the van, opened the door with the key and stepped inside. The limousine drove away slowly. The Senator's head disappeared as the tinted window rose with a muted whir.

Trixie wanted to spend some time in her camper writing before going to see the Dalai Lama that evening.

The Sun was ducking behind the trees, covering itself with a blanket made of buildings, birds, Maples, and Laurels. This was the saddest time of the day for Trixie, but it was also the time she felt the most inspired.

She turned on the wall-mounted lamp, pulled her journal from under the mattress and began to write:

All these years I was told that women have no power, but I have come to believe otherwise. We have more power than we realize, but most of us will not acknowledge that power. We strive to be at par with men, as competitive as men. Many women, I believe only end up becoming manly. There is no distinction between them and their male counterparts. They are not desirable. They are lonely. They are, in a sense, freaks. There is a distinction between being powerful and a woman and just being powerful and sexless. A powerful woman acknowledges her power and her womanhood. A woman who is simply powerful is lost in a void between men and women. Women will never be welcomed members of the Good-old-boys club. Nor should we want to be. It is a club that is deeply established and deeply flawed. We can, however, get close to it and manipulate it as we can a man. A woman who wants to be successful in a man's world has to acknowledge these facts. Our net worth can be in the millions of dollars, but the first thing a man will always think when he meets her is whether she is a moaner or a screamer, whether her nipples are innies or outies and whether she takes it in the ass or not.

Is it fair? No. Should it be? No. To conquer an enemy you must respect it first. And we must quest for balance, greatness and enlightenment. I have to go to the Schnitzer to see the Dalai Lama. Tonight I will be reborn again.

Chapter 34

Rich walk towards April, hoping to intercept her before they got inside. She quickly stepped out of the car, slammed the door and walked fast towards the house.

As Rich, got closer, he started to speak. "April, I can explain, I was downtown—"

"Rich, you don't want to talk to me right now." She did not make eye contact with him.

"Don't be like that, April," Rich pleaded.

"Be like what, Rich? I was in the middle of a presentation this afternoon when I got the call. I had to ask our clients to wait while I took the call. What Should I be like, Rich?"

"I'm sorry about that April. I was doing a shoot—"

April interrupted Rich before he could continue. "You know, Rich, I don't want to know what you were doing. All I know is what you WEREN'T doing. And that is taking care of your children."

"Jesus, Christ, April, you make it sound like this happens every day and it doesn't."

"It seems like something happens every day."

"Now you're being cruel, April."

"Well, I'm pissed. This is embarrassing."

"How do you think I feel…am feeling right now."

"You should have thought about that while you were out there doing whatever it was you were doing."

"I told you, I was—" April put up an opened hand and looked away.

"—Rich, I told you, if I know that you were involved in another of your crazy schemes, it will only make me angrier." She was yelling.

In the corner of his eye, Rich could see the Peasleys, standing, staring into space, still NOTHING going in their heads, both still two bails short of a haystack. They didn't respond to April and Rich, but Rich was still uncomfortable arguing in front of them.

"Okay, April. I give. If you don't want to talk about it now. Fine. Think what you want. I'm going to cook dinner for the children. I'll do one of those SOMETHINGS that always happens. If you want to be pissed, be my guest."

"Thank you. I appreciate that fact that you would allow me that luxury," she responded sarcastically.

Rich continued, "But don't expect me to drop my drawers and talk about this when you feel like it. I'm not like you, April. This pissed-for-hours thing gets old. If you're going to be pissed, lay it out on the table and let's get it done. Then we can go on with out lives. You in your infinite perfection. Me, a fuck up artist wannabe. As long as we have our roles defined, we can save ourselves a lot of grief."

April didn't know what to say. The argument was heading down a street she didn't like. She took a deep breath and said, "Rich, that's not how it is. I know you don't mean that. Look, this phone call could have cost us the account. I got a lot of grief over this at work and I don't know who else to blame."

"April, this is me. Do you think I would do something like this deliberately to embarrass you or make you lose your job. I'm sorry."

"No, I don't think you would do something like this deliberately, but I do think your passion for these little projects you get yourself involved in causes you to be inconsiderate."

"I can't argue with that. I'm the first to acknowledge my faults. But that doesn't make me an evil person."

"It makes people who care about you bad people, because we get so frustrate. And we…I, love you so much I don't know what to do."

"Look around, April. Is our life so terrible that it's worth getting so frustrated over."

April looked intensely into his eyes. "No, Rich, our life is not terrible. We have a good life. We have everything I ever dreamed of. I guess my dream was an imperfect one. There wasn't room for fault in my dream. I didn't imagine that the prince in my dreams would have imperfections, would be an artist, would not be completely bought into the American dream, 401ks, always punctual, always considerate, always thinking about everyone else's needs. The prince charming I imagined wasn't a real person. But the prince charming I got is."

"And I'm doing the best I can, April. I know I'm not perfect."

"I know, Rich. Neither am I. But I'm close."

Rich and April laughed. "Can we kiss and make up now?"

April hesitated then said, "Sure, Rich. I don't want us to be mad at each other."

Rich smiled at her and remembered why he fell in love with her at the moment. The evening sun glistened in her eyes. She was beautiful, and she could turn on a dime and surprise him.

"But, Rich, if I ever get another call from school, I'm going to personally hunt you down and kill you, then hang your dead body in Washington Square so all of Portland can spit on you and crows can eat your eyeballs out and rats can feed on your entrails. Clear?"

"Clear." They hugged and kissed.

The Peasleys turned away at this sight.

Chapter 35

Nighttime crept slowly over the quiet streets surrounding the silent van as Trixie struggled to put words to paper. The act of writing wasn't the problem. The emotions her words brought up were.

While writing in her journals, she alternately laughed and cried or sank into pensive moods or felt exhilarated. Her journals were her confessionals, her communion and her counselor, and over the years she had amassed quite a collection of them, which she stashed in her apartment.

As she scratched out the last words in her journal and closed it, she felt exhilarated. She thought about the Dalai Lama. She was hoping to see the Dalai Lama for almost six months. Now she would get her chance.

She gathered her jacket, purse, and stepped out of the van. The streets were quiet. Trixie walked to the intersection and caught a southbound bus that took her to the 32nd block of southeast Portland, then across the Hawthorne bridge to S.W. 10 Street and the Performing Arts Center, a majestic old theater turned concert/lecture hall.

Rich was glad April had calmed down before they entered the house. An angry woman in a confined space, even one as big as a house, was what Rich imagined was God's idea of Hell, if such a place existed.

Fortunately, April had her daily quotient of being angry at Rich, and she did not have the strength to stay angry. During dinner, Rich reminded April that he made plans to see the Dalai Lama. She simply gave Rich another look, this time one that said, WHY THE HELL WOULD ANYBODY PAY TO SEE A MONK IN A BATHROBE?

The kids took turns thinking of words that rhymed with Lama and had a great laugh over the whole topic.

Rich also reminded April that he was attending the writer's conference in Long Beach, Washington that weekend, where, he said, he hoped to finish the novel he'd been working on most of the year. At this news, Rich was given another look, the one that said, SO IF YOU WRITE A NOVEL WILL IT HELP PAY THE GAS BILL?

Rich could read all of Aril's looks. Sometimes, she didn't need to speak at all to communicate loudly and clearly.

Rich left after dinner and arrived at the Performing Arts Center minutes before the lecture was to begin.

The center was one of Portland's best theaters. It was originally part of the Orpheum family of grand Vaudeville showplaces that had been made-over for modern uses. The foyer had high ceilings with grand chandeliers. Black and brown Italian marble created a checkered pattern on the floor. Along the wall of the main floor were water fountains with plaster cherubs for bases and a wide half clamshell with a stream of water shooting into the air.

The wallpaper was gold and silver paisley patterned, typical of a 1910s theater, and the centerpiece of the lobby was a grand staircase with deco style carpet that led to the second and third floors and balcony seating. At the base of the stairs was a brass call box once used by wealthy patrons to call their personal valets. It now served as a useless but stunning antique fixture.

Rich's seat was on the main floor towards the front. A soft bell chimed to indicate that the doors would be closing soon. Rich rushed in and found his seat.

Immediately, a hush came over the auditorium and the Dalai Lama walked on to the stage to a lone microphone in the middle of the expansive stage. There was only silence. Then a tentative clap rang out from the back the theater, which prompted more claps.

The Dalai Lama simply smiled, held out both hands and moved them up and down ever so slightly. With that minute gesture, the clapping stopped. Silence. Every seat was filled with a body but no one was breathing, fidgeting or even scratching. It was as if they feared any slight movement might disrupt the fabric of space.

The Dalai Lama began to speak softly.

Trixie had a front row seat, practically at the Dalai Lama's feet. She sat, mouth open, jaw nearly touching the ground. Crazy thoughts passed through Trixie's head.

Throw your panties to him. Stand and scream as loud and as long as you can like at a boy band concert. She had been to a One Direction concert and knew what those were like. She knew what 30,000 teenage girls screaming at the top of their lungs for hours sounded like. She wanted to run onto the stage and try to kiss him. But that would only get the attention of the burly security guards who stood sentry at both ends of the stage. Instead, she suppressed her emotions and listened intently.

After a spellbinding hour-long lecture, the Dalai Lama simply walked off the stage. Most in the audience did not want to acknowledge that he had finished. They were mesmerized. It was not until the Lama was practically off stage that the thunderous applause erupted, like the monsoon rains of Indonesia.

The sound was deafening. Whistles and whoops were mixed in

with the claps, and the standing ovation continued for 15 minutes after the Dalai Lama left the stage.

Once the exit doors opened, most people orderly proceeded into the lobby and up the stairs to the second floor lobby where there was a bar and where the Dalai Lama was rumored to be making a visit.

Those who marched up the stairs had the same purpose in mind. Get as close the Dalai Lama as possible.

Rich decided to go along for the ride and make his way up the stairs. He was more curious than anything.

Trixie felt like a smitten teenager, dumbstruck and light headed. She could not move from her seat. She did not want the lecture to end. The Dalai Lama's words had touched her soul and she wanted to preserve the feeling she had forever.

She soon became aware the auditorium was emptying quickly and she did not want to be the last person in line to see the Dalai Lama.

She jumped up and raced to the exit to catch up with the last persons in the line leaving the cavernous room. She pushed some people aside, saying, "Excuse me. Pardon me. So sorry" as she worked her way up the stairs.

At the top of the stairs, Trixie met with a wall of bodies and no forward momentum, like an L.A. traffic jam of warm bodies. She jumped up to see what was preventing them from moving forward. Her first jump showed rows of heads with a bald brown one several feet away. This was the Lama. He was answering questions and shaking hands.

Rich saw the crowd and, instead of following the pack, he turned left at the top of the stairs towards the bar. At the bar, Rich ordered a single Chardonnay from a uniformed bartender with a toothy smile and friendly manor. As he paid for the drink a well dressed man walked up to the counter next to him and ordered a Slo Gin Martini, shaken not stirred with three olives instead of one. Rich was about to walk away when the gentleman asked him, "What did you think of the lecture?"

"Terrific," Rich answered.

"Have you ever heard him lecture before?"

"Nope. First time."

"I've seen him in Napal, Madrid and Singapore. Each lecture is different. But he's always a commanding presence."

"I was impressed."

"Names Sunny, Sunny Manns," the gentleman said and volunteered a handshake."

"Franklin, Rich Franklin's my name."

"What do you do Rich?" Manns asked, perhaps a little too forward, Rich thought. But he answered anyway. I'm a publisher, writer and a paperboy."

"All at one time?" Manns asked.

"Everything except the Paperboy part. Can't pitch and write at the same time."

"I'm a literary agent," Manns offered.

"No kidding."

"No Kidding. What's the matter, don't I look like one."

"Well, of course you do. I mean, literary agents look like everybody else don't they."

"Not really. Many of us look more like sharks or weasels."

Rich laughed. "So I've heard."

Rich looked Manns over closely for the first time. Horn-rimmed glasses complimented his chiseled face. His nose was aristocratic, pointed. Unusual for an African American unless he was of Indian descent. He was tall, well over six foot, and his double-breasted, tailored suit fit him better than butter on bread. It was dark, business like, but he wore a red turtle neck. A statement, Rich thought.

"So, Rich, what do you write?"

Rich hesitated before answering. Did he want to talk about his writing now. Not Really, but it was better than nothing.

"Non-fiction, articles, novels, shopping lists."

"Tell me more about your shopping list. I have a major publisher who's been asking me about authors."

Rich laughed. The ice was broken. Manns acknowledged that as well. "I'm working on a novel about a Paperboy who gets into some trouble. I'm still juggling plots, but I think I may be close to figuring that out as well."

"Do you have some samples I could take a look at."

"You mean now?" Rich sounded incredulous.

"Why not. You have a web site—and any samples posted there?"

"Well, sure, but you can't get to them from here."

"I don't see why not."

Manns pulled out an electronic device from his breast pocket, pulled out an antennae, pressed some buttons and said, "Voila. We're connected."

"Portable wireless. That's excellent."

"Here, check this out," Manns said as he leaned forward and showed Rich the screen. "You have a web site."

"Sure, and I have a some sample pages posted there. I hoped one day I'd be able to send links to an agent."

"Someday is here Rich. What's your URL?"

Rich gave Manns his URL. Manns pressed some buttons with a thin black stylus and reviewed the sample pages while Rich watched.

"This is good Rich. You know, I've got another agent friend who might have a publisher looking for something like this. When will it be finished?"

"I hope this weekend, maybe," Rich said, uncertain.

"Well, I have enough here to show. I'll pass it along. Here's my card." Manns handed Rich a card, finished his martini and said, "I gotta go Rich. Got a plane to catch. Nice meeting you Rich."

"Nice to meet you, too," Rich said, not quite sure what to make of this brief, chance meeting.

Across the room, Trixie struggled to see the Dalai Lama. She was too short to see over the myriad of manes and bald spots, and too small to bully her way to the front. Frustration turned to anger. Anger turned to despair.

She turned away from the crowd in frustration and glanced over at the bar. A tall handsome black man was walking away from the bar leaving another gentleman she had seen that afternoon going into Jake's standing by himself. Curious, Trixie walked towards him, fully intent on striking up a conversation to find out what was going on at Jake's that afternoon.

Rich took another sip from his drink and thought about the conversation he had with Manns. Where would this lead he thought? Seconds later he felt a tap on his shoulder and the familiar scent of China Rain. He turned to see Brenda, his favorite make-up artist and Phil crony, batting her beautiful eyelashes at him. They hugged.

Trixie stopped when she saw a tall, dark-haired, strikingly beautiful woman walk up behind the man she had seen. Competition? She thought. She felt a strange, uncomfortable, ping of jealousy as she watched Rich and Brenda's face lit up with the warm expressions of recognition.

Trixie walked to the bar, past the two strangers and stood a few feet away, observing and eavesdropping on their conversation. They were friends. They had both been at Jake's that afternoon. She recognized them both now. They were not lovers. But, judging by their body language, they could easily be. He's married. She is not. A beautiful woman and a married man. Perfect formula for trouble. She's striking. What man could resist her?

Brenda was surprised to find that Rich was interested in Buddhism. She grilled him about it.

"You know, Rich, we've know each other for years and yet we don't really know that much about each other. How does someone get to know you?"

"Brenda, I'm not that complicated. Nor am I so interesting that I deserve that question. If anyone is interesting here, it's you."

"Come on Rich, don't flatter me. Let's be honest with each other. Bring your barriers down, especially here in the midst of such great spirituality."

Rich studied Brenda intensely without saying anything. She stared into his eyes, barely blinking, probing for clues. She would not speak until he gave her an honest answer. This was scaring Rich. This is how romance started, with feigned honesty, locked stares, that point when you look into each other's eyes and one day see desire.

Brenda was transforming before his eyes from Brenda the quirky, creative makeup lady to Brenda the sultry, sensual, desirable woman. They were moving quickly to that danger zone.

Brenda's eyes followed his. She was looking deep into his soul, into his bowels, he felt. He was vulnerable. What should he do? He was a married man.

His cell phone rang. Thank God. Technology to the rescue.

"Hold on Brenda, I have to get this."

As Rich spoke, Brenda moved to the bar and stood dangerously close to him, practically perching one of her perfectly formed breast on his arm. She was already comfortable with him, but now she seemed downright uninhibited. Maybe it was the wine.

Trixie enjoyed the show. She watched Brenda maneuver. She could tell

Brenda had a burning interest in Rich, but there may have never been an opportunity for her to learn more. Now, that opportunity presented itself. There were hormones at work here that only women knew about. Trixie, was not disappointed any more, only amused now. She continued to watch and eves drop. Man's moral dilemma at work, she thought.

"Brenda, I've got to go," Rich said after ending the call. "Scott just called and said they need a piano player tonight at Jazz De Opus. His keyboard man is sick. I told him I'd sit in."

"Is that Scott Forbes, the drummer?"

"Yeah, you remember we met him at Phil's loft party. You're welcome to come down and see us tonight." Rich said, wondering if he was making a terrible mistake. Too late. It came out.

"Sure, Rich, I'll meet you there later. I've got to go say goodbye to some friends."

"Cool. You know where it is."

"On 3rd and Washington?"

"That's the one. We start at 10:00. I can only do a couple of hours then I got to get some sleep. Gotta deliver some papers in the morning."

"How's that going? Paper delivery I mean."

"It's going. You know me. I'm trying to be the best God damn paperboy in the world. And to prove it, I'm writing a book about it."

Brenda gave Rich a hug that would linger for weeks. Then she was gone. Rich left his glass on the bar and headed for the club.

Trixie, no longer distracted by the exchange, turned her attention back to the now dispersing crowd. The Dalai Lama was gone. She had missed him. She felt a deep sadness swelling inside of her. She had missed her opportunity to be blessed by the Dalai Lama, and she was disappointed that he was not as approachable as she thought he would be.

Trixie left the building, and as she walked past a side door, she felt tears forming in her eyes. she did not want to cry in front of so many stranger, but she was sad deep inside. She walked around to the back of the building and sat on some stairs near the back doors. She began to openly cry, deep heart wrenching sobs. She cursed herself for being so sensitive.

Trixie covered her face with her hands and pushed her face down hard onto her knees.

"Why are you crying?" a voice asked. Trixie thought the soothing voice was an illusion at first, coming from her head. She did not hear anyone approach. But the voice asked again, "Why are you crying child." There was a thick accent and the voice was familiar. Then a large hand touched her head.

As she looked up, she saw two sandaled feet first, then a golden silk and maroon robe draped over a small brown man who was smiling behind wire rimmed glasses. Trixie wiped away the tears that blurred her vision. The tears made the man seem like a blurry phantom.

The man reached down and gently gripped Trixie's shoulder. He lifted her up and held her close to him, hugging her while she sobbed. He was real, The smell of incense emanated from his robe. He stroked her head, comforting her.

"There is a great deal of pain in you child," The Dalai Lama said, carefully choosing his words. "I can sense that you are wise well beyond your years, beyond your lifetime, beyond this physical existence. Those of us who have inherited the knowledge of generations have a terrible burden to bare. Along with the pleasure we experienced in past lives, we have also inherited the pain, the misery, and suffering brought on by greed, envy, lust, and war. We cannot be what is considered normal. We, in essence, know too much. We are the divining rods of existence, of history, of knowledge. So, my child, you have everything and nothing to cry about. You and are one."

The Dalai Lama, held Trixie's face with both hands, then kissed her forehead, clasped his hands together, turned and walked back inside.

Trixie was in shock. The encounter for her was the equivalent of seeing Elvis for some. She never imagined she would find herself so close to greatness.

At that moment she felt a new power and sense of urgency. She had been affirmed, blessed, endorsed. She, at that moment, decided it was time to make a change. She would confront Delbert. She would let Chico go. She would give up her van. She would acknowledge her existence and stop living on the fringe. She had some money saved that would help her go to college.

She was smiling and happy as she waited for the next bus to take her to her Cully neighborhood, to her van, where she would gather her few personal belongings, leave the signed-off title to the van in the windshield, and walk away from that life she was living forever.

Chapter 36

Jazz De Opus occupied a corner of an older part of downtown Portland called Old-Town. The 1895 building was a classic Italianette structure that had been a coffee bar, a restaurant, then a coffee bar, then a fish market, then a cafe, then a restaurant, then a restaurant Jazz Bar.

When Rich opened the door, huge puffs of smoke bellowed out like the smoke stack of a Great American steam engine. The heavy hand hewn wooden doors were uncharacteristic of a jazz bar, but Jazz De Opus was uncharacteristic of a jazz bar.

Inside, Scott Forbes and other band members were sitting at the bar. They had finished a set without the benefit of a piano player. When Scott saw Rich, he stood up immediately and walked over to greet him.

"Rich! What's happnin'?"

"You," Rich answered as they exchanged hand shakes. Scott was the blackest white man Rich had ever met. He talked black, thought black, played black. Rich thought he may actually be black if his hair wasn't blond and a barely noticeable blond mustache wasn't threatening to show itself on Scott's face. Scott had been trying to grow it for five years. Scott was of slight build, almost frail. At 45, he'd been playing drums for a long time. He was old fashioned; wore a suit and tie whenever he performed, and music was the fuel that stoked his lifestyle of fresh cigars and whiskey, and sophisticated women.

"Rich, we're dying here. Thanks for showing up on such short notice," Forbes said, "Rich, you're always there when I need you. How the hell do you do that. You're like a God damn super hero. Appearing. Disappearing. You play piano like a God damn prodigy but you don't consider yourself a piano player. Shit, Rich, I love you man but you freak me out your so God damn talented."

"I'm here Scott, Jesus Christ, you don't have to kiss my ass. I know who you are and where you're coming from."

"Kiss my ass Rich. Just get the fuck up there and kill those damn keyboards."

Scott escorted Rich to the bar where the other musicians were nursing drinks. "All right kids," Scott announced, "We can make some real music now."

"Rich, what's happnin brutha," said Bobby Gonzolez, who was in his 70s, only drank Gallo wine, and didn't play trombone like he used when he played with Count Basie. But he could still put most players to shame.

"How you doin' Tipsie," Rich responded. "How's that leg."

"Oh, my bunyons been actin' up again, but I can still blow and

I can still fuck so I can't complain."

Everyone laughed at that thought.

"Tipsie, why you want to go and plant that picture in my head," Said Charlie Greyson, "I'm not gon be able to concentrate all night. God damn, make me lose my appetite!"

"Hows it goin Highnote?" Rich said to Charlie.

"It was going all right until Tipsie started talking about that nasty shit."

"Rich, your ready to jam," asked Jimmy "Smiles" Treehorn, the sax man. Treehorn was the darkest of the group. When he smiled, all Rich saw was teeth. That's why they called him smiles. He was a retired physician, pushing 75 years old. He was Rich's favorite.

"Fingers," the elder statesman of the group was quiet at the end of the bar. He was the bass player, Jackie Walker. He would not reveal his age, but some thought he could be nearing a hundred. Rich walked over to him, placed a hand on his shoulder and asked, "Mr. Walker, sir. How are you?"

Fingers looked up from his glass of milk and said, "Rich, you know Snoop Doggy Doghouse, Iced Milk, Piddy Diddy, you know all those rappers. They ain't really musicians. Theyze imposters. Miles, Ellington, Parker, all those cats I used to play with. They was musicians."

"Mr. Walker, I agree with you." Rich said. "Let's not forget Mr. "Finger's" Walker, lead bass man for Count Basie's Orchestra from 1960 through 1970."

"You ain't like them other young musicians, Rich, you know your history. You got to know your history. Time was a Negro couldn't play in a place like this. Young peoples got to know your history."

"Mr. Walker, sir, it would be an honor to play a set with you."

Fingers smiled. He was of mixed race, a White mother and a Black father. His hair was straight, thinned on top, but pressed flat on the sides with hands full of Afro Sheen, like Cab Calloway.

"Help me over there Rich. I ain't as young as I used to."

"Pleasure, sir."

Rich allowed Fingers to put a hand on his shoulder while they walked over to a stool on the stage that was next to an acoustic upright bass.

The other members of the band shuffled, limped or hobbled over to the stage. It was sight. The Portland Jazz Ensemble had to cumulatively be the oldest Band in the World.

Quiet couples and contemplative barflies were scattered at tables in the bar, illuminated only by single, red, glowing candles at each table. Layers of smoke criss-crossed the room as the musicians tuned their instruments. Before the band began, the door opened and in walked Brenda, radiant, intimidating, and her smile beamed across the room like a lighthouse when she saw Rich.

All Rich could think of was that he was in trouble.

Scott whispered to Rich, "How about Round Midnight?"

"Waltz for Debbie," Rich responded and winked at Scott.

"Yes, sir Mr. Boss man." Scott responded.

Bill Evans was Rich's specialty because Evans was complex, unpredictable and subtle at the same time. This was how Rich characterized himself. This was the persona Rich had carefully crafted.

As they eased into the intro, Rich's mind went blank. There was only sound and emotion now. He closed his eyes.

Partway into the song, as Highnote started his solo, Rich heard some unusual sounds emanating from behind Highnote. As Highnote blew each note, the familiar squeaking and trumpeting sound of gas escaping from his behind could clearly be heard by Rich. Rich opened his eyes and listened more intently.

Highnote was indeed farting a symphony along with his playing. Scott had warned him about this months earlier, but he'd never actually witnessed it. Rich looked at Scott. Scott hunched his shoulders as if to say, "I told you so."

Rich's thought was this was a whole new definition for Scat. It was amusing at first, but when the smell began to overtake the cigarette smoke, it started to become a problem.

But it didn't interfere with the creative process, Rich thought, so he chose to ignore it.

Rich played for 40 minutes, then, after the set ended, he joined Brenda at her table. He was surprised to find that she still had that look in her eyes, but she did not press for information like she did at the lecture. Their conversation was more casual, more familiar. He told her about the writer's conference that weekend, some of the other projects he was working on, and they talked about music for a while. It was all innocent.

But the look was still there. And that made Rich subconsciously uncomfortable. He had to keep asking himself, "What does she want from me?"

It was getting close to midnight and Rich had to get home. Although he had not told April what time he wold be home, she knew that in two and a half hours, he would have to wake up again and put on his best face and be ready toss his route.

Chapter 37

It was still close to midnight, when Trixie returned to her van. Delbert was scheduled to arrive at 12:30. Tonight would be different she thought. Tonight she would be liberated. Tonight she would reverse her roll in their relationship.

At midnight, Chico awoke in the shower, cold, smelly, sick to his stomach. He had not moved in hours. Cockroaches screwed their courage and crawled all over him, nibbling on his semen and scurrying over his body.

Chico jumped up and shuddered, letting out a scream in the process. He quickly turned on the shower, releasing a stream of icy cold water that sent his system into immediate shock. He screamed again and jumped out of the shower.

The hundreds of scrambling brown dots were sucked to their wet grave as water splashed around the tub and halted their frantic escape.

Chico slowly became more aware of the time and his surroundings. He also became aware of the lingering anger the days events had raised in him. When the water warmed, he stepped back in the shower and washed his body quickly. He turned off the water and stepped out of the tub. Before wiping his body with his towel, he shook it. Brown dots fell to the ground and scurried behind the toilet.

Chico continued his ritual. He retrieved a beer from his refrigerator, snorted a few lines of coke and jerked off to his big-tit magazines, dressed quickly, splashed on enough Brute to bath in, dressed, and went to his closet. He reached up into the upper shelf and retrieved a shoebox. He set the shoebox on the table, removed the lid and took out the black object that was stashed under some crumpled papers.

The revolver was a silver .22 caliber Saturday night special, better used for shooting sparrows than for self-defense. But for Chico, this revolver made him feel as if his cock had grown to sizes.

The feel of the metal in his hand caused his penis to become erect and push at his underwear and his khakis. Chico pointed the weapon at the wall and made a *bang* sound. He check for bullets. The carriage was full.

Chico shoved the gun in his pant pocket and rushed out of the apartment. He was invincible with his peacemaker. His only worry was that the gun might go off and shoot his balls off. He stopped briefly and took the bullets out of the gun and shoved them in his other pocket.

Chico wobbled up 42nd street and turned on Going, where he new Trixie would be. When he reached the van, he saw the Jaguar XJ-6 parked behind it. Chico locked his crippled 15 speed bike to a nearby stop sign and crouched in the bushes to wait for the car to leave.

Delbert arrived on time in his usual state of arousal, anticipating what he might do to this young, nubile girl in the dark of night. For Delbert, this rendezvous was the closest thing to adventure in his life. He knocked on the door.

Trixie, being cautious, yelled, "Who is it?"

"It's me, your daddy," Delbert said. Trixie opened the door.

"Come in Delbert," Trixie said. Delbert's grin turned to a frown when Trixie said his name. He also sensed the mood had changed.

"I asked you not to call me Delbert," Delbert scolded.

"Fuck you Delbert. I'll call you any God damn thing I want to. Delbert hoisted his bulk into the van and it leaned to the side as he settled into the small chair near the front of the van. He breathed heavily through hairy clogged nostrils. Trixie sat on the bed, staring at Delbert, confident, knowing exactly what she had to do.

"Delbert I know what you do to your daughter. And I want to tell you that you are one sick mother fucker."

"What are you talking about Trixie?"

"Delbert if you were half as smart as your ass size, you would have figured out that I'm not the idiot whore you make me out to be."

"Honey, have you had too much to drink this evening? Why don't you let me come over there and comfort you."

"Stay where you are Delbert. We are finished. I can no longer see you. And my advice to you is to leave your daughter alone. I know all about it and I have recorded everything you've said in my journals."

Delbert's mood changed immediately and he turned ghost white. He knew the risk of his action, but he never considered the consequences.

"Trixie, look, whatever you may think I'm doing is a figment of your imagination. I see you so I will not do those things to my daughter. Don't you see, you are helping me."

"No, Delbert, you're helping yourself, and I'm only helping you to feed your sick obsession. In my desire to help you, I'm afraid I may have done you and your family a great disservice. A man like you can only benefit by intensive counseling. And, unfortunately, the recivity rate for a child molester, adulterers and sex addicts all rolled into one is very low."

"What the fuck are you talking about. Are you some kind of undercover analyst or something. That's all bullshit," he said, sternly, starting to raise his voice. Trixie had cut deep.

"You're a fucking whore and you don't know shit about me. I pay you good money so I can fuck the shit out of you, not to listen to your smart ass mouth tell me how fucked up I am."

Delbert stood up and slammed an open shelf closed causing a loud bang and stomped over to Trixie and pointed a finger in her face.

"You're the fucked up one here you fucking whore bitch. Just 'cause you read a few psychology books doesn't mean you know shit about me? All you have to do is spread your legs, take your money and shut the fuck up."

Trixie was shaking and trying not to show her fear, but she was more afraid of Delbert than she was of Chico. She took a deep breath then continued.

"I talked to your daughter, Delbert. I know all about it and if you harm me in any way, your wife, your friends, and the Police will all know about it."

Delbert's eyes were bulging now. Rage was building inside. Should he believe Trixie or not? Was she just the dumb whore he thought she was or not? Should he punch her face in or not? As he thought over his options, Trixie reached over and pulled out a small piece of paper from under her mattress. She handed it to Delbert. He took it, read the numbers, then turned and stormed out of the van. Before closing the door, he took two thousand dollars out his wallet, crumpled it and threw it at Trixie.

"Here you fucking whore bitch. You come near my family again and I'll kill you!" He slammed the door closed and seconds later his tires squealed as he sped away.

Chapter 38

The house was dark and silent except for the hum of the furnace in the basement. Rich checked on the kids first, walking to their beds, careful not to step to heavily, kneeled over them and rubbed their heads. He gently placed a hand on their chests to feel their hearts beating, then he kissed them each and went into the master bedroom where April was sleeping. He could hear her muted breathing but he couldn't see her. He slipped quietly into bed.

The neon green cd-alarm clock screamed one a.m., and Rich cursed to himself. What the hell had his life turned into? His life, he thought, was like a coin that had been tossed up in the air but never landed. Instead, it rotated in the air incessantly. If it were ever to land, he thought, it would probably land on it's edge. Two hours sleep were better than none he decided.

As he lay there, unable to sleep, he considered what his life must look like to April and how it must look like a pretty screwed up picture. He final drifted into a deep sleep and the alarm clock went off.

"Shit! Rich yelled." He reached over and hit the snooze button hard. It was three o'clock already.

Rich dressed quickly and went to the station.

Chapter 39

After Delbert left, Trixie couldn't breathe normally or relax at all. What was she doing? She was afraid yet she wasn't. She was tired and hyper at the same time. She had no more appointments for the night. And she was not going to look for any. She was finished with this life. She decided to take a nap before gathering her things and returning to her apartment. She would leave a note for Chico on the door of the Van and probably never see him again

A half block away, Chico couldn't figure out what he had just witnessed. He could tell the John was angry. What had Trixie done to him? Chico wanted to storm over to the van and confront Trixie, but he was afraid. She scared him. He had to build up his courage. He would ride his bike for a while and chase feral cats. If he caught one he would kill it like he did the night before to boost his courage. Then he would confront her.

When Rich entered the station, Jimmy, looked at him and raised an eyebrow. "Hey buddy, I don't know what you did, but Ted called this morning looking for you. He told me to make sure you didn't leave until he got here."

"Did he say what he wanted."

"Nope, just said to keep you here. Somethin' I need to know about?"

"Not that I know of Jimmy. I'm just the paperboy."

"All right chief. Tuesday is money day. I put a stack of customer invoices by your station."

"Thanks Jimmy."

All the carriers were there, including the African king. There was a comfort in the rhythmic sounds of papers being folded, bagged and tossed in the carts. Rich joined in.

Fold. Stuff. Toss. Paper number one. Three hundred to go.

Outside, Rich heard the familiar sound of the Pimber mobile and footsteps approaching the entrance. Ted walked in, turned towards Rich and said, "I need to see you in my office."

They walked towards the rear of the building, opened a door with a sign on it that said MEN/WOMEN, both men stepped in and Pimber locked the door. Ted turned on the fan and pulled out a four inch long joint and lit it. He sucked in deeply, holding his breath and blowing the smoke up into the exhaust fan.

"Look Rich, I don't know who you know or what you know, but I want you to know this is not my fault."

He took an envelope out of his back pocket and handed it to Rich.

Rich looked at it, puzzled.

"Ted, I don't know what this is about, but if you want to fire me, we don't need to do this in the toilet."

"No, no, Rich, you got this all wrong. Open the envelope."

Rich opened the envelope and pulled out a check. It was made out to Rich and was for $600.

"Ted, what's this for."

"It's for you Rich."

Ted sucked on the doobie again.

"Your checks have been a little short. I got a call from accounting and they said I needed to give you this amount. They told me they wouldn't ask any questions as long as I took care of this today. You apparently have a great customer with a little bit of pull. I'm sorry, Rich, I was going to surprise you with a bonus in November."

Rich didn't make the connection right away. Then he remembered his conversation with James Walker.

"Ted, I don't know anything about this, but I will say thank you, regardless of the circumstances. I could use this money right now."

Ted held out a hand. "So we're square?"

"Sure Ted. As square as we can be." They shook hands.

"I'm going to finish this. Would you excuse me for a moment?"

"Sure thing Ted." Rich unlocked the door and walked out, closing the door behind him. Ted sucked on the last inch of his joint as Rich closed the door.

Chapter 40

Herbie Hancock was reverberating in the cab as Rich tossed his route. He was in the zone, halfway through. He would be on his home stretch in no time.

As he turned onto Going Street, he saw a flash by the van that was usually parked there. A pop, like a firecracker followed. Rich thought he blew a tire, so he slowed before passing the van. The van door seemed open, and a figure soon emerged and ran out into the street in front of the Rich. Rich slammed on the brakes and the truck screeched to a stop inches from the figure.

The figure stopped, held out it's hands as if they could stop the truck from crushing it. One hand held a wad of bills and the other held a small pistol.

The figure pointed the gun at Rich. Rich took a deep breath but couldn't let it out, even as his heart pumped loud and hard, trying to push more oxygen to his body.

Rich could see the figure was pressing the trigger but there was no flash, no sound, no shattered windshield, no bullet entering his chest.

The figure ran out of the headlights, crossed the street and disappeared into the night.

Rich felt a pain in his chest. Did he really see that? He should be dead, he thought. He pressed the accelerator to the ground and sped away. What had he just witnessed? A robbery?

Rich stopped at a 7/11 two blocks away. He sat in his truck with his head on the steering wheel, gripping tightly, rerunning the scene through his head. Sweat dripped on to the steering wheel. He still had trouble breathing. A Mexican American. A gun. A robbery. Should he get involved? Or should he finish the route and go home. A quick, anonymous call maybe. Do it. Finish your route and go home. It was just a robbery.

Rich made the call. He hung up without giving any personal information. They'll look into it, Rich thought.

Rich had more streets to toss before he finished his route. He turned up Herbie Hancock and continued his route. He was disoriented so he missed some houses. He was distracted by the image of the gun pointed straight at his face. He couldn't help think he'd been lucky that morning.

Chapter 41

Detective Bob Grimsley's day started early at the Public Safety Center gun range in Clackamas, on the outskirts of Portland. The range was designed for police officers and their families. It was plush, well ventilated, air conditioned and far removed from the gritty gun ranges of the past. It even had a game room, massage room and a tanning salon.

Grimsley liked the range, but had some trouble with the tanning salon when it opened. Once he saw how many police officer's wives actually used it, it started making more sense, and he didn't mind having more women around the joint as he called it, to pretty up the place.

The range Grimsley used had a plaque on the wall that read THE BOB GRIMSLEY / ELMORE LEONARD RANGE – DEDICATED TO THE BEST DAMN CRIME SOLVING AND SHARP SHOOTING DETECTIVE IN THE BUSINESS.

This was his gun range, dedicated to him by the owner of the range, J.D. Veckman, a retired police detective Grimsley had known for 30 years. J.D., as a joke, added the Elmore Leonard reference after seeing Grimsley's library, which contained thousands of crime novels from Raymond Chandler to Leslie Ann Rule. And Grimsley quoted regularly from Leonard novels. Rumor had it that Grimsley had written a novel of his own at some point. He wrote plenty of crime scene investigation handbooks. Any mention of a novel to Grimsley, however, was met with vehement denial.

"Why try to improve on perfection," he would say, "If a writer's name ain't Leonard, he's a hack, a copycat and a fraud."

Grimsley laid out his department issue Glock 45 caliber semi-automatic with a seventeen round clip, a Smith and Wesson 38 caliber revolver, a Colt 45 revolver, and a hand musket from the revolutionary war, complete with fuse, leather powder bag and hand made musket balls. Leaning against the wall on the floor, was a long leather pouch that held a breech-loading Winchester rifle that he claimed was from the battle at Little Big Horn. Each of the handguns lay on top of a custom leather pouch next to a box of ammunition.

This collection of guns, though impressive, represented a SMALL portion of his vast collection. Grimsley had hundreds of weapons in his Laurelhurst mansion. Many were rare firearms he'd collected during his early years as a national arms rep for Winchester and Smith and Wesson.

Grimsley would draw crowds to watch him shoot, especially the day he brought in the antique 40-40 that was owned by

Hemmingway and used for big game hunting.

No crowds gathered this morning. It was too early, five a.m. The range was opened for Grimsley's private use at this time. He couldn't sleep.

A solid gray head of hair graced Grimsley's head, partly obscuring the ear plugs. He was tall, six feet three, but he claimed he shrunk a few inches when he turned 62. His facial features were severe, hawk-like, but his blue, friendly eyes countered that severity and inspired trust. He was lean, fit from regular sessions on the racquetball court and he dressed like a sheriff from a small town in New Mexico, big silver southwestern style, belt buckle with Pueblo Indian designs in coral and turquoise. His boots were custom made Louise Lamore's, red and brown with a BG just above the heel.

This was his uniform. Everything was complimented by jeans, a button down shirt and a haring bone tweed jacket.

"Civilization is built on establishing patterns, rules," he was know to say, "That's how we live. That's how we survive. That's why we solve crimes." That was also the opening to his lectures at the University of Oregon where he taught courses on crime scene investigations and forensic sciences.

His classes were always full. Students sometimes attempted to sneak in and sit with friends in the same seats. A security guard had to be posted to keep unassigned students out.

His classes consisted of stories, demonstrations, visiting novelist and, on occasion, reformed criminals. On one occasion, a national media circus ensued when Grimsley arranged a roundtable with Johnny Cochrine, Mark Fermine, Marcia Clark and O.J. Simpson on satellite feed. They were all intimately aware of Grimsley's reputation and all did not hesitate to appear.

Time to shoot. Grimsley started with the .45 and fired six shots. Never fire the seventh. Bad luck. Each slug slammed into the target within an inch of the center. Grimsley pressed the red button to his left to retrieve the target. The electric motor whirred as it reeled in the target.

"God damn it," Grimsley said when he saw the results. "Can't shoot worth a damn."

A hand touched Grimsley's shoulder. It was J.D. Veckman, the center manager.

"Grimsley, how the hell are you, you old goat?"

"Well," Grimsley started, "I'm shooting like a 4-year-old and it ain't pretty."

"You're too hard on yourself. From the looks of your target

there I'd say you still got the touch that got you that gold medal."

Grimsley gave J.D. a slight smile. "That was a long time ago J.D."

Looking at the musket, J.D. inquired, "You going to shoot that thing or just keep it there for show."

"Oh, I'm going to shoot it. But you better have the block evacuated. Nothing closer to a hand-held cannon than a revolutionary war musket. Our boys were chewed to pieces with these sons of bitches. I like to fire of a few of these a year so I can get a feel for what they must have gone through. The ball didn't cut, it tore away the flesh and smashed or shattered anything in it's way. Even a leg wound could be fatal 'cause there was no way to close the wound. God damn ingenious. Claymore mines are the modern equivalent. If you took a bunch of scrap metal and shot it at a crowd, that's what it would be like. God damn brave sons of bitches to walk single file into a hail of musket balls. God damn brave sons of bitches."

J.D. listened, waiting to deliver the news. "Listen, Grimsley, I just got a call from precinct. There's what looks like a routine homicide they want you to take a look at."

"What the hell is a routine homicide?" Grimsley belted out, fully aware he didn't expect an answer. "God damn it. What the hell is this world coming to. Any details J.D.?"

"Not much, sir. A young prostitute in Northeast Portland. No ID, possibly a runaway. She's a Jane Doe."

"Shit. I hate those. If you can't find out who they are, you can't find out who killed them. If they have no history, no past, you can't track the patterns, associations."

"Sorry to have to interrupt your shooting this morning."

Grimsley said, "No, no, J.D. Not your fault. But it looks like I'm going to have to fire this cannon another time."

"I'll keep the fire department, FEMA and everyone else on alert."

They laughed at that thought.

Chapter 42

Rich had a lousy run that morning. When he finished, there were 10 extra papers in the passenger seat and he had no idea who they belonged to. The complaints would start coming in to the station at around 6:30. Jimmy would delivery the papers with his bad leg. He would not be happy about that. That, however, was the least of Rich's worries right now.

Rich went to his den, closed the door and tried to process the events of the morning. The image of the gun was stuck in his head. His brain was out of sync with his body. He paced. He bit his nails. He recreated the scene over and over again, wondering who the Mexican American was, what he was doing, and did he do the right thing by calling in and not giving a name?

He sat at his desk, head buried in his hands, sweating, the scene stuck in replay mode. His computer was on, so he decided to e-mail Kyle. He needed to talk to someone. His e-mail buddy indicator showed that Kyle was online. He wrote:

"Yo! Black! Sup!"

Kyle wrote back seconds later:

"Nothing broham. How you be?

Rich replied:

"Fucked up man. Saw some shit this morning. I think I almost got shot."

Kyle wrote:

"You bullshitting me?"

Rich wrote:

"Hell no. Mother fucker came running out from behind a van. I almost ran him over. Pointed a piece at me and pulled the trigger, man. Swear to God, mother fucker was serious. Had a roll of bills in his hand like he just hit someone. What do you think of that shit?"

Kyle responded:

"Get the fuck out of here. That's some serious shit. What did you do? Did you report it."

Rich wrote:

"Well, sort of."

Kyle wrote:

"What does sort of mean. Either you reported it or not."

Rich wrote:

"I called in an anonymous report. No name. From a phone booth."

Kyle wrote:

"What! Nigga, what if that mother fucker just offed someone or, comes by your house. If you saw the maafucka you'd be able to point him out in a line-up."

Rich replied:

"I know. I know. I feel like shit for it, like a coward. My life is fucked up enough, the last thing I need is to add another layer of shit to this mess I created here. Police asking all sorts of questions, digging into my shit."

Kyle wrote:

"Nigga, now you got another layer whether you want it or not. You got another secret you gotta keep. And you don't need no more secrets bro. Secrets gonna grow inside of you like a cancer, or cause you to do some crazy shit. Secrets lead to lies, lies lead to other lies, and eventually somebody gets hurt."

Rich wrote:

"Shit."

Kyle wrote:

"Damn straight. You know not only did you see that mother fucker, but he saw you too. And my guess is he lives somewhere in your neighborhood. You got to watch you back bro."

Rich wrote:

"I didn't think about that. He ran. Didn't see a car. Ugly mother fucker too. Flat Mexican Aztec looking head, short, probably small dick insecure mother fucker."

Kyle replied:

"Just watch your back. You may want to call the police and fess up or they might be lookin' for you for whatever shit that mother fucker did."

Rich said:

"I can't do that."

Kyle wrote:

"Don't say I didn't warn you. Anyway, what's the word on that novel?"

Rich replied:

"I'm making some modifications to the story. Met an agent who's interested in it, so I'm going to submit the manuscript as is and do some rewrites this weekend at this writers retreat I go to every year. Maybe I'll include some of this crazy shit that happened tonight, get it off my chest. I already added a few characters based on my friends."

Kyle wrote:

"That's great Rich. Not too many people can actually finish a novel. If you put me in the book, make my name Kyle Shaft Mackdaddy Williams, the baddest mother fucker in Portland. I want a purple duce and a quarter with one of those purple spare tire holders. Imagine that shit, pimps changing flat tires. Why the fuck did they have those damn things on there anyway. Pimp woulda had a hoe who was a mechanic. Problem with his ride, he be standin' over her with a coat hanger yelling 'Bitch, you two points off on the timing. Motherfucking mixture is to rich Bitch. What! What you talking bout' Don't be talking that auto mechanic differentiation, carbon monoxide college shit. Shit don't sound right. Jus fix the mother fucker. Anyway, I want only the finest hoes, and I want to be mean, pretty, and a poet, like

Dolimite."

Rich replied:

"*You one crazy nigga. I thought about how I might portray you. I love you too much to make you a pimp, so I made you a plumber.*"

Kyle wrote:

"*Mother fucker! I will come through the Internet and personally kick your ass!!*"

Rich wrote:

"*Okay. Okay. You're not a plumber. You're a college professor who pimps in his spare time. Your name is Dr. Kyle Pimpdaddy Williams. Your students call you Dr. Pimpdaddy, much to the chagrin of the faculty. But you're a bad mother—*"

Kyle responded:

"*Shut yo mouth*"

Rich said:

"*But I'm talkin' 'bout Pimpdaddy.*"

Kyle said.

"*We bad. Gotta go Rich. Give hugs all around. See you when I see you. Remember, watch your back. Motherfuckers crazy out there. Those kinds of people don't give a shit about you or your family. They just care about themselves.*

Signing off: Dr. Pimpdaddy!

Rich thought for a moment about what Kyle said. He made sense. He shuddered at the thought of his family being at risk. He banished that thought as quickly. He couldn't call the police. He retrieved the business card he was given at the lecture and typed in the e-mail address. He attached his manuscript, typed in a note and sent it to the agent. He logged off. Time to get the kids up.

Chapter 43

Chico had never seen the movie *Marathon Man*, but he'd heard about it. As Chico ran, he thought of Dustin Hoffman, running like his life depended on it, his baggy pants shifting down to his thighs. He tugged at them as he ran, trying not to trip, frantically wiping the sweat out of his eyes at the same time.

The first block, the sweat flowed down his forehead like a boxer in the twelfth round. The stinging sweat in his eyes made him angrier as he ran. The second block, his legs felt like a fire had ignited inside of them and they would explode at any moment.

Chico never ran. It was against his nature. But he was scared. Fear lifted each leg, forced each breath. White puffs of warm condensed air shot out of his mouth. Spittle ran down Chico's chin. His breathing was not rhythmic. It was erratic, forced, desperate.

It was still dark, so no one saw Chico as he turned on Wygant street. Home stretch. That's when Chico saw them. They were in the middle of the street, waiting for him, eyes glowing, reflecting the faint light from the street lights. Chico froze.

Four feral cats blocked his path. They didn't run like they usually did. They stared at him, defiant. They were all black, so he only saw their eyes, floating, shifting position, staring, taunting, teasing him, threatening him.

Chico's mouth hung open and his eyes widened at the sight. His clothes were drenched with sweat and spit. He folded over as his stomach constricted and dry heaved. Chico tried to puke, but couldn't. The cats moved towards him in unison.

"Mother fucking son of bitches. Kiss my mother fucking assholes you fucking cats."

Chico turned to his left and cut through a yard, over a chain link fence that surrounded a dirt brown ranch style house and a beater Camero, past darkened windows, to Alberta Court. He turned left and headed towards 42nd street, full stride now. Almost home.

His feet felt like lead. Chico's run had turned to a forced shuffle as his legs threatened to cramp up. Pain. Great pain were the only thoughts that went through his head. He reached his apartment, forced himself to run up the flight of stairs, opened the door, slammed it shut. Safe now. Exhausted, he fell to the floor. He hadn't the strength to make it to the couch. It was at that point that he thought about his bicycle. He'd left it a block away from the van, locked on a stop sign. He reached into his pants, and felt for something. It wasn't there either. The journal was gone.

Chapter 44

The only sound that could be heard on the street where Trixie's body lay was the faint whisper of an autumn wind blowing through the tops of the tallest Douglas Fur trees. Occasionally, a sparrow sang out, a signal for the other birds to wake up.

Trixie's body grew colder. The life drifting out of each cell, drifting, drifting off to nothingness. The signals that gave them purpose faded.

Then they started arriving.

They appeared from under shrubs, silent, bouncing stealthy towards Trixie. The feral cats gathered around her body. They sniffed and rubbed against here and meowed as if to mourn for her. The meowing grew louder as each cat arrived. They were all shapes, sizes, colors. Thick fur, short hairs, Persians, calicos, scruffy Tomcats and a few kittens. In minutes, there were 10 to 20 cats surrounding Trixie, wailing, sniffing, some perched on top of her.

The energy continued to drain out of Trixie as, blood cells, desperate for oxygen, expended the last electrolytes in an attempt to survive. The neurons were abandoned. No signals came from the brain. If they could get a signal, they were healthy, strong and could still pick up their body and movie it. But no signal came. Only the cats meows and the subtle breeze.

In Trixie's brain, there was chaos. Seconds after the bullet entered, her nervous system shut down from the shock. There was only blackness. Minutes, maybe hours, or even seconds later, Trixie's body shuddered. There was consciousness. Some systems attempted to recover. The craniospinal system attempted to communicate. It sent out a signal but was unable to complete any connections. Trixie's consciousness was still there but was slipping. Towards what? She didn't know. But for a few seconds, she was aware. She could hear the wailing of the cats. They were singing for her, she thought, saying goodbye, wishing her well on her journey. She was scared. Where am I going? She thought of Jill Cohn singing "I am free / I am free...Then blackness.

In that instant, the cats stopped wailing. There was a bright light that covered Trixie's body. It was joined by a red, blue and white flashing. They turned towards the light then froze. The sound of a powerful engine and rocks crunching under tires could be heard, then the sound of a door opening followed by footsteps.

One by one, the cats returned to where they had come from, reluctantly at first, but eventually they all disappeared into the night. All except one, a pure white cat with ghostlike qualities. It sat, perched on top of Trixie, defiant, possessive, daring anyone to come near it.

Chapter 45

Grimsley arrived at the scene around 5:30 a.m. As he drove up, the sun was peaking over the horizon as it started its morning display. There was a pandemonium of bodies and lights surrounding the beat up old van. Who the hell are all these people, Grimsley said to himself? He parked his Bronco about a hundred yards from the crime scene. He stepped out into the street and walked towards the flashing, bustling scene.

Grimsley's walk was slow and deliberate. As he approached the scene, he looked around, smelling and listening as he walked. He had spent time on an Apache reservation, studying with their expert trackers, learning their customs, understanding their ways, their relationship with the earth. He had been on many vision quests, and participated in tracking contest when he was younger. Technology could never replace the incredible ability of the brain to analyze what the senses absorb. He took mental notes as he walked. He stepped. Stopped. Like a wedding procession. Step. Stop. Listen. Smell. Observe.

A boyish looking detective noticed Grimsley approaching. He turned and walked towards Grimsley. "Inspector…er…captain," He yelled, "I'm sorry, sir, I don't know which one to—"

"Shhhhhh," Grimsley said, holding a finger to his lips. "Listen for a moment, son. What do you hear?"

The young detective furrowed his forehead and looked around, hoping to see something.

"Um, nothing sir." He hoped that was the right answer.

"Exactly!" said Grimsley. "What's your name son?"

"Paulson, sir," he replied, "Detective John Paulson."

"How many murder cases you handled, Paulson?" Grimsley asked, now standing over Paulson, a full foot taller, looking down at him with his hands in his pockets.

Paulson knew all about Grimsley and nervously answered, "Well, sir, I never really handled any on my own. I've been a detective for two months, and I—"

"Well, son, don't sweat it. Man's got to start somewhere. The road to greatness starts with the first step. Who would have believed that Lincoln spent his younger years picking the wings off of dragonflies in summertime and who the hell could have know heed been a bedwetter. That kind of stuff never gets in the history books."

"Yes, sir." Paulson didn't know how to respond. Grimsley continued his procession towards the van and Paulson fell into stride alongside him taking two steps for Grimsley's one. He held a notebook in one hand and a pen in the other.

"Paulson," Grimsley asked, "What the hell are you gonna do with that pen, shoot somebody with it. Put that damn thing away. Notebook too and pay attention."

"Yes, sir," Paulson shoved the pen in his breast pocket along with the notebook.

"Tell me what you got."

"Routine—"

"Stop right there, son."

He stopped, faced Paulson and sternly said, "No such thing as a God damn routine murder. Lose that word right now. Murder is murder. There are no routine, typical, standard, ordinary, usual murders. Just as you cannot be more dead. You cannot be typically or ordinarily dead. The first step to manhood is to clear your head of the junk you've been fed all your life. Give it to me straight. I want the facts."

Rattled, Paulson, reached for his notebook.

"Forget the notebook, son. Let's see what you remember."

"Errr, well," Paulson's broke said as he tried to regain composure. "Single female victim, age eighteen or nineteen. Single gunshot to the head. Estimated time of murder between 4 a.m. and 5 a.m. Reported by anonymous caller around 4:30 a.m. Signs that the victim may have been a prostitute. Condoms in the drawer. No ID. No signs of drugs or drug paraphernalia. No track marks on the victim. When we arrived at the scene, big white cat on the body, sir, kicked up a fuss when we got near the victim. No collar, just bigger'd any cat I've ever seen. Ran away after a few minutes. Did not retrieve the slug, sir. It penetrated went through the window and looks like it ended up in those bushes over there, sir. Got a few men searching for it. Pretty thick. Could be needle in a haystack, sir."

Paulson, paused, placed his hand to his head, thinking. Grimsley stared at him. "Um, sir, I can't think of anything else off the top of my head."

Grimsley continued to stare, then he smiled, "God damn, you remembered all that? You're one smart son of a…" He didn't finish.

"Paulson, there's hope for you. Let's go take a look."

Paulson smiled and let out a sigh of relief. As they neared the van and Grimsley saw the body, he said, "Jesus Christ, what kind of cruel bastard would do that to a kid.

He walked over to Trixie's body, kneeled down next to it and stared for a moment. He touched her hair, rubbed her cheek, then looked at the rest of her body. He observed the beaded necklace.

Underneath the smell of urine and blood he caught the hint of China Rain. He recognized it right away, it's sweet, musky smell was like no other smell.

A tear trickled down his left cheek. He removed a handkerchief from his breast pocket and covered his nose. With a slight gesture, he wiped the tear away from his cheek. No one noticed. The death of young girls always cut deep for him. In most cases, they were innocent and defenseless, weaker than the murderer. All most desperately wanted was love of their fathers and the security of a safe home. The murderers usually only wanted sex or money or control.

Grimsley stood up.

"Paulson, this is a God damn shame. Now, Paulson. Tell me what you don't see here?"

Paulson was on the spot again. He straightened his jacket, shifted his shoulder holster. Seeing his discomfort, Grimsley said, "Relax Paulson, that's not a trick question. Look at the scene here. Tell me what happened or what you think happened. Then tell me what else you don't see here that might help explain what really happened. Take your time, son."

Paulson looked around, thought about the facts, than answered. "Young prostitute lives in and works out of this van. Picks up a John, brings him back. He's an addict. Robs here. She chases him. He pulls out a piece and shoots her. He runs."

"Congratulations Paulson, you are absolutely wrong."

Paulson looked down, embarrassed.

"But don't let that scare you. My first murder case took me 10 years to solve. Every murder is a puzzle with multiple redirects, either intentional or unintentional. Let me show you something, why there's more than meets the eye here."

Grimsley walked back over to Trixie, knelt down again. Paulson did the same.

"No bruises, or sign of a struggle. Did you find any makeup in the van?"

"No, sir."

"Make up is subtle but it's there, blush, mascara, eyeliner. She put it on somewhere else, carefully, with skill, so she does this every day. Feel her hair."

Paulson reached over and touched her hair. "What do you feel," Grimsley asked.

"Nothing, sir, just hair."

"Conditioner, Paulson. Lots of it. She showered or bathed, meticulously and put on makeup somewhere else. Not just at a YMCA.

This kind of pampering takes hours, a stable environment, an environment for leisure. Girls are that way. Any change of clothes here?'

"No, sir." Paulson answered, the lightbulb finally going off in his head. "No personal belongings, no makeup, no tampons, nothing of that nature, sir. No purse. No food."

"And Paulson, she's not a drug addict. That fact alone elevates this murder to another plateau. Walk with me Paulson."

Chapter 46

When Enison returned to his office just before 9 a.m. he found Baker sitting in his chair with his feet propped up on his desk grinning like he just discovered the cure to baldness.

"So glad you could show up Enison. You're late."

Enison walked around the desk and stood beside Baker, peering down at them. In one swift motion, he kicked Baker's feet under the knees, causing the joints to bend enough and his feet fell to the ground jerking Baker's body forward.

"And you're still and idiot Baker. Get the hell out of my chair."

Baker jumped up and backed away from Enison's chair.

"You just assaulted me Enison. I don't have to take that from you. I outrank you here."

"You do...and you don't," Enison responded.

"What's that supposed to mean, Enison."

"You figure it out Baker. You've got a PH.D. Isn't that what you do, figure things out?"

Baker tried to straighten his coat but it kept leaning to one side. Frustrated, he gave up.

"You know Enison, you may think your excrement doesn't emit a putrid odor, but I know better. And you can only hide under the bosses skirt for so long before you're found out. You're up to something Enison and I'm going to find out what it is."

Enison was tired, cranky and his patience was running thin.

"Baker, within that deluded little mind of yours must be an even smaller demented mind. My advice to you is to get the hell out of here before I stand up, walk over to you and kick your ass from here to Bakersfield."

Baker smugly asked, "Are you threatening me Enison?"

"I don't make threats, Baker. I don't have time for threats. I make guarantees. And I guarantee you that if you are not out of my office in the next five seconds I'll kick your ass out of here."

"That's a threat. That's insubordination Enison and a gosh darned threat."

Baker reached for the speaker phone, pressed the page button, "Reception can you hear me. Call security and come in here. I need a witness. Enison just threatened me!"

Enison stood up, and, in two steps had Baker by the back of his oversized jacket. He lifted him up on his toes, like a cat carries a kitten and escorted him to the door, opened it quickly, threw Baker into the hallway, slammed the door shut behind him and locking it.

Outside of the door, Baker was screaming, "He threw me out.

He threw me out. Did anybody see that! I need a witness!"

He pounded on the door with his fist.

"Enison, this isn't over. I need your expense report by 9:30. The boss is going to hear about this."

Baker looked around him. Several agents had stepped out of their offices and were peering down the hallway at him. Baker tried to compose himself. He licked his hands and matted down the sparse crop of hair on either side of his head. He smoothed his suit with his hands, turned, chin up and extended and marched back to his office.

Enison almost felt bad about what he'd done, but even he had his limits. He unpacked his notepad, hooked it up to his flat screen monitor and a collapsible keyboard, plugged in an ethernet phone line and wend to work. Later, he scored some strong coffee and had a short meeting with his clients.

He didn't hear from Baker again. At 11:15, Enison put his coat and hat on, logged on to his anonymous e-mail account and sent short a message to Baker.

The subject header read: *Expense Report for Idiots*. The text area read: "*Kiss my ass.*"

He punched enter, scooped up his notepad, portable keyboard, briefcase and walked quickly out the front door, winking at Sara on the way out.

Baker had been sitting in his office simmering for the entire time, thinking about how he could nail Enison. He was humiliated beyond reproach and was feeling vengeful. He cleared his e-mail in-box earlier that morning and there were no new e-mails to read, so when Enison's e-mail arrived it jumped out at him and he reached for the mouse immediately. He knew it was Enison from the subject header "Enison, you fuck," he yelled, putting his hand over his mouth and looking around, expecting to find his father there waiting to slug him for cursing or feel the fingers of his mothers hands closing on his ears, dragging him to the bathroom to wash his mouth out with soap. He pushed his chair back and ran for the door, almost tripping over his pant legs as he neared the door. He ran down the hall to Enison's office and pushed the partially opened door in.

"Enison, where are you!" He screamed. "I'll get you for this!"

Baker was feeling pure, non-diluted, unadulterated rage, the kind felt when a husband catches a wife cheating with his best friend. He was beside himself figuring out what to do next. He needed a plan. He needed more information. If he was going to beat Enison at his own game, he needed to know more. He went to Enison's desk and riffled through each drawer, sifting through files, looking for clues.

Nothing.

Chapter 47

"Your a stupid butthead cheese head butt."

"Don't say that stupid idiot butthead!"

Rich was lost in his thought and barely noticed the crescendo of insults that flew back and forth between Juan and Antonio.

"Stop saying that Juan," Antonio screamed. "I'll sock you weenie head stupid!"

When Rich heard weenie head he snapped out of his trance and yelled, "All right boys! That's enough! Stop that yelling and eat your breakfast! We've got to go!"

"But he started it dad," Juan yelled. "He called me a butthead."

"And he said I was stupid," Antonio countered.

"Did not!" yelled Juan.

"Did too!" Screamed Antonio.

"Not!"

"To!"

"Not!"

This went on for several more rounds. Rich looked at them alternately and wondered if this were some kind of brother initiation ritual. The NOTS and TOOS came in rapid successions.

"Not-not-not-not-not-not."

"To-to-to-to-to-to-to...."

"Enough!" Rich yelled and stood up. "The next person to say a word will be taken out of here by his ears!"

There was only silence after that. Juan and Antonio stared at Rich, scowling with mouths grinding the cereal like cows at a trough. Silent, not daring to disturb the peace. They knew all the signals. Rich allowed them a lot of latitude to be boys, but they knew better than to call his bluff when he'd had enough.

Both boys occasionally peered at each other over their bowls and one would thrust out an insulting tongue at the other. Rich sat down and continued reading the morning paper. He scanned for news reports of robberies but didn't see anything on the front page. In the background, the slurping and crunching continued, seemingly orchestrated in some alternating, rhythmic patterns.

After the boys were dressed, Rich sent them out to the truck, did a list-minute light check, then walked out of the front door to the truck. He peered into the truck through the side window. The back seat was empty.

"Where's Antonio," Rich asked Juan.

"Iono." Juan answered.

"You don't know. Juan, he's your brother. You're responsible for him. Did you see where he went?"

"No." Juan hunched his shoulders.

"Oh, for the love of...Antonio!" he shouted. No answer. "Antonio, where are you?"

Seconds later, Antonio came running around the side of the house with something in his hands.

"Antonio, what are you doing over there?" Rich scolded.

"I saw something," Antonio answered. "I went to get it."

"Well, get yourself into the truck. What is that anyway? Give that to me."

Antonio walked past Rich with his head down and reached up an arm to hand the book to Rich. The binding was handmade paper with a matted leaf on the cover.

Rich was in a hurry. Any delay would mean missing the bus. He walked to the back of the truck, lifted the glass window and tossed the book into the bed. It landed amongst a collection of balls, empty newspaper baggies, nylon ties and crumpled Burger King bags. Rich found so many things during his route, his habit was to toss everything in the truck and sort it out later. Rich took the kids to the bus stop.

Chapter 48

Grimsley and Paulson stood up and carefully stepped around the myriad of footprints surrounding the body. Grimsley led and Paulson followed. They lifted the yellow caution tape that was attached to the end of the van and walked around the van and into the street. Grimsley was silent. He alternately rubbed his chin and scratched his head. A large red and white emergency vehicle drove up with lights flashing and parked about 50 yards from the scene. The side of the truck read MULTNOMAH COUNTY CORONER.

Through the shrubs, rose bushes and thicket of trees of the houses that lined the quiet street, Grimsley could see the movement of uniformed police officers who worked their way from door-to-door to inquiry if neighbors had seen or heard anything. Others were searching through the thick brush that was directly across from the van, trying to find the slug that ended the victim's life.

"Paulson," Grimsley broke the silence, "it's too bad real life isn't like the movies or those God forsaken crime shows on TV."

They stopped in the middle of the street and faced 47th Street.

"Why do you say that, sir?" Paulson inquired, confused. He stood beside Grimsley, looking down the street. The sun had fully risen over the landscape and Paulson and Grimsley could survey the entire scene. The street was a remnant of what was once an old growth forest, adulterated by houses, apple trees, rhododendron bushes, roses, pavement, grass and camellias. The Douglas Furs towered over everything else like sentries protecting their domain.

"So beautiful, this country of ours," said Grimsley, ignoring Paulson's question.

"Sir?" Paulson asked.

"Never mind Paulson, I'm just thinking out loud again, trying to get a handle on all of this."

Grimsley surveyed the pavement, knelt down, put his nose to the ground and sniffed, rubbed the ground with his hands, then walked over to the back of the van, knelt down and sniffed the ground, rubbed it with his hands, then began walking towards 47th.

"10,000 murders take place in this country every year," Grimsley said, not looking at Paulson, but expecting his full attention. "But only 70% ever get solved. And only 50% of that 70% are successfully prosecuted. You know why that is Paulson?"

Grimsley led Paulson away from the van, towards the corner at 47th Street.

"No, sir, I don't." Paulson said, sounding confused. He didn't know where Grimsley was going with this and wasn't sure he wanted to play Grimsley's game. "But, sir, the crime scene is over there." He pointed to the van. Grimsley stopped and peered at Paulson.

"Paulson," Grimsley barked, "Pull your head out of your ass. You're a bright kid. Your parents both graduated suma cum lada from USC. You graduated first in your class from Brown, but I'll tell you this, being smart doesn't amount to a hill of beans if you don't know to change your underwear when you shit your pants."

Paulson was flustered again, embarrassed, "What I meant..."

"Save it Paulson. Your real education starts here and now. Forget all that crap you saw on TV and all that bullshit they taught you in detective school. That's a seventeen, maybe eighteen year old girl over there who's life has been snuffed out by some God damn loser who was more concerned about his own ass than that girl's life. If we don't find him, he'll do it again. Next time, Paulson, it may be YOUR daughter or maybe even you."

As quickly as Grimsley started his tirade, he stopped, turned and continued to walk.

Paulson was angry. He was not used to being spoken to that way by anyone. His first impulse was to scream, KISS MY ASS! But he knew better. He stared at Grimsley's back, then started to turn towards the van, but stopped.

He glanced again at Grimsley's back as it grew smaller the further away he got. Grimsley did not look back. After a few seconds, Paulson, walked quickly towards Grimsley, caught up with him and said, "Sir, may I speak to you a moment."

Grimsley turned towards Paulson and in an impatient tone said, "Speak your mind Paulson."

"Sir, your right. I was out of line. I did not mean to show you disrespect. I just thought there might be more at the crime scene to analyze than over here."

"And you know what Paulson," Grimsley said. "You're probably right." Grimsley softened his tone slightly. "The crime scene is there. But the murderer is gone. He's out here. The most important thing we can figure out right now is how far he may have gone. I can't tell you how many times I've been at a crime scene and learned that the killer turned out to be one of the bystanders or only a few hundred feet away in the bushes or in trees above the crime scene. For criminals, this is a God damn game and most figure they're smarter than us. And many of them are. And because of crime shows like *America's Most Wanted* we can catch more criminals, but more criminals see what they need to do to get away. After all is said and done, the crime scene will help us prove the case, but to find a killer we rely on the bigger picture, what happens out here. And I can tell you right now that this is going to be a bitch of a case, but if we solve this one, we prove that there's hope for this Godforsaken world."

Paulson was silent. He was processing what Grimsley had said. Then he answered, "Yes, sir."

Grimsley reached into his coat pocket and pulled out a cigarette pack. He padded his other pockets and found a lighter.

"Also," Grimsley added, "I had to have a God damn smoke. Clear my head. This poor girls is a Jane Doe and probably a prostitute and that means the full resources of the Portland PD will *not* be diverted to this case."

Grimsley lit the cigarette and sucked in deeply and exhaled. "Nasty habit…so if whoever murdered this girl is going to be found, you and I will do it. Not the Portland PD."

Paulson was still silent, listening, not daring to respond yet.

"Paulson, right now you may be thinking 'what the hell can I learn from this old, wrinkled, cigarette smoking White man?'"

Paulson hesitated before answering, then said, "You're right sir."

"You're probably thinking I'm one of those good old boys who uses the word colored when I'm out with my buddies. And you probably think I would never let my daughter marry one of your kind because of the scandal it would raise with my friends and neighbors."

Paulson was prepared this time. "That's right sir."

"The problem with you black intellectuals is that you have figured us old White men out and now have the power and influence to do something about it, politically, socially, even in art, and literature."

Paulson was standing at attention, chin up, poised, ready for a fight now.

"That's right sir."

"Well, Paulson, you could be right about some of that. Which of it, I'm not going to tell you. But you could be wrong, too. I'm not going to make it easy for you, son. You have to figure that out for yourself. I will tell you this though, Paulson, that I couldn't give a hang about what color you are on the job. I know all about you. You've got what it takes to be a great detective. My only question for you is do you want to be?"

Paulson was still on guard, heart beating rapidly now. Paulson's dark skin contrasted with the white shirt and glistened in the morning light. His deep set eyes were fixed on Grimsley, studying him, trying to figure him out.

"Sir, I'd like to be as good as or better than you some day." Paulson said.

Grimsley stared at Paulson, then, for the first time since they met he offered a toothy, sincere smile. "I'll be God damn Paulson. For a colored fella, you got quite a set of brass ones."

Paulson, recognizing the compliment and Grimsley's sarcasm, conjured a smile and said, "God damn right sir."

"Let's stop dicking around here Paulson, let me tell you what really happened here."

Chapter 49

It was ten o'clock and Chico awoke with a shudder. He had passed out on the ground near his door and had not moved for hours. Dried saliva strips streamed down the ends of his mouth. Thick green crust caked the corners of his eyes and the acrid smell of urine filled the room as Chico observed the dark brown areas of his pants where he had wet himself.

The memories of the nights events slowly crept back into his head like a slow motion movie playing frame by frame as if being edited. The memories were a jolt for Chico. When he came to the scene with Trixie lying on the ground, blood splattered all over the van and the piles of puke next to her lifeless body, he panicked. He jumped up, ran to the windows and peeked out, expecting to find a full orchestra of police cars and swat teams, lights flashing, creeping up the stairs with guns drawn, waiting for him, waiting to blow his head off. Nothing. Only some Black kids from the apartment riding their bikes in circles, laughing and talking smack.

Chico felt nauseous. He paced back and forth by the window, then he stopped and padded his pockets, feeling for the gun. He felt it and took it out of his pocket.

"Stupid son of bitch. I thought I took all the bullets out of the this mother fucker."

Chico jammed his other hand into his pocket and pulled out a fist full of bullets and counted them one-by-one. When he got to four, he yelled, "Shit! Shit! Shit!" And threw the bullets against the wall. He opened the carriage of the gun and inspected the holes. They were all empty!

"Son of a…"

Chico ran to the closet, retrieved the shoe box and shoved the gun into it. Then he collected the bullets and put them in the box as well and covered them with newspapers. After he put the box back in the closet, he walked over to his coat and took the crumpled bills out and counted them. They were hundred dollar bills, two thousand in all.

Once Chico realized how much money he had, he puffed out his chest again and said, "Stupid bitch. Fucking with me, keeping my money. This is my money. People always fuckin' with me. I'm the baddest mother fucker ever lived."

Then Chico started weeping, "God damn Trixie, why you do that shit. This didn't have to happen. Chico covered his face and tried to dry his tears with the hundred dollar bills.

"I didn't mean for this to happen," he said between sobs. "I didn't mean for this to happen."

Chico fell to his knees, tears streaming down his face, snot running down his nose. The bills became soft and sticky in his hands, the smell of urine burning at his nose.

Chapter 50

Grimsley and Paulson had reached an understanding that morning. In the two tense hours they had spent together, they had gone beyond the old, prejudice, burned out cop, young, proud, black man stage and arrived at the mentor, protege stage.

Grimsley left Paulson at the crime scene after taking one more pass through the van. Grimsley drove downtown to the university campus, where he was scheduled give his guest lecture to a group of pre-law students.

That morning he was lecturing on how to be a perfect murder victim. The lecture was based on a reference book he had written years earlier. The book, if it hadn't received as much critical acclaim, could easily have been considered a satire. Instead, amongst the criminal law community, it had attained the status of E.B. White's *Elements of Style*.

The lecture hall was stamped out of the thousands of lecture hall molds on campuses throughout the country. It resembled a miniature half coliseum with rows of stairs and seats leading up to three doors spaced evenly at the top row between the groups of stairs.

The podium was attached to a table that included a sink and a burner for science lectures. The seats were filled to capacity with fresh faced students of all races, most shifting in their seats softly talking to their neighbors. All were eager for the lecture to begin.

Grimsley stood in front of the podium and looked out at the students.

"Good morning everyone," he said in a commanding voice that echoed off the walls. Most of the students answered good morning in unison.

"Welcome to my world."

His comment was followed by giggles and chortles. Nothing quite like this, Grimsley thought.

"Most of you have no doubt read my book. Let's start out with your thoughts. Anyone care to comment?"

A pretty young blonde with bright green fingernails with glitter on them and too much make-up sitting three rows up in the center raised her hand first, followed by several others.

"Yes, Ms…" Grimsley consulted his class list. "Ms. Bentley."

"Mr. Grimsley, I've read your book several times and each time I, like, discover something new."

She chewed on her gum as she continued, "I, like, have to admit that I still have a hard time thinking about what I, like, would do if I ever found myself in some of the situations you described, like, you know, talk about."

"You're not alone Ms. Bentley. But all of the cases in my book are real. While I don't propose waking up every morning saying 'I feel lucky today. I think today is the day I'm going to be a murder victim.'"

The class burst into laughter. Grimsley waited.

"I do ask people, especially young girls, to ask themselves, 'If I were to disappear today, would anybody know what happened to me? Ms. Bentley, would you care to tell your classmates which of the stories you found the most difficult to imagine."

Ms. Bentley thought for a moment.

"Well, like, the one that stands out for me the most is the girl who was kidnapped and locked in a trunk. She, like, bit her lip and wrote the name of her killer in blood on the inner wall of the trunk with her tongue."

"Ah, yes. That case was fascinating in that had it not been for that revelation, the murderer, a pissed off former boyfriend, would never have been prosecuted. All evidence was circumstantial up to that point. The boyfriend was sure he'd gotten away with it and he had a decent alibi. The victim had the wherewithal to write, JACK B. KILLED ME. The words were discovered by an alert state trooper during a routine traffic stop and inspection for drug paraphernalia. Thank you Ms. Bentley. Other comments?"

More hands went up immediately. Grimsley picked a sandy hair boy towards the top row.

"Yes, Mr. Peters."

"Mr. Grimsley, I think your book is a work of genius. And I don't say that to make you feel good, sir. My aunt was murdered by a total stranger, a random act of violence. But as you said in your book, sir, most random acts of violence are planned. The randomness relates to who the victim is."

The boy paused, carefully choosing his words.

"My aunt kept journals. Nobody knew about them. In them, she described things in her neighborhood; you know, cars she didn't recognize, new people she couldn't place, or people she thought seemed out of character. She made it a game to write character sketches of strangers she'd met or saw. She mentioned this to me a few times, but we didn't think she was serious. She wasn't a writer, but she said she'd hope to be someday. As it turned out, sir, the murderer had been casing my aunts neighborhood looking for single women to kidnap, or rape and ultimately murder for months."

"So, Mr. Peters, your aunt used her observations to catalogue things out of the ordinary. And this was an exercise for her. How did it ultimately help solve her murder."

"Well, sir," the student choked up. "Sorry, sir."

"Not at all, son. Take your time."

"The dirtball broke into her house around midnight last summer, tied her hands and wrists to the bed post and raped her repeatedly. Then he cut her throat and left her for dead."

"I'm sorry, son."

"Thank you, sir. The murder investigation went nowhere, sir, a few false starts, but the only one who saw anything was the neighbor who saw a black van. Eventually, we had to sell her house and it was on the day that I was packing her stuff that I found them, sir. Twenty books in all. All hand written. All had descriptions of unusual people she'd seen and cars she'd noticed. Plus, plain old observations about life. All the entries were dated, up to the day of her death. I checked the entry made the day before her murder and I discovered that my aunt had described in great detail a black van parked two blocks away from her residence. She'd noticed it on her morning jog. She had written down the license plate number and also described the van and the driver down to the very last detail. Mr. Grimsley, the police found the van, found my aunts blood in the van, matched the murderer's DNA. Found the murder weapon and found that this dirt bag had killed as many as 10 women throughout the country the same way."

"I'm sorry to hear about that, son."

"That's not the best part, sir. The same day I found her journals, I found your book next them. And there were pages marked. The section marked was the one where you recommend beating the bad guys at their own game by observing the world around you and taking notes or writing journals." The boy sniffed and held back tears. "Thank you Mr. Grimsley."

The class began applauding. Grimsley blushed and held up his hands, motioning them to stop.

"All right. All right. Thank you. Thank you for that story, son. I'm sorry about your Aunt. Your story validates what we're doing here, but this is a college course not a celebrity talk show people, so let's get down to business. I want to start out by talking about crime and criminals in general terms. Then we'll dig more deeply into the book and look at some other real life scenarios. Everybody okay with that?" Heads nodded in unison.

"All right, let's start with the mind of the murderer."

Chapter 51

Heavy gray clouds rolled into Portland that afternoon. They were quiet and ominous and customarily quiet. The autumn rains, once they started, continued sometimes through July.

Rich sat at his desk watching the walls close in on him. He couldn't concentrate on any of his work. The only thing he could hear was the constant trickling of the water as it dripped down the rusted gutter in the ventilation shaft near his window. That was big selling point for his downtown office. The gutter sounded soothing, like a backyard water fountain.

Rich couldn't get the picture of the Mexican American out of his head. Nor could he stop thinking he'd done something wrong. False guilt ate at his conscious.

The phone rang. Rich ignored it. His cell phone rang. He checked the number. Collectors. They could wait. He knew what they wanted.

He sat staring at his desk. It, by far, offered the best comic relief. Rich had dug this one out of a dumpster that summer. As usual, he poured a coat of polyurethane over it. It looked like it had been pulled from a dumpster and drenched with a coat polyurethane.

Rich reached for the phone and picked it up. He pressed "0" for the operator, *Verizon Operator Assistance may I help you?...*

"Yeah, um, sure, could you give me the number for the Portland police department please."

"Which precinct, sir?"

"Um, I guess Northeast."

"Is this an emergency sir?"

"No, I wouldn't say that. I..."

"I can give you the community policing desk at the North Precinct."

"Okay," Rich replied tentatively.

"That number is 503-555-5223. I'll connect you at no additional charge."

"Thank you."

Rich heard the first ring.

"Hello, Portland Police Department North Precinct this is Sergeant Sara Ferguson how may I help you?"

He hung up without replying. He cupped his hands and rubbed them nervously. Then he stood up and walked to the window and stared at the hundred-year-old stained and chipped red bricks.

The phone rang suddenly and jolted him back to the small room. Rich turned and stared at it as if his stare might force it to stop ringing. After 10 rings it stopped. There was an ominous silence. Rich felt relieved but still on edge.

Chapter 52

Towards the end of Grimsley's lecture, his spirits were lifted by a lively exchange with his students. Most had actually read his book and seemed genuinely interested. It still disturbed him, however, to see one student secretly talking to someone on a cell phone or another student obviously playing games on a handheld computer.

When he observed the student on the cell phone, he barked, "Ms. Tempey. Would you care to share what you're discussing on the telephone with the rest of the class?"

Startled, Ms. Tempey, a delicate redheaded girl with bright red lipstick contrasting against pale skin and freckles, scrambled to remove the mobile headset she was wearing, and said, "Mr. Grimsley, I'm sorry. Um, I…"

"Ms. Tempey, it is insulting and rude to distract your classmates and your teacher. One might think you were not instructed on the very fundamentals of respect for others, and, um, your elders. My advice, Ms. Tempey, is to, as you young people would say, LOG OFF, HANG UP, and engage yourself in what is taking place here in front of you. Lest you find yourself walking up to the podium on graduation day and being handed a blank diploma because these three required credits are missing. Then, Ms. Tempey, we shall be forced to spend a never-ending summer together, you and I, while your classmates have departed to make their mark upon the world. So, whatever you may think is so important to discuss on your cell phone during this class, I would advise you to reconsider. Do I make myself clear Ms. Tempey?"

Ms. Tempey's complexion no longer contrasted with her red lipstick. She was flush. On the opposite side of the room, another student secretly turned off a cell phone and stuffed it into a backpack, while others snickered, thankful they had not invited such attention from Mr. Grimsley.

"Yes, sir, Mr. Grimsley. Sorry," Ms. Tempey said sheepishly and turned her attention to the book in front of her.

"Let's continue our discussion about complex clues."

Grimsley pointed to a student in the first row and continued, "Mr. Nichols has asserted that the theories in my book relate directly to much larger historical phenomenon, such as the fall of the Mayan empire or unraveling of the mysteries of the Pyramids. He says that the rulers of these empires wanted us to know what happened but they were also covering up gross atrocities. These atrocities required that their history be a puzzle, one that only the astute scholars can decipher. I say he has a valid point."

Grimsley walked around to the podium, opened his book and said, "If you'll turn to page 88, you'll see where I write about the complexities of the psychopath mind. Many psychopaths have extremely high IQs. And, unfortunately, some psychopaths have become leaders of entire civilizations. We somehow have come to believe that leaders of ancient civilizations thought differently from us. But that is patently untrue. Itzcoatl, King of the Aztecs, could easily have been like Hitler. In which case, he may have been extremely intelligent, extremely violent, ruthless, genocidal, and would not want his people to document all of his atrocities. It would then become the challenge of the oppressed and violated people to leave us clues as to what happened to them. Some say fear was so absolute that no one dared attempt to formally document what happened to the Mayans or to the Aztecs under Spanish rule, but every day we find more clues that tell us more about the crimes that were perpetrated against these people. Now, how does that relate to us today? Ancient, mysterious civilizations may have as much to hide as they have to share. In common kidnappings, fear and secrecy is absolute. Control is essential, and that works to the advantage of the captor, the ruler so to speak. So, that's when you must be creative as a victim. We've all seen those crime movies like *Seven* and *Silence of the Lamb*s, but they're not so far fetched. Only in these cases, the criminal was leaving cryptic clues to lead the police on a wild goose chase. A hostage or kidnapping victim can do the same to achieve the opposite effect."

A hand went up in the front row.

"Yes, Mr. Pham."

"Mr. Grimsley, I hope you don't think this is a dumb question, but I've heard this used numerous times and there may be some relevance for our discussion in the answer." He paused, unsure of whether to ask the question of or not. "Can you tell me what exactly is a wild goose chase?"

The class burst into laughter. Grimsley joined in.

"Excellent question Mr. Pham. Now your thinking like detectives."

Grimsley returned to the front of the science table and sat on the edge, folded his hand across his lap and continued, "It's excellent, because as a detective for 30 years, I've been on many of these. A wild goose chase was a type of 16th century English horse race where the rider of the lead horse, instead of going around a track or prescribed route, went off in any direction he chose. Other riders had to follow at precise intervals, like wild geese following a lead goose. The term has since evolved into different meanings, the most relevant here being a useless or hopeless quest or to be misled or misdirected in the WRONG direction. Believe it or not people, we've had this done to us by criminals AND victims."

"Why would a victim deliberately mislead an investigation," Mr. Pham asked, puzzled.

"We don't always know," Grimsley answered. "But we do know that in the case of murder suicides, the perpetrators, instead of telling us outright what the situation was, want the public to feel sorry for them. There are also some victims who know they're tempting fate with their lifestyles, so they bury answers…"

Grimsley paused. His thoughts shifted elsewhere for a moment. "…they bury answers around them in complex clues."

"Wouldn't they want their murders to be discovered?" Pham asked.

"They do, in most cases. But as I mentioned, not all criminals are incompetent boobs like you see on *Caught on Tape*. The victim may be giving clues to us but ALSO protecting herself."

"So, victims who find themselves, for whatever reason, in a situation they can't get out of may want to leave clues, but not be obvious about it because they fear for their lives."

"Or, Mr. Pham," Grimsley said, "They may want to make it interesting for us. Remember, our minds are complex. The ability to create puzzles feeds the ability to solve them."

Grimsley returned to the podium. "But we'll talk more about that next time. Time to wrap things up. Next time, let's start out with this subject and talk about dictators, despots and dirtballs, how clues have helped us unravel their secrets. Class dismissed."

As the students shuffled towards the exits at the top of the lecture hall, Grimsley, reached into his breast pocket and pulled out his cell phone. He punched a button and said, "Paulson, that you?"

"Yes it is, sir," Paulson answered.

"Where's the van from this morning?"

"Precinct impound, sir."

"It's been dusted and samples collected?"

"From stem to stern, sir."

"Any clues to ownership?"

"Non, sir. No plates. Vin number has been wiped. Hasn't had a tune-up, new tires or parts for some time. Barely runs, sir."

"Paulson, go back to the van and check for any graffiti, any numbers or initials you might find. I'll meet you at PPD impound. You can let me know what you find there."

"Teii captain." Grimsley hung up and rushed to PPD impound

Chapter 53

Chico worked himself into a state of grief-stricken, drunken, masturbating panic. Like a caged animal, he paced from one corner of the cramped and cluttered room to the other, alternately slurping on beer and stopping to peek out the window.

After the fifth beer, he decided on a bold move. Fuck it, he thought. He wasn't afraid of nobody. He needed his bike. No public transit for Chico. Too risky. He would go get it now, see what was happening by the van. Then use Trixie's...his money to stay in a cheap hotel until things cooled off.

Chico was more confident now. No one knew him. No one knew what he looked like. He was like a vampire; rarely came out during the daylight hours. He had no friends. The only one who saw him was the driver of the truck. Fucking paperboy he thought. He had seen him before. Cars at that time of night were conspicuous. Chico knew all the cars in the neighborhood. He knew everyone's schedules. He knew the paperboy. And he knew he'd seen a truck like it parked in the neighborhood before.

Find the paperboy. Scare him. Stop him. Kill him or end up in jail again. Chico couldn't go back to jail again. He had all but blocked out the images of Pedro Montoya, a Crips kingpin he shared a cell with in L. A. County jail. Every night Montoya forced Chico to pull is pants down and bend over the small stained sink while he forced his dick up Chico's ass. While Chico whimpered like a child who'd lost his favorite Teddy, Montoya grunted and cursed at him, threatening to kill him if he made a sound or told anyone.

"Take my big cock up your ass you pussy bitch. When I get ready to cum, I want you to turn around and lap it up like a dog you bitch. Drink it like you love it mother fucker," Montoya would say.

Chico remembered the smell of shit and cum and crotch as Montoya pushed his penis deep into his mouth and squirted his cum into his throat. Chico would gag and dry heave.

"You throw up on me mother fucker and I'll slit your pussy throat right here," Montoya threatened. To show his dominance, Montoya forced Chico to tag along behind him during the day; treated him like a slave and beat him if he spoke out of turn. Then other gang members would take turns violating him in secluded areas around the prison, in the shower, in the laundry room, anywhere they wanted.

"Chico, you got the sweetest ass in L.A. County," Montoya would say. Chico was broken, humiliated, somebody's bitch. He couldn't go back. He couldn't go through that again.

Find the paperboy. Kill the paperboy. Paper slinging mother

fucker. Chico left the apartment. Maybe he'd find the journal too. He backtracked his route from the night before.

Chapter 54

PPD impound was an open parking lot in Northwest Portland. The large lot was surrounded by a six foot tall fence with spiral razor wire on top. Cars sat in uneven rows alongside Triple A branded tow trucks, most confiscated from drug dealers and awaiting auction. Next to the lot was a brick warehouse with creeping ivy lining the walls, where vehicles were dismantled or stored if needed for evidence in criminal investigations. Trixie's van was outside, parked next to a cherry red Lamborghini Testarosa.

Paulson stood next to the van as Grimsley passed through the security gates, pulled into the lot, parked next to Paulson's squad car with the red rose and Portland Police on the side. Grimsley got out and walked to the van.

"Detective Paulson," Grimsley barked, "Why the hell is this van outside?"

Paulson was getting used to Grimsley style and was prepared, "I called Captain Holister and inquired, sir, and his response would make Richard Pryor blush."

Grimsley rubbed his chin, "What did say?"

"Well, sir, he said nobody gives a shit about a whore. He said we get charged for storing cars inside by Triple A towing so since this is a low-level priority murder..."

"Low-level priority," Grimsley interrupted. "Now I've hear it all. Low-level, routine, typical...Jesus, what has this country come to."

Paulson waited.

"I'll deal with the captain, Paulson, "Grimsley said. "You looked for what I asked you to?"

"Yes, sir, I did. I think we may have found something." Paulson walked towards the open door of the van.

"Over here, sir."

Paulson stepped into the van. Grimsley followed.

"We've cleaned it up a little, sir, so it's easier to stomach. Over here."

Paulson moved a mattress away from the wall of the van and pointed.

"There sir."

Grimsley's eyes opened wide.

"Don't see a damn thing Paulson. This some kind of joke?"

Paulson smiled at Grimsley.

"At first glance, there seems to be nothing there. But I wanted you to see that, first. Here, allow me."

Paulson reached into his pocket and pulled out a flashlight with a dark blue screen.

"You remember the black lights of the 60s and 70s?"

"Course I do Paulson."

"Well, this prostitute was very clever, sir. Watch this."

Paulson closed the curtains on the windows, turned on the flashlight and as the beam crossed over sections of the panel, small evenly spaced, neatly written letters appeared.

"Well, I'll be God damn," Grimsley said, "You read the whole thing, Paulson?"

"Yes, sir I did."

"Break it down for me young man."

"It's a message. Non-specific, very well written. Not the writing of an uneducated person. Bits of philosophy, Descartes, to be exact. Quotes from Kant, Hillary Clinton, Mao, the Dalai Lama, and one you might be particularly interested in."

Paulson, slid further onto the platform and shined the light on a small section in the corner near the back window.

"You have to read this one yourself, sir."

Grimsley read it out loud.

"It is assumed that we are all afraid to die. But ignorance feeds that assumption. Some of us feel we have suffered enough or done enough good deeds that we are comfortable with the idea of death. Some of us even look forward to death. With death comes peace. With death comes life, another chance. I am not afraid to die. I have tempted fate, and perhaps I deserve to die a terrible death. If so, who should be held accountable? Will I have gotten what I deserve? Or should my death be avenged. I don't know. Whatever the case may be, I have left a trail..."

The note ended.

"What the hell," Grimsley said.

"It doesn't end there, sir, it just gets more interesting," Paulson said. "Over here, sir."

Paulson backed off the bed, Grimsley moving backwards at the same time. Both men stood up as much as the could. Paulson opened a cabinet where Trixie kept here China Rain. He shined the flashlight into the dark cabinet. The same block letters covered the back wall of the cabinet. The note was preceded by an ellipses and continued.

"...The trail is complex. I am nobody and I am somebody. If I remain nobody, I will still be somebody. As Bob Grimsley said in his famous book, 'Subtle clues are much more interesting than the obvious. Some victims like to think that even after they die, unraveling the complexity of their lives gives them a great deal of satisfaction.' So they (I) have left some deliberate, subtle clues about my life, my habits, my associations and the myriad of scumbags who inhabit the night. Looking under my mattress will get you started. The rest is up to you..Love Trixie."

Grimsley was beaming.

"Trixie," he said, "Just as I thought. There's more to you than meets the eye. Good work Paulson. Write it all down. Get what pictures you can. I'm going to see the captain. Low-level priority murder my ass."

Chapter 55

Chico pulled his stocking cap tight over his head so it mostly covered his eyes. He walked up 42nd street to Alberta Street, turned left and walked halfway down the block then cut through two small houses to Wygant, where he thought he dropped the journal. He found the wire fence he had jumped over and foraged through some overgrown grass. The journal was nowhere to be found.

He gave up his search and cautiously emerged from behind the big three-story house and headed east on Wygant to 47th street, then south one block to Going. As he approached Going, he slowed at the corner and glanced over to where Trixie's van was parked.

It was gone. There was nothing there. There was no evidence of the events of that morning. Chico's heart was racing. His arm pits were dripping sweat. Chico glanced a half-block up on 47th, past Going, where he had chained his bike. He froze as his eyes fell on the bike.

The bike was still there, but a large white feral cat circled the bike. It was sniffing and rubbing against it. Chico's fear turned to anger immediately.

He darted across the street, quickening his pace as he got closer, he glanced around suspiciously as he approached the bike. Just before he reached it, he shoved his hands into his coat pocket and removed a key to the kryptonite lock.

Seeing the menacing Mexican American approaching quickly, the cat froze and stared at him. It's short hairs stood straight up on its hunched back. It hissed at Chico, daring him to come closer. Chico thought he might be able to reach over the cat and unlock the bike, but as he reached over the cat, it hissed and leaped at his hand, swiping its claws across his fingers.

"Mother fucking sons of bitches!" Chico screamed as he drew back his hand. The gash was deep and blood streamed down Chico's hand.

"Get the fuck out of here you piece of shit cat. I just want my fucking bike."

The cat didn't back down. It hissed louder. Chico was amazed at the size of the cat. He'd never seen one that big. It was the size of a Bobcat, so Chico didn't dare try to grab it and strangle I like he'd done to so many others. He looked around for a stick of weapon or rock to smash over it's head and put it out of its misery.

As he looked for a weapon, Chico was thinking this was taking too much time. Fucking cat, he thought. Chico saw a branch near the aluminum fence of a sheet metal yard about 10 feet from where his bike was chained. Perfect, he thought. Bash it's little head in and leave it for the ants.

He ran over to the stick, picked it up and turned to face his nemesis. But as he looked at his bike, he was amazed to find that the cat was gone. Chico looked in all directions.

"What the shit," he mumbled. Chico couldn't believe that it could have vanished. But it was nowhere. Relieved but miffed, Chico said, "Fuck with me again mother fucker and see what happens."

Chico threw the stick aside, ran to his bike, quickly unlocked it, took a running start and jumped on the bike, landing hard on his crotch and groaning as the seat sunk into his scrotum. He found the peddles and, with all the energy he could muster, peddled towards 42nd street, then west on Prescott towards downtown.

As he peddled, the front wheel still wobbling from the wreck he had the day before, and his muscles burned with pain as he once again used muscles he hadn't used in 20 years.

To add to Chico's misery, the dark imposing clouds opened up a torrent of heavy, wet raindrops that beat down on Chico like a shower from a giant fire hose.

"Fucking sheet!" Chico screamed. He repeated this mantra as he pumped the peddles, the pain, cold and wet adding to his despair.

Rich left work early, around 2 p.m. and returned home. The house was quiet, eerie. The events of that morning made things feel different. Rich was tense and paranoid. As he entered the dark house, he checked behind doors after entering rooms, turned on all the lights, and kept the music off so he could hear any stirring if anyone had entered the house and was hiding.

He thought it was silly, but he did it anyway. He even checked the basement. The sound of the heavy rain pounded on the windows and the gutters played their water sonata from every corner of the house.

He went to the den and turned on the computer. While it booted up, he made a cup of his caffeine sludge, five teaspoon full of coffee in a drip coffee maker that has never been cleaned.

By the time the pot brewed, Rich was connected to the Internet and there were five messages in his mailbox, one from the agent he'd e-mailed that morning. Another reject letter he thought. He clicked on the message to open it and started reading. The message turned out to be anything but a reject letter.

Dear Mr. Franklin,

I have reviewed your manuscript and think it is brilliant. This morning I made a presentation to a publisher and we all agreed that we'd like to publish your book. We are going to fast-track publishing your book, with a 10,000 run and nationwide marketing and distribution. Attached is a contract with favorable terms, negotiated by Mr. Sunny Manns, who referred you to us. We will also be sending you a small advance or $5,000 as incentive to complete all rewrites by next Tuesday. We look forward to working with you Mr. Franklin. Please call at your soonest convenience.

Sincerely,

Barry Siegel
Siegel & Associates Literary Agency

"No fucking way!" Rich yelled. Rich's heart was pounding. "Jesus fucking H Christ. This can't be real!"

Rich stood up and circled the room, came back to the computer and read the message again. He mouthed the words as he read them, still not ready to accept that the message was real. He sat down at his computer and typed a short reply.

"Is this for real?"

He clicked the send button.

Seconds later, a reply appeared in his in-box. Rich opened it.

"Yes, Mr. Franklin. Shall we talk? I'm in the office, please call me if you'd like to discuss this now."

Rich clicked the REPLY button and frantically typed in a message. Not wanting to appear too anxious he wrote, *"I'd like a minute to read the contract and think about this."*

"No problem," Siegel replied. *"I'll be in all afternoon."*

Rich opened the attached word document and sent it to the printer. As each page appeared, he snatched it off the printer then slid it under a neat pile.

He intermittently bit his nails as the printer queued up. Once the printing was complete, Rich stared at the stack, then, after gulping the last of his coffee, he read the contract from beginning to end, without pausing.

Chapter 56

Grimsley walked past Captain Holister's receptionist without stopping for his usual pleasantries with Mildred Snagle, Holister's receptions; a stoic woman with a beehive hairdo, bifocals, dark pant suit and a stare that could tripple-freeze ice.

"Captain Grimsley," She called. "Sir! The captain is busy. Grimsley continued walking, ignoring Ms. Snagle.

"Can I make an appointment for you, sir?" she asked.

Grimsley reached the door that was made of dark stained wood and had a frosted glass pane with CPT. HOLISTER in removable vinyl lettering in the middle. He turned the doorknob and pushed in the door.

Captain Verl Holister sat behind his desk with his feet propped up on one end. He did not bother to look up at Grimsley, but instead, sucked slowly on a massive cigar, relishing each toke. Smoke swirled around his thick, wide, crooked nose, past his deep, dull gray eyes, and around his pimply shaved head.

Grimsley peered at Holister, waiting for him to acknowledge his entrance. Grimsley observed that Holister's white dress shirt seemed too small to contain his muscular, bulky torso.

As Holister raised the cigar to his mouth, his biceps strained against the fabric. Grimsley knew that Holister, at age 55, still pumped weights for three hours a day and competed in local amateur wrestling matches under the name Darth Vadar. Holister ruled by intimidation. But Grimsley was not phased.

"Close the door Grimsley," Holister said, not bothering to look up. "I've been expecting you."

Grimsley closed the door, shoved his hands into his pocket and walked around to the side of Holister's desk to face him. Holister peered up at Grimsley.

"Grimsley, I'll break the ice here because the sooner your ass is out of my office, the better."

He looked at Grimsley and blew several rings of smoke in his direction and grinned through yellow stained teeth.

"I don't like you. You don't like me. We're good that way."

Holister pulled his feet off of the desk, slammed then on the ground and stood up. He was a full two inches taller than Grimsley and twice as wide. He leaned closer to Grimsley face, close enough for Grimsley to smell his rancid breath.

"We're both captains. That's fucked up to begin with. And the fact that I have no authority to fire your ass really pisses me off. This, um, arrangement you have with the mayor smells like shit."

Holister picked up a cup of aging coffee, gathered up a ball of spit and squirted it in the cup and set it back on the desk. Then Holister picked up his cigar, took another deep toke, placed the cigar in the ash tray, turned and walked toward the window, blowing smoke as he walked. He placed his hands on his hips and with his back to Grimsley.

"I know what you want. I can't help you. I got a mandate here Grimsley. Two girls are missing. White girls. Wholesome, upper class, high school drill team girls with families who have lots of friends and lots of money. Doesn't matter if the girls are probably dead. Probably fucked and buried somewhere in the Olympic National Forest. Mushroom food. Doesn't matter. Mayor says to do what I need to do. So I gotta make it look good. And in order to do that, I can't delegate resources to your two bit whore who gets her head shot off by some nigger pimp."

Holister glanced at Grimsley as he finished his speech, looking for a reaction. Grimsley did not respond.

"Come on Grimsley," Holister said. "You're the fucking intellectual giant here. Shoot your best shot. I'm a prick, a bigot, a goddamn sonofabitch...what else is new. But I'm in charge this time Grimsley, and there's not a God damn thing you can do about it."

Grimsley pulled a cigarette out of his breast pocket and patted his jacket for a lighter.

"Mind?" he asked.

"Fuck no. You see my stogie."

"Let me ask you something, Holister," Grimsley started, and sucked on the cigarette and blew smoke into the air "What do you have against prostitutes?"

Holister turned away from the window, towards Grimsley, walked to his desk, placed his hands on the desk, leaned forward and said, "God damn cesspools of disease, breeding sick half breed scum. Bustin' up god Christian families. I'd like to take them all out into a field and shoot them. That answer your question, Grimsley?"

Grimsley turned away this time and reviewed Holister's book shelf. The shelves were lined with police manuals, survival guides, and one entire row of hard-bound volumes of Republican presidential biographies. You CAN judge a man by what he reads, Grimsley thought.

His back to Holister, he asked, "You know a cesspool of disease called Misty Knights. Has a penthouse on King Hill. Cute brunette. Into the kinky stuff?"

Holister's didn't move or react, but his jaw tightened, flexing the muscles in his temple and around his neck and the blood vessels in his eyes turned bright red.

Grimsley turned and walked towards Holister. One hand in his pocket and the other holding a cigarette.

He continued, "Misty—that's not her real name of course—is a very intelligent girl. Was valedictorian in her class. Maintained a 4.0 average all throughout high school and college. Has a degree in microbiology and raises orchids as a hobby."

Grimsley paused, glanced at Holister, who stood straight up now, loosened his tie and collar and peered angrily at Grimsley after clenching his fist.

"Misty is fascinated with the Internet. Loves the technology. Those God damn little Blink mini cameras are the rage. She's got them in every room and has the entire penthouse wired for sound. She films everyone she sees and posts pictures on here little web site…sometimes. Some faces are obscured and some are not in the videos. Through her little web site and a few discreet appointments every day, Misty clears about $1.2 million in income every year."

Grimsley chuckled. "I'm not a biologist or a God damn mathematician, and I don't encourage anyone to break the law, but I'd say Misty is one of the smartest cesspools of disease I know. Much smarter than you Holister. Seems a while back, you and…"

Holister pounded his fist on the desk. The banker's lamp jumped up a few inches, then fell over, shattering the frosted green glass.

"Cut the shit Grimsley, you fucking bastard. What do you fucking want?"

Chapter 57

Senator Jack Niel was having a stressful day on capital hill. A bill he had introduced to allow logging of 400,000 acres of old growth forest in Idaho was close to being defeated. He spent the morning frantically calling his colleague senators to see if he could gain more support. But the growing unpopularity of his bill and others like it, caused most senators to steer clear it. So nothing was working. Niel had to make it look good though. To get into office as a Vermont Senator, he had accepted soft money from major timber companies. And their lobbyist had been putting pressure on him to delivery a bill.

His tiny office was tucked away in the obscure wing of the capitol building. Niel sat at his desk, a large ornate antique, mahogany roll-top that was next to a sprawling faux Victorian era drawer-less table. When he hung up the phone with the latest senator to tell him no, Zach Temple, his personal assistant walked into the room with a concerned look on his face.

"Senator," Temple said, "We've got a situation."

Temple wore a conservative, navy blue Armani suit, white Tommy Polo shirt and dark tie.

"What kind of situation do we have Temple?"

"Trixie, sir. She's been murdered."

Neil's face went flush as he looked in horror at Temple. He stood up, walked over to Temple and in a lowered voice asked, "How did it happen?"

"As far as we know, single gunshot to the head by an unknown assailant."

Temple talked in formal, flat, even tones while standing at attention with both gloved hands holding his derby in front of him as he spoke. His steel blue eyes looking straight at Neil.

"Temple, you have someone on this."

"Yes, sir, I have a man in the PPD who's keeping me informed. And I've got people checking out the crime scene and scouring for clues in the neighborhood. Don't worry, sir, I've got this under control."

"What the hell could have happened here Temple. I mean, I know she was taking risks, but what the hell happened?"

"Nothing concrete, sir. Only theories. Early morning robbery. Probably a junkie on PCP. Out of his mind. We don't know who, sir. Blew her brains out, sir."

Neil said nothing. He looked at Neil with unconcerned curiosity. He marveled at Temple's detachment and lack of emotion but knew he could depend on that as well. Niel had good reasons to hire temple. Temple had been his personal assistant for 15 years. Temple was a former navy pilot, former CIA operative a Jet Ken Do black belt, and could be trusted to keep Neil's many secrets and get any job done. In spite of his quirks and obsessions for James Bond and Bruce Lee, Niel trusted Temple implicitly. Niel asked him about the Derby on one occasion and Temple responded simply, "Double O seven, Goldfinger, remember. Oddjob." Niel simply said, "Ooooh," and left it at that.

"Have they ID'd her?" Niel asked.

"Not yet, sir. But Grimsley's on it, though, which makes matters a little more complicated."

"Shit! That can't be good." Neil rubbed his chin nervously. "Temple you have to make sure she can never be traced back to me. Otherwise…well, take care of it."

"So far, she's a Jane Doe. Pressure is on to find a couple of missing high school girls, so this murder is being de-prioritized. That buys us some time, sir."

"Temple, I don't have to remind you that I have a wife and family and constituents to serve. And my job here provides a more than comfortable living for you."

"Sir, I completely understand."

"Go to Portland and take care of this. Do what you need to do and report back to me. I want a status report every hour on our secure cell. This thing CANNOT get out of control."

"Yes, sir." Temple had no need for further questions or answers. He simply turned and walked towards the door. Niel, arms folded, with a worried look on his face said, "Temple."

Temple turned and answered, "Sir."

"I do mean do ANYTHING AND EVERYTHING you need to do."

"Don't worry, sir, I know what to do."

Chapter 58

"Mr. Siegel," Rich started after the phone picked up on the other end and a voice who identified himself as Barry Siegel answered. "I read your contract. Even signed it. Got it in the fax machine right now and my index finger is hovering over the send button. Mr. Siegel, I'll be straight with you. I figured that someday I might find myself in this position again and wondered what I'd do. Sell my soul or leave my writing unpublished for my children to discover in a shoebox in the closet. Either way is okay with me. So, Mr. Siegel, I just need five minutes of your time; time enough for you to help me decide whether to press this button or buy a bigger shoebox."

The receiver buzzed over the silence, then Siegel cleared his throat and responded with a clear, confident New York accent, *"Mr. Franklin, first let me say, I've done my home work here."*

"How's that, Mr. Siegel"

"I know as much as I need to know about you to assure you that this is the right thing to do."

"Give me the one minute version Mr. Siegel."

"Well, I know you're no dummy for starters. You were never a straight A student in high school or college, but you had a talent for writing and were born with the gift of gab."

"Any astrologer could make those kinds of assumptions Mr. Siegel. Tell me something I don't know."

"I read the columns you wrote for the Kansas State Collegian. Even at age 19, Mr. Franklin, you showed promise. Had a way with words. Your professors, Bill Brown, Bob Bontrager, Carol Okrup and Bob Adams recognized this and tried to push you into newspaper journalism. But you never fancied chasing ambulances and writing obits."

"Go on."

"I acquired copies of your humor magazine, Rabid City Humor magazine from the Library of Congress. You thought they were special enough to register them at age 21. I got more copies from an old friend of mine, David Friedman, president of the Rocky Mountain Writers Association. You were a member back in '82. I read some of your early, humorous works, Bruce Why Interrogatory Spy, Chase Cable, Ace Public Eye and Private Parts and Manikin Depressive...Shall I continue, Mr. Franklin?"

"Sure. It's just getting interesting."

"So is your life, Mr. Franklin. Your were 21 at the time. Young. Confused, but writing cutting edge humor that only you and a loyal band of some 500 subscribers actually got. But you wrote without fear and to a certain extent without much aforethought. But that's what made it interesting. You were practicing. I'll fast forward, Mr. Franklin, because I don't want to bore you with *what you already know. Right here and now is an opportunity to validate everything everyone who has every known you knew. What you know, and that is that you've been practicing for years and now you're really good. You've got a story to tell. And your time to be recognized could be now. That's what the public wants. And, Mr. Franklin, that fact that you're an African American is a trump card for you."*

"How does my being African American factor into this?" Rich asked sternly.

"Don't take it the wrong way Mr. Franklin, this contract is not being extended to you JUST because you are an African American, but partly because you are an African American writer. It's being extended mostly because you are a damn good writer with a unique story from a unique perspective. And part of that perspective happens to be African American."

"There are thousands of good writers with good stories. I don't want to be published just because I'm African American."

"Don't worry Mr. Franklin, you're not. Listen, are you sitting down."

"Sure."

"Let me tell you a little about how the publishing game is played. My publisher, Putnam, is not in the business of losing money. They are in the business of publishing books to sell books. The publishing machine today is very different from the way it was forty years ago. First, we have 200 readers and editors on call every day who read our manuscripts and give us detailed ratings. We can print practically finished books on demand in minutes. Glossy covers. Fancy looking, and send proofs to every media outlet in a matter of hours. That's hours Mr. Franklin. Not months. Not years. Not days. We get commitments in advance for reviews and interviews from major talk show host, and, in some cases, this all happens before we even make offers."

"What are you telling me Mr. Siegel. That publishers have the equivalent of a hit machine, like those music executives and their boy and girl bands?"

"Sort of, Mr. Franklin. But it's a little more sophisticated. We're dealing with literature. Our audience is a little more mature. We have to be very careful. Major talk show hosts rely on us to deliver intelligent, insightful writers to them and, in turn, they agree to deliver them to the public."

"Mr. Siegel, you've had my manuscript for one day. What could possible have happened in one day?"

"I'll tell you. One copy sent to my contact at Putnam. She sent 25 copies via e-mail to our reader / raters. Another twenty-five copies were mailed to several major talk show host and publicist. And, of course, I kept one copy for myself."

"The only talk show host I care about is Oprah," Rich said, half joking. "She's the only one who understands."

"I know you may be joking Mr. Franklin, but Oprah read the first 10

chapters and gave us a thumbs up."

"You're kidding me, right?"

"I'm dead serious, Mr. Franklin. Many people purchase books based on Genre. Based on personal experience. Based on race. Based on gender. Your book is a murder mystery about an African American, written by an African American. We got an ace in the hole with three major interest groups. And I will admit, Mr. Franklin, there are a lot of lousy African American writers out there that we will not touch. You, Mr. Franklin, we think we can work with. We can hang our hat on you. People are souring on books by former gang leaders-rappers writing about, well, themselves and their reformation. Your book is closer to the experience of your generation. You're NOT from the ghetto, not a former gang leader, not a black militant, not necessarily angry at anything. You just want your stories to be normal stories about a black person dealing with ordinary AND extraordinary bullshit. AS a black person would. Rich, you're human. And that's what you want people to see. And that's what you managed to do in your book, and you wrapped it in the blanket of a murder mystery."

Rich was silent. He wasn't sure what to say next. Siegel was right and he knew it. Then he said, "Mr. Siegel, if I read this contract correctly, you own me for the next five years."

"That's correct Mr. Franklin."

There was silence.

"And you have first rights of refusal for everything I've ever written or published, even graffiti in the bathroom?"

"That's correct Mr. Franklin. Is there a problem with that?"

"Not necessarily, if you can deliver what you say you can."

"Correction. Not a problem if you can delivery what I think you can."

"I can delivery Mr. Siegel."

"Then there's no problem."

"Only one."

"What's that Rich?"

"I need to use a pseudonym."

"Well. That's not recommended."

"Why not?"

"Because it's very difficult to sell one name and interview with another. And there will be many interviews."

"But I'd like to remain anonymous, to protect my privacy."

Rich was really thinking about how to hide from creditors and keep the book deal secret for April and Enison and use the money to pay off his debts secretly.

"Mr. Franklin, allow me to be frank with you. Whether wanted or not, with success comes, in many cases, fame. With fame comes loss of anonymity. Trust me, Mr. Franklin, even with a pseudonym, you may not be able to hide. Let's keep

your real name on it. Give you something to show your mother. If you send her a book with a ridiculous pseudonym on it like U. R. Busted or Theamericanpeople Trustus, people are going to think you're an idiot."

Rich laughed. "You've got to be joking about that last one, right?"

"No, sir. Look it up on the Internet." Siegel said, chuckling. *"Political writer dealt the death blow to his treatise on American history with that one. It was dead on arrival. He turned out to be a bit of a psycho as well. He'd heard presidents and politicians use the phrase, 'The American People think...' you get the picture. He wanted to be able to say he WAS the American People and rebuff all the misquotes."*

"He actually published with that pseudonym?"

"Not only that, but he had his name change and ordered vanity plates. What a schmuck."

"Mr. Siegel, you've made a compelling case. Thank you. I just pressed the button. You got yourself a writer."

"It's coming through now. I'll process this right away and let the publishers know you're in. Now, let's get down to business, shall we."

"All right, boss. What do you need."

"Our editors will email the revisions to you today, so you'll get it by 10 a.m. tomorrow morning. We need all revisions back by Tuesday morning, so the book can be on the presses by Wednesday of next week. Once the new release reviews come in next Friday, we'll know whether you're on your way and know how many additional books to print on demand. Expect a 5,000 check from us within 72 hours."

"Perfect timing," Rich said. "I'm going to a writer's retreat this weekend in Longview, Washington. I'll take the manuscript with me and finish the edits there."

"That's fantastic, Mr. Franklin. I'm looking forward to a long, prosperous relationship."

"We'll see, Mr. Siegel."

"And Mr. Franklin," Siegel said, *"you really are a very talented writer."*

"Thanks, Mr. Siegel. I'll look forward to receiving your email."

Rich hung up the phone and finally too a deep breath. His eyes were blurry and his ear hurt from pressing the receiver too hard against his head.

He stared at the framed photograph of a battered fire hydrant hanging on the wall. He thought about the day he took the picture; an oppressive gray Winter day in Kansas City, Missouri. Union station was abandoned, decaying, fenced off from the rest of the city like a diseased building while city officials decided whether to tear down the eighty year old institution or resurrect it. The building was concrete gray, with rusted gutters and a moss spotted tiled roof. The fire hydrant was like a flower on the concrete parking lot, a thing of beauty in a desolate, dark landscape. He recalled how lonely and abandoned the building was, and he thought he captured, with a single click of his lens, the essence of its desolation.

Now, ironically, he was the happiest he'd ever been, but was also consumed by dread; felt desolate and alone when he should have been celebrating. He was the fire hydrant in the parking lot. His secrets were compounding.

Chapter 59

Chico cursed loudly as he peddled frantically, wobbling and weaving the entire way as the rain beat down on his head, soaking the Raider's cap, his coat and his shoes. Water dripped down his face and sometimes obscured his vision, forcing him to steer with one hand and wipe his face with the other.

Behind Chico, a black Lincoln Towncar cautiously followed, its driver obscured by dark tinted windows. Chico didn't notice it, but when he slowed or stopped, it slowed and stopped. Chico had managed to attracted the attention he was running from.

Chico rode from Prescott street to Martin Luther King Jr. Boulevard, took a left on MLK Blvd. and rode south to Burnside Street, then crossed the Burnside bridge and turned on to First street into Old Town.

First Street led into Chinatown. The streets were bustling with shoppers and derelicts, the lost and the looking curiously ignoring each other and coexisting.

Chico stopped at the first hotel that looked like a cheap, anonymous place to hide, where few questions would be asked. It was the Olympic Hotel. He peered in the front door. A single clerk flipped through a *National Inquirer* and ignored the pathetic parade of characters that slid in and out the front door. Chico locked his bike against a parking meter and went into the lobby.

The desk clerk barely look up from his *National Inquirer.*

"Help you?" he said.

Dark stubble stood out against pale olive skin. He spoke with a slight middle eastern accent.

Chico wiped the water from his face.

"Yeah, like, you got a fucking room."

The clerk raised an eyebrow and took a drag from a cigarette he'd been nursing in an ash tray. Unfazed by Chico's aggressive demeanor, he asked, "How long you want for?"

"I don know," Chico answered. "Couple days."

"I got day rates. Week rates. Month rates. Day is $20. Week is hundred dollar. Wad you want?"

"Gimme a week."

Chico stood up straight, trying to make himself taller so the counter would not obscure his face.

"Give me hundred dollars!" The clerk demanded.

Chico reached into his pocket and pulled out a crumpled hundred dollar bill and threw it on the counter.

"What is name?"

"Tito," Chico said.

"Last name."

"Tito Puente."

The clerk peered at Chico and raised his other eyebrow. He knew who Tito Puente was.

"Room 305. Sheet and bed change every day at noon. No cooking. No parties. You pay for everything you break."

He threw the keys on the counter.

He was trying to tell Chico what to do, Chico thought. What made him think he could do that? He was being bossed up by a total stranger. Chico stuck his chin out and leaned his head back, squinting his eyes to look intimidating.

"Don't want no fucking bed change and I fucking do what I want mother fucker."

The clerk stood up, reached down for a bat he kept at his side. He raised it and waved it at Chico.

"You do the fucks what I say or you get throwed the fucks out on you asses."

Chico raised his hands.

"Ait. Ait. Don't get all bent mother fucker. I was jus kiddin'."

Chico backed away from the counter. He'd lost again.

"Get the fucks out of here before I throwed your son de bitch ass out of here."

Chico backed away and walked towards the elevator. The clerk returned the bat to it's position under the counter, picked up his cigarette and his *National Inquirer* and continued to read as if nothing had happened. He chuckled as he read about the Martian baby twins. To him, this was all routine.

The black sedan parked in front of the hotel and a tall dark figure in a dark suit and dark hat emerged. He walked into the lobby and talked to the clerk. He slipped an envelope from his pocket and handed it to the clerk. The clerk slipped it under the counter and waved the man on. The dark figure took the stairs to the third floor, to Chico's room.

Chapter 60

The first thing Rich did was e-mail Kyle with the news. Before he told him the news, however, he wanted to vent, so he launched into a new tirade.

"Yo Bro," Rich started, "Got some shit to tell you."

"Nigga, you ain't got shit," Kyle responded.

"Got mo shit than you mother fucker."

"Kiss may as mother fucker, I got mo shit than shit itself," Rich wrote.

"Bullshit!"

"How long can this shit go on?"

"Til I come over yo house and kick the shit outta you!"

"Yo Kyle, you sure we educated niggas? We sound like a couple winos down there on 9th street."

"Nigga, we educated. Education don't always mean talkin' proper and shit. Education jus mean you know what mother fuckers is up to."

"I hear you black," Rich replied, "Thas why they don't want to educate niggas. 'Cause then we be hip to they bullshit."

"Damn straight black. Say, lemme run this one buy you. You know gentrification is fucked up. You know what the first thing White folks do when they move into a Black neighborhood?

"What black?" asked Kyle.

"They draw a white line through the neighborhood. You know what that white line represents?"

"Give the 411 cuz."

"It's a bike lane. You know what the bike lane is for?"

"Naw nigga. What the fuck is it for?"

"To protect White people from niggas while they riddin' they three thousand dollar bicycles through the poorest black neighborhoods, and to keep niggas from runnin' over they asses in they deuce and a quarters."

"Fo real?"

"Show you right, black," Rich typed, "Did a mother fuckin' impromptu, impartial survey. Sat my ass on a kona in the King neighborhood and watched who was ridin' bikes in the bike lane."

"Was you sippin' Mad Dog while you was doing your survey mother fucker?"

"You got that damn right! Tell you what I seent. I seent 75 White girls, hunnert and fifty White boys and no niggas riddin' in the bike lane."

"Where was all the niggas riddin they bikes?"

"Saw one nigga. No helmet. Liddy biddy dude on a fucked up bike with leopard skin plastic banana seat."

"No shit."

"No shit," Rich wrote. "Mother fucker was ridin' OUTSIDE of the bike lane, then cut across to the wrong mother fuckin side of the street, up on to the grass and into a got damn restaurant."

"Fuck naw!"

"Fuck yes! Then he rode his mother fuckin' bike up a got damn tree, ran over a mother fuckin' bird, cussed it out for being in the mother fucking tree, then you know what he did?"

"Naw man, what?"

"Rode on the got damn sidewalk!"

"Get the fuck outta here!"

"BACKWARDS!"

"Fuck me!"

"Niggas will not ride bikes in bike lanes. This they neighborhood. Been ridin' bikes all over shit for a hundred years. And they be resenting all those polite, bike lane ridin' white folks all sudden come in they neighborhood drawing the white line of gentrification. Plus all them white folks, specially them white gulls be wearin' tight spandex Speedo shit. Most niggas can't even afford that shit and resent these mother fuckin' tight shit wearin, titty floppin' jogin. bike ridin' bright close wearin' mother fuckers comin' into they neighborhood, trying to fuck things up by whitifying and politifying shit!!!"

"Yo, Rich, settle down. You get yoself all worked up and shit.!

"And what's even more fucked up…errr, umm, uuhh, where am I? Oh, I, I', sorry. I kind of lost it for a minute. I was in trouble for a second or two. I think I got blacked up. You know, I blacked out. All the black built up inside of me and I just needed to get it out. But I'm okay now. I just needed to say some shit."

"I know what you mean, black. So, how was your day?"

"That's it. Don't go gettin' all White on me. I still got some black left in me!"

"Say it loud brother! Nice to have you black."

"Now we can talk about, you know, normal shit. I do have some good news mother fucker."

"Need some good news after all that bullshit you just laid on me. All that angry Negro shit is turnnin' my screen black.?"

"Got a book deal."

"Get the fuck out of here! No shit!"

"No shit. Signed the contract today."

"Man, o man. I told you mother fucker. You got what it takes."

"Oprah read part of my manuscript and liktit it."

"Liktit it. That's some shit. If she just liked it, that wouldn't mean *nothing. But if she liktit it thas sayin' some shit."*

"No mother fucker, my shit."

"Congratulations blood. I'm happy for you. And I know you didn't tell anyone, especially not April if there's money involved."

"How did you know?"

"Nigga I know you."

"And don't tell me it's going to catch up with me. I can handle this shit."

"I know bro. I'm not going to rain on your parade. This is probably one of the happiest and important moments of your life and you can't tell the person that's closest to you. It's all good. Remember Denzel. Training Day?"

"Oh yeah. Cat was tough."

"You know he meant well; maybe. But you could never really tell. Cat had too many got damn secrets. His secrets caught up with him."

"You lecturin' me mother fucker?"

"Naw nigga. I ain't yo mamma. When do I get to see the printed book?"

"By next friday."

"Send me an autographed copy."

"What the fuck you talking about? You can buy it at Amazon.com like all the other mother fuckers."

"Funny mother fucker."

"Jes kiddin' You get the first copy I touch bro. Second one goes to mom. I got it all figured out. I need a week to take care of this shit and it will all work out. Then April will get a copy after it's established. The subject matter is too close to home. I need time to smooth things over with her. You know. Set the stage. There's some heavy shit in here. It will work out. You'll see."

"Ait bro. Gott go. Stay black and stay out of the bike lanes mother fucker."

"Ait bro."

"And by the way. I think I seen that same bike ridin' nigga ridin his mother fuckin' bike on the moon. Nigga gets around."

"Check you. Got to go pick up the kids."

Chapter 61

Baker was never good at managing anger, paranoia or anxiety. They had been thorns in his side since he could remember. Enison had lit a fuse in Baker that could not be put out. A fuse Baker would not allow to be put out. Baker couldn't understand Enison's audacity and insolence. It was inconceivable that a man of his education, accomplishment and stature could be dismissed and disregarded by a man who barely graduated from college and who's family came from the wrong side of the tracks of St. Louis.

Baker's revenge had to be precise. Had to be absolute. There could be no holes in his logic, in his proof. After he left Enison's office that morning, he placed a phone call to Skip Chambers, one of the firm's top investigators. He arranged a meeting at Skates On the Bay, a popular East Bay restaurant that sat perched over the water on the Bay in Emeryville. When he arrived, Chambers was already there waiting.

They sat facing each other in an isolated booth with high cushioned backs and wide Oak wood tables.

Chambers sized up Baker. They were not friends or friendly. They had never worked together, but Chambers knew who he was and acknowledged that he signed his checks.

Chambers was an old-school private detective. A Phillip Marlow fan. He was clean shaven, with granite textured skin from too many gin and tonics at Sam's Grill in San Francisco. He wore a trench coat, the best defense against San Francisco winds and kept a small office in the Woolworth building at Market & Powell in the city.

"What's this all about Baker?" Chambers asked, curious about Bakers need for secrecy.

"I need a favor, Skip," Baker said. He ordered a strawberry daiquiri from the pretty waitress in the tight black pants, white blouse and a 25% tip smile.

"Christ, Baker, what the hell is that?" Skip asked.

Baker, puzzled, asked, "What is what?"

"That drink. How can you drink those damn things? That's not a drink. That's an abomination, a bunch of fruit juice and some rot gut."

Baker responded timidly, "It helps me relax."

The pretty waitress, smile intact, brushed her hands through her hair, working both Baker and Chambers as she returned and stood over them like a Greek goddess valley girl.

"You need a few more minutes, gentlemen?" she chirped and leaned forward, partially exposing round inviting breast snug in a pink push up bra.

Chambers looked at the waitress, alternating between her cleavage and her eyes and said, "Hold on to your knickers sweetheart, your tip is safe with me."

He glanced back at Baker, "I'll tell you what will help you relax Baker, and Christ knows you need this. Sweetheart, bring us two double malt Scotches. Forget that pansy strawberry daiquiri whatsashit. And make it quick, honey."

Skip snapped his finger twice as he barked the orders. The pretty waitress stood up straight, turned quickly, hair flapping behind her and disappeared, her 25% tip smile fading to a scowl as she turned away from Chambers.

After the drinks came back, Chambers held up his drink for a toast and said, "First for the day."

Baker followed. Chambers downed the Scotch in two gulps. Baker hesitated then took a large gulp. He gagged and part of the drink overflowed out of his mouth and on to his shirt while he scrambled for a napkin.

"Keee-rist," Chambers said, rolling his eyes slightly. He gave Baker a chance to clean himself up before pointedly asking, "Baker, what can I do for you?"

He eased his tone slightly, now feeling a little sorry for Baker.

Baker wiped his face off again, patted down his tie and jacket, looked at Chambers, cleared his throat and said, "Enison's up to something and I need to know what it is. I need to take him down."

Baker's voice was slurred, tenuous and not in the least convincing, the strong Scotch going straight to his head and clouding his thoughts processes.

When baker finished his explanation, Chambers sat stone faced, staring at Baker. At first he responded with a smirk. But then he was unable to hold back the compressed chortles. Then he burst into outright laughter. He couldn't help it. The words from Baker's mouth sounded like execution orders coming from a Smurf imitating Woody Allen.

Chambers apologized after his outburst. He composed himself and heard the rest of Baker's plan.

Chapter 62

The Rose and Raindrop bar was ironically next to the Saint Vincent's Mission detox center on southeast Grand Avenue. Temptation was only short steps away. Paulson and Grimsley agreed to meet there at 5 p.m to catch up on the events of the day.

When Grimsley arrived, Paulson was already at the bar nursing a Scotch. The happy hour crowd was thin, but growing and only a few stools were occupied at the massive elaborately carved Oak bar. The space next to Paulson was empty except for a small glass with the potent brown liquid.

"For you," Paulson said, smiling and pointing to the glass as Grimsley stepped up next to him.

Grimsley picked up the glass and in a single gulp emptied it. Glenlevit, double malt, aged 15 years.

"Can you afford that kind of Scotch on your salary?"

Paulson raised his glass to Grimsley.

"Your welcome," he said and finished off the drink without flinching.

Grimsley held up his finger to the bartender.

"Vick," he yelled, "Another round here."

Vick, a pudgy, balding man with a cherub face said, "Sure chief, just keep an open credit card on these and maybe I can retire sooner than later."

"You try to retire, Vick, and I'll hunt you down, stalk you, break into your house and order drinks from you while you're trying to take a crap."

"Grimsley," Vick said, smiling, "you know as well as I do that my Scotch will be kept in a safe next to my Smith and Wesson. You get the Scotch, you also get a slug in the ass."

Grimsley and Paulson laughed. Vick slid the drinks in front of them.

"How the hell are you Paulson?" Grimsley asked.

"I'm fine, sir. I have some new information to report on this Jane—"

"Not that Paulson," Grimsley interrupted. "How the hell are YOU." He pointed a boney finger at Paulson.

"I…I'm…okay," Paulson answered sheepishly. He wasn't' sure how much to tell.

"How's your wife? Your house? Your family? Your friends? It's customary in our society to participate in small talk about our lives before diving into business. For those of us who have personal lives anyway."

Already feeling he effects of the first drink, Paulson sipped the drink this time, instead of gulping.

"Well, sir, Donna—that's my wife—is doing fine."

"She's a registered nurse at OHSU, right?"

"That's right sir. Been there a couple of years now."

"She's African American, isn't she?"

"Of course, sir," Paulson replied, seeming offended by the implications.

"You sound put off by that question."

"A little," Paulson replied.

"Nowadays, that question is not so unusual. It's almost expected, what with everybody marrying everybody else. There's a cross-cultural craze going on right now. White guys vowing only to marry Asian women. White women swearing off White men. Hispanic women who will only marry White men. It's quite an interesting development, don't you think Paulson?"

"Yes, sir, I do," Paulson started, "The cultures are blending and cultural identities are being blended...and lost at the same time."

"You sound like you have a problem with that."

"I do." Paulson hesitated before continuing. "I think there was some comfort, some security in races sticking with their own. Black culture is not what it used to be. The support networks are broken and we've lost our sense of family."

"I see," said Grimsley, "so the black community no longer goes to the same Baptist church and sings the same old Negro spirituals they used to and talk about how oppressed they are and happy they are to have their own community that's isolated from the rest of the world like inner city reservations."

"That's a simplistic, racist view."

"It is. But so is yours. If I wasn't mistaken, I'd say that deep down inside you are a closet racist."

"That's not true, sir, I just believe we should stick to our own kind."

"Paulson," Grimsley said, "I've heard too many Klan members say the exact same thing."

"That's bullshit sir. It's not the same thing."

"Show your fangs Paulson. Don't hold anything back. I call it like you see it, but it's not bullshit. I've spent enough time around White people AND Black people to know a racist when I see one. You're not a classic racist in the sense that you don't want to round up all the White people and ship them back to England. You're what I call a reverse racist. You want all the benefits of this society but you think we should all be separate. You're an equal-but-united-and-separate racist."

Paulson laughed. So did Grimsley.

"That's funny," Paulson said. "If you put it that way, there's some truth to what you say. I can't deny the benefits of assimilation."

"You mean Borg style assimilation?"

They laughed again.

Paulson was warming up to Grimsley.

"No. Not quite like that. I mean, acting, thinking, seeming part of this culture. But at the same time maintaining our identity," Paulson said

"You mean like the Chinese and the Russians and the Eastern Indians?"

"Yes, like those cultural groups."

"Problem Paulson."

"What's that?"

"African Americans don't really have a culture."

"I don't agree."

"African Americanism is like Catholicism. A lose set of rules to identify everyone as associates. And not everybody follows the same rules. With Black culture, you're born into it. Your skin color gets you in the front door. After that, all there is is the victim mentality, Negro spirituals, fried chicken, diabetes, Dolomite, Superfly, Michael Jordon, rap, a form of dialect called Ebonics and..." he paused, "and the pursuit of White women."

"Jeesus, Grimsley," Paulson said, shocked, "Your brand of social theory doesn't leave much room for logic does it."

"So tell me I'm wrong. What is black culture?" Grimsley prodded.

"Well, it's a sense of community, of feeling a part of something special, unique, something for young people to identify with..."

"I rest my case."

Paulson did not answer. Instead, he sipped his drink, looked at Grimsley, who was staring at him intently.

"All right Grimsley, that sense of black community may be as nebulous as the sense of White community. And the reason White people are so angry is they are also trying to hold on to something that doesn't really exist and that they don't really own."

"What's that Paulson?"

"You either aptly or offensively portrayed Black culture. Now it's my turn."

"Fire away."

"White culture, or Bubbaism is clinging to any Anglo-originated religion, bowling, skiing, operas nobody gets, Camaros with loud mufflers and mag wheels, duck-billed caps with farm implements on them, bad teeth, cancer, Volkswagens, cluelessness, hanging out in expensive restaurants talking about absolutely nothing, incest, pedophilia and—here's where you really stand corrected—White women in pursuit of black men."

"I'll be God damn," Grimsley said. "Paulson, you may be an African American, but you're as sharp as they come."

They laughed together and ordered another drink.

"Now that we've broken the ice—or made it thicker," Grimsley said, "What have we got on this young girl with a taste for intrigue?"

Chapter 63

Rich was ecstatic. He needed music to match his mood. He rifled through a plastic drawer organizer that held all of his CDs. He took out Jeffrey Lorber's greatest hits CD and put it in the player.

In seconds, the funky bass and synthesized piano filled the room. Rich cranked up the volume. The ground vibrated under his feet and Rich began dancing around the room, snapping his fingers, shaking his hips and thumbing an imaginary bass.

Lorber's music, Rich thought, was the ultimate happy music, made by a jazz funkafile who learned from the masters—Ramsey Lewis, Herbie Hancock, George Benson and the funkmaster of them all, Bootsie Collins.

Rich couldn't hear the phone over the music. But he saw the red call indicator flashing. In his excitement, he decided not to screen his calls. He pranced over to his desk and picked up the receiver—and immediately regretted his actions.

"Rich," the voice of Sam Enison boomed, *"How ya doin?"*

Rich's heart sank and his stomach knotted up. Enison was the last person he wanted to talk to. But he was committed. He couldn't hang up. Being rude could upset the fragile understanding he and Enison had.

"Rich," Enison repeated again. Rich did not answer. *"Rich, you there?"*

"Yes, sir Mr. Enison," Rich responded. "I'm here."

"Hey Rich, maybe you could turn that music down a little so we can talk."

"Uh, yeah. Hold on a second."

Rich set the phone down, and walked across the room. When he turned the music down, the silence was oppressive, stifling. Rich wanted to turn and run out of the front door and never come back. Instead, he picked up the receiver.

"Hello Mr. Enison, how can I help you?"

"Rich, it sounded like some kind of party. You celebrating something?"

"No, sir Mr. Enison, just getting ready to go out."

"I see," Enison said. There was silence.

"I won't keep you long Rich. We need to talk. Got a minute."

Rich knew he couldn't say no.

"Yeah, Mr. Enison. I've got a minute."

"Good," Enison said. Rich bit his finger nails as Enison continued. He had a feeling this was not going to be good.

"I've been getting some pressure from my manager here who's been getting pressure from our client. He says that we're going to need a payment sooner than next Friday. Rich, can you help me out here?"

Rich was stunned. He debated. Tell or don't tell. If he told, Enison would want his full advance. If he didn't, he'd have to make up some kind of lie.

"I don't have any extra money Mr. Enison. I'm tapped out."

Enison didn't answer immediately. He waited. Rich could hear his breathing in the receiver. Sweat formed around the ear piece as he pressed it harder against his ear, waiting for a response.

"Rich, that's not what my manager is hoping to hear me report back."

"I'm sorry Mr. Enison. I'm working three jobs right now," Rich jumped in. "There just isn't anything left over."

"You know Rich, I like to think that you and I have become sort of friends. That kind of thing happens when people talk as much as we do."

Rich tried to anticipate where Enison was leading with his comments so he could defend himself. Feelings of despair stifled his thoughts. The profound sense of joy he felt earlier had turned to dread.

Enison continued his gentle reaming that was both friendly and condescending.

"And Rich, I have to tell you, I'm more than a little disappointed."

"I'm sorry, Mr. Enison," Rich said. "I don't know what to tell you."

"Rich, please call me Sam. You disrespect me when you're so formal."

"I'm sorry Mr....Sam, I really don't know what to say. I promised to send you more money at the end of the month. I thought we had an agreement."

"We did, Rich," Sam said, *"but you had another agreement that carries more weight. An agreement with your credit card company to pay your bills on time. And you broke that agreement."*

"Look, we've been through this. I said I was sorry and I'm doing what I can to pay you back."

This call reminded Rich of the first difficult phone call he ever had with Enison. They were complete strangers then. Enison was angry. He did his best to bully and humiliate Rich and over the hour that they talked, Rich mostly listened and tried to convince Enison he would come through and only needed a little more time. Eventually, Enison gave in and cut him some slack.

But Rich could tell something else had changed and Rich could sense it and hear it in Enison's voice. It wasn't just the client or the manager as Enison said. Enison was too tough for that.

"Rich, I've been given an ultimatum so I have to give you one as well. My client has asked for a $4,000 payment by Wednesday of next week."

"What!" Rich yelled into the phone. "Mr. Enison, Jeesus Christ. Where am I going to get that kind of money from."

"I don't know rich," Enison said, "but if I don't receive a payment, I've been instructed to file the necessary papers to bring a lawsuit against you and your wife. And Rich, I don't have to remind you that you AND your wife are liable here. If you lose, her wages can be attached and we can force you to sell your property or take out a loan to pay back this money."

"Mr. Enison. Listen. You gotta give me some more time." Rich pleaded.

"Sorry Rich, there is no more time. A check must be post marked by 5 p.m. this coming Wednesday or all bets are off."

As Rich talked, he caught a glimpse of his face in a small hand-painted mirror hanging on the wall over his desk. He could see the fear in his eyes. He was trapped, like a rabbit cornered by a grizzly bear.

"All right. All right. Mr. Enison, um, uh, let me think about this..."

"Rich, you know I went to bat for you," Enison said, "But this one is out of my hands. You come through for me this week and I'll see what I can do. Right now, Rich, it's still you and me. But if we don't get a payment this week, you're going to need to bring your wife into the picture. We already know there's enough equity in your house and money in her retirement fund to resolve this matter today."

"No," Rich snapped. "This is not her problem. I created this problem. It's my problem and I need to deal with it."

"Rich. Come on. Be reasonable. You need all the help you can get."

"Look, Mr. Enison. I'll figure something out."

"You sound pretty sure, Rich. You come into some money?"

"No," Rich snapped.

His answer was quick, but not quick enough. Enison knew he was lying.

"Okay Rich. Take it easy. I believe you. Remember. Wednesday. Don't disappoint me."

Enison did not wait for an answer. He hung up. The sound of Enison's voice replayed again and again in Rich's ear as the dial tone hummed in the background. Rich carefully placed the phone on the receiver, sat in his chair and buried his face in his hands, not sure whether to cry or laugh.

When he looked up, the clock read a quarter to 3:00. Time to put on his family face and pick up the kids. Later he would give the performance of his life. He would pretend everything was all right as he suffered quietly. He thought about the book. The rewrites had to be perfect. Nothing could interfere with the advance check. It was too important.

Chapter 64

Chico listened to the creaking cables of the 80 year old elevator as it laboriously moved upward. It jolted to a stop almost causing Chico to lose his balance. He was prepared to scream if the elevator plunged unrestrained to the bottom of the shaft.

The thick main door slid to one side, leaving the metal folding door. Chico gripped it and shoved it aside and walked out into the hall. As he passed the metal door, he sneered at it as if it had offended him in some way.

Chico became aware again that his clothes were wet. The rush of adrenaline from his encounter with the front desk clerk had pushed his situation out of his mind. In an instant it was back. He wanted to get out of the wet clothes, get some food, get some big tit magazines, some Coors light and relax.

As he walked past the doors in the hallway, he could hear television talk shows, music, the wailing of a baby and a man yelling in Hindi.

The carpet was dirt brown, stained and neglected, and the walls contained brightly painted tags from made up gang names, nothing Chico recognized. Gang member wannabes, Chico thought. "Fucking losers," he growled as he passed the tags.

Chico held up his key and checked the room numbers on the doors as he passed. When he reached the end of the long, dreary hallway, he found the door that matched his key. He pushed the key into the scratched and battered lock.

As Chico stepped in and turned on the light switch. The light and the smell arrived at the same time, the distinct odor of urine, sex, shit and chlorine assaulted his senses. This was familiar and foreign to Chico. The difference was these smells were not his. They were offensive, repugnant and this territory was marked by another male, a predator and a competitor.

Chico shuffled into the room and surveyed it. The single hotel surplus lamp with the large bulbous green floral print base was the only real color in the room. Next to the lamp was a dirt brown sofa-bed. A small desk and chair occupied a corner window. Next to the desk was a darkened bathroom.

Fucking shit hole, Chico thought. But it was only one shit hole gold star removed from his apartment—and he knew it.

Chico walked to the bathroom and pulled the light switch that hung from the ceiling. The dull bulb illuminated an ancient, stained sink, a molded shower big enough for one, and a toilet that hissed and occasionally refilled by itself when enough brownish water leaked out of the tank, triggering the float to refill the bowl.

Chico turned on the shower and a thin stream of rust-colored water sputtered out of the head. After the air pockets cleared, a solid stream of clear water flowed out and disappeared down the partially plugged drain.

Chico took off his wet clothes and draped what he could over the bathroom door. He took his pants into the living room, pulled the single chair from the desk close to the steam heated radiator and hung them there, along with his coat.

He would feel better after a shower, he thought. The dread he felt would go away, and the aching in his heart would subside.

Through the thin walls, Chico recognized the music of Cubanisimo. Chico was not political. He rarely read, and knew nothing of history, but he had respect for Cuba and Castro. Castro was his hero because he shook his dick at America. Chico listened to salsa and afro Cubano music whenever he could. When he listened to their music, he felt as though everything was right; everything would be okay.

As Chico walked to the shower, he did a Latin three step, holding up his hands as if dancing with a partner and simulated a turn. Fuck Trixie. Fuck the pigs. Fuck everybody.

"Cubanisima is some bad motherfuckers," Chico said. Mimicking the song he heard, Chico sang, "Tiem Bien Passo, Tiem Bien Passo, be my mother fucking bitch asshole." Chico substituted the real words with profanities.

He entered the shower.

Chapter 65

"All right Paulson," Grimsley barked, "We've wasted enough time getting to know each other. What did you find out?"

"I love you too Captain," Paulson said sarcastically.

They both sipped another drink before Paulson continued.

"Sir, we canvassed the neighborhood. Folks on that block keep to themselves. Most have seen our girl but none have ever spoken to her."

"Any descriptions of visitors, cars, acquaintances."

"No, sir," Paulson answered. "One neighbor said the van his been there about a year. Most goings on take place after midnight. Senior citizens mostly. No insomniacs in the bunch. Most sleep like rocks sir."

"That's not helping us solve this Paulson."

"I know, sir. Our girl kept to herself. She was either sleeping during the day or somewhere else."

"I'm betting somewhere else Paulson," Grimsley said. "But the only way we can find that somewhere else is to find out who she is or find somebody who knew her or saw what the hell went on there at night."

"Any luck with Capt. Holister, sir?"

Grimsley's mood soured at the mention of Holister's name. "God damn illiterate son of a bitch. Paulson, if you remember two things in your life, remember this: "Stay away from Turkish prisons and Capt. Holister. That bastard will try to screw you any chance he gets."

"I figured as much, sir. He's been riding me ever since I joined the force two years ago."

"He's like those God damn thumb thumbs in the Spy Kids movie. You see that one, Paulson?"

"No, sir," Paulson said, smirking at the thought, "sounds like a kids movie. Don't have any kids."

"Keerist Paulson, you don't have to have kids to see kids movies. Some of these movies are great. Look at Siskell and Ebert. They see every God damn movie there is. Maybe I should say three things to remember, the last being, never grow old."

"I'll try to remember that, sir."

"Anyway, that's beside the point. Holister will give us some breathing room, but we get no media exposure, no reward drive, no picture because she may be a minor."

"Doesn't sound like we get anything at all, sir."

"Almost, but we get a little. We get full lab resources. I get you full time. And we get the full treatment if we uncover an international conspiracy involving a national threat."

"What kind of threat, sir?"

Grimsley cleared his throat, "Well, Paulson, nuclear war ought to do it."

"If you weren't serious, I'd say that was funny, sir."

"It's God damn funny Paulson. Permission to laugh. Paulson, we're missing something, so I want to go back to the crime scene in the morning. You go home and get some sleep. We've got a busy day tomorrow."

"When are you going to the scene, sir."

"Three a.m."

"I'll be there sir. "

"No, Paulson, you stay home and sleep off this fine bourbon with your wife. You can report to the office at 9 a.m. tomorrow, punch in and wait for me."

"I don't think so, sir." Paulson replied, "If we're going to solve this, sir, I need to stick to you like..."

"Like what Paulson?"

"Like white on rice, sir."

"Like a tick on a cows ass." Grimsley added.

"Yes sir. Like that too."

"You son of a bitch." Grimsley said. He finished his drink, regarded Paulson's offer and his insult then continued, "Don't be late or I'll come drag your ass out of bed. Don't care if you're trying to catch a quickie with your wife before you leave. You say you'll be here, I'll hold your ass to it."

"I reserve the right to come drag your ass out of bed too, sir, even if you're doing whatever it is you old fuckers do with yourselves before you get out of bed in the mornings."

Grimsley couldn't contain himself any longer. His outburst of laughter caught the attention of the entire bar.

"Grimsley," Vick yelled from the end of the bar, "go the fuck home. I'm starting to lose business 'cause you and your little friend there are so God damn annoying."

"Hey Vick," Grimsley yelled, "meet me on the gun range tomorrow. I need a target you fuck."

"Get the fuck outta here!" Vick answered and winked at Paulson as he gave him a sly grin.

"Let's get the hell out of here Paulson before it gets ugly."

Chapter 66

The dark figure slipped the key into the lock of Trixie's apartment door, opened it, stepped inside and gently closed the door.

The setting Sun's rays beamed through one open window, refracting throughout the room and blending with the pink and lavender hues of the paint on the walls, furniture and shelves.

The dark figure examined the room.

Fastidious, he thought, much like himself, a girl who reveled in the complexities of human nature. He recognized many of the book titles on the shelves. Fromm. Shakespeare. Bombeck. Stein. Her interest covered the gamut of subject matter. How, he thought, or why did she decide to take her life in the direction that she did.

As he walked past the futon bed with the pink down comforter, he wondered who may have lay in that bed and what kinds of things she did with them. He touched the comforter gently and smiled. He was curious and he was aroused at the same time. But he also had a job to do and he didn't want to linger any longer than he needed to.

He walked to the shelves and began removing books and examining their contents. One after another, he carefully flipped through each page, checked the binding, held each book open by the ends of the spines and shook the books. Lose papers, mostly bookmarks and receipts for purchase of the books fell out on to the floor.

The dark figure gathered them up as they fell out and examined them. He loved invading the privacy of others. As he flipped through pages, he thought about the secrets he had discovered during the years he indulged in this passion, including the secrets he had discovered about his first wife—now ex-wife, and the bizarre and kinky rendezvous she had while he traveled.

He had misjudged her, he thought. He had trusted her. A mistake. But she was human, and she, like all weak humans, gave away her own secrets by trying to hide them. Over the years, the clues became more and more obvious. She became more distant, more irritable, and more elusive, and he became more aware. Like any good hunter, he thought, he could sense fear, and as each day of her deception passed, she became more afraid.

It was easy to find out what she was up to, once he decided to. That's what he was good at. That's what he got paid to do; find out what people did—what people didn't want you to know. And he had an arsenal of the most sophisticated equipment at this disposal.

He set the trap before taking a protracted business trip to Afghanistan on a counter espionage job. Before leaving he set up five micro cameras with motion sensors in his bedroom, one in every other room in the house, and voice activated throughout the house. They all to feed into his computer.

On top of that, he bugged every phone in the house, including her cell phone. She would not suspect that, he thought. And, he install a GPS tracking device in her mini van that was enhanced with a high sensitivity listening and filtering device that monitored noise levels automatically and was capable of interpreting and clearly recording and separating sounds within a 50 yard radius based on pre-defined algorithms. It could filter out cars, animals other interference, break them into categories. He had programmed the filter to listen for, fucking.

Brilliant, he thought. The database driven programs searched the Internet for sounds to compare and found 10,000 examples to filter against. And it could display the location based on a geographic and topographic satellite link.

Even more brilliant, he thought.

He considered it comical that his most sophisticated and efficient surveillance operation would be on his own wife.

As he thought about her, his mind hesitantly used the word wife or ex-wife, because other words like slut, bitch and whore clawed their way into his consciousness, pushing out any pleasant thoughts that may have existed before. He fought the same battle he always did and pushed those words out of his head. As much as he hated her, he still loved her and blamed himself for everything that went wrong.

His attentions focused back on his task when he noticed a book that seemed out of place. The jacket was too big to fit the book, a quarter inch too thick and a half inch too tall.

He removed the book from the shelf and opened it. There were no publishers markings. He removed the jacket and observed a handmade green and red binding with an abstract pattern made from multi-textured rice papers.

The dark figure grinned as he realized that he had found what he was looking for. He flipped back to the inside cover and saw, in the upper left hand corner handwriting that said TRIXIE, Book #25. His elation quickly waned when he read the number this book placed in the series. He flipped through more pages and scanned the neat even-spaced writing.

Read them later, he thought. Find the other books. He continued checking every book on every shelf. By the time he came to the last book on the shelf, he had discovered five more journals, all of them filled from beginning to end with stories, observations, graphic details of sexual experiences and the longings of a little girl forced to grow up too soon, and most importantly, names and backgrounds of her customers, including his client.

Next he checked drawers, behind pictures, careful not to overlook anything or miss any secret hiding places.

He had to erase any evidence that might identify certain parties. His discipline was complete. Execute precisely. Finish the task perfectly.

When he finished his search, he removed a cell phone from the breast pocket of his black double-breasted jacket and punched in a phone number.

"Hello," he said to the voice on the other end. "I'm finished. Send a truck."

He listened intently and when a nervous voice responded he barked firmly, "20 footer. Fifteen minutes sharp. Get over here."

He pressed the stop button. He didn't argue. He had no penchant for exaggeration. He dealt in facts and realities. Theories were only relevant when they related to achieving an assigned task.

He was well versed in philosophy, economics, politics and art. But none of that was as real as telling some piss-ant who worked for him that his orders were never to be questioned. And a screw up or breach of trust was the equivalent of a death wish.

He liked to control things that way. He controlled his wife that way, which is why her departure from what he considered normal was so extreme, so dramatic and so bizarre.

She knew the rules, and he liked that fact that she was afraid of him. That was power. And he assumed his indoctrination was so complete, that she would never dare cross him because of the fear he had instilled. She called him sir when they were in the house and she knew to pleasure him whenever he demanded.

Unquestioning service and obedience, he thought, was true love. Plus, if she did everything he demanded, he would not beat her, like a dog he had when he was a young boy. Women had to be retrained to think that they are only bitches after all. Good for sex, child bearing and all things domestic. All a husband needed was sex and exceptional service and he was happy.

But he had missed something. He had miscalculated something. She strayed for some reason and he could only blame himself.

When he cleared the call, he thought about Trixie. He envied her in a way. She had brains, money and true power, power she still wielded even after death.

While he waited for the truck, he stared at the sunset; brilliant, golden, fractured into shades of blue, orange and red.

Then his thoughts drifted back to his ex-wife and her transgression.

When he returned from his trip to Afghanistan, he, at first, refused to review the audio and digital recordings captured in his absence. He wasn't sure he wanted to see what was on them. But he was driven by voyeuristic instincts and his Machiavellian nature. The tapes represented power, power he needed, power he loved, and power he could use to destroy someone who he suspected had defied him.

It took a quarter bottle of Jack Daniel's to screw his courage and another fifth of Knob Creek to guide his legs to the control panel and editing station behind a carefully camouflaged section of his book shelf.

It was 2 a.m. Everyone was sleeping. As he drank, he listened to Rachmeinonof. The drama of his hunting symphonies complimented his mood.

He approached the keyboard and the glowing 30 inch plasma monitor that hung on the wall above the desktop station. He typed a password into the input field on the screen and pressed the return button. He could hear the hard disk cycling up and the hourglass on the screen indicated that the system was engaging. He had programmed the system to launch the video cataloging and editing program and access all wave and mpeg files that had been saved since the last time he accessed the program.

He typed in another set of commands that asked the system to display all files with associated audio and cataloged the segments by the first ten words in each segment. He could review all video files and search for irregularities.

When the search ended, the displayed 50 segments, each with 10 words and an ellipses on the end. He scanned them all. There was nothing unusual about the segments.

The system wasn't fool proof. If non of the cataloged segments were extraordinary, he would have to search by keywords. Or he could do another random search. The powerful processor could do these searches in seconds but it required choosing the right keywords or a little luck.

He clicked on random audio entries. Most involved the children. Dinner. Bed. Lunch. Then his eyes fell on one entry and froze there, glued to the words. It was logged at 10:10 p.m. on a Sunday. It read, "It's okay, they won't hear us..."

He moved the cursor over the entry and hesitated before double-clicking on the line. He was apprehensive about what this line might be in reference to. A visiting girlfriend perhaps. A family member staying over night. He would not think about any other possibility. Not yet any way.

His eyes were bloodshot and his coordination was tentative. He took another long drink from the bottle of Knob Creek. His mouth was dry and his breath as fierce as the contents of the bottle. He could feel his blood boiling as the alcohol ran through his veins, denying his body oxygen, forcing his system to overcompensate.

With a few keystrokes, he found the associated audio-video file. He pressed the button on the mouse and the file opened instantly. He stood emotionless watching the images on the screen. He didn't blink. He even seemed to stop breathing.

The audio track continued, "I'm sorry, I didn't mean to be so loud."

A lamp near the bed clearly illuminated the two figures. On the bottom with legs spread wide like a swans wings flapping ready to take flight, lay his wife. In between her legs was a man with pale tight buttocks, thrusting himself in and out of her as she groaned and gyrated with pleasure, matching her motions exactly. Her legs shuddered as he pushed in and out of her and he moaned with pleasure.

When she reached around and gripped his buttocks and pulled him deeper inside of her, he could take no more. He stood up and threw the bottle at his book shelf, hard enough for it to shatter into tiny pieces. Consumed by rage he dashed over to his desk drawer, opened the small drawer and took out a document and slammed in onto the top of the desk.

He walked to the door of the den, opened it and walked to the end of the hallway, where the master bedroom was, threw it open and walked around to the side of his bed where his wife slept soundly.

She screamed as he grabbed her by the hair, lifted her up and drug her off the bed, forcing her to stumble and cry as he dragged her out of the room to the den and forced her face into the monitor that displayed her prone, being fucked by a man he neither new nor cared to know.

She wept and screamed, "I'm sorry! I'm sorry!"

She was dead to him. To him, this was an irrevocable offense. He needed no explanation. No apologies. He had no time for that. Still gripping her hair, he lead her to the chair beside his desk and shoved her into it. He walked to the leather executive chair, sat in it, turned it to face her and stared at her as she sobbed and buried her face in her hands.

"You fucked up," he said as a matter of fact, not a matter for debate. She refused look at him.

"You only get to do that once and live," he continued. "I don't want to know how it happened or how many times you did it or who that fucking asshole is. I just want you the fuck out of here."

He pushed the document over to her and said, "This document is your salvation. You will get to see your children. I will not deny you that. You get a hundred thousand dollars to do whatever the fuck you want with. I don't give a shit. But if you don't sign this now, you will not live to see your children graduate from high school and I will make sure that your life is a living hell before you die."

She raised her head and stared at him through disheveled strands of hair. The lack of emotion in his voice and the calculating tone assured her that he was serious. She reached over and pulled the paper close to her and started to read it.

"Don't you fucking dare," he yelled. "Sign the God damn document and get the fuck out of this house."

She winced and fixed her eyes on him again. Her natural beauty was diminished by the intense fear in her eyes. Her hazel eyes were dull and dead. She was ghost white except for her nose, which was red with snot smeared below it. She did not speak.

She signed the document. He wrote her a check for one hundred thousand dollars and handed it to her.

"My lawyer will contact you with all other necessary arrangement. I'll collect the shit you can take."

She started to speak, but he cut her off, "I don't want to hear another word from your fucking mouth. You have nothing to say to me.. Get...The...Fuck...Out...Bitch."

He turned his chair away from her and stared out the picture window into the night as she crawled down the hall, packed a small bag and left the house.

Across the room, his ears focused in on the faint sound coming from the computer, the sound of couple climaxing together then silence, the satisfied couple falling asleep curled in each others arms.

His anger turned to feelings of victory and satisfaction and power. He didn't indulge petty emotions for too long. There was too much to be done.

When his wife read the contract, she would find that it was complete. No holes had been left out. It also assured complete confidentiality. That he was sure of. He had been wrong about her before, but there would not be a second time.

His thoughts were interrupted by a knock on the door. He

looked through the peep hole. When he opened the door, two men, one a wiry middle-aged man with dark mustache, extreme overbite and the look of a second year cop. The other was heavy set, frumpy and built for bowling and drinking beer. His pock marked face was flush from too much gin the night before. They resembled a White trash version of Laurel and Hardy as they wheeled in a dolly stacked with flat boxes.

"Gentlemen, you have three hours. Everything needs to be in boxes and in that truck and gone. NOTHING is to be left behind. You understand?" he asked.

"Yeah, sure," the wiry man Neal said. Larry followed with the same.

"I'll take care of everything at the front desk. Wash everything down. Scrub everything. I want it to look like NOBODY lived here."

The men did not say anything this time. Nor did he expect them to. He left the room as Laurel and Hardy went to work erasing this part of Trixie's life.

Chapter 67

The crowd was thinning at Skates as Chambers, more amused than anything with Bakers demeanor and inability to hold his liquor, considered his proposition. Baker continued blabbering about anything and everything, slurring his words and spraying droplets of spit over the entire table in front of him as he spoke.

Baker pointed a long skinny finger at Chambers, leaned in towards him and said, "Between you and me Mr. Chambers, I'm going to let you in on a secret."

He looked around for prying ears but it was late and the booths surrounding them were empty. Confident no-one was listening, Baker continued, "The Return of the Jedi was the best of the Star Wars series."

"That's it," Chambers said abruptly. "You're fucked up Baker. Time to get your ass home."

Chambers stood up and whistled at the waitress with the 25% tip smile. He'd been feeding her tips all evening and she had warmed up to his course style.

He learned her name was Sara. Sara bounced over to Chambers and said, "Mr. Chambers is everything okay here. Her smile was magnificent, chiseled out of sorority girl stone and perhaps finished by direct descendents of the Goddess of glamour models herself. She placed a hand on Chambers shoulder. "Is there anything I can get you, sir."

"Sure sweetheart," Chambers said, taking her beauty in. "Come with me, I need to talk to you."

Chambers placed his arm around her waist and led her to a spot two booths away from where Sara didn't seem to mind Chambers' hand and leaned into him, rubbing her breast and hips against him as they walked.

Baker sat, dazed and confused by himself.

"How old are you sweetheart?"

"Twenty five," she answered and flashed another brilliant smile.

"Listen, honey, don't get the wrong idea with the question, but do you have a boyfriend?"

She blushed. "Not right now. I'm in between boyfriends."

"What a shame. You're very easy on the eyes, you know that?"

"Thank you," She said, looking down, afraid to make eye contact and blushing slightly.

"Look at me sweetheart." He lifted her chin with his index finger until their eyes met, "I'm an old fuck, probably 10 times your age, but I still know a beautiful dame when I see one. If you're not doing anything after work tonight, I want to ask you do something for me."

She hesitated, twisted the end of her mouth, shifted feet, then said, "I don't know."

"It's not what you think sister"

He turned and pointed at Baker.

"See that fuck."

"Yeah," she answered.

"He's an idiot. But he's my client. He's drunk. I have to get him home. But I'd also like to talk to you some more, so here's what I want you to do."

He reached into his pocket and pulled out a set of keys.

"In the parking lot is a black 2002 Lamborghini Testarosa. You know what I'm talking about."

"Like Magnum."

"Smart girl. You know your cars. Cost me a years wages but it keeps me honest."

She laughed at the thought.

"Here are the keys. I'm going to drive dip wad home in his Pinto."

He dropped the keys into her hand.

"I want you to meet me at Prego's at around midnight."

Sara's eyes lit up.

"Prego's. Can you really get in?"

"Sure baby. I got some markers to call with the owner."

Sara shivered at the thought of getting into Prego's.

"Now, I don't want nothin' from you. You're young. You seem like a bright girl. I got a little cash I need to spend, so do you think I should spend it on you and make a kid happy?"

She wasn't sure how to respond.

"Well, sure...I don't know."

"Well, the answer is yes. You know, I can't take it with me when I die, and I'd rather spend it on a pretty girl than that prick over there."

Sara giggled.

"Drop by your apartment and put on your Sunday best will ya. I try to dress like a fuckin' king and the bastards sometimes give me a hard time. We have a deal?"

Sara was beaming now.

"Sure thing Mr. Chambers."

"All right then," Chambers said, "I gotta go. And by the way, thanks for being a sport about my being such a asshole. So many young girls today got no sense of humor. You. You're okay."

He kissed her on the forehead.

"See you later."

Chambers, walked to the table and pulled Baker up from the seat. He continued blabbering nonsensical gibberish. Chambers led him towards the front door. As Sara returned to the table to clean it off, Chambers glanced back at her and winked, put on his vintage Stetson and hauled Baker to his car and his home.

Chapter 68

Rich bluffed his way through dinner, feigning normalcy. He hated these times in his life. Times when he was angry that he had made such stupid mistakes, and was frustrated that he couldn't reveal his secrets. And because his children and April made him happy, he was angry that he couldn't be sad and sullen and somber. He couldn't just disappear; get in his car and drive for three thousand miles until he came to the smallest town he could find in Pennsylvania and start all over again, no questions asked as he'd done when he was younger.

He was stuck but wanted to be stuck and hated being stuck at the same time. He desperately wanted to say he didn't have a care in the world, that all was right and the only thing left to do in life was watch his kids grow, retire and die.

The reality of Rich's life was that he always chose the hard things; never wanted the easy way out and was a risk taker. He loved the chase for success but wasn't much good at handling it.

He retired to his den after dinner to think about his dilemma. Delivering newspapers made it impossible to stay up past 8 p.m. for more than a day and he'd gotten two hours of sleep in two days. Something had to give.

Rich put Pat Matheney's CD *As Falls Wichita, So Falls Wichita Falls* into the CD player and turned it on. It matched his mood, contemplative, complex, distant.

Pretending took a lot of emotional energy and Rich was exhausted. Within seconds after the song *Ozark* filled the air, Rich had settled into the felt-cloth covered armchair and was sleeping soundly.

Rich was awakened by a strange sensation in his ears. As he uneasily opened his eyes, he found Juan sitting in his lap with his fingers in Rich's ear and manipulating Rich's face with the other hand.

Rich grabbed Juan in a bear hug and pulled him close. Juan giggled.

"What are you doing you little sneaker?"

"Making faces with your face," he said between giggles.

"What do you think I am some kind of puppet?"

Juan reached out and pushed up the ends of Rich's mouth, "Sure daddy, you're a clown."

"That's it!" Rich said, "you're in big trouble now."

Rich tickled Juan and he squirmed to get away.

"That'll learn you."

Rich stopped tickling and hugged Juan.

"Hey Daddy," Juan said.

"What sport."

"Your were drooling."

He giggled again.

"Is that so?"

"Yahaa," Juan answered.

"And you never drool when you sleep?"

"Not me daddy."

"I beg to differ," Rich said sarcastically, "When you were a baby, we used to have to put buckets under your mouth because you drooled so much."

"Na-aaaaa!"

"Absolutely. In fact there was a flood in Portland back when you were a baby. Devastating. Homes destroyed. Mass hysteria. People running for the hills, floating away in bath tubs. It was terrible."

Sounding slightly older than his six years, Juan twisted his face, rolled his eyes and asked, "Duh, dad, what's that got to do with drooling."

"Duh, you," Rich said, "That was you buddy. Waves of spittle from your mouth, devastating Portland."

"Naa—aaah. You're telling a big fat one."

"Well, maybe there is a bit of exaggeration, but you get my point."

"Dad, you're delmmous—, um, what's that word?"

"Delirious?"

"That's it. Come on dad, I'll take you upstairs. Mom says you gotta come to bed. And so do I."

Juan led Rich upstairs, yelling "Mommy" at the top of the lungs the entire way. This, thought Rich as he watched the small human escorting him to his room, is why he had to make this work.

Chapter 69

Grimsley wasn't big on sleep. He considered it a waste of time. He'd read biographies on great men and observed that most great men seldom slept, drank whisky often and bedded women incessantly. These were common traits. The drawbacks, of course, were that their greatness and achievements were often coupled with reoccurring instances of insomnia-induced BAD decisions, multiple cases of venereal disease and plague-like occurrences of liver disease.

Grimsley did not want to go out that way. So he made some compromises in order to stay alive. He slept three to four hours every night, limited his intake of spirits and avoided young women, most of whom rarely had the intelligence to match their ability to fuck like rabbits and cause chaos for men.

He wasn't a misogynist, but he was a master of emotional self-defense. Young women unintentionally created chaos for men simply by being women. Older women, he established, deliberately manufactured chaos for men because they were angry at being born women, a wrong they hoped could be corrected by some waving of an evolutionary wand.

Grimsley stood by his Bronco on Going Street near where Trixie had been murdered. He listened to the sound of the night. Everything and almost everyone was sleeping, a natural cycle. Plants. Birds. Animals.

The afternoon downpour left the night air moist and fragrant with the rusty smell of decaying fall leaves. There was a hint of burning wood in the air from still smoldering fireplaces.

It was pitch black because thick clouds still blanketed the stars and threatened to again send more waves of rain down to cleanse the earth. Nature's wash-o-matic, Grimsley thought. Too bad rain couldn't wash away the dregs of the earth, the scumbags who lurked in the night, shooting young girls in the head and cowering in the dark corners of the earth waiting for their next victims.

Grimsley could hear Paulson's car approaching two blocks away. As it turned the corner onto Going Street and approached him, he took out a cigarette and lit it.

Paulson turned off his headlights and killed the engine. He stepped out of the car and walked over to Grimsley, wondering what kind of mood Grimsley might be in. Paulson could see the crimson bead of ash of Grimsley's cigarette moving up and down as Grimsley took evenly timed drags off the cigarette. They could not see each other's faces.

"Paulson." Grimsley said flatly.

"Captain."

"Walk with me." Paulson didn't answer. Grimsley turned and walked towards 52nd street. Paulson walked alongside him. Both men said nothing. What a pair we are, thought Paulson.

Grimsley broke the silence. "Any luck finding that bullet?"

"No, sir."

"I saw a fella in the school park around the corner with one of them metal detectors. Hobbyist, probably. But in some cases, those fellas are X military mine sweepers. Many from Nam. If they were in country, they could read brush the same way you and I read books and they can find a flea on a Buffalo's ass if they needed to. Tomorrow, you find that fella and tell him we need to find chunk of metal."

"But, sir, we've had men trampling all over that area. It will be much harder now and we've had our best men looking for it."

"Bunch of pricks," Grimsley said. "You find this fella. Offer him a thousand bucks."

"Yes, sir."

The two men fell silent. Only the sound of their footsteps echoed in the night. Grimsley lit another cigarette.

"You read the newspaper Paulson."

"I do, sir. Every day."

"What do you like about the newspaper?"

Paulson braced for a confrontation.

"I like the comics, sir."

Paulson couldn't see Grimsley's face, but he knew he was smiling.

"Me too," said Grimsley, "plus, I get a kick out of all that liberal crap they print too."

Don't you think it's a little early for a confrontation? Paulson thought but the words never made it to his lips.

"What time do you get your paper, Paulson?"

"I don't really know, sir. Well before I get up in the morning."

"What do you think, two thirty, three thirty, four o'clock."

"Well, it wasn't there when I left, so must be some time after three o'clock." Paulson said.

"Sounds about right," said Grimsley.

"You notice anything about this block?"

"Well, sir, I observe a lot of things. Are you leading me to something here, sir?

"Of course Paulson," Grimsley answered, "I'm always leading you to something. What kind of God damn mentor would I be if I wasn't?"

"What are you leading me to, sir?"

"Well, it wouldn't be much fun if I told you, now would it?"

"I guess not, sir." Paulson thought about Grimsley's questions. "All Right, Grimsley. You win."

"How's that, Paulson. Giving up so easily?"

"Don't count on it, sir."

Paulson paused for effect, seeing if Grimsley would take the bait.

"Murder occurred between three thirty and four thirty a.m. This street has mostly curbside newspaper tubes. Most customers pick up their papers around 6 a.m. I was a paperboy, so that much I know. Plus, that's the latest my paper should be delivered. Last night I observed that no papers were delivered either before or after the murder."

"Humm," Paulson said. "What does that tell us?"

"It's either a staggering coincidence that the carrier accidentally missed this block altogether or decided to skip it because of all the activity."

Humm," Paulson said again. "Or—"

"The paperboy saw something and panicked."

"Or—"

"The Paperboy did it."

"Or the God damn butler Paulson," Grimsley barked, "Keerist. You were doing great until you got to that one."

"Just exploring the possibilities, sir."

"I'll bet you are. Make the call Paulson, we need to find out about a paperboy."

Chapter 70

When Rich arrived at the station, Jimmy grabbed him by the arm and escorted him to the bathroom office. Jimmy would not reveal the nature of his sudden need to talk in private.

"Buddy," Jimmy said, "I don't know what kind of trouble you got yourself into. Ain't my business neither, but the Police was her looking to find out about you."

Rich started to tell Jimmy what happened, but decided not to. Instead he said, "Jimmy, I don't know what they want. What did you tell them?"

"I told them what I had to. You all right, Rich? I don't need no trouble from mister man," Jimmy said.

"You gave them my address?"

"The one I have. Here's a card. Negro police man came by. Lieutenant. You know a Negro got to work a long time fo them stripes. Educated too. I admire you young peoples. Negro got to kiss a lot of ass—"

"Jimmy, Thanks," Rich interrupted, not wanting Jimmy to lecture him about Negroes and colored folks. He was panicking and needed some air. The bathroom office was the last place anyone should spend more than a few minutes.

"It's nothing, Jimmy. Listen. I've got to get to my route."

"You best give that officer a call. Police like to take care of they business."

"I will, Jimmy. As soon as I finish my route. You remembered that I'm gone this weekend?"

"Yeah, I remembered," Jimmy assured Rich. "Got a newbie to come in and fill in."

Rich reached for the bathroom door.

"Oh, Rich, somebody else called asking about you earlier. Didn't say nothin' about who he was. Just asked if we had a paperboy who drove a white truck and was delivering yesterday on Going street. I told him who you was before I realized I bed get some mo information. When I asktit him who he was, he hung up. Strange voice. Sounded like one of them secret agent fellas, all sneaky and everything. You know. Could have been the police too. But I don't think so."

Rich was dazed and confused now.

"Um, uh. I don't know. Uh, Thanks."

Rich needed to think. As quickly as he could, he stuffed all his papers and started on his route. As he rounded each corner, he slowed and looked for anything suspicious, anything out of place.

Rich was particularly apprehensive about Going Street. He

already had a list of misses, all on Going street from the night before. To miss them two days in a row would be disastrous and obvious. He kept his music lower so he could hear everything and could think clearly.

As he approached Going Street, he slowed. Before he reached the intersection, he saw the Bronco parked near the corner and his internal alarms went off. He knew every car on the block except this one.

Instead of turning into Going, he drove slowly through the intersection. He couldn't see anyone. But that was to be expected. The darkness would have hidden anyone standing anywhere in the block. He could drop the papers at the end of his route instead.

Grimsley paced up and down Going street observing what time lights went on in the houses and what time cars left driveways. It was four o'clock and all houses were still dark and no cars had left. Grimsley was heading back to his Bronco when he saw the headlights enter the intersection, slow at first, then continue on.

Grimsley smiled. He already knew who it was. He needed a little more information though. And he would wait for a proper time to question him. Let him go home to his wife and kids.

Even though Paulson had insisted that they bring him in for questioning before he finished his route, Grimsley would not allow it.

"And who is going to delivery the papers, Paulson?" Grimsley had reminded.

Grimsley also reminded Paulson that a family man and homeowner is not likely to disappear and he reminded Paulson that the more you know before questioning anyone, the more likely it is you'll get the answer you already know you're going to get.

"Can't ask the right questions if you don't know the right answers already," Grimsley told him.

Chapter 71

Chico walked to the corner market and purchased beer, a dozen big tit magazines and some blow from a junkie who hung out in front of the store. Chico was feeling better about his life. His short term memory was taking over where long-term memory failed him. The events of that morning were fading fast, washed away by half a case of Coors Lite.

Within one hour after arriving at his hotel in Old Town, Chico had scored all the necessities of a man of his position and importance; shelter, booze, drugs and porn.

He still had money in his pocket, too, so to Chico the world was at his feet giving him a blow job. His only source of irritation now was the clerk in the lobby.

"Fucking son of bitch," Chico repeated to himself. He had been disrespected for the millionth time in his life, and that wasn't right. If he could figure out a way, or if he had the courage, he would teach the man in the lobby some respect. This, was now Chico's latest obsession.

Chico was incapable of ever being happy. His brain was not wired that way. He was an angry clone, manufactured to be angry at the world and everything in it. There was always somebody trying to fuck him over or jack him up. He merely needed to identify who the mother-fucker of the day was. Today it was the hotel clerk.

Chico was sure he was an A-rab—he emphasized the A, and separated if from the RAB—a Sand Nigger he called them, Maybe a camel jockey or just a mother fucking A-rab asshole. Whatever the case, he was the target of Chico's wrath today.

Chico sat on the couch and picked up a brown paper bag that lay on the coffee table. He reached in and removed the contents and carefully laid them out on the table. The magazine covers had big-breasted smiling women spread eagle, exposing all their private parts and inviting Chico to play.

"I'll show that mother fucking son-of bitch what I'm all about," Chico said, sneering at the same time. He picked up one of the magazines and smiled as he read the title out loud.

"Big Tit Arab Babes," he said, "Mother fuck you clerk mother fucker. I'm gonna fuck your women then cum in their faces."

This was Chico's way of exacting revenge on his adversaries. For Chico, it was like a voodoo ritual. If he could cum all over a picture or possession or something that represented the object of his wrath, he could destroy them. He thought cum had the same mystical powers as a voodoo doll, so he made it a point to cum on anything that represented anything of value to the people or things he hated the most.

Throughout his lifetime, Chico had cum on car seats, on buildings, on pictures, in cat magazines, on grocery store shelves, on police cars. He once even broke into the offices of a public television station and sprayed his cum in the desk of the station manager—twice.

This was the source for Chico's power. Each time he did it, he became more powerful, more viral, more smarter as he described it.

Chico unzipped his pants, and reclined on the couch with his dick in one hand and the big tit magazine in the other hand. As he flipped through the pages, he pounded harder and harder on his diminutive organ.

"A-rab mother fucking bitches. Suck my mother fuckin' dick. Kiss my ass you mother fucking sand niggers."

He groaned in between expletives.

"Big mother fucking tit bitch mother fuckers. Suck my dick. Drink my mother fucking cum!"

Chico's body shivered as he neared total climax. He gyrated and bucked as he cursed and began drooling and clenching his teeth in anticipation. He pounded faster and faster.

"Mother fucking fuck you you cock-sucking A-rab bitches," he yelled, not caring if anyone could hear through the thin walls.

Chico was close. Just a little more. He leaned his head back in anticipation and closed his eyes and started a slow, continuous groan of complete pleasure.

Partway through the groan a figure emerged from the bathroom and, without making a sound, made its way to the couch where Chico lay, oblivious and in ecstasy.

The knife sliced cleanly through Chico's throat. Blood immediately squirted from the deep open wound and mixed with air from Chico's severed windpipe. There was a deep gurgle of bubbles as Chico's last breaths escaped from his dying struggling lungs.

Chico's body was in the throws of full orgasm, and his brain hesitated to acknowledge that it was about to die. His body jerked one last time, shooting Chico's semen out with such force that it landed on his face and ran down his nose, past his open mouth and into the open gash under his chin.

Chico's white muscle shirt turned red as it soaked up the blood. Seconds after Chico's orgasm, urine flowed from his penis and his hands fell to his side. His breaths were short.

Chico's panicked eyes focused on the dark figure that hovered over him. He had only seconds to live. He mouthed something to the dark figure then his eyes closed.

Chico was gone.

The dark figure wiped the knife on the couch, folded it, slipped it into a zip-lock freezer bag, then shoved it into the pocket of his hip-length black leather jacket. The tall dark figure walked to the door and quietly slipped out, closing and locking the door behind him.

As the dark figure walked down the stairs to the back exit, he couldn't help but be amused at Chico's last words.

He had seen men die before and was never surprised by unusual dying declarations. But Chico had him stumped. Reading lips was a skill necessary for his profession, so he was sure about what Chico had said. He just couldn't figure out why.

What, he thought, would possess a man to say, "Kill all the mother fucking son of bitchin cats" as his last dying declaration. Not only was it grammatically incorrect, but it was stupid. He was miffed. But based on what he knew about Chico, he also thought good riddance. Another retard scumbag gone.

It was a great day for mankind.

Chapter 72

Ali Muhammad owned the Olympic hotel for 25 years. He paid for it with cash. Cash he smuggled out of Iran after he escaped the wrath of a new regime that did not take fondly to Western influenced Iranians.

As a General in the Shah of Iran's army, Muhammad had been a target of the Ayatollah Khomani for corrupting the souls of Persian youth. If he had not escaped to America and asylum, he would no doubt have ended up rotting away in a shallow grave in the Dasht-I-Kavir desert or in a dark, moldy prison cell. And he knew he would have deserved either of those fates.

As a high ranking general, it was his job to manufacture corruption and fear. He was no stranger to death. And twenty five years later, there was still very little he would not do for money.

His hotel was his sanctuary and his hiding place. He had fled the country with enough money to purchase the hotel, a restaurant and a house. And, still fearing that the families of people he had executed would be hunting him, he preferred to spend his days babysitting the lowlifes of the earth anonymously behind the counter rather than spend time in such a visible place as a restaurant. Plus, he found that prostitutes would do anything for a free nights stay. Those activities fed his appetite for kinky, hard, rough sex.

He knew Chico was a loser the minute he set eyes on him. So, the decision to accept money to allow the stranger into his room was not a hard one. It was not the first time he had allowed someone access to a room for a significant cash payment. The stranger had also offered a sum of money that would help him buy a second hotel, the Majestic, a run down roach infested flop house he had been considering two blocks away. Transient hotels, he learned early, were very profitable because maintenance was general not expected.

As part of the condition for letting the stranger in, Muhammad agreed to check the room at 6 a.m. the following day and call the police and report a homicide. He had been carefully instructed on what to say. Muhammad took no notes. He was Harvard educated. Remembering things was not an issue.

As a general, his memory served him well. He never forgot his enemies. And never forgot to destroy them if they got in his way. Chico had made the wrong enemy today.

Muhammad picked up the phone and made the call. He said only what needed to be said and hung up the receiver. Without hesitating or much reflection, he picked up his *National Inquirer* and snickered as he read about the man with two penises who was hatched from a giant egg.

He lit another cigarette.

"God damn fucking Americans," he said to himself, "makes me laugh they can make up such crazy shit. I love this country."

Grimsley's cell phone rang around six thirty a.m. It was Paulson.

"Talk to me Paulson," Grimsley said curtly.

"Sir, I completed the background search on Franklin. Nothing unusual there except some collection agencies chasing him for credit card debts."

"Who isn't being hounded by credit card agencies. Worst goddamn thing ever happened to our society. Credit without guilt. Credit without responsibility. And Credit without consequence. It's unconscionable."

"Yes, sir," Paulson said, verbally rolling his eyes on the other end of the line.

"Well, sir, these debts are pretty significant. $50,000 dollars from two agencies, along with some local businesses trying to recoup money for some ad placements that never happened."

"Whoah. That is hefty. Any priors?"

"Nothing, sir. Good upstanding citizen. Not even any moving violations, parking tickets. Clean all the way around."

"Makes me want to cry. A 40 year old kid without a criminal history. Our job is done, Paulson. We can turn in our badges at the end of the day."

"Very funny, sir. Shall I pick him up?"

"I'll take care of it Paulson. You find that mine sweeper. We need to find that slug. And those salaried dipwads from forensics are not going to help us."

"I'm on it sir."

"I'll call you later and—"

Paulson interrupted and said, "Oh, by the way sir, there's—"

But Grimsley was quick to cut back in.

"Paulson, I hate that goddamn line 'Oh, by the way.' Don't ever use that again. Either be a goddamn straight shooter, or don't shoot at all. You got something to say, just say it. Spit it out. That phrase means your tenuous, unsure, hiding something, slipping it in. I'm not your bitch Paulson, you don't have to distract me before you fuck me. Now, you got something to say, say it?"

There was silence on the other end of the phone. Grimsley could hear Paulson's breathing, heavier than normal, with slight stutters. The silence seemed to drag on while Paulson decided whether to accept this most recent reaming.

He continued.

"We got another homicide last night."

"Great Paulson!" Grimsley yelled. "You somehow think that a few credit card debts are more important than another murder!"

"Well, err, I thought your—"

"Paulson! Don't try to read my thoughts! Better clairvoyants than you have tried and failed. A murder is always important. 'Oh by the way' was bad enough. Now I learn you 'Oh by the way'd' a murder. Oh, by the way Paulson, that's bullshit. Now, give it to me straight. What do you know?"

Paulson cleared his throat, recovering from his embarrassment. He took a deep breath and told Grimsley about a Mexican American John Doe discovered in a transient hotel with his throat cut.

When Paulson mentioned the name of the hotel and Ali Muhammad, Grimsley interrupted and said, "I'll be down there in 15 minutes."

He hung up the phone, jumped into his Bronco, placed the magnetic emergency light on the roof, turned his flashers on and sped towards Old Town.

Chapter 73

Grimsley parked three blocks away from hotel on 2nd Street in front of the House of Louis restaurant and Seafood Market. Discarded ice used to pack frozen fish covered the sidewalk and the pungent smell of fish assaulted his senses.

Grimsley could see the flashing lights and pandemonium of the crime scene in front of the hotel. The sidewalks between the hotel and where he stood glistened from the morning dew and above, the heavy, clouded, dark sky threatened another rain storm.

Grimsley stepped out of his car, lit a cigarette and walked towards the hotel, carefully examining each building as he passed the darkened windows or deserted entranceways.

He stopped on each corner, and looked long and hard in both directions, carefully scanning parked cars for any human shadows that may be loitering where they shouldn't be.

It was six a.m. in one of the seediest parts of town. Most professional criminals would be in bed by 5 a.m. Any car that didn't belong would stand out. And Grimsley knew that in five out of every ten cases he had solved, the killer observed from a close distance, especially if he was confident he could never be suspected of the murder.

First block was clear.

Grimsley walked another block and was one block away from the hotel, standing in the middle of the street, halfway across the intersection when he saw the black Lincoln Town Car on the eastern side of Hoyt, idling near the farthest corner.

The windows were heavily tinted. It was washed and waxed. And it had a fresh coat of Armorall on the tires. It did not belong on a street with closed restaurants and gutter rats at this hour.

Bingo, thought Grimsley. Today was his lucky day.

He made a mental note of the license plate numbers, turned and walked towards the car. Before he completed his first step, the lights of the car blinked on. It roared to life and eased away from the curve, u-turned and proceeded towards Front Street, where it turned and disappeared.

Grimsley did not take the second step. There was nothing he could do. Mentally, he ran through the possibilities. New Lincoln Town Car. Black to be less visible at night. Driver probably owned a police scanner. Rented new luxury car. Not a two-bit criminal. Low rent crooks and rent-a-thugs only rented the economy car of the day, probably brightly colored, conspicuous Dodge Familycar or the Ford Domesticbliss. Crime scene buff? Probably not at this hour.

Grimsley reached into his coat pocket and took out a pen size digital recorder and recorded the license plate and what he observed. This, he thought, was interesting and he was anxious to get inside now that he had a lead before he even knew the details of the crime.

Chapter 74

When Chambers woke up, he was surprised to see the sun. It was September in San Francisco, the rainy season. He was used to waking with the fog and going to sleep with the fog.

His flat, nestled on the side of a hill in North Beach, had a birds eye view of the Transamerica building as it silhouetted against the orange and pink ball of sun that barely peaked above the horizon.

Beautiful, he thought. This was why he could never leave the city.

He caught the scent of China Rain with a hint of sweat and glanced across the bed. Delicate blond hair was draped across the silky bare back of the waitress with the 25 percent tip smile. He smiled as he thought about the night before. And without warning, he could feel the yearnings and desires swelling up inside and under the sheets. He pressed his body against hers and felt the full length of her tight body.

She moaned, lifted her head slowly and met his eyes.

"Be still my heart," he said. "Good morning doll face."

She giggled and said, "Good morning."

"How'd you sleep last night?"

"Not very well."

"Well, why not precious? Are my accommodations not comfortable?"

She propped her head on her hand and, while blushing, said, "Your accommodations are perfect."

She looked around and giggled again. Noticing the sunrise, she said, "Oh, that sunrise is gorgeous too. I just didn't get much sleep last night."

"And I know why, sister. You're an animal. Kee-rist. I invited you over for a nightcap not thinking it was going to be me. Listen baby," he leaned towards her and kissed her gently on the nose, "I'm an old man. I don't have many of those kinds of nights left in me."

"Well," she said and paused, looking towards the pillow and brushing her hair back with her free hand, "I want all that you have left."

She giggled again.

"Kee-rist," Chambers said. "You're fucking adorable and dangerous as hell. Come on baby. I'll make you some breakfast and we can eat out on my deck and watch the sun come up. I'm not a religious man. But this kind of morning is a gift from God. And before I go to work, I want another gift from God from you."

He winked at her.

"What ever you want," She said. "I had SUCH a good time last night."

"That's great cupcake. I'll get you connected and you'll do all right. Then you can meet some young stud your own age who can keep up with you."

"You do just fine. I have never met anyone like you before. You were fantastic."

"That's great baby. I can feel my balls growing right now. I'm a regular Don Juan. Listen to me sister and listen good."

He paused, thinking about how to say what he had to say without ruining the mood.

"I'm an old guy. I seen a lot of things and been with a lot of women. As much of a prick as I am, I know that a beautiful woman is a work of art. You don't fuckin' piss on a Picasso. I'm no good for the long haul, but I know I can make you happy for a little while…until my fuckin' bad attitude gets in the way. And sure as I'm sitting here, baby, my fuckin' bad attitude is going to come out."

She looked puzzled. Chambers thought he was losing her. She was quiet and drew invisible patterns on the sheets with her finger.

Then she said, "Listen, Chambers, I get you."

Not showing his surprise, Chambers cocked his head back and asked, "How's that pudding?"

"I'm young, but I've seen those Jimmy Cagney, Humphrey Bogart and Clark Gable movies. You're one of those guys. Especially like Bogart in Casablanca, African Queen, or Maltese Falcon. A tough guy with a big heart."

Chambers was shocked to hear her say that. He'd given his 'bad attitude' speech to lots of women. Most just kept quiet and played along so they could enjoy his Ferrari for a few days longer, while others grilled him about loving and needing to be loved. Then some tried to use the only weapon they had on him. They pitied him. Dozens upon dozens of times he had heard the line, "I pity you…" That was usually when he stood up and told them to get their shit and get the fuck out.

"My head is not where you think it is, Chambers. I'm a fan. The reason I didn't have a date last night was because most of the boys my age don't have a clue what the word intrigue means. They have no sense of self, of mystery of persona. They don't know anything about props and language and theatrics or how to treat a girl. All they know about is text messaging, drinking a lot of booze and trying to get laid. That's all good, but there's nothing romantic or ironic about that. But you. You're simple and complicated."

She paused and searched for a reaction. But Chambers just stared and listened.

"Chambers, as they say in those old movies, I'm not some dame who doesn't appreciate a Joe like you. But don't go thinkin' I'm just gonna go get all soft on you without you having to work for it. If that's what you're thinkin' then brother you can take a hike."

Chambers burst into laughter and so did she. They were communicating.

"You win, sister. I'm a freekin' dog with a bark and no bite. Come on. Mimosas and scrambled eggs. That was brilliant, the cutest thing I ever heard from a broad."

Chambers took her hand and helped her stand up. When she stood up, the sheet fell away from her body, revealing a sleek physique, with a studded navel ring, round breasts and curly blond hairs highlighting two long sensuous legs.

Chambers stopped and stared.

"Goddamn work of art. Here baby, put something on. He picked up his Stetson and placed it on her head. "Perfect."

He picked her up and carried her to the balcony.

Chapter 75

Baker woke up thinking his head would explode from what seemed like silent mortar shells exploding in his head. His eyes were unable to focus on anything in his apartment. The pain was excruciating. It was a 6 a.m. He was usually in the office by that time. As he regained consciousness, he could see that he was till wearing his suit. Only his shoes had been removed. And the memories of the night before at Skates began to dance in his head. Broken puzzle pieces at first, but then they started to coagulate and make sense. Vague scenarios and pieces of conversation became cohesive pictures. Chambers. Scotch. Pretty waitress. Star Wars. Enison. Revenge. Disdain. Destroy. Destroy. Destroy. The vengeful feelings towards Enison rushed to the surface like an erupting volcano.

Baker sat up quickly. Anger helped suppress the pain. Revenge helped him stand up. Disdain helped him drag himself to the bathroom. And too much Scotch helped him puke his guts out for the next 15 minutes.

Baker was a wreck of a human, the embodiment of an unnatural disaster. But as terrible as he felt, he would not stay home that day. He had to be near Enison. He had to follow up on his master plan. He had to do what he could to destroy Enison. That was his only purpose now. His life had new meaning. Vengeance supercharged him. These feelings that surged inside of him helped bring him closer to all the non-fiction books he'd read about Hitler, Mussolini, and Machavelli. He was alive now.

Get Enison. Get Enison. He repeated this over and over in his head until it was the only thing he heard. He showered, retrieved one of his 10 big suits and draped it on. His suits had been ordered from the J.C. Penny's catalogue. His mother always ordered from the catalogue and he honored her by doing the same. If the product was defective or the wrong size, his mother never returned it. She "made due" as she called it.

When all 10 of the suits he ordered arrived and they were five sizes too big, Baker could not return them. His mother would be ashamed. He made due. And to his surprise, he actually found the oversized suites attractive. His warped sense of style overruled. He considered himself a "natty" corporate dresser.

Even though the memories of the night before were forming, Baker found that they were not quite complete. There were gaps in his mental tapes, like the Nixon tapes, so he would call Chambers and find out what they had discussed. After he ate two pieces of toast and an egg sunny-side up, he called Chambers.

Chapter 76

As Grimsley entered the Lobby of the Olympic Hotel, two uniformed officers turned and look at him. One after the other, they each touched the bill of their department issue hats and said, "capt'n" and nodded.

Grimsley could see Mohammed's dark probing eyes in between the broad shoulders of the two officers, who were a full foot taller than he was. His eyes met Grimsley's. Grimsley did not acknowledge Muhammad. He didn't have to. He knew who he was. And Muhammad knew who Grimsley was. Muhammad broke eye contact and sucked on his cigarette and continued talking to the two officers.

Grimsley walked down the long narrow lobby to the elevator and stairwell entrance. The back exit door was ten feet past the elevator. Convenient. And the door could be seen easily from the front counter. A bright red sticker with white lighting said EMERGENCY EXIT - ALARM WILL SOUND. No one could get in or out without being detected.

On the third floor, the coroner waited outside of the room with his gurney, pristine and neatly organized. Two more uniformed officers stood outside of the opened room door, as light bulb flashes blinked from the open room door. Along the hall, doors were partially opened, some with heads and arms sticking out as curious tenants observed what was possibly another murder in the building.

Grimsley grunted at the officers as they said "capt'n." He was not in a good mood. Inside the room, Paulson, the coroner, Jack Sleighton, a wiry man with thick glasses and lean body, who took pride in his tailored suits and spit shined shoes, waited patiently. The dead, he felt, now had all the time in the world.

Chico was a sight to behold. As Grimsley observed Chico, his first thought was that this was the worst possible position to be caught dead in. Chico's tiny limp dick was still in his hands. Cum streaks stained his face. Dark blood stained his muscle shirt, and his frozen eyes stared up at a killer who was long gone.

Strewn across the table were Chico's big tit magazines, a half empty can of Coors and a small neatly wrapped tiny aluminum square of cocaine.

The smell bit at Grimsley's nose. And for a few short seconds, he questioned why he bothered to be a police officer. Most, he thought, never had to witness a scene like this. And his job, perhaps, was to see that they never did. The doubt he felt about his job was fleeting. This, after all, was not the worst thing he'd seen. And the fact that he could stomach it without flinching gave him a calming sense of superiority over common mortals.

"God help us all," Grimsley said to himself as he scanned the room.

Paulson walked up to Grimsley and, not wanting to look at him directly, still reeling from their phone exchange, began to dryly describe the scene.

Grimsley, not taking his eyes off Chico, listened intently.

"We got a Mexican American, throat cut. Pro job. Mid 20s, Registered under the name of Tito Puente."

Paulson paused and Grimsley raised an eyebrow. On that cue, Paulson continued.

"Not his real name. Real name is Chico De La Toro Rodriguez Espanoza—"

"I thought he was a John Doe?"

"He was, sir. No Tito Puente matching his description." Paulson paused again. Grimsley raised the opposite eyebrow and peered and continued staring at the body. Satisfied he had Grimsley's attention, Paulson continued.

"On his back, sir, a tattoo across his shoulders. I shifted the body slightly after we recorded the crime scene. His full name is tattooed on his back."

"I'll be God damn. Looks like every other detail about his life is covering the rest of his body," Grimsley said, more animated now.

"That's about right, sir. Birth date, Family names, Mother's maiden name. Shoe size. Gang affiliations. Everything we need to track his life history," Paulson said. "No need for Facebook profiles. It's all here."

"Not too bright. These people cover their bodies with tattoos and wonder why they're so angry all the time. I wouldn't be surprised if he had a tattoo on his pecker."

Paulson tried to suppress a smile.

"Possibly sir. But it's extremely small. Plus, how could they do that. Wouldn't they have to be, you know, aroused for some time while enduring a bit of pain."

"Paulson, I've been all over the world. Enduring pain and maintaining an erection is thought to be the ultimate test of manhood in some cultures. With a good porno video, a hooker and a couple thousand bucks, you too could have the declaration of Independence tattooed on your prick if you wanted."

Paulson winced at the thought.

"Ouch," he said.

"Paulson, have a look see."

"You mean, check his dick for tattoos."

"Sure," Grimsley smiled.

"Shouldn't we leave that for the coroner?"

"Could. But if there's something there, we need to know now."

Paulson, glanced at the Coroner, who was smiling and nodding.

"All in a days work, Paulson," Grimsley said.

"I'll take care of it," Paulson said. He turned to the two uniformed officers and barked, "Simmons!"

"Sir," the officer responded immediately and walked towards Paulson. "Yes Lieutenant."

"Make yourself useful. Put on some gloves and check this man's dick."

With a puzzled look on his face, Simmons responded, "Hugh?"

"His Pecker. His boinker. His manhood. His pithy grit rod. Check his cock for tattoos."

"Oh, oh, sorry, sir. Um. I see. Right away, sir."

Simmons retrieved thin rubber gloves from his pocket, slipped them on and walked over to Chico. Holding his nose with one hand, he leaned over slowly and reached into the dark hairs and gripped Chico's penis by the head and attempted to stretch it.

Both Grimsley and Paulson looked on sternly, recognizing that they could not smile or show emotion. A young officer's reputation was on the line. An incident like this could ruin a young policeman's reputation and lead to intensive locker room razing and years of therapy.

Chico's penis head slipped out from in between Simmons' fingertips. There was still wet cum covering the areas where Chico's fingers had been. After two attempts, Paulson stepped toward Simmons and whispered, "Simmons, I asked you to examine it not jerk it off."

Paulson looked around the room. The two officers gawked from the open door. Grimsley, scratched his head, embarrassed for Simmons.

"Simmons," Paulson, said, loud enough for everyone to hear, "Let me show you."

Simmons took a step backwards. Paulson took a pair of gloves and a pair of sutures out of his pocket, leaned over and gripped Chico's penis head with it. There were dark letters covered by the crusty semen. He reached into his pant pocket and took out a white cotton swab and cleared the lettering. He looked at Grimsley but said nothing.

Grimsley raised both eyebrows now and asked, "What'd you find Paulson?"

"Well, sir, do you believe in coincidences?"

"Never have and never will."

"Well, then what we have is a bona fide clue."

Grimsley moved towards Chico and Paulson and leaned towards Chico's dick. In elaborate letters, Grimsley read the words TRIXIE'S DICK.

Chapter 77

Chambers and Sara were rounding the corner on their third mimosa, quickly forgetting the lingering hangovers that threatened to dull the brilliant sunrise that painted Chambers' small deck shades of amber, purple and gold.

As the champagne took hold, their smitten glances and uninhibited touching, like two school kids in love promised another go-around in bed and possibly another few weeks together as they laughed and talked about old movies, private dicks and politics. It was with some reluctance and irritation that Chambers answered the antique black dial phone after it refused to stop ringing.

He grumbled as he stepped inside the sliding doors and picked up the phone.

"Some day I'll have to get an answering machine or voice mail."

"Hear the car is going to revolutionize transportation, too," Sara joked, giggled and sipped her drink.

"Chambers here. Talk to me," he barked.

A meek male stumbled over his words as he said, *"Uh, Chambers, um, hello, it's Baker. How are you?"*

"Grouchy, irritated and pissed that someone would call me before seven a.m. and disturb my…" Chambers hesitated, glanced outside at Sara, winked, and continued, "sleep."

"Oh, I'm sorry," Baker said, *"I just. I just, um, uh, I—"*

"Kee-rist! Baker. Can't you say what's on your mind. You're on the clock here. Every call is a conference call and costs you five hundred bucks a minute. Now what can I do you for?"

"I wanted to know when we get started on the Enison case."

Chambers' back straightened up and he furrowed his forehead.

"Listen Baker. *We* are not a *we*. I am an I. You are a you. I don't work for you or with you. We don't work together as us. And we don't do nothin' as a we. If I needed you're money, we'd be in deep shit and YOU'D never find out what you need to find out. I'm doing this as a favor for a company that's been very profitable for me over the years. But I'm self-sufficient now and I can tell youz guys to fuck off if I want to. So, Baker, let's understand each other. YOU don't fuckin' call me. I'll fuckin' call you. You stay out of my ass and I'll stay out of yours. You fuckin' call me again and I'll make you regret the day you was born. Now hang up the fuckin' phone, take a shower, jerk off, and have a nice day!"

Chambers hung up, walked outside and kissed Sara on the forehead and said, "How you doin' cupcake?"

"Fine," she said.

After hesitating she asked, "Was that the guy from the bar?"

"Yeah," he answered, not meeting her probing stare. "That was my client."

Puzzled, Sara said, "Sounds like you were pretty mean to him."

"That's right," Chambers said, not volunteering more information as he quietly mixed another glass of orange juice and Dom Perinon.

"Is everything okay?" She asked.

"Yeah, baby. Sometimes you have to set the precedence, establish what the relationship is going to like up front. Otherwise some jerk-offs start gettin' big ideas and thinkin' for themselves. The last thing you want to do in life is be beholden to some pencil dick executive who doesn't know his ass from an apple, and doesn't know boundaries."

Sara looked down. She could see the anger in Chambers eyes and it scared her. Chambers, seeing her reaction, reached over to her and lifted her chin up. Their eyes met.

"Listen. I'm the last guy in the world you need to be afraid of."

Sara flashed a perfect 25 percent tip tentative smile.

"It's pricks like him that you gotta be afraid of. A frustrated momma's boy who is a closet misogynist with an inferiority complex; the kind of guy who cuts women into little pieces and leaves them in freezers and secretly prefers little boys."

"So, why do you work with him?" she asked.

"I owe somebody a favor."

Sara considered what Chambers said.

"I understand."

She cupped his face with her hands and pulled his lips to hers and kissed him deep and hard.

"By the way," she whispered in his ear as she nibbled on it. "I love it when you talk tough like that. Makes me hot. Would you please make love with me NOW!"

He looked at her and smiled.

"Aye aye sugar cane. Let's go."

Chapter 78

Grimsley and Paulson examined Chico's dick closely as they processed the implications of what they learned.

"Capt'n," Paulson said, "If there are no coincidences, this is a clue. But we don't have much to tie him to our girl."

"True Paulson," Grimsley admitted. "Is there an address?"

"Sort of, Sir."

"Where?"

"On his ass."

"I'll be God damned," Grimsley said.

"His ass has a tattoo that reads, 42ND STREET REGENTS GANG."

"What the hell is that?"

"Gang affiliation, sir?"

"Not likely. I know every gang name and every member in Portland. There's no such gang unless it's a gang of one."

"That might explain it, sir."

"If it's a gang of one, then the name is derived from the primary street in the residing neighborhood, a landmark, a building, an apartment, or some stupid ass name some pissant thug blurts out just before he OD's on crack."

Paulson snickered. Grimsley gave him a disapproving glance before continuing.

"Here say is that the gang name 'Cribs' was derived from their original founder—if you could call it that—who's mother used to beat him even when he was a teenager. He used to run to his room and cry like a baby in a crib. One day, he decided that since he cried like a baby, he would start a gang and call them the cribs."

Paulson looked at Grimsley, who stepped around Chico as he spoke, and blurted out, "That's bullshit, sir!"

Grimsley, stopped, stared at Paulson again and said, "What's the matter, Paulson, can't you take a joke? Crime is serious business. But it's times like these that you have to have a sense of humor."

"I suppose so, sir."

"Well, look at us Paulson. We're here fingering a dead man's dick and his ass looking for clues. There has to be some levity somewhere. Anyway, back to work. What's the next step Paulson."

"Northeast 42nd Street. Check for buildings, apartments, anything with the word Regents. Find a permanent residence for our boy."

"Get on it Paulson. I'll finish checking things out here."

Chapter 79

Rich welcomed Fridays. Fridays represented a break from his life, from his worries. And most important of all, a break from the unwanted phone calls. The bill collectors would play golf or go boating or drink themselves blind while exchanging war stories about how they intimidated another pour soul.

They would leave Rich alone for two days.

On weekends he never had to worry about April possibly getting a call on their home phone from a collector. Rich had diverted them all to his cell phone.

In a sense, he could almost relax. Perhaps that was the purpose of the weekend after all. A chance for people who had screwed up their lives to forget about their troubles, to retreat into an illusion of normalcy; to play with their children as if nothing were wrong, participate in family outings, eat with friends and talk about politics and education and love.

Meanwhile their worlds were collapsing around them. That weekend could perhaps be the last one they enjoy before all hell breaks lose, the last one before being condemned or before that single thing goes wrong that would unravel the web of deceit they had spun. Seventy two hours to enjoy his life before it started all over again. Every weekend Rich could experience real joy. But Monday always came. Every Monday the trial began again.

After delivering the Children to the bus, Rich proceeded home to pack for his trip to the Annual Writer's retreat in Ocean Beach. His manuscript corrections arrived at 10 a.m. in an email He quickly reviewed them, grabbed his single travel bag, sleeping bag, pillow, laptop, and put them in the truck.

Before leaving, he scratched a short note to April and rushed out the door. As he drove towards 42nd Street, he couldn't avoid the feeling that he was a fugitive stealing away to avoid some terrible fate.

He brushed off that notion and turned on to 42nd Street and went North towards the I-205 onramp.

Two blocks before he reached the Interstate on-ramp, he saw the flashing lights in his rear view mirror. He pulled over, expecting the flashing red lights to pass him by, heading for some emergency of some sort.

Instead, the lights slowed behind him and stopped. And that's when Rich knew his world was closing in on him.

Chapter 80

Rich' grip tightened on the steering wheel as he pulled his car closer to the side of the busy road. Most vehicles didn't bother to slow down at the sight of the small flashing light on top of the Bronco behind Rich. As the engine idled, Rich glanced in the rear view mirror and waited for someone to emerge.

Dust swirled around his truck as semi-tractor trailers roared by, causing his truck to lurch slightly as they passed. Rich turned the engine off, a show of good faith he thought. As he waited, the palms of his hands began to sweat and ache as his grip tightened on the steering wheel.

Finally, the door to the Bronco opened and a wiry man stepped out and walked towards his truck. The policeman seemed to prolong arriving at his window by pausing every other step and glancing around. He almost seemed paranoid. Rich thought that was unusual behavior for a policeman. It made him even more nervous. Rich could see the slight bulge in the officer's hip where some type of weapon was holstered.

As the officer came closer, and his features became more distinct, Rich suddenly recognized the officer from various news reports on TV and in the newspapers.

This was not good he thought.

Rich rolled down the window as Grimsley walked up and stood just behind the opening.

"Mr. Franklin?" Grimsley asked, as he leaned up against the truck.

"Yes, sir, Captain Grimsley."

"So, you know who I am?"

"Yes, sir. And you know who I am?"

"That's correct Mr. Franklin."

There was silence. Rich couldn't think of anything to say that wouldn't sound cliche or condescending. He figured police officers were sensitive to things people heard on cop shows. So, Rich, in a bold maneuver nervously said, "Captain, I wasn't speeding. I haven't committed any crimes. You're the chief of police. And I'm a nobody. So I have to assume that you don't need to see my driver's license and registration."

Grimsley looked over Rich, wanting to see him sweat more than he already was.

"That's right, son."

He didn't volunteer any additional information.

Rich focused his attentions on the gravel curb ahead of him, thinking. Thinking about his next response. Preparing a defense if he needed it.

He turned to Grimsley.

"So, that means that you are one of the ones who have been asking about me?"

"That's right, young man," Grimsley answered, still not saying any more than he chose to.

Rich's heart was beating so hard, he found it difficult to breath and he had to consciously push air from his lungs into his windpipe to form the words he needed.

"And I probably should have contacted you this morning first thing. I'm sorry about that. But I've got to get out of town this morning and..."

Rich paused, suddenly realizing how his excuse sounded.

"Un, huh," Grimsley said, raising an eyebrow.

"Listen, captain, I know how that sounds. Um, that's not what I meant. I've got a writer's conference to go to this weekend. I need to finish rewrites on my novel, and, I wasn't going to—I mean, I'll be back Monday and that's better—I'm not running from anything. I—"

"All right, Mr. Franklin," Grimsley said, wanting to spare Rich any more humiliation.

"Listen, Mr. Franklin, I want to invite you over for dinner on Monday night. You and your wife get a sitter and come on over. Got a pen?"

Rich's mind was reeling now, processing.

"Dinner?" he asked as he reached above the sun visor and retrieved a pen and a note pad.

"Yes, Mr. Franklin," Grimsley responded. "I understand you're not a bad jazz pianist."

"Well, sir, I do all right."

Well, I got quite a collection of Coltraine, Rollins, Mingus, Miles and Parker. You can check it out, let me know what you think."

Rich couldn't figure out what was happening. He wrote the address and phone number as Grimsley recited it. After he wrote it, he peered up at Grimsley and asked, "You mean you stopped me to invite me to dinner at your house so we can listen to Jazz?"

"Not exactly Rich." Grimsley looked away, then back at Rich. "We also need to talk about a dead girl."

Grimsley turned and walked away. As he did, he said, "See you Monday night. Don't be late."

Rich was about to ask WHAT DEAD GIRL but Grimsley's departure was so abrupt, he did not have a chance to get the first word out.

Rich sat, dazed and shocked, thinking about what Grimsley had said.

What could he possibly know about a dead girl. He thought Grimsley must be mistaken. He must be thinking about someone else. Then Rich remember the Mexican American. The gun, his life flashing before his eyes. The impact and implications of what he'd witnessed had been so traumatic he pushed the memories into the deepest, darkest recesses of his brain. He reluctantly retrieved them for a moment, moment enough to come to a realization: If he were trying to simplify his life, he wasn't having much success. This was not what he needed right now.

He buried the memories once again, determined not to let them interfere with his recent stretch of good luck.

Chapter 81

As Rich passed over the bridge that spanned the Columbia River he was oblivious to the majestic flow of water two hundred feet below and the light mist that covered the shores of the Washington and Oregon banks.

Above him, passenger airliners glided into Portland International Airport, one after another like paper airplanes with blinking lights and swirling trails of condensation behind them as they cut through the low-hanging clouds on their way to deliver their bounty of vacationers and weary salesmen hungry for their next deal or cocktail.

Rich couldn't see the orange and red patches of leaves juxtaposed with rich green foliage of the Dogwood, Maple and Douglas Fur trees that lined the highway. The dreary gray day was not enough to mute the brilliant fall colors that filled the Pacific Northwest countryside rivaling any autumn shows around the world.

But all Rich could see were the flashing lights of Paulson's truck and his unsmiling stoic face looking at him as if he knew something that Rich didn't know about.

Rich replayed the incidents of the night before over and over and created wild scenarios in his head. His thoughts were on overdrive, his imagination running at hyper-speed, blocking out all surroundings, only focusing on words, pictures, ideas and emotions locked in his head.

It wasn't until Rich reached Longview, which was 20 miles north of Portland, that he snapped back into the here and now.

He nearly missed his exit. He quickly signaled and exited onto highway 4, which took him northwest into the hills alongside the Columbia River, to Raymond and Ilwacco, and ultimately to Ocean Park on the Long Beach Peninsula.

Rich, turned up Pat Matheney's *As Falls Wichita, So Falls Wichita Falls*. Pat Matheney was calming to Rich. His thoughts focused back on the manuscript. He flipped on the switch in his head that did writing and opened the creative valves as he described it. Two and a half hours of pure thought. he would know exactly what to write when he reached Long Beach.

That, he thought, was the miracle of his itinerant genius. It was not constant. He had to summon it. Conditions had to be perfect, like the mating season for Coho Salmon. And there were times when it was simply out to lunch. But when it worked, it worked really well.

Chapter 82

When Grimsley walked away from Rich's truck, he smiled.

This was a game he enjoyed playing. He enjoyed having most of the cards and he enjoyed playing them at his whim. He didn't want to ruin Rich's weekend, but he did want him to squirm and lose a little sleep, so that he could confront him on Monday.

He was already figuring out how to approach the dinner he set up. Whether to take the direct approach, whether to embarrass him in front of his wife, or whether to make chicken tar tar or grilled salmon with a butter dill sauce.

These were the dualities of life, the incongruities that create mysteries, and, he thought, the absurdities that make life interesting.

Grimsley needed to go back to the hotel where Chico's body was found. Something was eating at him. He'd missed something. And he hated missing things. He hated the idea that he might have made a mistake. Most of all he hated the cliché of the idea that he might have made a mistake.

Too many God damn cop shows on TV, he thought. Can't do his job without thinking about those God damn shows and movies. They were the ingrown toenails of Grimsley's life. CI: Miami, Homicide, Law and Order, Magnum reruns, the old classic Mannix, Eddie Murphy Beverly Hills Cop, and the lowest of them all Columbo.

Every God damn crime scenario and detective type had been featured on TV or in the movies. There was nothing left for the public to imagine. He could see it in the faces of the crowds that gathered at crime scenes. When they saw him, a figure of authority, they wondered. Was he a Columbo typo, a bumbling, forgetful, stumble-on-the-answer type or a hard boiled nail-eating-bully-the-suspects-Mel-Gibson type? Or was he in line to star in Naked Gun 17?

Grimsley didn't hate movies and TV shows. He, in fact, had in his library bootleg copes of Mannix and had seen every detective show ever made from Charlie Chan to Mary Kate and Ashley.

It was his way, however, to be over analytical and critical. After all, the story-telling bar had been set by Raymond Chandler, Louis L'amoure, Pete Seeger, and Sojourner Truth. Most everything else created was crime sacrilege. Why Sojourner Truth, he asked himself, continuing the mental dialogue. Because by disguising escape plans and schedules in songs and stories, Sojourner Truth had saved thousands of lives with story-telling.

What greater purpose could there be for story-telling, but to affect change in thinking, purpose, actions and society, or to save lives. Otherwise, he thought, it's just a bunch of God damn noise, words, fictional pontification by caviar-fed intellectuals with nothing better to do with their time but to sit around and make up a bunch of God damn outrageous lies.

You're so full of shit, he told himself. Let's get on with this murder investigation.

Grimsley started the Bronco, put his light on the roof, did a wide U-turn and sped back to the hotel.

Chapter 83

Rich arrived at the retreat center less wound up than when he'd originally started his journey. He drove through the gate of the retreat, past the caretaker's modular home, and followed the dirt road to the main lodge, which was nestled on a hill overlooking the open field that was the main outdoor activity area. The field had a play structure for kids, a small wooden gymnasium and small log cabins scattered around the edges of the field.

In one section of the field was a small group of trailers that were used for overflow when the lodge was full. There were 10 old 30-foot Streamliners, and early model Prowlers, along with a few nondescript double decker models from the seventies. Several were painted with wacky themes, including one that was called the African Queen and was painted with murals of Humphrey Bogart and Kathryn Hepburn.

Rich hoped the lodge was full. He wanted one of the Streamliners. Most had two separate rooms and plenty of space and isolation to get plenty of work done.

He parked in a small lot near the front entrance of the lodge and a calm washed over him. He made it. The familiar surroundings of the retreat and the promise that his future held almost made him giddy. He pushed Grimsley, paper tossing, the collectors so far back that it was now possible to focus only on writing.

As he got out of the truck, he was met with a light mist, heavy fog he called it, which was a constant by the ocean this time of year. It wasn't immediately cold, but if he stayed outside long enough he would eventually feel the effects of the mist and the autumn chill.

He grabbed his sleeping bag, pillow, black leather bag that held his manuscript and his laptop bag and walked towards the front door. Others were arriving as well. He greeted some of the regulars with a curt "howsgoing?" There was little chit-chat.

It was understood that if you drove to this retreat—many came from as far as Idaho—you were there to spend a weekend writing, talking about writing, eating writing, sleeping and breathing writing. The environment was conducive to doing that. Small talk was not necessary. A pensive, staid attitude was required. And that was that.

As Rich entered the front door, he heard a familiar voice yell, "Rich. Oh my God. I'm so glad to see you!"

Before he could say anything, he felt arms surrounding him and squeezing him tight. His natural reflex was to wrap his arms around the mass that was a woman. Thick brown hairs covered his face and scent of China Rain overcame him. He was dizzy. And he could feel the two mounds that were breast pressing into his chest.

As she squeezed, he felt another natural reflex occur. He was stunned, so the reflex was not immediate, but when it happened, it was genuine and full. He smiled. Only because this could be the best thing that could happen to him or the worst.

Brenda loosened her grip on him and looked in his eyes.

"I'm so glad you could make it, Rich. I wasn't sure you would."

"Brenda, nice to see you. I...how... what are you doing here?" Rich tried not to sound surprised, but wasn't sure he pulled it off.

"Well, when you told me your were coming here, I though I'd check it out. You know, I've always wanted to write. Painting is my first love. Writing is my second. And I've been writing a journal for years. I thought this would be the perfect opportunity to learn more and to spend some time with you."

"I see. Well, that's great, Brenda. I'm glad you're here."

Inside, Rich was happy and angry. He had been ripped from that pensive, dark, brooding, writing place and into a social, human interaction, emotional place. He wasn't prepared for this. He had to process and transition.

They stared at each other, smiling.

Finally, Rich said, "Okay, well, this is the best place to explore writing. This is my sixth year coming here. I never miss it. It will be great to explore writing with you."

Rich was shifting back to the writer. The temporary shift from writer to human was almost complete.

"Once you get settled in, we can meet back up here at the lodge and throw some ideas around."

Shift back. All Writing. All business.

"That's great Rich, but we don' have to meet back up here. We're sharing a trailer, one of those stream ones."

"What!" Rich said, surprised again.

This time he had no opportunity to adjust, so he tried to recover.

"I mean, what do you mean?"

"Well, I got here early and started talking to Pat, the director about you. I told her we were friends, and she told me you liked the stream thingies. So, I asked if we could share on. And she said no problem. They're big enough for two people have two separate rooms. Isn't that great? This is such a cool place."

That's bad. That could only spell trouble, Rich thought. But I have to be strong. I can do this.

"Yeah, Brenda. That's great. Um, Okay, well. Alrighty then.

Have you taken your gear down yet?"

"Not yet. I was waiting for you. Oh, Rich, I'm so glad we could be here together. You are such a wonderful person."

"Um, I'm glad too, Brenda."

Rich didn't know how to handle his situation exactly, so he went along.

"I think you're great too. Come on. Let's get settled in. There are some great seminars tonight."

"Okay, Rich."

Rich started to turn away and pick up his bags, but before he could do so, Brenda pulled Rich toward her again. Rich could see it all in slow motion, her body screaming towards his and then a collision, body parts smashing together, hair whipping in his face, chest, thighs, shoulders, breasts, loins crashing together becoming entangled, clinging together, causing yearnings to surge from deep inside. Rich breathed in deeply and sighed. He could smell the sweet scent of t-r-o-u-b-l-e.

Chapter 84

Grimsley returned to the Olympic Hotel and his first stop was the front desk where Muhammad stood, reading *Star* magazine, sucking on an unfiltered cigarette and nibbling on a slice of pita bread with feta cheese.

Muhammad smirked as he read, shaking his head and mumbling, "God damn sons of bitches." He did not look at Grimsley as he approached.

"Captain Grimsley, sir, how can I help you my friend," he said, still not looking up.

Grimsley stopped at the counter and stared at Muhammad, waiting for him to make eye contact. He needed to take a quick reading of how much Muhammad was willing to lie, not IF he was willing to lie.

Muhammad quickly glanced at Grimsley and immediately looked back into his paper. That was Grimsley's queue.

"Tell me what went on here Muhammad."

"I don't know what you mean," he answered, still not looking at Grimsley and taking a drag of his cigarette.

"You know what I mean Muhammad. Give me the real story."

"I am a simple business man trying to live the American dream in this glorious United States. It pains me so when low lives break the laws and murder each other."

Grimsley leaned on the counter, reached over and gently pulled the magazine down so it was flat on the counter, forcing Muhammad to look at him.

"Muhammad, you're a lying, thieving scum bag and a war criminal. You disgrace the term American, and if I could run your ass out of this country I could. But since you are an American, I have to protect your rights as if you were a law abiding citizen. But we both know better than that don't we?"

Muhammad, expressionless, fixed his gaze on Grimsley now, eyes full of contempt. He now wore his general's face and prepared for battle.

"You want a piece of me don't you Muhammad?"

Muhammad did not respond.

"Well, we both know that's not going to happen. I know too many people who would still like to skin your ass for all the handiwork you did in Iran. Now tell me what happened here."

Grimsley's words sank in and burned at Mohammed's composure. But he would not yield. He was always a phone call away from four goons who lived in room 101. He could take anything

Grimsley could throw at him.

"Respectfully, Captain Grimsley, I do not know what you are talking about. I am trying to run a legitimate business here. I am not responsible for the actions of every low life in this city. I think, Captain Grimsley, and forgive me for saying this, that you are barking up the wrong bush."

Muhammad calmly took another drag of his cigarette. He was cool, calculating and fearless. Grimsley knew it would take some kind of miracle to get Muhammad to back down. He was a formidable, calculating psychopath and not afraid of Grimsley.

It was a stand off.

"All right, Muhammad. Let's try something else. How badly do you want that second hotel?"

Mohammed's disposition changed immediately and a broad smile crossed his face, showing brown, rotting teeth. Muhammad was beaming with anticipation.

"So, Mr. Grimsley, you have a proposition for me?"

Grimsley reached for the registration pad, took a pen from his pocket and scratched out some numbers and pushed the pad to Muhammad. Muhammad read the note and grinned as if anticipating a blow job from a high priced hooker.

"This will buy you *some* information, but not all. Information, as you know, is very expensive."

"That's all you get Muhammad. Give me what you've got."

Muhammad wrote a series of numbers on the pad and pushed it back to Grimsley.

"Please deposit the cash into this account and I will delivery a copy of a gold leaf hand bound book of quotations from Allah."

Grimsley took the sheet, folded it and put it in his pocket.

"A man came in and requested to see Mr. Puente. He was a White man, over six feet tall, well dressed in a black suit. He drove a black Lincoln. I gave him Mr. Puente's room number and that was the last I saw of him."

"How did you happen to find the body?"

"Mr. Puente and I had some disagreements and I was concerned that he might damage the room."

"These flea traps could use some damage. Might improve their livability."

"One man's castle Captain Grimsley?"

"What else?"

"Well, there is not much more. I found the body in the state you saw. I must tell you, Captain, in all my years as a business man, I have never seen such a thing."

Muhammad paused for effect.

"Mr. Puente seems to have had some issues, if you will, and some enemies. They both seem to have gotten the better of him."

"Did you catch a license plate?"

"No, sir, but Mr. Puente chained his bicycle outside." Muhammad pointed at the door and Grimsley looked, immediately recognizing the bicycle as the one from Going street. It was covered in mud and the front wheel was visibly bent, but he could see it was the same bike.

"Hoooooly shitstorm," Grimsley said, anxious to examine the bicycle.

He turned back to Muhammad and asked, "How much did he pay you Muhammad?"

Muhammad held up his index finger and waved it from side to side.

"Tisk, tisk, Mr. Grimsley, there must be some honor amongst businessmen. I'm afraid that I cannot share that information with you. But let us say that I am much closer to my new hotel than I ever hoped to be by this time."

"You're a piece of work, Mr. Muhammad. A real piece of work."

"From you, Captain Grimsley, I take that as a compliment. Please to have a nice day," Muhammad said and picked up his *Star* and continued reading where he left of, smiling and unconcerned.

Grimsley called Paulson on his cell phone as he walked out the front door.

"Paulson," he said, "get down to the Olympic Hotel and pick up a Shwynn chained in front of the hotel. Also, this thing is bigger than it appears, so don't talk to anyone about what you and I know. There are some pros involved here and I don't like the smell of it. Our boy Chico must have been in the middle of some kind of shit. Let me know when you find an address. I'll be at the gun range."

Without saying goodbye, Grimsley hung up his phone and went outside to examine the bike.

After Paulson and forensics examined the bike and removed it, he headed to the gun range to let out some steam. He felt as though he had looked in the eyes of evil and had made a deal with the devil in dealing with Muhammad. But 30 years of crime fighting had taught him that money was the best way to beat criminals at their own game. Was he funding crime by buying information? No, he answered to himself. Crime had its own economy. And in order to get something out of it, you had to occasionally invest in it. There was such a thing as conscientiously investing in crime as well as in stocks.

Paying snitches, offering certain protections, and ignoring minor infractions were the investments police had to make to keep ahead in the crime market.

Muhammad was evil. But he was also retired. His network was still far reaching. As much as he hated dealing with him, he preferred to know where he was and know that he had access to him. Although Muhammad had lied to him, he had given him enough information to work with without risking his own neck, which he valued.

Grimsley knew, too, that everything he was told, was well scripted with whomever paid Muhammad. This was the game he played everyday. Invest in the crime market and see if your stock goes up or down.

All the big players had influence enough to know your every move before you made it. Grimsley was in the game now and he had to be careful. Whoever was playing, was playing for keeps. And they would stop at nothing to save their own necks.

Chapter 85

Chambers parked his Ferrari a block away from the exit of ACS's parking lot. He could see all the cars that entered and exited. Enison got to work early and was still inside.

Chambers took the time to catch up on his phone calls and type some reports on his pocket PC. He loved his gadgets, which were all wired into his car. His car was the centerpiece of his technological world. He didn't believe in voice mail and kept an antique phone in his apartment, but his car was rigged with more gadgets than the average Bond car. But you had to know how to find them.

At his side was hand held receiver with an ear plug running out of it and into Chamber's ear. A power cord ran from the receiver to the cigarette lighter. And on the seat next to him was small hand-held video monitor.

Chambers smiled.

This was the life he dreamed of. Private dick with lots of gadgets giving the elusion of being a leadite.

For years, Chambers had access to the ACS offices. He installed miniature cameras and bugs in every office and could easily monitor everything that went on inside at his leisure. He didn't particularly target ACS. He had other clients. They were similarly monitored, some with systems Chambers had custom designed.

He played the tough as nails private eye well, but he knew he had some smarts, including a degree in mechanical engineering from MIT and held several patents for surveillance technology and software.

But who needed to know that?

Layers, he thought. Let people think what they wanted, view him as they thought they should. Layers, like Baklava, he thought, made a man interesting. Like a gaudy Greek wedding cake. Like the big breakfast pancake stack at I-HOP. Like…his thoughts were interrupted by sleek black Jaguar that emerged from the parking lot. It was Enison.

Show time thought Chambers.

As Chambers started his engine, he was shocked to see a green Ford Escort emerge from the parking lot behind the Jaguar. It was Baker.

"God damn It! God damn it!" Chambers shouted. "God damn prick."

Chambers gunned his Ferrari and made a screeching U-turn, nearly colliding with an Oakland city bus. The driver angrily honked his horn at Chambers and threatened to get out and come after him if he stopped. Enison was driving fast. Too fast.

Baker couldn't keep up. When Chambers got close to Baker, he flashed his high beams and honked his horn, all the while, pointing to the curb, gesturing Baker to pull over.

When Baker finally got the hint after recognizing Chambers, he slowed, eased into a curbside parking space and put on his emergency lights.

Chambers emerged quickly from his Ferrari, leaving the door open and marched up to Baker's window.

"What in God's name do you think you're doing!?"

Timidly, Baker answered, "I…I'm…following Enison. I didn't think—"

"Kee-rist almighty Baker, you want to get your ass sued!? He's a God damn employee for God sakes. You can't just go around lurking behind him like you're some kind of private eye. Now get your ass back to the office and try to do the job you were hired to do. Let me do the job I was hired to do."

"I, I'm sorry Mr. Chambers."

Baker kept a tight grip on his steering wheel and refused to look at Chambers. He acted less like an executive and more like a kid caught shoplifting a stick of gum, speaking barely audibly and stuttering. Chambers thought Baker was actually going to start balling right there in front of him.

Shaking his head in disbelief and disgust, Chambers turned and marched back to his Ferrari, slammed the door shut and watched as Baker signaled and turned his car around. Baker seemed so small and frail in the driver's seat, his dark suit draped over his shoulders, thinning hair pushed forward and the Ford spewing smoke as it struggled to reach the speed limit.

Chambers put his head on the steering wheel and sighed. No reason for ever making that piece of crap car…or that idiot Baker, thought Chambers.

Chambers opened the glove compartment and took out another device about the size of his pocket computer, only black, with a small plasma display. He turned it on and it beeped.

On the screen, was a color map with a red dot traversing a grid of Oakland streets. The blinking dot changed directions and the red display below the screen showed longitude and latitude. Baker had placed a GPS beacon on Enison's car.

Backup he thought. Always have backup.

Chapter 86

Rich and Brenda deposited their sleeping bags into the tiny rooms, one in the very back of the trailer and one in the middle. As was customary with all the retreat trailers, the owners had not changed anything in them since they parked them there twenty years ago.

The burgundy and green plaid curtains were worn, faded and dusty. Some had lose threads hanging from the ends as the fabric threatened to unravel from countless thousands of residents tugging on them over the years.

In the tiny living room towards the front of the trailer, a small, yellow, Formica-topped, metallic-lined table surrounded by matching chairs was the centerpiece surrounded by a brown and green sofa sleeper with tattered edges from cats sharpening their nails and perhaps a slumber party too many.

A low, battered, bulky, coffee table was littered with *National Geographics*, *Writer's Journals* and *Newsweeks* from the 70s and 80s. To add to the nouveau tacky look, there were small wicker baskets holding dusty, fake daisies and begonias strategically placed around the living. The scene was surreal, one that survived for decades in this metallic silver time capsule with wheels.

The tiny kitchen was fully functional, with a small propane stove, an aging Westinghouse refrigerator and a slightly browned, stained sink.

Past the kitchen was the aft bathroom, linen storage, and Rich's room. Beyond that was the furnace and the master bedroom and bath. The bathroom was one-person closets with a miniature toilet, coffin-sized shower/bath combination and a sink the size of a small cooking pot.

Rich welcomed the extreme tackiness of the trailer. To him, it provided a glimpse into the past. It was all offset by his favorite feature of all, the textured wood paneling, some buckling in spots from years of extreme weather conditions and condensation.

For Rich, the soft, brown, Oaken tons of the walls reflecting the incandescent light were soothing and gave the trailer a Craftsman's den-like character amongst all the kitsch.

The only things missing, Rich thought, were the Pink Flamingos.

Brenda emerged from the master bedroom and stood close to Rich. The room suddenly got very small, and Brenda's perfume clashed with the smell of mold and dust, countering the classic ode de olde trailer.

For the first time since Rich arrived, he was feeling relaxed. He had accepted his circumstances, reflected on his wife and family as the best thing going in his life right now, buried the idea of a dead girl and any possible involvement, distanced his other problems and found the presence of Brenda and her quirky sense of self and humor a welcomed juxtaposition to the tacky environs and the serious booknicks who came to bury themselves in their manuscripts.

Brenda wore a psychedelic turtleneck sweater with jeans so tight it was hard to distinguish skin from cotton. They were pre-washed, pre-shrunk, pre-frayed, pre-tattered, pre-bought, pre-sold, everything that could possibly be done to jeans to appeal to, premadonnas and pre-teens who wanted to pay a premium for pre-worn clothing. They fit Brenda nicely.

Her devil-may-care black zip-up boots were covered by the tight flares and the three-inch heels made Brenda stand a glorious five feet eleven, every inch an angel. Her dark hair flowed like a black waterfall, splashing onto her shoulders and framed the evenly toned skin on her face. Her cheeks were lightly blushed, and here ruby, red lipstick created a stark contrast against her skin, accentuating lips as full as rose petals.

Brenda hugged Rich again.

"Rich, this is great. I'm inspired already. Now I see why you come here. This is perfect."

"I know," Rich said, smiling. "Once a year I come here to get recharged. It last me the rest of the year, so it has to be perfect."

"It is," she replied.

They looked out the rounded picture window over the sofa bed and said nothing. The gray clouded sky was darkening as dusk approached and the Ocean mist continued to fall, creating unmoving droplets on the window, obscuring the view leaving only a Monet-like impressionistic image of the dense woods beyond the expansive, open field.

Brenda finally broke the silence by asking, "Rich, you're not disappointed that I came are you?"

Rich tried to camouflage his surprise and said quickly, "Oh, no Brenda. Not at all. I'm sorry if I may have given you that impression. I'm, well, I'm just a little nervous is all."

Brenda said, "Oh, Rich, is it me? Did I do that? I didn't mean to. I really wanted to get away and explore my writing. Really, Rich, I just thought—"

"No, Brenda, it's not you," Rich interrupted, "Well, I mean, it sort of is and it's not."

Rich faced Brenda and thought about what he wanted to say.

Brenda's piercing stare probed Rich like an alien examining a new species, searching for answers, wanting to be taken to their leader. He could tell she was curious and vulnerable. And so was he.

"Brenda, this is the one place and the one time of year where I may actually expose myself. I come here to bear my soul; try to resolve a lot of issues related to art, people, life. You know, I do a lot of soul searching. Plus—and no-one knows this yet—yesterday I got an offer from a publisher for my novel."

"Oh my God, Rich. No!" Brenda said excitedly.

"Yes," Rich said, trying to suppress a proud smile, "and I have to have the revisions done by Monday. I'm panicked and excited and worried and trying to maintain my dark brooding writer persona at the same time."

Brenda smiled.

"This is a very different side of you, Rich. You're always so cool whenever I see you, like some kind of secret agent. You know, like Shaft, always cool, never nervous, somehow saving the day just in the nick of time. I suspected but never thought about all the other stuff that might be going on. I can empathize with that. I have my own secret life."

"I appreciate your honesty. And I suppose the thing that makes me the most nervous about this is that we know the same people. I hope you won't blow my cover and tell any of our other friends that I'm actually, well, actually a human being behind my façade."

Brenda laughed again.

"Don't worry Rich. Your secret's safe with me. And you might be surprised to know that some people have already figured it out, like Phil and Rock. They talk about you all the time. I get bits and pieces, but they both love you a lot. And I'm beginning to see why."

"They feel the same about you, and so do I, Brenda," Rich said.

Not wanting her to misconstrue, Rich explained, "They think you're a brilliant artist and nice to a fault."

"Yeah, I'm sure that's why all my relationships dissolve like sugar in water. Too nice. You know, Rich, I don't get that. Why do guys always run away whenever things start to get serious?"

"I get it," Rich said. "You're beautiful and you're smart. Guys your age just want to get laid and guys my age are just looking for girls your age to lay because they feel they missed out on something when they were your age. They all want the beauty without the brains. In a way, they're playing the babe market, like stocks. Buy and sell, never accumulated."

Brenda blushed and her disposition suddenly darkened.

"You think so, Rich?"

"I know so. Brenda. You just have to learn to play the market. Listen, this is a weekend for letting out the demons, for putting all the cards on the table, so I'm going to let you in on something else. Aside from my fictional novel, I actually have several completed manuscripts for a few other crazy books. One is a relationship handbook, written from a layperson's perspective. I wrote it ten years ago and I've just been waiting for an opportunity to get it published. All my manuscripts are up for grabs by my agent, so I'm revisiting them all, and have a copy of it with me."

"You're kidding, Right?"

"I kid you not. Later tonight, let's talk about that. You show me yours and I'll show you mine."

"Rich, you don't mean…"

"No, not that. Writing. Show me some of your writing and I'll show you some of mine."

"Oh, I see. Okay. I brought a bunch of my journals. It's kind of personal though. But I think some of it is good."

"Well, that's what we're here for. And don't worry. You're secret's safe with me. I'm sure that in one of my former lives I was probably a Neanderthal, secret agent, pimp, politician and, most importantly, a woman, which is why I can speak to any circumstances that exist in life."

"That's quite a combination. And what might your name be now if all those personalities were to surface?"

"Good question. Maybe Ramona Grok Ace PrettyBoy Smithington the third?"

They both laughed.

Rich looked at the cat clock on the wall. And he noticed it was not plugged in. He reached over, plugged it in and the tail swung back and forth while the eyes moved from left to right.

"Oh, it's almost dinner time, Brenda," he said suddenly. "Let's head up to the lodge. Remember. Most people here are serious writers. Most have never been published and probably never will be, but they never give up. Try to look troubled, contemplative, and morose. Never, *ever* smile or they'll know you're not a self-absorbed literary geek. If anyone ask you if you've read anything. Unlike Nancy Reagan's advice, you should just say YES. The thing that scares a writer the most is finding someone who actually has read more than they have and knows more than they do."

Brenda giggled and said, "Rich, you'll protect me I'm sure. You won't let them spray me with melancholy and brand me contrite and banal, will you?"

"I am here to serve and protect commoners from the intellectual literate elite," Rich said as he held out his arm and Brenda gripped it tightly. You've been briefed, now come madam; the writer's labyrinth awaits. Shall we?"

Chapter 87

Grimsley braced himself for the next shot, aimed and squeezed the trigger. The explosion was thunderous and caused all the other shooters to stop and look in Grimsley's direction.

Swirling puffs of gray and black smoke that looked more like a cannon discharge than a rifle shot blasted out of the end of the barrel.

"God damn it," Grimsley said to J.D. as he set the rifle down and gripped his shoulder, grimacing with pain. "How in hell did anyone shoot more than one round with these God damn things."

J.D. smirked and answered, "I'll tell you one thing, there was probably a lot of luck involved. Get enough of those bullets in the air at one time and they have to hit something."

"You're probably right. But if everyone shot like me, we'd have probably lost the Civil War."

"Did you really win?" J.D. asked sarcastically.

"Oh for God's sake, J.D., you're not going to go there again. Are you?"

J.D. smirked and said smugly, "All I'm saying is the North may have won the war but they are losing the battle. Whites have lost all their rights in this country and—"

"J.D., you can can that shit right now. White people had it too good for too long and we all know payback is a bitch. We raped and pillaged and murdered and took whatever we wanted. Still do. All people want now is a chance to get some of what we've had and still have plenty of. So, don't start that racist shit. You can do that on your own dime," Grimsley raged.

J.D., looked away, scratched his head and his beard, and said, "You're the only sombitch I'd let talk to me like that."

"I know that J.D.," Grimsley said. "You're a proud man, and you were a great cop. Now you just have to figure out how to be a great, proud, understanding, semi-retired White citizen who accepts the realities that a true American is not just Southern and White. That's your Achilles heel, J.D. and if you die with that, well, you just die with it and God help the devil. And don't think for a minute that heaven and hell are segregated. If you believe in God and Satan and the afterlife, you have to accept that both are equal opportunity employers. And you have to think that Satan will have Blacks, Hispanics, Whites and, everyone else, sucking his cock every day like one big happy cursed family. Now, J.D., there's an African American cop six ranges behind you. Working hard. Serving and protecting your rights. J.D., you're smarter and wiser than that racist shit. Absolve yourself and go tell that officer thank you for having the courage and guts to serve the public interest like you did. Shake his hand and feel the touch of his flesh. He's human J.D., just like you and me. When he smiles, let it touch your soul, just like the smile from your grand children. If you do that, there may be hope for your eternal soul. And instead of sucking Satan's dick in hell with every other sinner and bigot, you can sip caviar in Heaven with the Lord Jesus Christ at your side and be at peace surrounded by a hundred billion Hispanics, Africans, Jews, Chinese, *and* Middle eastern fellas who's souls have made it that far."

"Good God, Grimsley, you're the biggest bag of wind I ever met," J.D. said. "But sometimes you do make a little sense. I'm sorry 'bout my comment. I wasn't thinking. I'm not saying I agree with everything you say. I'm just sayin' that's another way of lookin' at it."

"J.D., you always were smarter than everyone else. When you get through talking to that officer, please tell him I'd like to have a word with him."

"All right Grimsley."

J.D. turned and walked to the officer. Grimsley could see the officer smile as J.D. spoke. When they shook hands, J.D. turned and looked at Grimsley. With his free hand, J.D. saluted Grimsley with a raised middle finger, which he placed at his side, just out of sight of the police officer. The officer placed his weapon in the leather holster strapped around his chest and walked towards Grimsley.

Chapter 88

All Day Enison couldn't shake the feeling that something wasn't right. He was paranoid anyway because he felt his plan was more complicated than he thought it would be, and Baker had become increasingly more suspicious and agitated since their confrontation earlier in the week. He had to forge cautiously ahead. He was committed now. And a lot of people were involved.

As Enison pulled his Jaguar into the parking lot of Yoshi's, he contemplated his next move. He was having dinner with Jeremy Goldberg, the agency president.

It was a sunny, crisp fall day that was turning into a chilly Oakland night. No wind blew and vibrant green palms stood like sentries along the street with colorful Maples and Oaks, half naked as leaves continued to loosen and flutter to the ground.

Yoshi's was nestled in between two apartment complexes in a sleepy, residential neighborhood that bordered what was considered the good and the bad parts of Oakland. It was common ground between gentrification and the west, the only Sushi jazz bar Enison had heard of.

The cars in the lot reflected the clientele; BMWs, Lexus', Jaguars, and Cadillac's; an upscale, older crowd, which Enison appreciated. He felt right at home amongst the multicultural landscape of the restaurant and it fed his passion for what he called *real* music.

As Enison opened the door and entered the restaurant, he was not aware that half a block away, a red Ferrari parked on the corner, just within view of the restaurant. Its lights went off and slid into their hidden panels and no occupant got out. Even unaware of this fact, Enison's sense of foreboding clung like a statically charged sweater. As he entered the front door, he heard a voice break through the noise and chatter and saw Geremy Goldberg standing at the sushi bar being friendly with two attractive Asian women. When he arrived at the bar they all exchanged greetings and Goldberg pushed a flask of Sake in front of him and proposed a toast. This was all too convenient, Enison thought.

Chapter 89

After the evenings seminars and dinner, Rich and Brenda returned to the trailer and sat together on the dilapidated couch. Brenda faced Rich as he slouched there with stocking covered feet propped up on the coffee table. A small CD player, hooked up to amplified computer speakers was playing Dick Blake's rendition of *How Deep is the Ocean*.

"Rich, you may have saved my life earlier," Brenda said as she touched his arm.

He glanced her and smiled, "How so?"

"About the writers. Several tried to corner me and assault me with their smartness."

She giggled.

"And what did you do?" Rich asked.

"Just like you said. Never cracked a smile—except one time—and never strayed from the topic of writing, books, and agents—mostly though, I just let them talk."

"Weren't they suspicious?"

"Oh, no. When I was bored, I started talking about myself and that usually started a chain reaction."

"No kidding."

"Sure, once they realized I was talking about myself, they suddenly had to go find an invited agent or get another drink. It was great."

"I told you. You know, all these-I mean us—writers are self-absorbed, paranoid and at a great disadvantage today," Rich said

"What do you mean?"

"Well, consider this: many, many years ago, making a career of writing was considered fickle, frivolous, and a waste of good talent. If you had a propensity for carpentry, that's what you should make your life's occupation. And wasting time on writing was NOT considered an honorable pursuit."

"Art was the same way," Brenda said. "If you didn't have a commission from some royal family, pursuing art and expecting to make a living from it was a *futile* pursuit."

"Now, every Tom, Dick and Jan wants to make a million dollars writing. They want to be the next like Tom Clancy and Dean R. Koontz or Terry McMillan," Rich said. "They want to become the next hit machine. It's very different now. And let's face it. Most people are hacks. Maybe even me."

"So, why do you write, Rich?"

Rich thought about Brenda's question.

"Don't know really. But I just know I write because I'm

compelled to."

"That's sufficiently vague. Care to elaborate?"

"I'll do my best."

"We've got all night, Rich," Brenda said smiling.

Rich looked into Brenda's eyes. There was that look; the look of someone sincerely interested in what he had to say; fascinated almost, and a look of pure infatuation. He looked way, to the cat clock on the wall and studied the paneled room. It would help him stay focused.

"I can't really explain it, Brenda. I'm not really looking to get published necessarily. I've always had good jobs. Made good money or started magazines and made good money where I was in charge and was independent. There have been, well, some setbacks. But in general, making money has never really been an issue for me. All I know is that whatever my circumstances, ever since I was a teenager I knew there were stories inside of me that needed to get out. Journalism was my ticket, my training, so to speak. But I definitely didn't intend to chase ambulances all my life. I thought working for daily newspapers and publishing magazines was a great community service. But there were always crazy ideas dancing around in my head all the time; wild, bizarre thoughts, visions, themes, inventions, characters and stories. If I didn't learn to think and write, they would be trapped there and, who knows, I might very well have gone insane."

"So, what did you do?"

"College was an exercise for me, four years of studying human nature, relationship, exploring logic and philosophy, theory and learning some solid writing skills. But the real world provided the canvas for my creativity and has been leading me steadily up to this point in my life. I'm sure you can relate to that."

"Sure, Rich. I viewed college in much the same way. I think I'm a loner like you, Rich; always thinking, analyzing, looking for an angle. And it never stops."

"Brenda, that's no accident. That's something phenomenal. That's something all great dreamers, thinkers, and artists share. It's the one thing that distinguishes the hack from the true artist. Inspiration for us comes from some cosmic place, some mysterious source and it's channeled, in a way, through us. There are writers out there who know the rules of writing from top to bottom. Writing is like designing a new McDonalds. They have to think about every sentence, every punctuation, every grammatical rule before committing a sentence to paper. Brenda, for us it's not like that. I had writing down after English 101. And I took English 101 during the summer before my senior year in college. Lyman Baker, my professor, saw that. He knew he only had a few months with me, and he made sure it counted. In a sense, that's all I really needed. The rest was icing on the cake. Brenda, without thinking, I can produce thousands of pages of almost perfect prose. Without pausing to think about it much, I can create bizarre stories and ideas. The talent and the stories are there. And those facts have fueled my career. And it's that same talent that's allowed me to survive in the corporate world all these years."

Rich propped one leg under the other and thought about what he wanted to say next.

"I'm a little older now. A little more serious, perhaps a little more selfish or self-absorbed like, well, like *them*. And I feel ready to take on societies morays, to deal with those inner conflicts that have driven me; to explore the injustices of life and to, well, take a closer look at love and see if I can't become more intimate with it."

Rich was suddenly aware that his words were pouring out of his mouth as Brenda sat patiently listening. Felling more self-conscious, he said, "But I'm babbling again like I always do."

"Oh no, Rich," Brenda said sincerely, leaning towards him and smiling.

"I appreciate your honesty. I rarely get to interact with anyone on this level. Just these few hours we've spent together shows me that superficiality is rampant in my life right now and it shows me how isolated I've become. I'm stimulated—bombarded by other people's noise every day, messages and ideas and theories that barely scratch the surface of thought. It's distracting in a sense, and when I decide I want more, there seem to be only two extremes. The intellectual zealots, who can only communicate on an intellectual level and are so completely absorbed in their own ideas that I can't relate, or there are truly stupid people who only react to the world and never really analyze it."

"Yes," Rich agreed. "The key is balance. I will never say that I'm better than anyone. I am cursed with the gift of observation and interpretation, so I do have to make fun of people. That's the itinerant comedian in me. But I know there is some of everyman and everywoman in me, from the trailer trash in rural Washington to the Publisher of the *New York Times*."

"Rich, you're a breath of fresh air. Our quest seems to be the same. That's why I'm here this weekend. I think that's why we have always gotten along so well. Rich, I'm younger than you, by a few years—"

"Quite a few I'd say," Rich interrupted and laughed.

"And I'm also cursed with the gift, as you might call it. Only I've known it since I was five and everyone else has known it and I've never been allowed for a minute to forget it. And everyone else, from my surgeon father, former debutante and beauty queen mother to all of her non-profit benefactor cronies. It's been a real struggle to find myself amidst all the hoopla. You see, Rich, once wealthy people realize they have a potential Pollock or O'Keeffe or Frida in their midst, they scramble like sperm seeking an egg, a frenzy of pampering, giving, helping, nurturing and worst of all sheltering. They erect what I call the Caucasian shield of support that's forged by money and power, classism and racism. When you're behind the shield and you don't mind it, it's cool. You have everything you need. But when you're behind the shield and you want to get out and experience the world, it's miserable. Rich, I was one of the miserable ones. I could see that there was no way I could grow as an artist spending all my time with White wealthy matronly grandmothers and their heirs who always spoke in terms of them, they, and those people versus us."

Brenda paused and looked down at her fingers, which she was scraping nervously with her fingernail.

"So, I rebelled, Rich, and it was the most painful—maybe best thing I've ever done. But sometimes I wonder..."

Brenda's lower lip began to quiver as she thought of what to say next. Rich, seeing her discomfort with the subject and hesitation, leaned toward her and rubbed her shoulders gently to encourage her.

"What is it Brenda? You can talk to me. I'm not here to judge, only to listen," Rich said, concerned.

"Rich, I am in exile in my own country," She said, sniffling, fighting to hold back tears. "I dropped out Julliard and walked away from my family close to two years ago. They were smothering me, trying to make me into something I did not want. I hated them for that. My father is an arrogant bastard who only cares about himself and the family name. And if any of them knew I was here in Long Beach, Washington, alone in an beat up old trailer with a Negro, they would try to have me committed."

Glistening droplets appeared under Brenda's eyes and rolled down her cheeks, leaving shiny stripes on her face. Rich got up, went to the bathroom and emerged with toilet paper.

"Sorry, this is all we have," he said, handing it to her as he sat down on the couch again, this time, closer to Brenda. Rich turned towards her again, shifted his body slightly and wrapped his arms around her and pulled her close to him. She hesitated at first, a natural defense for her, but seconds later she gave in.

"Don't be afraid, Brenda. Remember, I am everyman and everywoman," Rich said softly. "In me is the compassion of ages. Comforting, nurturing are second nature to me. And one thing I've learned by having kids is that we adults never stop needing the same things we needed as kids, somebody to hold us and say it's going to be okay."

Brenda's crying became more pronounced as she buried her face in Rich's shoulder. Rich was silent. This was no time to talk. When someone was feeling so much pain, they should be allowed to indulge in it, to realize it. The soothing array of complex piano signatures of Dick Blake's rendition of *The Touch of Your Lips* filled the room. Rich listened to the music, Brenda's soft sobbing, the heater knocking loudly in the back of the trailer and thought about the many impromptu magic moments in his life. This was perhaps one of the best.

Chapter 90

The police officer shooting a Glock six stalls away from Grimsley and talking with J.D. approached Grimsley cautiously.

"Grimsley, sir, I wasn't sure whether to call out the bomb squad or just duck for cover," Paulson said.

"Hold your ears and duck for cover son," Grimsley said, glancing at Paulson and surrendering a slight smile. "More people went deaf using these things than were killed by them."

"And your friend back there," Paulson said, while gesturing towards J.D. "He's a real racist isn't he?"

Grimsley, stopped, looked hard at Paulson, smiled and asked, "How could you tell?"

"At first I thought he was being sincere when he thanked me for protecting the 'people of this great nation.' But he blew it when he said 'some of your people have proved to be great American citizens and patriots.' Where do they make people like that?"

"Eastern Washington," Grimsley answered. "I thought you knew all about that. You know, Walla, Walla is the hive and Kennewick was the birthplace. The ancient remains they found there were of the first racist that ever lived in North America, which is why the Natural History Museum and the Klan are both interested in it."

"Seriously Grimsley," Paulson responded, "do you consider him a friend?"

"I do, Paulson," Grimsley returned. "But I don't agree with his politics or his views on race and I remind him of that every day. Best God damn cop I've know though. Used to be captain of the northeast precinct—your people's neighborhood. No-one was more passionate about creating a safe environment for your friends up there—and I don't mean that negatively. No one did more to make your neighborhood safe. So, the only question that remains here is can you be a good, noble, well intended person, even a God damn hero and still be a racist? If you free the slaves but still promote segregation, what does that make you? That's a classic historical dilemma. And we still don't have an answer for that one. Washington liberated our country but was a slave owner. Was he a good person or a bad person? Lincoln freed the slaves but didn't want them fraternizing with White people. Good or bad? God created us in his own image but somehow gave his followers the idea that White people were different, better, special and therefore superior to ALL other races. Good God? Bad God? And finally—and you'll appreciate this one—12 to 15 million African men, women and children were kidnapped and sold into slavery by their African brethren. Africans: Good? Bad? And, by the way, aren't you a little pissed about that?"

"I see your point, sir," Paulson said, "But you can't use history to protect one man's racist attitudes."

"On the contrary," Grimsley disagreed, "you can use history to justify and understand his views and tie that back to human nature. Now, will understanding human nature and history change attitudes?"

"I don't know."

"I'll answer that one. It did for me. And I will tell you this, son, that's coming from the son of one of the largest plantation and slave owners in Virginia. JD's heart and actions are in the right place, but they occupy a different place than his views. Good person? Bad person? Should I hate someone because they—like you—believe in the archaic idea of separate but equal?"

Paulson had no retort, and sensed he was being baited—again. He was not prepared for any intellectual sparing right now and anxious to change the subject. He both admired and was uncomfortable with Grimsley's, at times, impeccable logic and knowledge about history and audacity.

At that point he decided he was going to try to level the playing field if he could. He would take a crash course in world history and politics and be ready the next time Grimsley tried to pin him against the wall with some grand argumentative soliloquy.

Examining Grimsley's collection of weapons, Paulson asked, "What kind of guns do you have there, sir?"

"You interested in antique guns?" Grimsley asked.

"A little. What cop isn't?"

"You'd be surprised at how many gun control freaks we have in our ranks Paulson."

Grimsley picked up one of the guns neatly lined up on the counter as if they were newborn babies.

"I'm not one of them, sir. What's that one?"

"This, Paulson was the true peacemaker that never caught on." He gently handed it to Paulson.

Paulson examined the unusual pistol.

"What is it?"

"That, son, is an experimental Winchester rifle slash pistol. Twenty two caliber bolt action, cast brass rec with gold gilding and walnut grips with mother of pearl inlay. Deadly accurate and rare. Too bad too. Just never caught on. Colt .45 was just too popular. How much do you think that gun is worth?"

"Don't know, sir."

"Try ten thousand on for size. Only a few of these made."

"Ten thousand!" Paulson said, surprised, "You sure you want to shoot with this or donate it to a museum?"

"What's the point of having guns if you can't shoot them?" He took the gun from Paulson. "You know who was the best gun-maker in the world?"

"Don't know that either, sir, but I think you're about to tell me."

"German fella named Johann Adam Kuchenreuter. Made the most perfect weapon of the time."

Grimsley picked up a pistol and showed it to Paulson. "Anybody with the right tools could make a weapon. Kuchenreuter made parlor pistols and dueling pistols used by royalty. Called them Kingly Bavarian court-gun-makers. Original, rare, and brilliantly crafted Kuchenreuter pistols still pop-up in personal estates in Europe all the time. Finest craftsmanship I've ever seen."

"What about Winchester and Colt?"

"Keep in mind, son, we didn't start making guns on our own until well after the Chinese, British and Germans. Americans, like with everything else, built for sturdiness and volume not necessarily high quality. Can't imagine a jewel encrusted, mahogany stock Colt forty five. That's kind of dandy, don't you think? But a king did not hesitate to order a set of Ebony handled, pearl-inlay dueling percussion pistols, complete with mahogany, gold-trimmed case, and a muzzle scroll engraved with the maker's full name and the court's coat of arms on the stock. Needless to say that faulty manufacturing under those circumstances could cost a gun maker his head."

"Thanks for the gun lesson, sir, but do you want to talk about the case? I have some good news for you."

"Sure Paulson. You haven't talked to anyone else about what you know yet, right?"

"No Sir. Only fed the uniforms the obvious stuff. What I have for you is strictly between you and me."

"Here, put this on," Grimsley said, handing Paulson a pair of ear muffs with a built in radio receiver and a flexible microphone mouthpiece, like a bulbous telephone headset used by professional football coaches on the sidelines. Grimsley placed one on his head. Paulson placed his one his head.

"Can you hear me Paulson?"

"Loud and clear sir."

"Good," he said as he picked up the large cannon-like rifle and held it up so Paulson could see it.

"This is a forty four caliber M 89 Marlin musket. Only 67 of these were made. Blow a God damn hole in the side of a freight train. I'm going to fire off a few of these. If this knocks me on my ass, ignore me. I'll be okay. Think you can fill me in while I do this?"

"I think so sir. And I think you're going to find what I say very interesting sir."

Grimsley pointed the weapon at the target and squeezed the trigger. A paralyzing blast echoed throughout the range as the target was instantly shredded, again attracting the attention of every other shooter in the building.

"God damn it. Son of a bitch kicks my ass every time," Grimsley barked.

"You all right sir?" Paulson asked through the headset, as Grimsley set the rifle down and held his shoulder, rubbing it gently.

"Yeah, Paulson, I'm all right. It'll take me a few minutes to recover and to reload this thing. Tell me what you know Paulson."

Chapter 91

Temple sent an encrypted e-mail to senator Neil telling him that Trixie's journals had been shipped to him and that Chico was no longer a threat. He regretted to inform the Senator, however, that several months worth of entries were missing, which indicated that there my be one or two journals unaccounted for; entries that might include information about the Senator.

Temple's cell phone rang immediately.

"Hello Sir," he said, "you got my e-mail?"

"Yes, Temple, and I'm concerned."

"I understand, sir."

"Any ideas about where that, um, those journals might be?"

"Only a few people may have had access, sir. Chico, Grimsley or Paulson. I also tracked the anonymous report to a paperboy named Franklin. Called in the shooting and ran. Means he probably saw something or knows something. But I can't get to him. Grimsley's got him in a box."

"What about Chico? The police don't know anything more than what they're supposed to know. There were no lose ends, sir."

"The stakes are high here Temple. We're not the only ones with a lot to lose. You need to find those other journals before anyone else does. Get to that paperboy and shake him down. Find out what he knows. And if Paulson or Grimsley get in your way, you know what to do."

Temple loved that kind of talk.

"I know what to do."

"And if you get caught?"

"I know, sir," Temple said. "I verified the funds. If I don't do anything stupid I can serve my time and be out in time to withdraw the principle and all interest and write my own ticket for the rest of my life."

"That's right, Temple. All courtesy of this great nation you've served so proudly."

"Don't worry, sir. This will all be over soon," he assured the senator and hung up.

Chapter 92

Rich felt the warmth of Brenda's body and heard her quietly sigh as she continued to sob. Delicate, warm, wet tears landed on his neck and tickled as they rolled down to the collar of his T-shirt. The China Moon perfume was intoxicating and made his head light.

They sat listening to the sound of their nervous breaths, neither feeling it necessary to speak, listening to Blake's melodic piano strokes. Blake's music brought back memories of watching a brilliant sunrise on Venice Beach in California many years earlier while listening to Nat King Cole singing the same song that was now playing. Rich softly sang the words as he remembered.

> *...And when my life is through*
> *And the angels ask me to recall*
> *The thrill of them all*
> *Then I will tell them darling*
> *I remember you...*

Brenda's sobs subsided as she listened. She turned her face slowly towards Rich; their faces barely an inch apart now. The soft, brown incandescent glow of the table lamp reflecting off the wood paneled walls made Brenda's face seem surreal as the light glistened off the tears that formed in her eyes.

Her hair partially covered one eye, but both were fixed on Rich. He could feel her hot breath on his face as their eyes remained locked in a hypnotic stare. Rich could sense the sexual tension growing inside as Brenda became visibly flush and her breathing more rapid. Rich's heart beat faster, like a kettle drum as he anticipated and intellectualized what might happen next.

An invisible magnet seemed to pulled them closer together as their lips locked in a deep passionate kiss, tongues delicately probing in their mouths, exploring, teasing and tempting, speaking an ancient mating language. Brenda pulled him closer and he could feel her firm breast against his chest and feel himself growing more and more aroused.

Brenda used one hand to guide Rich's hand under her loose, fitting silk T-shirt. Her warm breast completely filled his hand and her nipple peaked up between his fingers as he squeezed gently. Brenda closed her eyes and moaned.

The thrill of them all, he thought as the song ended and Blake eased into his rendition of *Tenderly*. Rich hesitated briefly as common sense kicked in. This was wrong he thought. He repeated that over and over in his head. Stop now. But it felt too good. And who would know?

As he subconsciously rationalized, his hand moved over Brenda's soft skin to the other breast and he squeezed. He felt as if he was being guided by the puppeteer of desire himself.

As Rich's fingers explored, Brenda moaned and pressed harder against Rich as she squirmed with pleasure. Their bodies were pressing close together and mouths were locked in a deep kiss as Rich's hand explored; both breathing heavily.

The animal instincts that drove men and women together were taking over as lust boiled inside of them. There was no turning back now.

The loud boom seemed to shift the very foundation of the gun range as Grimsley fired another shot. Even through the ear protectors, Paulson's ear drums ached. Grimsley was groaning with pain and cursing.

"Shall I continue, sir?" Paulson asked.

"Sure Paulson. This will pass."

"We found Chico's apartment. Regent Street apartments on 42nd and Emerson. Sleazy slum of a studio that looked like it should be quarantined as an EPA super-fund site."

"That sounds about right."

"We did not find a weapon, but we found lots of big tit magazines, booze, and roaches the size of Buicks. Very few clues. He wrote next to nothing and owned next to nothing. Typical transient life. We also know about his L.A. connections and it appears Chico was in hiding, on the run from some very dangerous drug dealers. This could have been their handy work."

"Nope," Grimsley said as he cleaned the chamber of the rifle, "Don't think so. This is not how L.A. gangs work. One, they're not that sophisticated. They typically bring in 10 people, walk into the room and start shooting like a bunch of fuckin' idiots. They don't do knives. Knives are for putas. They have standard issue weapons, like the military, 38mm S & W semi-auto for larger gangs, 22 cal. pea shooters for smaller gangs. No Glocks, Walther PPK's or Rugers; those are reserved for the Aryan Nation and Skin heads. Mafia is a 38 mm Baretta; single bullet in the head. To the Mafia, it's personal, intimate, and they always say, 'fucking schmucks. I loved this guy' right before pluggin' a guy. Knives are, well, knives are typical used by NSA,

CIA, Special Forces and Ninja assassins."

"Why is that, sir?"

"You can shoot a guy 16 times and he can still live. You cut his throat or disembowel him, and he doesn't have a chance in hell. L.A. gang members have no training and couldn't hit their dicks even with a full woody and a sight scope trained on it. They could shoot off 100 rounds and maybe five bullets might hit something. And they haven't figured it out yet. That's great for us. No stress fire training. That's why so many gang members end up in jail or dead. Their victim lives to tell the tale. Mafioso on the other hand, go for the law of averages; fuckin' mathematicians, all of them. One out of every one million guys plugged in the head lives. And that one guy ends up a vegetable or too afraid to talk, 'cause a second bullet in the head really smarts. Know what I mean? And the law of averages is against him then."

"What about the Asian gangs and Russian gangs?"

"Don't get me started Paulson," said Grimsley, suddenly becoming more excited. "The bridge between the Asians and the Russians is a very short one and they have both learned from each other. Mao Tse Tung as you know was a student of Stalin and the cultural blending of Russia and Asia has been happening over centuries. Both cultures understand that there are a million ways to torture or kill a person, so it's very hard to ID these gangs based on MO. But if you piss off these guys, you just have to watch your ass and expect to die in some horrible, humiliating way. The act of killing does not bring pleasure or revenge, but securing a horrible, terrible, symbolically significant death for one's enemies brings honor among these gangs. And the perpetrator is honored in legend and song. Fuckin' bizarre if you asked me. Whomever did this was classically trained, a blend of Russian, Asian tactics to be sure. But because there were no symbols or clues left behind by the perpetrator, we can rule out the Russians and the Chinese. This is pure sneaky, clandestine shit. Probably NSA."

Sensing the conversation might stray, Paulson said, "Sir, we're getting a little of topic. Shall I continue?"

"Oh, sorry," Grimsley said as he aimed and pulled the trigger. BOOOM!!! "Jeeeeeez!" he yelled and said in the same breath, "You know how I love talking about this stuff."

Temple settled into his sprawling room at the Embassy Suits hotel. Temple was lying naked on the bed, remote control in one hand and his penis in the other. He had used the remote to order several pay per view porn movies and as the big silicone breasted bodies bobbed up in down on the screen and naked men rammed themselves into their delicate bodies, Temple gently massaged himself.

He felt power in being able to view porn as he pleased, being able to do what he pleased and being able to snuff out lives as he pleased. Lives that will never experience what he was experiencing now ever again.

A man pleasuring himself was the greatest show of power. Man was self sufficient. He didn't need women. With enough money and power, he could have as many children as he wanted. With a phone call, he could have 10 women to perform any services he wanted. But he did not want that right now.

He loved the idea of pleasure and women but hated women even more now. Women were for performing sex, chores and raising children. A man dependent on a woman was not a man. He would never rely on a woman for pleasure and he would never show any woman any level of acquiescence or vulnerability. Ball busters. All of them. There were times like these where a man had to be alone with himself.

On the screen, a pretty brunette sucked the enormous, erect dick of an African American.

"God damn, those guys are fucking horses. Where do they find those guys?" he mumbled, as he rubbed his erect penis harder.

The African American actor rammed his penis into the women and she screamed, "Oh my God, your so big. Fuck my pussy you Black stallion. Then fuck my ass. Oh, yes, your so fucking big."

Temple felt his heart racing, pulsating, sending torrents of blood to his throbbing member. He felt the power surging inside of him, the tingling deep in his gut, the rush as his body started to spasm. He thought about his now ex-wife and visions of the hundreds of women he had fucked swirled in his head.

The African American sprinkled oil on the woman's ass then rammed his penis into her tiny orifice, her hole offering little resistance. She screamed and bit the couch cushion as he pounded harder and harder as if trying to shove his huge member all the way through her.

In a frenzied fit of passion, he pulled his 12 inch penis out of her and straddled her as she turned over and in a plethora of lust and sweat and moaning and screaming and groaning began squirted cum all over her face.

Temple, at the same time, let out a guttural groan that was almost animal sounding; sustained and intense as the pressure built up inside of him, like some kind of demon possessing him and forcing its way out. The spasms were intermittent as hot cum shot out of his penis, landing on his stomach and on the bed, pumping steadily; sticky, creamy; raw power surging from inside of him.

On the screen, the African American slumped over the woman, sweat glistening off of his muscular, mahogany body, the brunette still wreathing with pleasure as the white sticky jizz dripped down her nose and onto her breast as she licked what she could from around her lips and rubbed the rest across her enormous fake breast.

Temple watched intensely but didn't move. He glanced at the sticky liquid that now covered his hands and body and thought, this is the way it is supposed to be. Man as a force. Man as the creator, the builder, the ruler, the keeper of the seeds of life. He possessed what woman wanted and that gave him superiority.

Temple turned off the TV, cleaned himself up, sat in the middle of the room with legs crossed and meditated on his dilemma, sorting and analyzing his problem and the solution.

He would remain there for hours. He would, in fact, sleep in that position. In the morning he would know exactly what to do. He took no notes, left no important information in his pocket PC. Everything was mapped out in his head. It was the only computer he relied on because it could never be compromised. The first order of business was planning an appointment with a paperboy that he had to keep.

Enison and Goldberg spent three hours together in Yoshi's upstairs jazz bar. Chambers found a corner at the Sushi bar downstairs and feasted on Sushi, Sashimi and sake while he watched the monitors that showed the bands performing and the crowed upstairs.

Ingenious, thought Chambers. You could eat downstairs and watch the jazz upstairs. When you finished eating, you could go upstairs and enjoy live jazz. Get all the bullshit talking out of the way and actually listen to the music, especially the young people on their first dates.

Chambers was positioned in front of two monitors; one that showed the stage and one that showed Enison and Goldberg at their table. Chambers could only see Enison's face and, while reading his lips, caught one half of the conversation, which made it difficult to piece together what they were talking about. He, surreptitiously recorded what he could into a micro-cassette player he kept in his palm that had an ear piece with a microphone attached. Most who saw him either thought he was schizophrenic or figured out he was talking on his cell phone.

After the first set, Darryl Grant walked off the stage and joined Enison and Goldberg. Grant sat with his back facing the screen. Their conversation became even more cryptic from there because Enison could now only catch one-third of a three part conversation. He'd have to study the tapes when he got home and fill in the gaps.

Chamber's cell phone rang, which caught him off guard. Few had the number nor even knew he carried a cell phone. He took it from his pocket and answered.

"Talk to me," he said in a gruff voice.

"Hi, it's me?," Sara's delicate voice answered. *"I hope I'm not interrupting anything."*

"Heya doll face," Chambers said, now remembering he had done something he'd never done before and given Sara his cell phone number. He found himself suddenly in a better mood when he heard her voice.

"Spookin' a couple suspicious corporate types. Howya doin angle cakes?"

"Fine. Thanks. I was just calling to see if you wanted to meet me after work."

"Sure, baby. I didn't scare you off this morning?"

"No, you didn't. I told you. I'm not one of those ditsy bimbos who wants to domesticate you like some farm animal and force you to commit and have a baby with me. I just want to spend a little time together. You make me laugh."

"Well, sister, that's just about the sweetest thing anybody's ever said to me. I been accused of a lot of things; bein' a jerk, a prick; even a great fuckin' cook; but never been accused of being a funny guy, so I'm not gonna fight you on this one. Meet me at the Top of the Mark in the city."

"Top of the Mark?" she asked, puzzled.

"Don't tell me you never been there? Top of the Mark Hopkins Hotel, the ballroom. Those smoes you been hanging around all been takin' you to the wrong places. It's in Union Square offa Powell. Take a cab, they'll know where to go and I'll cover the tab. We'll do a little dancin' then I'll take you to Napa tomorrow. All right?"

"*All right. I take it it's a fancy place so I'll dress to the nines, like a real lady.*"

"Yeah baby. We're on then. And make sure you don't give nobody this number. Most of these schmucks out here don't even know I have a cell phone. And there's a lot of sneaky bastards out there who'd love to know what I know. They'll hire children to come up to you and ask you personal question like if maybe if you know me. Maybe if you got a number for me 'cause it's some kinda emergency. Then they got their meat hooks into my business. Know what I mean? Took me years to get people to think the rotary dial phone in my apartment is all the technology I got. And I like it that way. See you later puddin' stick."

He hung up.

Chapter 93

"You we're right about the mine sweeper you saw. Turns out he's a professional treasure hunter. Name's Marvin Penderson. Spent two tours in Nam doing recon. Highly decorated. After Nam, he retired and eventually became a professional treasure hunter. A Kay Modgline and Mel Fisher protégé; helped locate some of the 1715 Spanish Plate fleet,"

Small caliber gunfire echoed in the background.

"I'll be God damn. Lucky guess I guess." Grimsley replied, still busying himself cleaning the handguns as he spoke and placing them in their leather pouches.

"Said he wipes his butt with a thousand dollars a day, but he'd take a look 'cause he knows about you and was happy to do you a favor. All he wants is to have a Scotch with you some day at Kell's and swap stories."

"No problem. So he took a look at the crime scene?"

"Yes, sir. After fifteen minutes a the scene he concluded that the bullet never reached the brush. It landed in the street and was either picked up on a unsuspecting car tread or the killer fished it from the scene before leaving."

"That so? I never thought of that," Grimsley responded, scratching his head. "Any clues about the caliber of weapon from the coroner."

"Still would not commit because the entry wound bore no conclusion. Twenty two or thirty eight could have made that mess. Without the slug, we're just guessing."

"All right, we know what we don't have," Grimsley said, somewhat exasperated. "What do we actually have?"

"Forensics has matched Chico's hairs found in the van, and DNA from the puke and the prints to Chico. They matched perfume residue on his clothing with the scented oil we found in the van called China Rain, to him as well. Residue was found on his hands and clothing. Unmistakable chemical make-up and only sold in one shop in town, the Body Shop. Perfect match. And finally, they found one of Trixie's hairs in his stocking cap."

"So Chico is our shooter?" Grimsley asked.

"It would seem that way."

"So who offed Chico and why?"

"Does it matter, sir?" This time Paulson was baiting Grimsley.

Grimsley, stopped polishing the Kuchenrouter pistol in his hands and studied Paulson, and, seeing through his question right away, he said, "You would think not, son. You would think not. One dirt bag knocks off another. Should we really give a crap? But I think you know the answer to that one. What's the big picture Paulson? You're holding out again, I can see it in your eyes. But at least this time it's well tempered, well timed. I like that."

Paulson smiled. He'd given it to Grimsley straight, as Grimsley had asked. And Grimsley was not buying. Now it was time to exercise his own brand of genius.

He continued.

"On one hand, Chico looks like our boy. And he may well be. But there are too many missing pieces to come to that conclusion. Trixie was too smart and elusive to be involved only with a dimwit like Chico. I think he was a pet project for her. Everything we've seen tells us there was more to her than meets the eye; an enigma, if you will, a very smart girl with a complex life she deliberately manufactured."

"Paulson, you have my undivided attention."

"Frankly, from what we've learned about Chico, I don't think he had the balls or the wits to pull something like this off. Apparently animal control in Compton had a rap sheet ten miles long on Chico. Cat torture was his stick. I'd say that whoever is complicit in this is smart, keeping a half step ahead of us, which indicates some inside intel. They're the sophisticated ones. And all fingers I think are too conveniently pointing to Chico."

"That's what you think Sherlock?" Grimsley asked.

"I think the hunt is afoot, sir," Paulson answered sarcastically, smiling, "And I also think we—meaning you and me and our paperboy—are in the middle of it, surrounded by whatever Trixie knew."

"What do you think Trixie knew?"

"As I said, sir, she was no ordinary prostitute. We've seen this before. She was smart. She knew how to protect her assets; how to use money to her advantage and she probably knew how to make a lot of it and be very discreet about it, even at a young age. A girl in her position sometimes has to grow up fast. Most people assume prostitutes and porn stars are uneducated sluts. But you and I know better. Nike has figured out how to make billions off of sports attire, prostituting the public in exchange for dreams of greatness. Surely a smart prostitute can appeal to that same sense of vanity and to men with too much money and not enough to spend it on. The writing is on the wall, so to speak, sir." Paulson said, subtly referring to the notes in the van.

Then he paused. Grimsley raised a customary eyebrow at his comment.

"More clues are out there," he said, "we just have to find them first. And I think we're running out of time."

"Good, Paulson," Grimsley said. Paulson sensed a hint of pride in Grimsley's voice. "Now, this is all fairly broadband. Let's narrow the band a bit. The sneaky bastards behind Chico's murder?"

"They're creating missing links, re-directing, sir, like you wrote about in your book. Playing a game of hide and seek and catch me if you can. But as careful as they were, we could tell that both Chico's apartment and his hotel room were meticulously, and carefully searched. We found where the dust shifted when objects that had not been moved in a year were moved and carefully returned to their original place. And based on what you told me about Ali, they have the cash to back up their efforts."

"Here's the question: did they find what they were looking for?"

"Don't know, sir. Can't really say. Because we don't know what they were looking for. We know it wasn't big tit magazines. Those were in abundance. But if I venture a guess, I would say they didn't."

"What could it be Paulson? The answer may save your skin and my skin and maybe even the skin of a paperboy who has two beautiful kids and wife and great future as a novelist; our customer."

Paulson was silent as he thought through the question and the clues.

"From what I've seen of these types of circumstances, sir, it's usually diaries or journals or call list or little black books that lead to this kind of murder and mayhem."

"Bingo, Paulson. You're now operating on all three pistons."

"Don't you mean four, sir."

"For you, three. I think the fourth will kick in sometime soon. We need to find that apartment, the second location. Any luck on that?"

"Nothing. Some clerks recognized her picture; even one bus driver, a particularly unsavory man who I wanted to arrest just for the hell of it. He recognized her but if he knew anything, would not offer any more clues. Said he recognized her but never paid attention to where she got off. When I challenged that, he got belligerent and told me to either arrest him or get the fuck off his bus."

"Customer?"

"Maybe. Or Trixie could have been toying with him and he's still pissed about it. Everything else is a dead end."

Grimsley did not speak, nor did Paulson until Grimsley said, "Say, Paulson, I'm having dinner with the paperboy Monday night. You and your wife are welcome."

Sensing an opportunity, Paulson said, "Sure, is this an interrogation?"

"Sort of. But not really. You like jazz?"

"I do, sir; mostly smooth jazz. You know, Kenny G., Yanni, John Tesh."

Grimsley raised both eyebrows, furrowed, lightly bit his lower lip and said, "Hate to burst your bubble, Paulson, but that's not jazz. I got some Miles, Mingus and Coltraine I think you're going to like."

"Oh, yeah, old jazz—"

"No, Paulson, real jazz," Grimsley interrupted, slightly irritated, but softening his tone to further entice Paulson. "Come on by, bring your wife. I'm cooking."

"Okay, sir. I'll be there."

"And Paulson, keep a man on the paperboy and the house."

"Taken care of, sir. Got a writer friend of mine, who's also a damn good investigator in Long Beach right now and a uniform on the house. I won't let anything happen to our boy or his family, sir. Like you said; our customers. We serve and protect."

"I've got some people working on ID'ing our assassin. But, Paulson, that's all I can tell you. These people are what I call Intel fathoms. They don't really exist for you and me. They make a good living providing information. They're like agents with no government affiliations. They're loyalties are unquestionable, and they're smarter than you and I combined. I've got one of my best on this one because you can bet your ass that even if we find him, he's already covering his trail right now. These bastards disappear as fast as they appear and there are a thousand ways from Sunday to get lost in the world if you can afford it. These guys can afford it. Know what I mean?"

"I think I get the picture, sir. I should assume that everything I do; everyone I know; and everything I say may be compromised. So, it's like a chess game. I make a move, anticipate a counter move and protect my people as best as I can without losing anyone.

"Yep. But we've already lost two, Paulson, our queen and a prick—er, pawn, so we're losing the game right now. But masters can win even without the queen. And, fortunately, our queen is still helping us posthumously. Let's show these sons of bitches how smart we really are Paulson. It's time to be on the offensive and not on the defensive. Get my drift?"

"Yes, sir."

Chapter 94

Rich woke up at two thirty in the morning, his mental clock refusing to turn off, even on weekends. He completed the re-writes on his novel by six-thirty and was giddy about the prospects the day presented.

What happened with Brenda the night before, however, filled him with apprehension, excitement and fear. He had completed a lifelong goal and may have possibly made the biggest mistake in his life all within twenty four hours.

All he could do was curse fate and himself while patting himself on the back. The irony was stifling and thrilling.

When Brenda awoke at seven, he invited her to take a quick walk on the beach before breakfast and the morning seminars and she excitedly accepted his invitation.

The morning mist had cleared, exposing a brilliant Sun. The ocean breeze was still chilly, though, and nipped at their faces as they hiked on a barely visible trail through thick woods that led to the beach.

Scrub Jays screeched out warning cries as they approached and tiny brown-headed towhees darted in and out of the brush like little dark rats with bills. The trees were draped with rich green lichen and moss that looked like ancient beards on elderly trees standing sentry for the beach. The beach was empty save hundreds of sandpipers racing away from the rushing tide as small groups of sea gulls pecked at vacant crab shells and rotting seaweed, scavengers foraging for scraps of sustenance.

Brenda and Rich were mostly silent as they hiked, only speaking to confirm the way to the beach or comment on the cold.

Halfway to the beach, Rich gripped Brenda's hand and led her through the high grass covered dunes that led to the flat expanse of the beach. They continued holding hands as they walked south, where they would warm up with a mocha or latte at a small coffee shop in Seaview. It was a mile away, so they had plenty of time to walk, talk, maybe sort out the awkward circumstance they had both created. Brenda broke the ice.

"Rich, I'm not sorry about last night," she said, nervously, then continued, "and, I...well, I just wanted to know how you felt. I know this is kinda weird."

Rich did not answer right away. He decided to let the tension build as he thought about his answer, and truth was, he was not sure what to say, so he finally said, "Brenda, I don't know what to say. I know many fancy me the Safeway answer man kind of guy, but right now I don't know what to say."

Rich looked out at the tumbling waves crash against the beach as they roared, grumbled and dissipated in rolling lines of foam and seaweed. He focused his attention on the graceful dance of the sandpipers, the sound of the waves, and the cries of the sea gulls as if they might have an answer to this dilemma. They walked slowly, Brenda's arms curled around Rich's. In the distance, they could see an approaching jogger with a dog at his side.

"Brenda, you want me to be honest, right?" Rich finally asked.

Brenda looked at Rich and reluctantly said, "Sure Richey. I would expect that from you."

Rich looked at her. And there was that look again. This time, she knew he knew, and she smiled a smile that made his heart race like a dirt bike and skip a beat at the same time. Rich was thinking, *she's magnificent.*

But his mouth said otherwise.

"Brenda, I'm excited, nervous, scared, happy, sad, depressed, frustrated, elated and cold, all at the same time."

Rich glanced at Brenda and smiled. She blushed. The rising sun created cast a warm glow on the beach.

"You're right. This is all pretty awkward, you know?" Rich said, "Who really knows what the right thing to say is in a moment like this. I suppose, the old standards work. You know, I had a wonderful time last night. You were great. I think you're really a special and wonderful person. But, Brenda, while I'm great at creating those conversations in my head, they never come out of my mouth that way. It never sounds right coming out of my mouth. I always feel like a puppet in a play or like I'm trapped in some kind of bad B-movie, unable to get out without forcing my way through a terrible script."

Brenda listened but did not respond.

Rich continued, "Brenda, I'm an aging African American—not Negro by the way—that's only used by anthropologists and southern republicans—married with two wonderful children. I'm almost fifteen years older than you. Fifteen years! I'm not Rich. I'm not famous. I'm shorter than you. I'm ten pounds over weight and could have tits of my own in a few years. And, well, I've got issues, scary issues, demons in my head, voices, multiple personalities that I can only expose in my writing."

Brenda smiled as she glanced at him. She didn't respond.

"On the other hand, Brenda, you're twenty five, in the prime of your youth, beautiful, talented, brilliant. Why in God's name would you be interested in getting involved with someone like me? I mean, don't get me wrong, I'm flattered. But you could have any guy you want;

could do so much better with less encumbrances. That's what I'm thinking right now. Why me? I don't get it."

Brenda thought for a moment then answered, "Because Rich, that was so well put. And if you have to ask that question then you probably understand why."

"I'm not followin'," Rich said.

"Well, Rich. I've been with all types of guys. The most alluring are the confident guys. Layer on creativity. Layer on intensity. Layer on mystery. Layer on handsome. Layer on unavailability. Layer on fearlessness. Layer on compassion. Layer on awareness. Layer on subtle cockiness—"

"And you end up with some kind of bizarre man meat hoagie." Rich interrupted.

Brenda and Rich both laughed at that notion and some of the tension dissipated.

"Okay, okay, okay, I'm not going to start viewing myself that way no matter what you say. I can't afford to. I have a thesaurus and I know it inside and out. And the two adjectives I prefer are unassuming and selfless. But I get your drift. I'm certainly not blind. But, Brenda, I prefer to do the complimenting around here, okay."

"You see what I mean, Rich, you're so damn charming and you won't even admit it. You're the kind of guy who is easy to fall in love with; like you walked straight out of a dream or something. I've always felt that way about you because I've seen you in action."

"I know, Brenda," Rich agreed, finally, "I've seen you watching me."

Brenda blushed slightly and a mischievous smile formed on her face.

"But, Brenda, you understand my dilemma. I may be all those things, but I also try to follow a strict code of behavior and have made some promises that I feel like I've broken. I'm feeling good and really bad right not."

"I know, Rich. I know." Brenda said sadly. "I'm sorry. I didn't mean to put you in such a spot. I know you would be good for me, Rich. I wish things were different. And I don't care that you're a colored guy. I don't see color when I look at you. I see a man, a wonderful man, and I think to myself, 'your wife is very lucky.' Your kids are very lucky. And I want what they have. And maybe I can get it from you now as opposed to waiting for Mr. Right to come along some other place. Some other time."

Brenda started to cry. They stopped walking and Rich hugged her.

"Brenda, it's okay. It's okay to want those things. But I'm not sure this is the way. You're great. I've grown very close to you this weekend and what we have can never be taken away. But I'm not available."

"I know, Rich. I know," She said, as she wiped the tears from her eyes with her sleeves, "I have to try to accept that. But it's not going to be easy. I've been falling in love with you Rich for a long time, and I'm sorry, but I've crossed over the line and I have to find my way back."

"No, Brenda, you don't have to find your way back. You just need to find *your* way, get comfortable within your own skin, make peace with yourself, your family if you can and invest in yourself; find the way that makes sense for you right now. This bond between us can never be changed and can never be broken, but the nature of our relationship can't continue down it's current path. Too many people could get hurt. And I don't think you want that on your shoulders; nor do I. We both already have too much to think about in our lives."

They continued walking in silence. Soon, they approached an opening in the beach that led to a blacktop that was partially covered by sand. A small building that housed a bathroom was on the left, and the small coffee shop called the Seaview Café was on the right.

"We're almost there," Rich said.

"Oh, that's a cute place. I'm so cold. A hot coffee will be perfect right now," Brenda announced between sniffles.

"Brenda," Rich asked, as they reached the bright lit glass door of the café. Beyond the door, several people sipped cups of steaming coffee at broad, varnished driftwood tables, "do you think we're going to be okay? Is this the beginning of a beautiful friendship ruined by a moment of weakness?"

Brenda looked at Rich and answered, "Rich, we could never ruin our friendship. I just think we're a little closer now. We understand each other a little more. And I think, like you said, we also both have a lot to think about."

"That's what I was afraid of," Rich replied, "Shall we get some Joe."

"Sure Rich," Brenda said, smiling.

Chapter 95

Rich left the writer's retreat early Saturday afternoon and found a wifi hotspot and e-mailed his manuscript from the Ocean Park public library. Then he returned to attend the afternoon seminars, spent another night with Brenda, then on Sunday afternoon, they bid each other an awkward and inconclusive bon voyage.

When he arrived home on Sunday evening, he felt a great sense of relief. Everyone was there. Everyone was all right. He hugged April and kissed her like he hadn't done in a long time and he gave the children extra long hugs as well.

He was home; everything was as it should be. The pandemonium of the house allowed him to drift back into father slash husband mode; the writer retreating back to his cave; the semi-intellectual retiring to his mental den; and the elusive liar and potential scumbag as he called them retreating to their prison cells; all convenient places in his head to house these seemingly multiple personas until forced to the surface again by circumstance.

That was his head, he felt, a prison for desirable and disreputable personalities and bizarre creative types, like a sleazy hotel for people who should never meet. That was one reason ten years earlier he had cut his alcohol consumption by ninety percent. When he drank too much, all the demons and personalities joined in one big freaky frat party in his head and had a mental intellectual food fight.

Staying sober allowed him to operate on a level playing field most of the time. His indiscretions now, could not be blamed on alcohol. When the cat was let out of the bag, so to speak, he willingly and consciously made those decisions. He was in control.

Or was he?

Chapter 96

Brenda's mood was sullen as she drove back to Portland. Instead of taking highway 30 along the Columbia River, she took the long way, Highway 101, through a progression of small coastal towns, then east on Highway 26 to Portland.

It was a slower route, but she needed to buy some time to think before returning to her expansive loft along the east river bank, alone to face herself and her situation again.

She was not sure how she felt about the weekend and what had happened with Rich. Crazy thoughts crowded out rational thoughts; manifesting emotions were clouding common sense and every conclusion she drew came wrapped in a question.

This could work. I've seen it work in movies. What about fatal attraction? He could love me. He could leave his wife. He won't. They never do. Could I be a mother to his kids and could we have kids or our own? He's too old. But he's so smart and cute. Our children would be beautiful. He could make me whole. I could make him whole. My father would not approve. But he would have to. I could handle it. Stand up to him. I could make him happy. We could be artist together.

All these ideas rushed through her head like the cars of a passing bullet train, disappearing as fast. Each thought created another questions, and each question created another question.

When the silence in the car collided with her rampaging thoughts, she decided to create a diversion, so she took Jill Cohen's CD out of here glove compartment and placed it in CD player.

For the moment, she was distracted by the soothing sounds of Cohn's voice. But it was only temporary. Her thoughts drifted again to the lengthy discussion she and Rich had about writing and the seminars they attended together.

Rich read some of her journals and told her they were good, but somewhat one dimensional; words piled upon words piled upon words.

At first, she was defensive, but he assured her she could do better and could get more out of them by going to the next level.

"Right now, you're merely documenting your experiences as matter of fact," he told her. "I can see the ideas here; the stories. Now, try adding some texture. Try being less of a transcriber of your days and more of a storyteller of your life experiences."

At first, she didn't understand. Then he explained, "Consider this: You could say in your journal, 'Rich and I really got to know each other this weekend. We talked about a lot of stuff. Then we returned to Portland.'"

Rich explained that he could read that and not be moved, not formulate any pictures or ideas; not understand the motivations or emotions of the characters; not really give a "Shit" as he had put it, with qualifying apologies for his French.

But, he explained if she wrote it this way: "Rich, a diminutive stump of a man with skin as black as French truffles, hobbled over to me on the first day and said, 'Prithee madam, I sense in you a desire to understand your true nature. Allow me to introduce myself. I am Cedrick, a black Smurf from the land of Chocolate covered Smurfs..."

They both shared a laugh over Rich's description. He went on to describe a fictitious experience between her and the chocolate Smurf and improvised the details of their relationship. As he talked, she drew pictures in her head and realized that the difference between what she wrote and what she could potential write were on two opposite ends of the spectrum.

After that, Brenda reread some of her entries out loud then ad-libbed how she would change them to make them better.

It was a revealing exercise for her, and Rich further explained the "we write to understand. And we write to help others understand. Use dialogue wherever possible to move the story along and give us a sense of the characters and how they interact. Use descriptive narrative only where necessary to move your story along, set the scenes or describe a character. But be thrifty so you don't bore the readers. Allow room for them to interpret and extrapolate. Readers like that. They're not stupid. Find a single story and focus on it rather than bury it or rush past it."

Brenda took all that he said to heart. When she got home, she decided she would practice what she had learned in her journal and on canvas. She would write a story about Rich and interpret that story in a painting.

Her thoughts were distracted by tiny droplets that appeared in her eyes and rolled down her cheeks and into her lap. She was thinking about how she might start her story. And the only thing she could think of was the old cliche "These were the best of times. These were the worst of times..."

Chapter 97

The dark figure sat silently in blackness of the Towncar as the engine idled. The heater forced warm air into the digitally controlled climate as the figure sat, still, staring, patient, like a leopard stalking his prey.

The Towncar was parked at the far end of the block, out of sight on the corner. Through the car speakers, the figure listened to the sound of a toilet flushing, then footsteps, a deadbolt being engaged, then he pressed a button on a small device that he held in one hand and heard the sound of an engine charging to life and the clear sounds of some type of funk music he was unfamiliar with and found rather annoying.

The bugs he planted in the paperboy's house and truck were functioning properly.

To eavesdrop was much too easy today. All he had to do was drill a series of tiny holes in the exterior of the building and place the devices in the holes in order to monitor sound in the entire house. Each device could be monitored through local area FM signals or WIFI, and he could listen to them over the car radio or on his PC. The receiver was no bigger than a Walkman.

The dark figure smiled as he listened and thought, these were the best of times for clandestine operations. Thank you Intel.

Rich's truck passed by seconds later, and just as the dark figure was about to turn on his lights to follow Rich at a discreet distance and look for the right place to make a move, he saw a pair of parking lights enter the intersection and stopped. Instinctively, he turned off the engine and ducked his head below the dash.

He cursed under his breath.

This would not be as easy as he thought. He did not have enough time to distinguish the make or model of the car. It was big, black, probably a government issue, a detective he thought. Not sure. But he couldn't risk following Rich. He couldn't risk being discovered. He would resort to plan B.

Grimsley was up early as usual. But instead of going to the firing range as he always did, he drove to the neighborhood where Trixie was killed. He had a hunch that time was running out, so he had to move quickly.

He came to a stop in front of a huge Craftman style home that was opulent by comparison to the other modest homes. Its grand porch with hand hewn pillars was imposing at first glance. Grimsley admired the bold architectural statement the house made. It seemed to say, *kiss my ass*. Grimsley liked that.

When Grimsley knocked on the door, it opened immediately. "Captain Grimsley," the figure of James Clarence Walker said. "I've been expecting you. Come in."

They shook hands and Grimsley, said, "Thank you Mr. Walker. We have to hurry. We don't have much time."

Rich arrived at the station his usual time, and Jimmy immediately started grilling him about the detective who came to see him Friday.

"You call that Negro police man like he say?"

Trying to avoid giving any details, he answered, "Yeah, Jimmy, I talked to them."

"What he want? You in some kinda trouble chief?"

"No, Jimmy, they just had some questions about the neighborhood; you know if I'd seen any suspicious characters around."

"Somethin' happen' I don't know about?"

"I don't know, Jimmy. But I gotta get these done and get out there."

"Ait chief. But don't forget Going street. Folks is havin' keniption fits on that street. And the newbie we had this weekend fucked everythin' up. You want a good tip this month, you gotta straighten all that up."

"Okay Jimmy, I'm on it. You know I can take care of this."

"I know. I know. And long as you takin' care of yo police bidness, you probly okay. You know Negro policemens don't take no stuff. Take them a long time to earn them—"

"—stripes, and we got to respect that. I know Jimmy," Rich said respectfully, not wanting to offend Jimmy.

He had grown fond of Jimmy and respected him like an uncle.

"I'm on it Jimmy. Everything will be all right."

At the moment, Africa burst into the room. He stopped at the door. His dark, angry eyes were bulging, chin high and extended. A bright, multicolored kenta cloth dashiki draped over his body. He surveyed the room as a king might survey soldiers who had showed cowardice in battle.

He announced, "I'm no gonna take these sheet no mo. I kanno do my jab if I kanno pak in de front of the bilding."

Most carriers gave quick, disapproving glances.

Africa merely stood, staring, awaiting a response.

Rich looked at Africa and their eyes met. He decided that today he was going to do something different.

Days earlier, Rich, curious about Africa's background, had done some research on the tribe Africa was from and discovered that Africa was indeed from royal lineage and had achieved the status of doctor. The internet site he found had provided some information on customs and greeting from Africa's country that Rich memorized.

Rich stepped from his post and walked to where Africa stood. He stopped in front of Africa, who's eyes were frozen on him now, piercing, unblinking.

This close, Rich could more clearly see the six tribal markings on his cheeks, healed scars from deep cuts, three on each side. His nose was wide and flared and the muscles twitched as he stood staring, breathing heavily.

He was at least a foot taller than Rich, which made Rich nervous. But he knew what he wanted to do.

Rich bowed to Africa and in the best Swahili he could muster, he said, "King Mamelo, I greet you and thank you for bestowing your presence on us."

Africa's eyes bulged even more, which Rich did not think possible and his deep breaths became more pronounced.

Having exhausted his Swahili, Rich continued in English, "Chief Mamelo, you are my brother and a king, and you may have my spot tomorrow and from this day forward."

He bowed again. Africa, tipped his head to the right, not sure how to regard Rich's gesture, then surveyed the room again. Jimmy and all the other carriers were staring in disbelief. Africa turned his attentions again to Rich and for the first time ever, a large, hauntingly beautiful, broad smile formed on his face.

Africa gave Rich a subtle bow and in Swahili, Mamelo said to Rich, "May you prosper and bear many children."

He stood erect again, thrust his chest out, chin high and forward and proudly stepped past Rich.

As he passed, he stopped, leaned over to Rich's ear and said in perfect English, loud enough for only to Rich to hear. "Thank you Mr. Richard Franklin. And, perhaps, Rich Franklin, you are a king as well."

He continued to his station and started bagging papers.

Chapter 98

April was intrigued but not thrilled about having to go to dinner at a stranger's house on a Monday night. The chief of police no less. Getting a sitter at the last minute was difficult and she was tired. And she was equally frustrated that Rich could not answer all of her questions as to why they had to do this.

"I don't know April," was all he could say when asked why, if the police wanted to ask him questions about something, didn't they just invite him down to the station during regular business hours.

"I think the captain is a jazz fan. And he didn't tell me anything more," was his response all the way to the driveway of Grimsley's home.

As they slowed and approached Grimsley's house, April suddenly became very quiet as she stared in awe at the expansive driveway that led to the Greek Revival mansion at the top of the hill.

Nighttime came early in September, so she was not able to see the carefully manicured landscape with Oregon grape, huckleberry and rhododendron bushes along with late fall blooming annuals that decorating the strip.

There were two cars in the driveway. One Rich recognized as Grimsley's, and the other he did not recognize. They parked behind Grimsley's Bronco.

The night air was damp, typical of Oregon's average 98 percent humidity this time of year, and rain could pour down from dark sky at any time.

They got out of the car. April wore a tight, dark green skirt with a delicate white blouse, both highlighting her petite hourglass frame. Her hair was tied in a bun and held there by a turquoise laden stick pin.

Rich draped her coat over her shoulders.

She was absolutely beautiful, he thought, especially for a forty year old mother of two. Maybe he was lucky after all he thought.

Rich wore all black, partly because it somewhat reflected his mood and partly because it looked good on him and gave away no clues. He had a feeling he needed be on guard tonight.

When they reached the front door after ascending a flight of fifteen stairs to reach the porch, Rich rang the doorbell which sounded like the bells of St. Patrick's relocated from New York City.

Rich surveyed the porch and the house. The exterior of the house was white. The porch was covered by a twenty foot piedmont and supported by four Corinthian style fluted columns with stiff-leaf capitals, all reminiscent of the entrance to some Greek temple. Both Rich and April felt as thought they should have worn formalwear.

Grimsley appeared at the door and smiled a broad smile. He was dressed in his typical blue jeans, Tony Lamas, plaid shirt and looked distinguish, intimidating and humble.

"Mr. Franklin, Mrs. Franklin, welcome to my home. Do come in."

"Thank you Captain Grimsley," Rich said as they entered the foyer and introduced April.

"This is casual, Mr. Franklin, Mrs., Franklin, please call me Bob."

"Thank you ,sir," Rich said, "and please call me Rich and this is April."

"Hungry?"

"Absolutely," said Rich.

"Starving," said April.

"If I may say so," Grimsley said as he led them down a long hallway, "You both look stunning tonight."

"Thank you," said April.

Rich was hesitant to respond. This was not the Grimsley he had heard about and the same elusive Grimsley who had stopped him two days earlier. The halls were lined with dark wood paneling, probably mahogany, Rich thought, and neo-classical artworks graced the walls along with some cubist and post-modern pieces; a real hodgepodge of different styles. They all seemed to be originals.

Their footsteps echoed off of the polished hardwood floors, which were old growth pine with Cherry wood inlays running along either side and composing intricate Walnut and Cherry geometric patterns in the corners.

In another room, Rich could hear John Coultrane playing on the stereo. Coultrane complimented the rich wood textures, Mission style furnishings, and mica lamp shades that covered decorative hand-carved and brass cast lamps in every corner.

The savory scent of garlic and roasted meat filled the air as they turned the corner and entered a sitting room with a coffee table in the middle of the room center over a large Persian rug, and huge ornate fireplace with a blazing flame.

The room was lit with two delicate Tiffany lamps and candle shaped sconces on either side of the fireplace.

Seated in one chair was a beautiful black woman in her mid thirties with legs crossed, wearing a conservative navy blue pant suit, with shoulder length black hair. Her features were soft, almost aristocratic and she sat, back straight, shoulders high and proud and smiled at them as they entered the room.

Standing next to the fireplace was a man with a friendly face, horn-rim glasses, handsome approachable features and all the self-assuredness and cautious mannerisms of a cop. He wore a blue Bronco, khaki slacks and pressed button down shirt and paisley covered tie.

Yep, Rich thought, a cop.

"Rich," Grimsley said, "This is Detective Paulson and his lively wife Amanda Paulson. They exchanged greetings and when Rich looked at April, she seemed relieved that there was another couple in the house, even more relieved to have another woman at this gathering.

Rich was relieved to see another black person in the house. We are a majority, Rich thought. But he also realized that there was no such thing as safety in numbers against cops.

After taking drink orders, Grimsley joined everyone in the sitting room where they exchanged small talk and broke the ice, then all migrated to an even larger room replete with an ornate Crystal chandelier, another decorative wood and tile fireplace, and it was conveniently located near a set of double-sided sliding pocket doors that led to the kitchen and to the hallway.

Grimsley seated everyone and proceeded to make trips back and forth from the kitchen to the dining room, each time with a new plate of food. There were four dishes in all, three pasta dishes and two meat dishes.

Soon, Grimsley was finished and joined them at the head of the table. In the corner was a speaker that now played Charlie Parker's *Kansas City*.

Grimsley taped on his glass and announced, "Ladies and Gentlemen, may I have your attention please."

Paulson, Rich, Amanda and April all focused their attention on Grimsley.

"Thank you for joining me for dinner tonight. This is a social occasion, mostly. Although there is a little business I need to discuss with Rich, but the reason I wanted to do this under these circumstances is because of what I discovered several days ago."

Grimsley stood up and looked at April.

"April, he said, you probably know this, and so I won't bore you with details, but I'll lead by saying the world is indeed a small place."

Neither Rich nor April had any clue where Grimsley was going with this, so the looked at each other with confused expressions on their faces.

"Twenty-five years ago I had the privilege of meeting your

father, Mr. Stan Hardwick."

April looked at Grimsley in shock. She was not angry, she was more surprised. Paulson was also taken aback. Grimsley had not told him anything about this. But it was making sense. That's why he would not allow him to pick up Rich or interfere with their household.

"You, you, knew my father?" April asked.

"Yes, mam. Not well, but well enough to know what kind of man he was."

"But how, where, did you meet him?" April asked.

Rich simply sat watching Grimsley, dumbstruck, wondering what other kinds of tricks Grimsley had in his hat.

"Mam, there are a lot of folks who know about guns in this country. But there are only a few who can actually be called experts. You can count those experts on one hand. So, we are in great demand. Mam, your father and myself were among the top two. So, we often found ourselves on opposing sides of the expert witness teams. Four or five times we went head to head, testifying about ballistics this and forensics that, bull-shitting—if you'll pardon my French—about what we thought happened as opposed to what the other team thought."

"How often did that happen?" April asked.

"Often enough for us to learn little bits and pieces of each other's lives, especially since we always made it a point to share a Scotch or two once the verdict was in and bullshit about incompetent lawyers and whatnot. Sometimes my team won. Sometimes his team won. But we had a lot of mutual respect for each other. Then we went our separate ways."

"When did you find out about April's relationship?" Paulson asked.

"Oh, I've always known for years that he had a daughter. He used to show me pictures all the time. He loved the hell out of you, mam. Always talked about his little Teddy Bear."

"That's what he called me," April said. "He hadn't called me that in a long time, not until just before he died last year."

"And, mam, I'm real sorry about that and I want to propose a toast to your old man and say that I'm honored to be able to share this time with you, your husband, and I hope some day I can meet those two little rug rats of yours—and I mean that in the best possible way. Here's a toast to your father. He was a good man."

They raised their glasses and all sipped.

"Now, enough with the formalities, let's dig in and get to know each other."

Chapter 99

Chambers arranged a meeting with Baker in Jack London Square in Oakland, near a one-room souvenir shop that sold tacky Jack London paraphernalia on the expansive concrete plaza, a stones throw away from where the Oakland Ferry docked.

He decided to take the Ferry from San Francisco to avoid the evening Bay Bridge traffic which backed up for miles into the city.

The fog rolled in early and blanketed the city with a heavy mist that diffused blinking lights, framing buildings, towers and making car headlights look like blurred UFOs skating along the city streets.

With the fog came a strong, icy wind that blasted in from the Pacific and sent residents scurrying for shelter and made unsuspecting tourist wish they hadn't been lulled into wearing shorts and T-shirts by the sunny seventy degree weather earlier in the day.

Chambers stood on the deck of the ferry as all other passengers huddled inside, unfazed by the wind as it threatened to blow his gray, wide brimmed gangster-style Stetson off of his head.

But he knew that would never happen.

It never happened to Bogart or Edward G. or Cagney. So it couldn't happen to him. He made sure of it. It was tailored to fit his head like a glove by his hatter Gino, who owned the last haberdashery on Union and Green Street.

His London Fog broke the wind and protected his tailored Armani suit. He stood, like a vision from Polanski's Chinatown, thinking about the disturbing news he had to share with Baker.

Temple parked his Towncar on Alberta Court, two houses and one street away from Rich's house, far enough away to be comfortable, but close enough for him to still see the upstairs bedroom window of the Franklin home through sprawling branches of aging, neglected cherry and apple trees.

He continued to monitor the listening devices he had placed in the house. No one was home, so Temple put a Rachmeininoff CD into his CD player to pass the time.

Temple loved surveillance. He considered it the best part of his job. He enjoyed eavesdropping on unsuspecting victims, learning about their conflicts, about their habits, listening to couples make love and he enjoyed being surprised by everyday couples abilities to be creative in the bedroom.

Mostly, though, he was amazed at how domestic life turned men into cattle and women into shrill, nagging bitches. When they thought no one was looking, they whined and complained and wondered around their little houses, bumping into each other like rats in a cage or cows in a corral.

Common boring lives he thought.

Temple read the obits every day to see who died and how long the lived and how long they were married. When he saw that someone like Abigail Irma Vanhousen passed away at ninety nine years old and had been married for fifty five years, he thought what a God awful shame. He was firmly of the opinion that man's quest should be to get as much young tail as he can before he died. Familiarity was a progressive disease that caused women to despise sex and only comply when they felt their husbands were desperate enough.

Fucking elderly cock teases, he thought.

Rochmeinenoff almost drowned out his disgust.

Was the idea to die with honor?

Fuck that, he thought.

When you are dead. You are dead. It only mattered how much money was in the bank and how much tail you've had. He then imagined what his dying words might be and smiled as he thought about the dramatic end to his life, which he considered was a perfect life.

He imagined the perfect eulogy, which he had already written several drafts of but never done anything with.

It simply read: *"I'm fucking dead. Fuck all of you. I hate all your fucking guts. I spent my life taking what I wanted and judiciously sharing it with those I had something to gain from. I was a liar, a thief and a murder and I loved my life. None of you get shit from me now that I'm dead. I'm taking every God damn thing with me. Don't any of you dare fucking cry. I know you all hated me and pretended to like me. And I don't give a shit. I fucked all the women I wanted and fucked over anyone who got in my way. I've set up a trust and left specific instructions with my lawyers to hire a construction company to put all of my money in my casket, encase it in a small pyramid and let the fuckers try to get at it. I will be buried like an Egyptian pharaoh. They say you can't take it with you, but fuck that. I fucking can."*

He imagined the looks of horror and anger on the faces of his so-called friends and family as they listened. The thought almost gave him a full woody.

Enison poured himself a Bushmill on the rocks and was sipping it as he looked out the large plate glass sliding door with a clear view of the Bay

Bridge and San Francisco in the distance.

His house was a palatial, modern building nestled on a hillside in the Oakland Hills and was one of the new houses re-built after the fire that destroyed most of the million dollar houses in the eighties. Firestorm 1989. In the background, he played Grover Washington's greatest hits and *Winelight*.

Enison was trying to relax but couldn't. He was irritated by the news he'd gotten earlier through a phone call from a police captain in Portland inquiring about one of his targets, Rich Franklin. Seems there was some trouble brewing in Portland that threatened to interfere with the money he planned to recover for his client.

Enison's track record was spotless, and he would not allow that record to be tainted. He needed to know more about what was going on. From what little the captain had told him, he deduced that there was more to his story than he was letting on. He did, however, find the captain affable. Enison shared what info he thought he should about Franklin.

He needed to know what was happening in Portland but he could not invest any time tomorrow. He had a meeting the following morning with a another potential large client, Citi Group, a potential multi-million dollar account. He needed to be in the office and needed to spend *all* day with the client, reviewing accounts and brainstorming about strategy.

So he decided to send someone to Portland to be his eyes and ears and assist where possible. He walked over to the phone, set his drink down and dialed the phone number.

Brenda spent an agonizing Sunday night sifting through her feelings. Not only was she torn about Rich, but their talks prompted her to reconsider the position she had taken with her family. She ignored all the messages on her answering machine except one from Phil, her mentor and benefactor.

When she called him, she could not keep herself from crying as she talked to him about her weekend. Phil drove to her loft that evening and consoled her. She told him everything and they talked for hours about Rich, art and what options she had.

Phil left shortly before ten o'clock and Brenda spent the rest of the evening practicing her newfound approach to journal writing. This, she found, was the best therapy for her, and at the end of her lengthy entry she resolved to accept the circumstances confronting her.

She would leave a note for Rich tomorrow explaining how she felt and what she had decided. Rich had mentioned that April leaves for work in the mornings. He usually stays home for a few hours after dropping the kids off for school. And he is usually the first to get home with the kids in the evening.

If she left a note for him on his windshield after nine o'clock, he would get it when he left the house and there would be no risk of April seeing it. Then she would take a trip home to Boston to confront her past.

She wrote the note, made reservations on Travelocity.com, packed, drank a glass of Chardonnay and fell asleep with Jill Cohn playing on the CD player singing *Kayenta*.

Baker was standing by the souvenir shop shivering as he folded his arms around his shoulders trying to hug himself to keep warm. When he saw Chambers approaching, he yelled, "Chambers! Chambers. Over here!"

He jumped up and down like an excited three-year-old who just spied his nana, his suit flapping in the pressing wind like the flying nun's habit.

Chambers rolled his eyes and thought about how pathetic Baker was and asked himself why he had agreed to do this job.

As Baker approached, Chambers held up his hands and said, "All right. All right, Baker, hang on to your shorts for God sake. We're trying to be discrete here."

"Oh, sorry, Mr. Chambers. I, I was just excited to see you."

"Well, I'm not excited to see you Baker. But a job is a job."

"Should we find someplace warm to talk?" Baker asked.

"Hell no," Chambers fired back. "This is the perfect place. No prying ears. And I don't want anyone but you and me to hear what I have to say."

Chambers looked around to see if any embarking passengers were lingering.

The towering fluorescent lights that surrounded the plaza cast a golden glow over the concrete concourse. Shadowed figures hustled across the open court, none stopping to unduly regard Baker or Chambers.

"Let's make this quick, Baker," Chambers said, "then I'm on that next boat back to the city. I got a date with a dame I'm sweet on. You know what I mean?"

"Sure, sure, Chambers. That's fine," Baker said excitedly. "What did you find out?"

"You were right. There's something big brewing. I followed Enison to Yoshi's and listened in for a spell. Plus, I did some digging. I don't think Goldberg knows anything about it. Enison's a sneaky bastard."

With this news, Baker's disposition changed and he gasped and almost squealed like a newborn pig.

"I knew it! I've got you know Enison."

Chambers rolled his eyes again, but the overhead light cast a shadow that partially hid his face and his frustrated expression.

Chamber's cell phone rang.

"Kee-rist," Chambers said. "What is this? Grand Central, or something? He took out the diminutive cell phone and said, "Chambers here. This better be important."

"Chambers," Enison voice registered, *"It's me."*

Chambers looked at Baker, who was staring at him through his thick glasses, his eyes bulging with excitement and anticipation.

"Yeah, what's up?" he asked, not wanting to give away who he was talking to.

"I got a situation I need you to handle," Enison said.

"Fire away," Chambers said, turning away from Baker and shielding the mouthpiece of the cell phone to muffle his voice.

"There's a paperboy in Portland, Oregon, who might be in trouble. I need some eyes there tonight because the situation looks like it might be getting complicated."

"What are you suggesting, um, er, my friend," Chambers said, searching for a vague term to refer to Enison, "that I catch a plane tonight."

"Yes, Chambers," Enison, answered. *"I'm sorry. You don't have to do this. But it's important. He's one of my accounts and I've come to like this kid. There's a Captain Grimsley there who you can work with."*

"The Bob Grimsley?" Chambers asked, surprised.

"Yes, sir, the same."

"Always wanted to meet him."

"So, you'll do it?"

"Is it freakin' raining there? You know how I hate rain. Being in Oregon is like taking one long fuckin' shower. Last time I was there I ruined two pairs of very expensive Florsheims."

"Rainy with a chance of showers. I checked. And I'll cover all your expenses, Chambers, even your shoes. But time is of the essence here. You know what I mean?"

Chambers knew Enison and knew he only asked for extraordinary favors if there were extraordinary circumstances. He glanced at Baker, who stood, shivering with his hands in his pockets, shoulders hunched, pacing while Chambers spoke.

"All right. But you owe me an explanation when I get there. When do I leave?"

"I have a flight leaving from Oakland International in two hours. Got a hotel and a car for you too."

"What the fuck? Taking some special liberties with my schedule aren't you?"

"Well, if I couldn't get the best damn PI on the west coast to do this, I would have to send our receptionist."

"Get the fuck out of her you rat bastard. That shit ain't funny."

"I'll fill you in on the account when you get back."

"What kind of car you get me? You know how particular I am about cars."

"Got you a Cadillac."

"Perfect."

"Cadillac SUV, Escalade."

"No you didn't fuckin' do that, my friend," Chambers said, irritated and unable to say Enison's name. "That's not a fuckin' car. That's a fuckin' tank. God damn Oregonians like to drive those bullshit vehicles, then slow to a crawl when they see a God damn pothole in the street. I'd rather drive a Pinto."

"Settle down Chambers. Give it a try. You won't turn into an Oregonian just 'cause you drive one. Plus, it's the only one with the extras you like, and you'll blend in."

"Yeah, like a snake in a rabbit hole. You'll pay for this one, em, my friend."

"Okay. And Chambers, I appreciate this very much."

"Fuck you. When I get back, you can personally kiss my ass."

Enison laughed before hanging up the phone. Chambers, was irritated, but he knew he would get over that. He walked over to Baker and said, "Fuckin' go home and I'll keep tabs on this. And remember, stay the fuck out of the way or I'll personally kick your ass."

"Oh, okay, Mr. Chambers. Where will you be?"

"Don't fuckin' worry about it. I gotta make a quick trip, but I'll be back. Just rest assured I got people lookin' into this. I'll get back to you in a couple days. Go home."

"But—"

Before he could finish, Chambers walked away and pressed the speed dial on his cell phone.

"Sara, baby, how ya doin?"

"Fine," she answered, I'm working right now, but I can call you on my break."

"No, no, you don't have to do that. I need a favor peach pie."

"Anything you want."

"So cooperative. I love that. Tell that prick of a boss of yours Espanoza you need to take care of something for a friend—me. If he gives you any shit, remind him I got markers on him. Go to the Ferry Plaza parking lot and pick up my Ferrari and take it back to the house. It's open. Key is under the floor mat. In my closet you'll find a silver case. Call OCEN 444-7000 and ask them to pick it up and call me. I'll give them instruction on how to get it to me. You can stay at my place the next couple days and use the car as much as you want. Take a trip if you want. I gotta go to Portland right now."

"Are you in trouble? Is everything all right?"

"Baby, I'm always in trouble. That's my business. And there's something brewing in Portland and I couldn't stay away even if I wanted to. But I'll miss you baby."

"You're sweet," she said. "I'll take care of this for you. And I'll miss you while you're gone."

There was silence. Sara spoke first, "Do me a favor?"

"What's that sweetness."

"Don't stuck your neck out too far and don't take any wooden nickels."

Chambers laughed.

"Okay. I'll call you in a couple days."

He hung up, called a cab and cursed Enison all the way to the airport *and* well after he received his fourth Scotch on the flight to Portland.

By ten thirty he was in the Hertz lot at Portland International Airport picking up the Cadillac SUV. As the huge white SUV pulled up in front of him, he turned to the attendant and said, "I'll be God damned. Looks like you can fit the whole God damn U.S. gymnastics team in that son of a bitch."

The anemic, dark-haired attendant, who looked too young to drive or even hold up the baggy black slacks and Hertz sport shirt said, "Yeah, it's big huh?" and smiled, his braces glistening under the lot lights.

Chambers scowled at him and said, "Guess I'll go mow down some old growth forest and fuckin' burn up some fossil fuels. God damn Oregonians are so hypocritical and pretentious. Bunch of fuckin' nature boys rapin' the environment with all their outdoor extreme sports, dirt bikes and mountain climbing shit. All these sons of bitches need to spend more time watching fuckin' Bogart movies and sippin' some good brandy instead of fuckin' protesting every God damn thing and bitchin' about nothing and everything and tearin' up the fuckin' environment."

The attendant stood frozen with his mouth agape, not sure how to reply, then cautiously handed Chambers his keys and slunk away after telling Chambers to have a nice day.

Chapter 100

As every one ate, Grimsley broke the ice, "Rich, you're a writer, right?"

"That's right."

"What do you write?"

"A little of everything, articles, non-fiction mostly, but I'm dabbling in fiction right now."

"A novel, right."

"That's right."

"I do a little writing myself. Who's your favorite author?"

"No one really."

"Oh, come on," Grimsley prodded, "Every writer has to have a favorite author, maybe the classics; Tolstoy, Hemmingway, London?"

"Not, me," Rich insisted. "I find the classic authors a bit staid, dull and culturally limited. You know, too safe, precise and outdated."

Grimsley did not respond but simply looked at Franklin intensely, then he smiled.

"God damn—pardon my French ladies—you're baiting me aren't you?"

Rich did not look at Grimsley right away, but instead glanced at Paulson who was staring intensely at him.

Rich winked at Paulson, who finally smiled, along with his wife. April was already smiling.

"Yes," Rich agreed, as he looked at Grimsley. "I'm baiting you. I'm classically trained. I have a masters in English literature and Journalism. My instructors beat the classics into me like my life depended on it. But to be perfectly honest, my favorites are Elison, Baldwin, Chandler and L'amoure. Their prose was simple, raw and powerful. All that flowery language in the classics gives me a headache."

"Spoken like a true rebel and an opinionated writer with his own ideas," Grimsley said. "And I couldn't agree with you more. People interact like this, like we are interacting now. Not in ten page paragraphs about fancy chandeliers and ten thousand ways from Sunday of describing the weather. Too many writers waste their time trying to be like Hemmingway. Waste of God damn time if you ask me. If you're going to tell a store, tell the God damn story and don't jerk the readers off."

"So what do you write?" Rich asked.

"Fiction," Grimsley replied. "Detective novels."

"I'd like to read some sometime."

"Sure. Sometime. You got any nibbles from a publisher?"

Rich, shifted in his seat. He sensed a lie coming on. He did not want to tip his hat about the book deal just yet. The timing was not right, so he answered, "No, not yet."

"That's funny," Grimsley said, "I talked to an agent friend of mine, a Mr. Abrahamson, and he said he's talked to you recently."

April looked at Rich, puzzled. Rich cleared his throat. Think fast. This was not happening. Somebody had turned up the thermostat in the room, he thought. It was suddenly getting hotter.

"Oh, yeah, he said," smiling at April, "We spoke. That's right. And we're working on something. But I'd rather not talk about that right now. You know, Don't want to jinx it or anything."

Grimsley took another bite and did not look at Rich. He had thrown this one out there and was enjoying the show.

April said, "Rich, that's great. You didn't say anything about that."

"It's all pretty recent, just in the last few days. And there hasn't been time."

Inside, Rich was seething. He was down one point and needed to make up some ground in the conversation, and he needed to be more on guard. Grimsley obviously was smart and new more than he was letting on.

Grimsley smiled and looked at Paulson and winked.

"Now, you and April have been married for ten years. I applaud you. That's a long time."

Rich quickly calculated all the different directions Grimsley's next comment or question might go and factored in the odds. He was ready.

Grimsley continued, "How do you find living in Oregon? You know, being a couple of different ethnicity and all. Especially given that Oregon, according to most demographic polls, is 84 percent white?"

Rich was ready. He had several ways to answer this question. He just had to chose his mode of attack.

"That's a good question, one April and I have addressed regularly. And we typically use the answer to educate people."

Rich paused, to build suspense and let the implications of what he said sink in.

"In 1845," he continued, "when the first British trade was set up in this area, Whites constituted only 1 percent of the population. Native Americans, African Americans, and Asians constituted the majority. Most early trappers married Native Americans, including McGloughlin, who is considered the father of Oregon. So, history weighs heavily in our favor in the Pacific Northwest. That fact has not changed. April and I see ourselves as pioneers. Only the demographics have reversed. Whites comprise the majority now. But no one knows how long that will last."

Rich became more animated as he spoke, saying each word with confidence, precision and determination, as if he were speaking before the house of representatives.

"And just as there was fear of Black and brown people back then," he continued, "White people today are still resistance to share the Pacific northwest bounty with people of any ethnicity other than Caucasian."

Rich again paused and watched Grimsley, Paulson and Amanda.

"But should that stop people of color from coming to Oregon to seek a better life? Absolutely not. Should we view ourselves any differently from settlers in the 1800s, black, white or other? Absolutely note. Should we fear White people because they are the majority? Indeed NOT. Should our experience here be any different from any other couple? Absolutely not. Is it different? Yes. I'm black and April is white. Blacks and whites will not allow us to forget this fact. Nor should we want to. But we don't give a good God damn about that—again, ladies, pardon mon Francais—we consider ourselves, contrary to popular belief, an all-American couple, perhaps even more so. We have to sift through all the subtle shit that's thrown at us every day of our lives. And we DON'T let that get in our way. We stand strong as a couple, as a family. We educate our children to respect people of all races and we do our best to affect the revolutionary, racial paradigm shift that's occurring in this country today. We came to Oregon because as Americans it is our right to go anywhere in this great God damn nation that we good and well want to. And, like the early pioneers, we're not about to let a few uppity white people get in our way."

When he was finished, Grimsley, Paulson and Amanda all sat, stunned. Even April seemed surprised, if not proud of Rich's soliloquy and was not sure whether everyone would clap or whether they should gather their coats and head for the door.

After a protracted period of silence, Grimsley was the first to speak.

"Did a little acting did you?"

"Yes sir," Rich answered without hesitation.

"Like the epics?"

"Yes, sir."

"Mr. Smith Goes to Washington?"

"Absolutely."

"A Few Good Men?"
"Ten times."
"JFK?"
"Four times."
"Denzel fan."
"God damn genius."
"Glory?"
"Yep."
"Malcolm X?"
"Phenomenal performance."
"Spike Lee?"
"All except Bamboozled."
"Couldn't sit through that one either."

Paulson, April and Amanda were silent, taking in the show.

"How is the meal everyone?" Grimsley asked, changing he subject. He looked at Rich, who had resumed eating and smiled, then winked at him and April while Paulson, complimented him on the meal.

"Rich, that was the most phenomenal piece of pontificating I've ever heard. And I have to say that everything I've heard about you is absolutely wrong,"

Rich knew Grimsley was leading into his next statement. Timing. He was a master of timing. Wait for the punch line.

"You and April are even more charming and intriguing than I had imagined. I propose a toast to all of you and want to thank you for breaking bread with me."

They raised their glasses and drank. Rich was relieved. His stomach was not as knotted as it was before and they all exchanged smiles.

"Now, I hate to put a damper on this dinner party, but I want to talk about something a little more morose.

As you know, my business is crime, homicide in particular. And we got a situation in your neighborhood that's got us stumped and we think there's more here than we've been able to figure out. Rich, you might be able to help us out since this homicide occurred on your paper route. Paulson here is our lead detective, so he's got a handle on all the details, so he's going to take a few minutes to fill you in."

Paulson started reciting the facts of the case, "Four nights ago a young prostitute was murdered. She lived in and worked out of an old van on Going street; went by the name of Trixie. Rich, she was on your paper route, do you remember her?"

Rich, looking uncomfortable again. Oceans of sweat seemed to form in his armpits and the room suddenly got very hot again. Who turned up the thermostat again, he thought. "

"Um, yeah, I used to see her on occasion; sometimes just walking around."

Rich hoped he didn't have to lie any more, but he felt himself backing into a corner and wishing he could have found some excuse not to attend this dinner.

"The morning she was murdered, we received an anonymous report from someone who had seen the murder scene either during or after the crime was committed," Paulson continued.

Uh, oh, here it comes Rich thought and his jaw tightened as he braced for either a colossal lie or the truth being forced out of his mouth.

Paulson explained further, "We don't really care that much about the anonymous tip. We always appreciate citizens calling in and while we prefer to know who they are, we are more interested in finding who committed this crime. Sometimes the person who reports the crime can tell us more then they think they might be able to."

Rich let out a breath the he'd been holding deep in his gut as Paulson continued.

"Now, we know there was a Hispanic American named Chico who may be the murderer, but unfortunately we will never get a confession from him. He was murdered a few days ago in a hotel downtown."

What are they getting at here, Rich thought. The Mexican American who could have killed him, killed a prostitute then is murdered. Case dismissed.

"On the surface, this looks like an open and shut case. Scum bag shoots girl. Runs. Another scum bag shoots scum bag. End of story. Not quite. There's more."

Paulson explained the notes found in the van, the possible involvement of an assassin and the missing link, the diary or black book. And finally explained that they were trying to find the Trixie's apartment but were not having any luck.

"You know, I usually saw her in the night. Never in daylight, so I never saw a clear picture of her. Do you have a picture available?" Rich asked.

"I do," Paulson said. But it's not the best picture. For all intents and purposes, she will not have a complete history until we get a last name and more information, so we only have pictures from the morgue. I had them photo-shopped to eliminate all the, well, gory stuff and enhance what she might look like alive."

"Can I see them?" Rich asked.

"Sure, I'll get them out of my brief case," Said Paulson.

Paulson stood, excused himself and went into the parlor. He returned with two eight by ten prints and handed them to Rich.

Rich stared at the pictures, trying to imagine Trixie's life and her death. Visions of the ghostly angel walking in the night returned to him. She was even more beautiful than he imagined and he was saddened when he saw the pictures. In the far recesses of his memory he saw an uncanny likeness of Trixie, radiant, intense, impossible to ignore walking in the night and standing in front of a hotel across from Jake's. He passed her quickly, but their eyes locked for an instant, long enough to acknowledge their existence, a brief attraction, a brief recognition, but not long enough to consider each other any more than that.

Rich said, "I recognize her from Going street…and I think I saw her downtown last week at the Empire Hotel, across from Jake's. It's a transient hotel, you know—"

"I know that hotel," Grimsley interrupted.

"Are you sure?" Paulson asked excitedly.

"I'm fairly sure," Rich answered. I was in a hurry. But she was looking at me. Something about her was familiar, maybe because I had seen her in the dark. But she was standing by the door, like she was waiting for them to buzz her in.

Paulson and Grimsley looked at each other. Paulson knew what he had to do.

"You don't need to say anything sir." He turned to his wife and said, "I'm sorry, but we have to go. Timing is everything. Each second could mean all the difference."

"I understand," she said. "You married a nurse and I married a cop. We both have a duty and impossible schedules."

"Paulson, call me as soon as you find out anything at that hotel."

"Yes, sir. No problem," Paulson said.

He gathered the pictures and he and Amanda thanked Grimsley and said good by to Rich and April.

"Rich, thank you," Grimsley said.

He walked Rich and April to the front door.

"This could crack this case wide open. But I also have to tell you, this could also make this whole situation more dangerous. There are some powerful forces at work here. Now, I can't see any direct connection to you, unless when this all comes out, you might be able to recognize a car or a person you've seen on your route, maybe even one of the residents, but keep your head down. Until we find whoever is behind this we know they will leave no stone unturned until they find what they're looking for. And they're as thorough as we are. They'll look for the most likely connections and act on them. Know what I mean?"

"I do, Bob," Rich said, "I've read enough detective novels to know how it works."

"Only now it's for keeps. Two people are dead and we don't want any more people dyin' on us."

"Rich, all this mysterious talk about assassins and missing diaries is making me nervous. What can we do to protect ourselves?" April asked.

"We've got a man on your house. We'll know if anything's going on. You folks go home and don't worry about this. We're taking extra precautions to make sure you and your children are not in any danger."

"We appreciate that," Rich said, "and thank you very much for the wonderful meal. The music is wonderful. Hope we can come over again and listen to more of your collection."

"Sure thing, Rich," Grimsley said as he lead them to the front door. "Next time."

Chapter 101

Paulson had no problems finding the Empire Hotel and gaining access to Trixie's room. The hotel manager recognized Trixie and was more than cooperative and explained that the room had been rented to her for three years until her father came by last week and said she was moving her back home. He had no reason to question him. He recalled that all her possessions had been moved out in a single day and he was given an extra thousand dollars to paint the room immediately.

The paint job would have been finished except, wanting to save money, he had hired his nephew to paint the room and instead of taking a day to do it, he had taken two days and the job was still not done and his nephew had made quite a mess. The manager expressed his frustration in colorful expletives as he lead Paulson to Trixie's room, opened it and left him there.

Paulson surveyed the room. The smell of fresh primer was strong and white blotches were splattered on the dark wood floor. The primer did not cover the deep nail holes and the light rectangles and squares where pictures once hung. Paulson called Grimsley and explained what he found and waited for Grimsley to arrive.

On the way home, April and Rich hardly spoke. April's silence was Rich's clue that she was not sure what to make of some of what she heard at dinner.

"So, Rich, you think this agent might offer you a book deal?" she asked, breaking the bottomless silence.

"April, I told you, I can't talk about it. You know, I don't want to jinx it. There are so many variables. Getting published is not so easy," Rich said, avoiding a direct answer.

He rationalized that not answering a question was not telling a lie. If he never told the lie, it could not be counted against him in liar's court.

"Well, is the novel finished?" she probed further.

"Yes, it is," he answered.

"Can I read it?"

"Um, uh, I don't know. You know, it's just too personal. You know, too much of me is wrapped up in it. You probably wouldn't like it."

"Oh, you never know. I might like it."

"I don't know. I'll have to think about it. Maybe it's better to read it when and if it gets published. That way, it's perfect. You know what a terrible speller I am. All those typos could be distracting."

Sensing that Rich did not want her to read his manuscript, April backed away from the question and said, "Well, I thought I'd ask. But you know I have all the faith in the world in you. I haven't read it, but knowing you, it's probably good. And I'm willing to wait."

"Thanks," Rich said, relieved.

They were silent again.

"I'm still a little nervous about this murder situation," April said, "that seemed a little too close to home. And the fact that you are out there early in the mornings makes me uncomfortable. Supposing that Chico character had seen you and came after you?"

Rich could not say anything. He was dumbstruck by her perceptiveness and by the vision of the gun pointed at his face and the desperate look in Chico's eyes as he pressed on the trigger and realized nothing happened.

Rich began to hyperventilate slightly as he thought about the encounter. To avoid April sensing his dread, he laughed nervously and said, "You know me. I move too quickly in the mornings. Something like that can't happen. You don't have to worry."

"I do worry. I have to. Rich, I wish you would find something else soon."

"I will. I will. Something will come through. Don't worry. Everything is under control."

"That's easy for you to say. But I know that it's taking a toll on you. You've been jumpy these past few days and not getting enough sleep. It would be great if you had a normal job."

"April, I'm not a normal person, so I have no concept of a normal job. Money is money. Sometimes We have to be creative to accommodate our circumstances."

"Yeah, if we create circumstances that are not normal. Rich, I just want us to be able to spend time together without you falling asleep in the middle of our conversations."

"I know. I know. I'm working on it. Like I said, I've got some things I'm working on. Things will be all right."

"I hope so," She said and repeated, "I worry sometimes though."

"I understand. If we stay strong, there's nothing we can't handle."

Rich glanced at April. She turned to him at the same time and gave him a look. This time it said, I TRUST YOU AND I LOVE YOU. He recognized it immediately. And for the first time since he returned from the writer's conference, he realized that his actions and his decisions could instantly turn that look he so loved to one that said, I HATE YOU YOU LYING CHEATING MANIPULATIVE SCUM.

Rich imagined the hurt and the disappointment and instantly played out the entire scenario in his head including the yelling and the screaming.

When he saw April slapping him in the face, he snapped out of it and convinced himself in an instant that that would never happen. She could never know.

He smiled at her and said, "April, no matter what happens, you know that I love you so much."

April wasn't sure what to make of his comment and smiled, then asked, "Is that a question or an answer?"

"It's a fact," Rich said.

She kissed him on the cheek and said, "I love you too Rich, even if you are a paperboy. You're the best paperboy I know."

Chapter 102

"Looks like we're too late," Paulson said, as he stood in the middle of Trixie's apartment. A dingy overhead light blanketed the empty room.

"Looks that way," said Grimsley, his baritone voice echoing off the bare walls.

"God damn sons of bitches are still one step ahead of us. You find anything at all?"

"No, sir, they were very thorough. Packed. Cleaned. Washed the walls. ServiceMaster's best could not have done a better job of mopping up this place. And the nephew is making a hell of a mess as well."

"You scan with that fancy little black light of yours?"

"Yes, sir. Didn't pick up anything."

"Maybe you need a bigger black light?"

"We could try that, sir. It's a little late to buy one though. All the head shops are closed."

"Let's borrow one."

"Just like that?"

"No, not just like that. We have to do some investigating first. Go door-to-door and sniff for weed and incense."

"How is that related to a black light?"

"Then listen for the kind of music you hear?"

"Huh?"

"If you hear any bands from Woodstock playing on the stereo, there will be a black light, probably velvet posters of African American women with big afros and an ounce or two of pot somewhere in the apartment."

"All right. I'll go check it out."

"And Paulson," Grimsley said as he opened the door, "We're asking for an unusual favor. You don't need to make any arrest. Thank them and hurry back here."

"Eye eye captain."

"And Paulson," Grimsley called before Paulson disappeared, "You do know who was at Woodstock don't you?"

Paulson smirked.

"Of course. Everybody knows who was at Woodstock. I have parents. Pat Boone was the headliner and Jim Neighbors was his special guest."

He watched Grimsley grimace again.

"There was also Hendricks, Jefferson Airplane, Otis Redding, Janice Joplin and Country Joe and the Fish," Paulson said.

Without waiting for a reply from Grimsley, Paulson shut the

door.

Score one for him. He smiled as he walked away.

Woodstock was his favorite case study at the Academy; a perfect example of anarchy, drug culture, crowd control and nudity control—a law enforcement nightmare.

He thought Grimsley's idea was outrageous, too, but he was not going to allow him the pleasure of questioning it in his presence. This was another one of Grimsley's little tests, he was sure, and it sort of made sense.

Somewhere in Grimsley's past he may have had to do something similar to solve a case. Even though he would feel like a complete idiot, perhaps a little like a drug sniffing canine, he would show Grimsley that he was not afraid to do what it takes. He would satisfy the little sadist perched on Grimsley's left shoulder who argued with the benevolent mentor and teacher perched on the other shoulder incessantly.

He commenced going from door-to-door, sniffing and listening to any sounds he could hear.

The first five doors were quiet. Then he heard the clear sounds of Bootsie's Rubber Band playing *Flash Light* and smelled whiskey, probably gin. Strike out.

The next door he heard a festive blend of disco and Persian instruments and smelled spices. Nope. The next door smelled of perspiration and piss and he could her the sad musing of Johnny Cash singing, "*I hear the train a comin…*"

No black light here he thought.

He continued around the corner past twelve doors, where he heard AC DC, Radio Head, KISS, Clint Black, Garth Brooks, Mariah Carey and Eddie Santiago, until he came to a door where he recognized the pungent smell of strong marijuana disguised by a nondescript pungent incense. He could hear Blood Sweat and Tears playing *Spinning Wheel*.

Bingo. He knocked on the door.

A meek, youngish voice sheepishly asked, "Who is it?"

"Police," he yelled. "Open up."

Chapter 103

Grimsley was examining the small, dark closet when there was a knock on the door. He instinctively reached for his Smith and Wesson which was snug in its shoulder holster. He undid the straps. He cautiously walked towards the door and with one motion, opened it and stepped back.

The hall was poorly lit and all he could see was the shadow of a dark figure standing there, still, confident, his six foot frame peering at him from under a dark hat, holding a large metallic case at his side.

"Who the hell are you?" Grimsley barked, as he kept his hand ready to withdraw the .357 magnum.

"Easy there chief," Chambers announced. "I'm one of the good guys."

"Like I said," Grimsley repeated, "Who the hell are you?"

"Chambers, Skip Chambers, private dick from Oakland. I'm here to help."

When Grimsley heard Chambers name, he recognized it immediately and relaxed his hand.

"Well, I'll be God damn. In the flesh?"

"In the flesh," Chambers said. "And you'd be Bob Grimsley?"

"In the flesh."

"Here tell you got some kind of mystery up here. Murder. Missing clues. Assassins. Whatnot? Word on the street, even down in the Bay Area, is you could use a hand."

"We didn't ask for it," Grimsley said, pausing, then continued "but if you're offering, I'm no fool my friend. I'm accepting, specially from a man of your reputation."

"I'm offering. It's free. And you can take that to the bank pal."

Grimsley looked him over

"You're a slick one aren't you?"

"Don't sound so greater-than-thou 'cause I'm a natty dresser Grimsley. I know all about you. As a young FBI agent, you looked like one of those God damn MIB impersonating sons of bitches, fresh faced, spit shined, ready to piss your pants at the sound of the first gun shot. You were wound up so tight you could crack walnuts in your ass cheeks."

"No Shit. No shit. Come on in," Grimsley said, smirking and gesturing for Chambers to enter the room and extending a hand.

Chambers stepped into the room. He scanned the space and shook Grimsley's hand.

"Pleased to make the acquaintance of the man who does his homework and is the same man who revolutionized surveillance equipment and software and refuses to take any credit. Not only that, but you live out your life as a PI for a collection agency while the world relies on your inventions to make it safer. You're a living legend Chambers. When we get near a pond, I want to see something; to see if you can actually walk on water like the rumors say."

That broke the ice.

Chambers almost smiled. Grimsley then closed the door.

"Let's get down to business, Mr. Grimsley. I have a feeling time is running out here. I made some phone calls. You don't need to brief me on background. Based on what you found in the van, I brought some equipment that might help here. By the way. Where's your sidekick, Paulson?"

"He's out sniffing for pot."

"Funny. That's very funny. I like that."

Chambers did not smile. He simply laid his brief case on the ground and opened it.

Inside the top half of the case was a monitor. A keyboard was nestled in the lower half, next to a silver digital camera surrounded by foam. He removed a camera that was small enough to fit in his palm, took out a small high-intensity spot light and attached it to the camera. He screwed a purple filter on the spot light then flicked on a switch.

The intense beam with the black light filter blasted a powerful blue light onto the walls. At the same instant the walls of the room appeared on the computer screen.

As Chambers scanned the wall, he pressed several keys on the keyboard.

"This filter picks up black light inks. I've written an application and modified the algorithms to capture and separate an latent images, anomalies...or writing in this case. The program will enhance them and automatically scan for familiar patterns. Got the equivalent of a Sun Spark server in this box. Processes at 5 gigahertz and I've got a 4000 gig hard drive. Christie's has been using this application to spot fakes for years. Our girls was smart. Black light ink is an old trick, but effective. Don't worry, with this kind of horsepower, not even the manager's jerk-off nephew can keep us from figuring out what's going on here. Watch and wonder."

As the image scanned, fuzzy letters began to form in blue hazy shadows. In the next half hour Chambers systematically scanned every inch of the room, saving and cataloging individual frames until he had more then fifty images.

"This is going to take a little to render and decipher. But I'll be able to tell you most of what's on these walls in 24 hours. Chambers packed his case, touched the brim of his hat and said, "I'm at the Benson. Call me if you need me, SEABREEZE-555-4000. Good day sir."

Grimsley did not say anything. He was not easily impressed. But today was an exception. He had seen the specter of greatness, a no-nonsense, certifiable genius who walked right out of Casablanca. Chambers disappeared as quickly as he appeared. Not big on small talk Grimsley thought, but didn't need to be.

Seconds later, Paulson entered the room through the open door proudly holding a six foot black light and excitedly announced, "Your black light, sir, and an ounce of pot on the side. Shook down a young University of Oregon student just moved here for the summer to be a bike messenger. Barely twenty. Can you believe that?"

"Don't need it any more," Grimsley said.

"What!?" Paulson responded. "I practically got a buzz sniffing doors for this."

"Don't need it," Grimsley repeated. "We got a little help. Private dick from Oakland named Chambers. And by the way, you passed the test. Let's get out of here."

Chapter 104

Rich didn't realize that Brenda decided to drop a note into his mailbox around nine thirty that morning. It landed on the ground inches from the base of the door. She saw his truck parked in the driveway and figured he'd get the note when he left for the day.

Rich got a call that morning from Phil. He wanted to meet for lunch at the Laurelhurst Bar and Grill in Hollywood. He agreed to meet Phil around eleven.

He worked in his den until around ten o'clock, then cleaned out the back of the truck. He removed all the empty plastic baggies, bundle ties, fast food bags and soda cups. He collected a stack of community newspapers and everything else and put it in the den. He would read as much as he could later.

The postman came at his usual time and dumped his daily cadre of bills and junk mail on top of Brenda's Letter. As Rich rushed out the front door, he stopped, scooped up the pile and placed it on the bench next to the door. He would go through it later when he got home.

Just as Rich was closing the door, the phone rang.

He hesitated, then locked the door anyway, deciding to ignore the ringing phone. At that time of day, he was sure telemarketers were calling, hoping to find someone home to make a pitch too.

When he turned on his cell phone, he found that there was a message waiting, but he was late and did not want to take the time to listen to it.

Probably more bill collectors.

All morning long, April had a difficult time concentrating on her work. Several of her co-works, noticing her lack of usual enthusiasm and asked if everything was okay. She was not comfortable telling what had happened and she did not want to worry anyone. So she begged off their concerns and tried to focus on her work.

Finally, in frustration, she gave up and told her boss she was going home for lunch. She thought, too, that it might be nice to meet Rich for lunch if he wasn't busy.

She tried his cell phone first but there was no answer. Then she tried the home phone. No answer.

Disappointed, she decided to go home for lunch anyway. She could at least think more easily in familiar surroundings.

She arrived home a half hour later and as she walked into the quiet house, she scooped up the pile of mail Rich had left, made a sandwich, a cup of Earl Grey, put on the Blues Travelers and opened the mail as she ate.

The Laurelhurst Bar and Grill was a popular brew pub in the central part of Hollywood, which used to be a city of its own before it was incorporated by Portland. Its streets were lined with turn-of-the-century buildings, coffee shops, banks and antique stores.

The centerpiece of the neighborhood was the Hollywood theater, which featured an ornate terra cotta marquee. The Lauralhurst Pub was one block away from the theater and nestled between the Medak real estate office and the Hollywood Senior center, where small busloads of elderly shuffled in and out to bide their time playing bridge, dancing or looking for love.

Phil was already in the restaurant when Rich arrived and he gave Rich a bear hug before they sat down.

"Richey, how are you buddy?"

"I'm all right. How about you?"

"Couldn't be better."

Rich noticed that Phil couldn't stop smiling.

"Either something's really wrong or someone's under the table sucking your dick, Phil. I know you. You can't stop smiling. That means you're brain is churning on something."

"Richey, you know me so well. And you're right."

"Well, what is it? Are you going to keep me in suspense?"

An earthy waitress with long brown hair, thick, untrimmed eyebrows and perfect teeth walked over to the table and said, "Can I get you something to drink?"

"Sure, I'll have the homemade root beer," Rich said.

"Hefeveizen, please," Phil said.

"I'll be back to take your order in a minute," she said.

"Rich, Rock showed me the first edits of the show and they're phenomenal. He burned a DVD for me and you. Here's yours."

Phil handed him a jewel case with a gold disk with the words, TWO GUYS HAVING LUNCH AND TALKING TOUGH EPISODE #2 written on it with a Sharpie.

Rich was distracted, but perked up when Phil mentioned the show.

"You think it was good?"

"Rich, I wouldn't say this if I didn't mean it. We may have something here. I'm going to submit it to OPB to see if they'll air it.

The president is a friend of mine and he might be able to pull a few strings."

"You really think they'll do that?"

"Rich, I'm telling you, it's first rate. How'd you like to get paid to have lunch with me?"

"I'd prefer someone with bigger boobs, but you'll do."

Phil laughed Rich joined him.

"All right, Rich, I know you'll never get too excited about anything, but that's you. And that's why you're great and that's why I love you."

"I'm sorry, Phil, I know you're excited about this. I am too. I was just kidding about the boob thing. I'd have lunch with you any day of the year—every day if I could. You're one of the few people I can honestly say I spend a LOT of time with outside of my family. If this OPB thing takes off, I'm there all the way. You can count on that."

"I know Rich. Don't worry about it. Just let me know what you think after you watch it."

The drinks arrived and Phil and Rich toasted the show and sipped their drinks. Around them, well dressed real estate agents discussed deals, and aging hippie types lingered in booths, cuddling up to journals, books or the local weekly *Willamette Week*.

"Rich," Phil said, changing his demeanor. "I need to talk to you about something else. This may be none of my business, but as a friend, I need to tell you about this."

"What is it Phil?"

"Brenda called me Sunday night. She was distraught, crying and babbling about stuff and not making sense, so I went over to see her to see if I could calm her down."

If Rich could turn white as a ghost, he would have at that moment. He stared at Phil with a look of shock, his heart racing like a jet engine before take off. All the blood was pumped to his head, making him feel as though he was hanging upside-down on monkey bars.

He said nothing.

"She told me about last weekend," Phil continued, pausing to make eye contact with Rich and gauge his response. Phil could see that Rich was speechless.

"Like I said, this is probably none of my business, but she told me everything and I had to talk her down. You know, she's a kid. Sweet. Smart. And she wasn't sure what to make of things."

Rich mouthed a question but no words came out. His lower lip was quivering.

"Rich, you okay?"

"Ye, ye, yeah, Phil. I just didn't think that…I, well, you know, I didn't know what—"

"Listen, Rich, take it easy. She's okay now. She said that what you taught her about writing changed her life but it kind of also flipped her out. Your suggestion that she go home and confront her parents freaked her out too. But once she started writing about it and talked with me more about it, she found that it made sense."

"You mean she just talked to you about her journals and what we talked about?"

"Sure, Rich. You know she's been toiling with this stuff for a long time. She said you helped her see that even as an artist and a creative person, she was living and thinking myopically. And that tunnel vision was holding her back. She was a prisoner in her own life."

"So, she told you about the trailer?"

"She told me everything?"

"Everything. You know, Rich, I don't know how you did that."

"I didn't mean—?"

"You know, being in the same trailer with such a beautiful women all weekend," Phil interrupted, wanting to finish before Rich responded. "You're a better man than I. You guys talked about journals and writing and all that other crap. Absolutely amazing."

When the bulb of realization went off in Rich's head, the imaginary color that had left his face, slowly returned, and he tried to regain his composure with a feigned laugh.

"It was a working weekend," he said, trying to be convincing. "I had to finish my manuscript. It had to be in my agents hands this week."

"You got an agent!"

"Last week, a referral. And he came with a book contract. The book gets published this week."

"No you didn't. Get the heck out of here!" Phil yelled. "Oh, my God. That's great! Come here!"

Phil stood up and picked Rich up by the shoulders and hugged him as hard as he could, laughing loudly.

"You sly dog you. When were you going to tell me?"

"When I got a copy of the book in my hands." Rich said, looking around at the stares, embarrassed.

He sat back down and Phil followed.

"It's all happening too fast and I've been distracted by some other stuff."

"Well jeez leweez. This is your week isn't it?"

"I guess so."

"Well, I need a signed copy."

"Okay, you got it," Rich said.

Phil looked at his watch.

"Oh, shoot, you know, Rich, I can't stay. I've got a meeting. I'm buying another historic commercial building in southeast Portland, the Huber building and I have a tour in about fifteen minutes. I gotta run."

He threw a ten on the table.

"Can you take care of the tab?"

"Sure, Phil, I'll let you know what I think of the show tomorrow."

"Okay, and remember, a signed copy," Phil said.

He gave Rich another bear hug and dashed for the door. Before he opened the door, he turned and said, "Oh, and Rich, did you get Brenda's note. She said she was going to slip it in your door this morning before she flew home for a couple days."

"No, I didn't get it."

"Well, I'm pretty sure she left it for you. She called me before she got on the plane. Said to tell you hello. She was a little embarrassed about the note but said you'd understand once you read it."

"I'll check when I get home."

"Okay Richey. See you later."

When the door closed, Rich's cell phone rang. At first he ignored it. Then thought it might be Grimsley or Paulson with some news. When he looked at the phone, he was shocked to see the phone number. It was his home phone number, which could only mean one thing.

"Fucking shit!" was all Rich could say. The phone went to voice mail before he could work it out of the holder. Knowing what might be happening, he left more money, ran out of the restaurant, to his truck and sped home.

Chapter 105

Chambers did not sleep. He, instead, sat staring at the computer screen, typing in instructions, manipulating each image and programming three dimensional flash renderings of Trixie's room.

As he slowly examined what was written on the walls, all he could gather was that it was gibberish. Then, as more of the wall was deciphered, he realized that Trixie was using a code, burying pieces of her messages on separate sections of the wall. So, in order to make sense of anything on the walls, he had to completely render every frame, which was slow and painstaking.

Chambers was patient. He only slept deeply when he had a dame to cuddle up to. He hated hotels and was always suspicious about their laundry patterns. Everyone knows, he reflected, that they never show Bogart sleeping. He's always up, working on something, meticulously dressed, solving something, slapping somebody, plugging somebody or having some fist-to-cuffs with a bad guy. That was fine by Chambers.

He did take a break to shower, brush his teeth, put on some new underwear and socks and shirt he had purchased in the lobby. He slipped into a new suit he had hastily purchased at the Men's Warehouse at Lloyd Center.

He distracted himself while the hard disk compiled the data by thinking about how he had acquired the suit so quickly. He could have called the hotel tailor, but there was no drama in that. And he wanted to see if all the commercials were really true. Turned out the Men's Warehouse commercials were true, only, he thought, they would probably not use his case as a real case study.

He imagined himself calling the Men's Warehouse and recording a message on the customer satisfaction hotline.

"Hello. This is Chambers," he would say, "This freaking jagoff executive calls me and says some Oregon schmucks can't investigate their way out of a freekin' paper bag. Says I gotta be on a plane in freekin' two hours. I ain't got shit. Ferrari's in the freaking Ferry building and my drawers is already a full day stale. So I gets on the freekin' plane with the suit on my back, a fifth of bourbon and a freekin' attitude. Knowing I can't wear the same suit two days in a row, I steps into the Men's Warehouse and says, "Get your hands off your peckers and Gimme a freeking Armani suite right now, cut to fit or I'm callin' every God damn radio and television station and screamin' false advertising you slubs. Well, I'll be God damn if this little turkey necked geek comes out of the back room with an Armani suit that's freekin' silk and everything and he measures and cuts it right there. In freeking one hour I'm walkin' outta there on clouds sayin' Men's Warehouse, You lucky fuckin' bastards."

Chambers sort of smiled, but it took minutes to get there. He felt his sense of humor was a little jagged around the edges. By eleven o'clock he had broken the code and began piecing together the messages. The puzzle was complex and showed a level of thought that impressed Chambers.

Based on what he was, he thought that Trixie, perhaps, could easily have been of genius level intelligence. But that was only half of it. He recognized some of the names, names that made even Chambers afraid.

When Rich got home, no one was there. He walked over to the dining room table and noticed the pile of mail. Most of it was opened and separated. Sitting alone was an opened pink envelope. A letter on top of it.

He looked at the half-filled cup of tea sitting next to strained tea bags in a small plate. Light waves of steam were still coming out of the tea cup.

But where was April?

Rich picked up the letter and read it.

"Dear Rich," It started, "Last weekend was the most wonderful weekend I've ever had. Rich, I wasn't sure what to make of what happened between us. On one hand, it felt so good to be with you, touching you and sharing with you. But on the other hand, I know it was wrong what we did…"

Rich stopped reading and could only imagine what April's reaction might have been reading these first lines.

He screamed, "God damnn it! Fuuuuuuuuuuuck!" and sat down in the chair, stunned by what the letter revealed. He laid his head down on his arms and rattled through ever variation of the Lords name with some profanity of some sort associated with it.

He continued reading after he'd exhausted his expletive options, "After some soul searching and talks with Phil and writing in my journals I know you're right. No matter how I rationalize it, a relationship with you could never work. April is very lucky to have a man like you. And even though I'm jealous of what you have found with her, I accept that I could never compete with that.

But I still love you very much, Rich, and hope we can still be friends. Even if I'm not with you, no one can take away what we shared this weekend. I'll always have that. I know that I'll always have you inside of me.

Today, I'm going home to confront my past. Wish me luck. All my love, Brenda."

"Holly fucking shit," was all Rich could say as he read the salutation. "I'm fucked."

He turned over the letter and found, written in April's handwriting and brief note that said:

RICH, YOU ARE A PIECE OF SHIT. I HATE YOUR GUTS. I'M GOING TO PICK UP THE KIDS FROM SCHOOL AND GO TO THE CABIN FOR A FEW DAYS WHILE I SORT THIS OUT. IF I STAY, I MIGHT DO SOMETHING THAT I MIGHT REGRET. RICH, I HOPE YOU KNOW HOW MUCH THIS HURTS ME. I FEEL USED, DIRTY IN FACT. YOU ARE A LYING, LOWLIFE, AND I'M VERY DISSAPOINTED. VERY DISAPPOINTED AND HURT! HOW COULD YOU?!

Rich read the note over and over. Each word cut through his heart like a serrated edged knife. This couldn't be happening? It was all wrong and it seemed so surreal.

But the emotional knot that was forming in the pit of his stomach was more than real. It made him feel sick. He ran to the bathroom and threw up until there was nothing left to throw up.

He dry heaved until he felt as if his stomach had turned inside out. Then he curled up in a ball and lay down on the floor, crying, agonizing, wailing as loud as he could; not in words, but in primal, unrecognizable screams of pure pain.

His world was falling apart.

Chapter 106

"Here's what we got, Grimsley," Chambers said as he pointed at several photographic prints of Trixie's apartment walls. "Safety deposit boxes, numbered accounts and pet names, all criss-crossed on opposite walls. The missing numbers and letters from this wall are visible on this wall. The missing letters from this wall are on that wall. I almost didn't catch it, but the program did."

Grimsley and Chambers were in a private booth at Huber's on Third and Alder. As Chambers spoke, James Louis, the great grandson of the original owner approached their table, and in Mandarin, said, "Mr. Grimsley, an honor to have you here, sir."

Grimsley replied in Mandarin.

"The honor is all mine, sir. Please allow me to introduce Mr. Chambers from San Francisco."

Chambers stood, bowed and in perfect Mandarin said, "Mr. Louis, I knew your grandfather. I am honored to meet you and humbly appreciate your hospitality."

Louis wore a navy blue double breasted, tailored suite. His dark, straight hair was meticulously trimmed and he wore a tightly-trimmed mustache that decorated his handsome, intelligent forty-year-old face.

"Gentlemen," he said now in perfect English, "Anything you want. It's on me."

Louis snapped his fingers and a waiter, decked in white vest, bow tie and black slacks, who was at the far end of the restaurant, immediately came to their table.

Louis placed a hand on the waiter's shoulder and gently said, "Take care of our guest. Whatever they want."

The waiter, an older, balding Asian man did not look at Louis or acknowledge his request. He immediately focused on Grimsley first and said, "May I take your order, sir."

Grimsley and Chambers knew the hierarchy of a Chinese owned restaurant. Louis request was a command. Huber's was the oldest and most respected restaurant in Portland and Louis ran the restaurant with absolute authority. Respect was unconditional. Position was earned and a job could be lost in a heartbeat. Likewise, Louis loved and respected his employees like family. A Chinese family, or course, was very different from any other family.

Two Irish coffees, Huber's institutions, invented by Huber's namesake more than a century ago, arrived at their table.

"What do these pet names mean?" Grimsley asked, focusing their attention back on Chamber's laptop.

"I saw a footnote on the arriving officers report that said there were cats gathered around Trixie's body when he arrived." Chambers said.

"That's right. We didn't make anything of it. We figured, they were strays come to see the show and sniff for food."

"The officer thought it was strange, right."

"That's right, hinted at some supernatural connection. You know, spirit leaves the body and at that moment is reincarnated as an animal or an ant. Buddhist philosophy."

"That wasn't in the report," Chambers said.

"I asked Paulson not to speculate on the supernatural in his report, just to stick to the facts."

"But do you believe in that sort of thing?"

"I believe anything is possible, Chambers," Grimsley answered.

"Tell you what I believe."

"What Chambers?"

"That Trixie was a cat fan. She fed the neighborhood cats at the same time every morning. She was killed a little before feeding time. The only thing predictable about cats is when they eat. She was not able to feed them that morning. On the four corners of her walls in the main room, near the picture molding were the letters, SPCA. The bus she took regularly, went north to Columbia or south to Hollywood. I'm betting she went north to the new SPCA on Columbia. Cat people are predictable. These pet names reflect her passion for cats."

"That's good Chambers. God damn, that's good."

"That's not all. She's a Buddhist, or wanted to be. I found a quote from the Dalai Lama, who, by the way, was in town last week. Some of these codes have Buddhist names, a little harder to decipher because I have to cross-reference the many Buddhist sects and Gods. Never seen so many Gods. How would you keep track of all of them?"

"Paulson can check out what you've got so far. It's going to take some time. We only got a handful of men to work with."

"Well, you've got two hours before banks and offices close. We better get busy."

Rich lay in the bathroom for four hours. He was unable to focus on anything, simply lay there, his eyes bloodshot from crying, his head pounding like an anvil being battered by a twenty pound sledge, and gut throbbing from dry heaving. His chest was so tight, he felt as though he were wearing a straight jacket with straps being pulled as tight as they could be by some muscle bound orderly. He felt paralyzed as he stared at the bathroom door.

If he stood up and walked through that door, he would have to facing the world, his screw-up, his pain, April, his children and the pain he had caused. He did not want to do it. But he had to.

He knew he had to face whatever was in store for him. Out there, beyond the door. He had to face it. He had to make it right if he could.

He owed April that much. He owed his children that much. And he felt he owed the people who maybe loved him that much.

Rich reached for the sink that was six inches from his head and pulled himself up. He could not straighten his body completely. The needles of pain that shot through his abdomen were extreme. He looked down, into the face bowl, avoiding the mirror in front of him.

When he finally looked up at his face, it frightened him at first. He looked years older, hair disheveled, brilliant red eyes, snot running down his nose.

Not the tough guy he always imagined he was.

He turned on the water and placed a finger under it until it was warm. Then he cupped his hands, filled them with warm water and splashed it on his face.

Rich was distraught, not sure what steps to take next; not sure what moves to make. He was not in control situation was looking like a complete disaster. He needed advice, but Dr. Phil was not on the air, so he thought about who else he could trust, consult in. After a few minutes he knew who to consult.

Rich, walked to the den and turned on the computer.

Dusk was approaching fast and tiny droplets of rain were forming on the windows. None of that mattered though. He needed to talk to Kyle

When the computer booted up and his modem had reached into that fantastic space called the Internet, he typed in Kyle's e-mail address and wrote:

"Yo Bro, I fucked up. I'm in pain. You out there?"

He pressed send.

"There's one more piece of information on these walls that scares the bejeebers out of me Grimsley," Chambers said, as he consumed the Huber's house specialty turkey sandwich. "The name of Neil, and what looks like a Swiss bank account number."

"The Senator Sam Neil?"

"Don't know."

"But I know a fella by the name of Temple. Neil's personal assistant slash murderer slash scum bag who's smart, clever and ruthless. James Bond fanatic. Fancies himself Odd-job. I've been following his patterns for years and so has the FBI but no one has ever been able to link him to anything. The books say he's clean, but I know too many people who know different."

"So what does that mean, Chambers?"

"Neil will protect the Senator's interest at whatever costs. That's what he's paid to do. And he's paid to deflect it from the Senator so he remains bulletproof. And there's no-one better at it than Temple."

"So, you think Temple is behind this? Is he our assassin?"

"Not a chance. James Bond. Remember. Walther PPK with a silencer or something ridiculous like a toe knife or hat with a saw or something like that. Real drama queen this Temple. Freekin' nut case with an IQ of two ten. He would never use a knife. Macho prick thinks knives are for sissies."

"So why hasn't anyone been able to pin anything on Temple so far."

"You know as well as I do that governments aren't the only ones who can kill and get away with it. People are murdered every day. Some look like accidents. Some are unsolved murders. Some we never hear about. The reason I'm on this end of solving crimes is because our only chance to get people like Temple is to be one step ahead on the technological side. If we design the systems we can understand them, and we can use them to our advantage. If the other side designs the systems we're screwed."

"But if they use our technology against us, doesn't that help them?"

"Yeah, it does, but don't think we don't have ways of tracing our technology. Every piece of software and hardware I designed also has an untraceable, impossible to detect back door built *between* the circuit board layers. That, my friend, is a secret only you and I need to know. Listen, I'll find out where Temple is and I'll try to crack this account code while you find out what you can."

"You can crack Swiss bank account codes?"

"Come on Grimsley, you've been spending too much time on the gun range. This is a new age. With a little information, some inside Intel, and the right application, you can crack into any computer out there. Computers are like people. If you peel back their fingernails enough, they scream like monkeys and spill the beans. They'll rat out their own mother board if you squeeze them hard enough."

"Chambers, I like you. That kind of colorful human slash techno talk gives me a woody every time."

Chambers pushed up the edge of his mouth, threatening a smirk, but stopped just short. His eyes, however, were laughing their ass off and Grimsley could tell.

"You're a cool one Grimsley. Very cool. And don't think I'm fooled by this country bumpkin act of yours. I've read every book and paper you've ever written. You've done all the hard work. I'm just here on the clean up crew, to take the bows for all your hard work. Let's get to work."

Grimsley called Paulson and Simmons and gave them the task of tracking the bank accounts, which meant they had to call each bank before closing then race from bank to bank before the bank manager left. It was less like an investigation and more like delivering newspapers.

Paulson pulled up in front of the bank, double parked, and both he and Simmons jumped out of the car and ran into the bank branch, presented the account numbers, jotted down notes, ran to their car and sped to the next bank. No single branch on Trixie's list was in the same neighborhood. Grimsley emphasized that all accounts had to be checked by six p.m.

Grimsley paid a visit to the SPCA and Chambers returned to his room to continue breaking the code.

Chapter 107

"*Mother fucker, wassup. Yo message don't sound right. You all right?*" read Kyle's message.

Rich could not stop the flow of tears as he typed his reply to Kyle, "*Shit hit the fan. I fucked up and got involved with a women this weekend and April found out. She's gone and she took the kids with her to the cabin in Lincoln City. It's all fucked up.*"

Seconds later, Kyle's instant message flashed on the screen, "*That's fucked up bro. Can't say I know how you feel 'cause I ain't never been through no shit like that. How you feelin'?*"

"*Like somebody just kicked my ass.*"

"*That sounds about right. Listen bro, I know you probably hurtin' right now, but you got to be strong.*"

Kyle next message read, "*Shit gets fucked up for people every God damn day. Mother fuckin' loved ones die in plane crashes, get arms and shit cut off, see best friends shredded to pieces in car accidents and they don't give up. They face that shit. That's what you got to do.*"

"*That's easy to say.*"

"*Of course, bitch, shit is easy to say. What the fuck you think I'm talkin' 'bout here.*"

Rich felt a smile forming on his face.

"*Don't be a fuckin' pussy and think your shit don't stink. You created this shit and now you got to fix it.*"

"*I'm sorry, you're right.*"

"*And you say you're sorry one more time, I'm gonna come there and bitch slap you mother fucker. The only one needs to hear that shit is April and yo chilren and all the mother fuckers you hurt. Nigga, you can't touch me. I know all about you mother fucker.*"

"*What you know nigga I ain't told you,*" Rich felt the strength returning to his fingers and could feel his pulse race as he read Kyle's words and responded.

"*I know you want to be a righteous mother fucker, but you don't trust nobody. You live in a world of your own design. You think you a mother fuckin' island and that shit is what's fuckin' you up. You ain't on no island, nigga, and the reality is that you can be honest with people and they won't fuckin' shoot your ass. You got to stop bein' afraid of bein' afraid mother fucker. Then you can start enjoying your life and allowin' people around you in.*"

"*Nigga you talkin' shit.*"

"*Ahh Ahh, no you didn't. You didn't say that shit. See what I'm talkin' bout. I'm tryin' to talk some sense and you booshitin' with me nigga.*"

Rich, realizin' his mistake wrote, "*I'm so...um, I didn't mean it that way. You right. I'm a multiple personality mother fucker and never know which one* to bring out and talk fo me and act fo me. I need to get all these mother fuckers together in my head and decide which one is me. Feel like I got that mother fuckin' To Tell the Truth game show going on in my head. Host be askin, 'which one of these mother fuckers is the real Rich Franklin?"

"Now you talkin' nigga. Don't take no psychologist to see the shit goin' on in yo head. Sept you the only one don't see it."

"Like I said, Kyle, you one bad ass mother fucker."

"I ain't," he replied, "I just say what's on my mind. Somethin' you need to learn. And I ain't going to let you go down mother fucker. If I have to prop your skinny ass up durin' a time of need, I'll do that."

"So, what should I do?"

"Nigga, you figure that shit out. I don't know. What you think, I'm the guru mother fuckin' Maharaja or some shit like that? Put your shit straight. Pull your mother fuckin' family together nigga. That's the most important shit' you got going on right now. You lose that and, well, shit you can always start over with somebody else. But that shit is whacked. Who wants to do that? That's like going out and selling a good BMW 'cause one of the windshield wipers don't work. Don't make no mother fucking sense, do it?"

"You right mother fucker. I know what to do. You right."

"And nigga, I expect to hear some shit from you every mother fuckin' day until your shit is straight."

"Ait mother fucker; every God damn day."

"Go take care of your shit. I'm out..."

Rich smiled. His mood was quickly shifting. Kyle's reaming was what he needed. It resonated in his head, and as he thought about his dilemma, he had a fleeting thought about what a Black therapist office should look like. Instead of having a couch in the office, they would have a barber shop chair. When niggas came in whining about shit, the therapist would verbally tear a nigga a new asshole and fuck up his hair.

He imagined that when the sessions was over, the therapist would say, "Thas fifty fi dollars. Now get the fuck out of here. Next time you come back, you bed not be whinin' 'bout shit and you bed have you shit straight or I'm gone fuck up yo head again."

| A PITCH IN CRIME | 500

Chapter 108

When Kyle logged off, he was deeply disturbed by the situation his oldest friend Rich had created. He hoped his straight-forward words of wisdom would help. But he wasn't so sure.

He had known Rich since junior high. He knew Rich would never ask anyone to do anything for him unless he could do double for them first. Rich had a weird thing about emotional debt.

Rich figured that by helping others, he accumulated emotional stock from them but never gave away any of his. Rich figured he could cash in this stock in some cosmic bank somewhere. But his theory, Kyle reflected, had the reverse effect than what Rich had intended.

Rich accumulated emotional stock and never gave out any of his own, so his emotional stock languished. Kyle explained to him in one email that some day he would be majority holder of a shit load of his own worthless stock. Emotional stock only gains value if you allow others to invest in it, he explained in colorful language. But Rich wasn't buying.

That was twenty years ago. Now, Rich was screwed up in the head a little, Kyle thought, so he had to do something. He couldn't do much here in Kansas.

Kyle's office was an enormous carpeted room with a huge plasma screen TV mounted on the wall, hooked up to banks of VCR, DVD players and amplifiers. His office acted as his screening and editing room. Next to the TV was his Mac editing station. A large leather couch graced the center of the room and each wall was lined with shelves and shelves of books. His desk was a dark stained, antique roll-top that was scattered with papers, pens and video disks. Kyle had two documentary scripts in the works and had recently sold a script to Sidney Potier's production company for a movie on Nicodemus, the only all black settlement in Kansas.

Once Kyle's first TV script sold, the work and the money came pouring in from Hollywood. But he refused to leave Lawrence, Kansas, because he did not want his family growing up in California and did not want to leave his teaching post in the University of Kansas film department.

He, instead, purchased this palatial mansion for his family and continued being a commuter Hollywood insider and outsider, making frequent trips to Los Angeles to consult with producers and pitch ideas while maintaining his Kansas roots and lifestyle.

He scanned his desk, looked at the word document with the cursor blinking in the middle of an incomplete sentence and said, "This is gon have to wait. I got to take care of an old friend."

He quickly logged onto Cheaptickets.com and found the only red eye to Oregon and made reservations. Then he walked downstairs and to talk with his wife.

The carpeted halls were lined with doors, all bedrooms for each of his kids. As he reached the top of the stairs, he could hear the frenzy of activity in the five rooms downstairs. PlayStation in one room, the clatter of dishes in the kitchen, and an argument about somebody teasing somebody in another room.

Kyle smiled. He loved this shit.

In the kitchen, Lisa, Kyle's wife, looked at him and immediately recognized something was wrong.

Kyle and Lisa married seventeen years earlier. Lisa's friendly, green eyes complimented her youthful face. Her reddish hair was disheveled, some hung lose and some was tied at the top of her head and she was still strikingly beautiful for her age.

"What is it Kyle?" Lisa asked. "The last time I saw that look on your face was when your mother died."

"Not that bad," he said, "but bad. Rich and April are in trouble. I've got to go to Oregon tonight, honey."

Lisa walked over to Kyle and looked up at him. He towered over her at six foot six, and his afro added another four inches. She reached up and hugged him.

"Are you sure?"

"Yeah, I'm sure. It's not good. And you know that nigga ain't never gon ask fo shit from nobody. That's why I got to go rescue his ass."

"How long will you be gone?"

"Just a day or two, long enough to take care of bidness. You gon be all right?"

"Yeah, I think so. I don't have to work at the lab until tomorrow night and we do have a sixteen year old in the house."

"Sixteen!" Kyle said, feigning surprise. "God damn, how in the hell we get a sixteen year old in the house? How many mufukin kids we got?"

Lisa laughed.

"Still only five."

"Five! Got damn, where all these kids come from?"

Lisa could see Kyle was only joking. This was his favorite joke. They had five beautiful kids, each with a unique sense of humor that always amazed them.

Even though physically, Kyle was intimidating, all the kids knew Kyle was there to protect, hug and try to make laugh as much as possible.

"You want me to drive you to KC?"

"Naw, baby, I'll take the Gremlin."

She laughed again.

"OK, but be careful. It started to snow out there."

"All right. I'm going to sneak out 'cause if I tell he chitlins they gon try to stop me. You know, pull out the spark plug wires, pee in the gas tank, slash my mufikin' tires. You know, them little…"

Lisa shot a disapproving glance at Kyle and he stopped, smiled and knew to quit while he was ahead.

He packed, kissed everyone goodbye and drove his Range Rover to Kansas City International where he caught a red eye to Portland.

Chapter 109

Now was the time for intense thought that would lead to specific actions Rich repeated to himself as he paced back and forth in the den.

Music. He needed the right music. What would work? What would be perfect?

Herbie Hancock.

Rich took the CD out of his vinyl CD holder and placed it in the tray. Herbie Hancock's *Chameleon* was first, base throbbing, clavinet, minimoog, all playing in unison, like a steam locomotive.

Think.

What next? Drive to Lincoln City tonight?

It was three hours away and he'd never make it back for his route in the morning. Plus, April, probably needed a cooling off period. There was no phone in the cabin and no cell service.

Drive out in the morning after my route? That's it. Now what? The book. What's going on with the book?

Rich checked his e-mails for any other messages. There was one from Emily Patterson. He did not recognize it, but recognized the URL. It from his agent's office. He opened it. She was letting him know the book is on target to be printed on Wednesday and will be in stores on Thursday.

Perfect, Rich thought.

Call Enison and tell him the truth. Call Grimsley and tell him the truth. Call Phil and tell him the truth. When you see April, tell her the truth about *everything*.

Rich was going to put his *shit straight* as Kyle had demanded. It wouldn't be easy. There would be questions, personal questions he'd have to answer. He'd have to dig deep.

Rich sat at his desk. He noticed the stack of papers and pamphlets he fished out of the truck earlier that day.

In his haste, he had not paid attention to the 10-inch deep stack of crap. But as he examined it closer, he noticed the thin, colorful book that was sandwiched in between the mess.

He reached down and pushed the other publications aside and picked up the book. It was a beautifully crafted journal with hand made rice paper binding and intricate patterns on the cover.

At first Rich didn't remember how or where he had acquired it. Then he remembered that Juan found it in the yard. He assumed it was empty, so, at first, he was not going to open it. He had other problems to deal with.

He was about to place it on the bookshelf when he remembered what Grimsley and Paulson had said about a journal.

Can't be, he thought.

He put the book on his desk and pushed the cover back. In the upper right hand corner of the first page was the name *Trixie, book #25.*

Rich gasped and sat up straight as he read the name over and over. The journal was started in January.

"Holly fucking shit," he said then turned the page and read more.

The handwriting was precise and neat. The tone of each entry seemed to depend on Trixie's emotional state. She was contemplative at times and intellectual at times, documenting facts about her life, people she encountered and in some instances, just ranting and cursing about life and the men she knew.

Rich could not stop reading until he read about Senator Sam Neil, who paid her ten thousand dollars a month to have sex with him and be his escort whenever he visited. Trixie documented each visit and included a small table showing the amounts she was paid.

In all, she had made $150,000 dollars, just off of Sam Neil. She also wrote about his assistant, Temple, who she considered a scary, angry person who's *Karma was all screwed up.*

Rich flipped through more pages and his eye caught the name of Delbert Debartola who she described as a pedophile who worked for the Standard Insurance company. She included his full name and address and also documented each visit as well, how much she was paid and the kinky things Debartola did to her.

Rich found an elaborately, decorated page that stood out from all others. Trixie used colorful markers to decorate the page with paisley patterns, butterflies' and rainbows. It was her birthday.

At the top of the page Trixie wrote, *Born to losers on this day eighteen years ago.* Her birthday was the day she died.

Grimsley's smoking gun. That meant anyone who had sex with her prior to her birthday would be guilty of statutory rape of a minor.

This journal, thought Rich, was what everyone was looking for.

Rich closed the book, picked up the phone and called Grimsley.

"*Grimsley here. Speak,*" Grimsley was leaving the SPCA building.

"Captain, Grimsley, this is Rich Franklin."

"*Mr. Franklin, How are you? How can I help you?*"

"Sorry to bother you, sir, but I have Trixie's journal and there are details here I think you want to see right away."

Chapter 110

Even before Rich finished speaking, Grimsley's cell phone beeped.

"Hold on Rich, don't say another word."

"Who is this?"

"Walker, Mr. Grimsley. You asked me to keep an eye on this number for any unusual broadcast. I just got my equipment in place and calibrated to that location. Franklin's land line shows one distinct broadcast and the house is broadcasting to another receiver, both within one block of the house."

"Holy shit!" he yelled, "hang on, I'm putting you on three way."

He pressed another button on his phone.

"Rich, Walker you both hear me?"

"I'm still here," Rich said.

"Loud and clear," Walker said. *"And captain, I hate to say this, but you're broadcasting too. Separate frequency. Somebody else is listening to you."*

"Shit," he said. *"Can you scramble all of us?"*

"Yeah, I can. Hold one. But I can't scramble the house."

Rich and Grimsley listened while Walker typed on his keyboard. Their lines beeped simultaneously.

"Got it. We're clean."

"I know this is a bad time for introductions, but you two already know each other. Rich, say hello to your best customer, James Clarance Walker."

"Hey Rich," Walker said.

"I don't believe this," Rich said.

"Believe it," Grimsley shot back. *"Now let's cut the small talk. Walker's helping us out. I asked him to triangulate your house from a satellite feed and scan for any unusual radio frequency broadcast. Sounds like we got two bogies about a block away from you, Rich. Those dots on Walker's screen, Rich, are our bad guys. Very bad guys."*

"Half block now," Walker said excitedly.

"Shit," Grimsley, said. *"Rich, lock your doors and windows. You got a secure room?"*

Panicked, Rich said, "Um, uh, okay, yeah, the den is the most secure, only one window with locking storms, impossible to get into easily.

"Go there, barricade the doors, turn out the lights, block the windows with a book cases, anything you can find. Call Walker on your cell phone and he'll make sure it's scrambled and we'll keep you talking. We have a plain clothes man who will be at your door in a matter of minutes. Keep your head down Rich."

"All right."

Rich gave Walker his cell phone number, hung up the land line, grabbed his cell phone out of his bag along with a portable head set and called Walker. Walker patched Rich through to Grimsley.

"*Rich,*" Walker said, "*you back in the Den?*"

"Yep," Rich said, breathless from running from door to door and window to window checking locks and panicking about the unwanted visitors.

"*That Herbie Hancock in the background?*" Walker asked.

"*Yep,*" Rich said hastily.

"*Turn it up?*"

"*Why?*" Rich said confused.

"*Rich, your phone lines and your house are bugged. These characters have been listening in for who knows how long. Your cell line is clean but we don't know where the other bugs are. We can talk safely if the music is louder.*"

Rich turned the music up and hit the repeat button so the CD would recycle the same song.

"*Rich,*" Grimsley chimed in, "*How much of the journal did you read?*"

"Enough to know it's our smoking gun, Mr. Grimsley," Rich answered. "Details about senators and local executives, payments, kinky stuff. She just turned 18 captain."

"God damn it. How did you find it?" Grimsley asked.

"My kid fished it from the back yard and it's been driving around with me all this time in the cab."

"*I'll be God...Chico must have dropped it when he left the scene...Rich, they're going to try to hit you fast and disappear in the night. One will take out the other if he has to. That journal can hang more than one person. And it looks like there are at least two parties who want it very badly. But we're not going to let that happen. We're on our way.*"

Rich was sweating profusely as he huddled under a folding table. He had locked the door and pushed the book case in front of it. The window was also covered by a shade and a flimsy bookshelf.

He was really scared now.

When Temple heard Rich announce that he had the journal, he knew he had less than ten minutes to move on him, to infiltrate the premise, eliminate the target and remove the journal.

Then he had five minutes to drive to the switch point, and a half hour to drive to Pearson's Airfield in Vancouver and fly his private twin-engine jet back to Washington where an air-tight alibi awaited him.

He was a man of action. He grabbed his hat, the monitor, which was attached to a pair of earphones, and dashed out of the car and into the back yard of the adjoining house.

He climbed over the redwood fence that separated the two yards. As he landed in the vegetable bed, he was giddy from the rush of impending violence. This was a competition, he thought, and there could be only one winner here, and it was going to be him.

At the same time that Temple heard Rich's announcement, a dark figure moved quickly out of another dark sedan and approached the house from 47th street. He was aware that a plain cloths officer was watching the house. He seated in a government issued Caprice, dressed in "cop" clothes.

The dark figure wore black tights, black ankle high sneakers, a black Al Mar jacket, and each pocket was filled with the tools of his trade.

Velcro strap around his thigh had pouches that contained his collection of tactical weapons.

He crept up to the black sedan and in one swift motion, opened the door, grabbed the unsuspecting officer by the head and snapped it around, breaking his neck instantly.

He kept track of the time subconsciously. Two minutes. Too long. He had to hurry. He did not hear Grimsley's conversation with Walker, but he could tell that they were aware that he was on his way. He had to hurry. Infiltrate, acquire and disappear. Collect his money and disappear even more.

He approached the front door, reached up and unscrewed the bulb in the overhead light. Darkness washed over the porch. He had a key and inserted it into the deadbolt, unlatched it and entered.

As he headed for his Bronco, Grimsley called a young detective named Fred Tanner, who he had posted to watch the Franklin residence. There was no answer.

"Shit," he said.

He reconnected walker's line.

"Walker, the detective I posted at the house is down. You're closest. Can you get there? I'm ten minutes away. That's not enough time. You're two minutes."

"I can do it. My system is portable. I'll be there in one minute."

Grimsley's gunned the engine and screeched onto Columbia boulevard, the emergency light flashing on top of his Bronco. His phone rang,

"Talk." He said.

"Chambers here. What's going on? I picked up a lot of chatter on the scanners a few minutes ago. "You need some help?"

"Franklin has the journal. And they know it. Two bogies closing in on his place. Nearest cruiser is fifteen minutes away. I'm ten minutes."

"He'll be dead in ten and they'll be gone by then," said Chambers. "I'm at Trader Joe's in Hollywood. Needed some food."

"You're three minutes, Chambers," Grimsley shouted. "Can you get there?!"

"Two and a half, my friend."

Chambers threw a twenty at the cashier, showed him the can of nuts he had and shouted, "Police business I gotta run. You can keep the change. Buy some Jamba juice or something."

He charged out of the door, climbed up into the Escalade and gunned it through the parking lot, straight up 41st street. One block later he was on 42nd and speeding north, past Prescott, then Going, than, turned the headlights out and eased to a stop in front of the Franklin residence.

The porch and the house were dark, except a single light in the back of the house.

He called Grimsley.

"I'm here. Where's our boy?"

"In the den. Back of the house on the left."

"Ask him to turn that light out?" Chambers said.

"I'll patch you in," Grimsley said. *"Rich, you there?"*

"I'm still here. Scared shitless."

"Turn that light out kid," Chambers ordered.

"Who are you?" Rich asked.

"Rich, this is Chambers a PI from Oakland. He's here to help too," said Grimsley.

"You got quite a team," Rich said.

"Quiet kid before I change my mind," Chambers barked. "I'm outside and I'm going in the front."

"Walker is on his way. He's patched in. He's got a portable monitor and is plotting their location based on their broadcast frequency. As long as they don't turn off their receivers we'll know where they're at."

Walker's voice broke in.

"I'm at the back door. No breaks, but a basement window is compromised."

"One came in the basement and the other came in the front door," said Grimsley, *"Can you tell which part of the house they're in."*

"No, they're too close. I just got one big ass dot here."

"You know what to do. Keep your line open, watch your back and take them out," said Grimsley.

"I'm going in too," said Chambers, gun drawn, crouched at the front door.

"Chambers, what are you packin?" Grimsley asked.

"Eight shot three fifty seven."

"Walker. What are you packin?"

"Spyderco and my whits. That's all I need."

Grimsley said, *"You both know how to ID weapons. Make every shot count. We need these guys alive if possible, but don't take any chances. They're not as concerned about your lives as we are theirs."*

"Walker, you know how to whistle?" Chambers asked.

"Sure, just put your lips together like this and blow." Walker blew whistle into his mouthpiece.

"I see they teach you young Harvard boys a thing or two about the movies. We get in a firefight, you whistle and I promise not to blow your fuckin' head off."

"Franklin, stay put and stay quiet," Grimsley warned, *"We'll get you out of this mess."*

Temple broke the basement window and slid in on his stomach. He landed on a large, dusty decommissioned oil tank, slid to the cold cement floor and crouched there on all fours, listening intensely.

He listened on his monitor and could hear nothing except music. It was conveniently too loud.

He cursed. Five minutes gone. Only five left. Check upstairs first.

He crept up the stairs and cautiously opened the basement door. The house was pitch black. The stairs that led upstairs were next to the basement door. Temple pressed his body against the wall, the excitement building inside of him. Most people go upstairs when they're scared. Perfect. Upstairs they're trapped.

He climbed the carpeted stairs.

He mentally shuffled through tense scenes he'd memorized from the movie *Gold Finger. Keep cool.* he thought. Like Dr. No. *Your invincible*. He crouched in the hallway at the top of the stairs.

The dark figure had memorized the furniture configuration from his earlier visit. He slipped in the front door and dove across the room, somersaulting once, which put him behind the large dark couch near the fireplace.

He crouched there. Listened. The music was too loud, he thought. Convenient and annoying. They knew something. They warned Rich.

Darkness shrouded the house interior.

He preferred it that way.

There were four rooms down stairs. Three upstairs. He could sense the danger. He assumed his counterpart was close.

Rich, he figured, was hiding somewhere.

Five minutes burned. Five minutes left. Not much time. Check every room. Start downstairs.

Three rooms, including the bathroom, were in between. The den was at the end of the hallway. Check them all. Thirty seconds in each.

He entered the first room, and, like a cat, slunk from one corner to the next, his senses heightened, smell, sight, sound, instincts.

He would need them all. He did not need a flashlight. His eyes were attuned to seeing in the dark. He was trained to recognize anomalies in the darkness. He was, in fact, trained to fight blind folded if he needed to. The darkness was his ally.

When Chambers reached the porch, he was tense and irritated. His shoes were wet and the porch conveniently dark. He hated Oregon and he especially hated dark houses with killers waiting inside.

Made him very uncomfortable.

Chambers turned the knob on the front door and pushed it open. He slid in and stepped slightly to his left and immediately rammed his knee on an end table.

He grit his teeth and held back a curse. Even if he screamed, the music was too loud. No one would hear it.

Weapon held straight up, he dared not use his pen light or he'd be an easy target. After his eyes adjusted, he could see the dark forms of tables, sofas.

It had been a while since he'd had to stalk someone under these circumstances, but the skills were there. He took a deep breath to calm his nerves and wiped the sweat that was forming in his palms on his coat.

He stepped out of the living room and into the dark hallway that separated him from Rich in the Den.

He did not like this. But he had to do it.

In a bold motion, he holstered his gun. He would need both hands. A shot would be a giveaway in the dark and Chambers knew that the person to fire first loses.

He moved slowly toward the first opening, stepped in and froze. His heart beating so loud he thought he was not the only one who could hear it.

He crouched.

The silk of his suit gave easily. He moved towards the window. He examined each corner. He examined every shape. When he finished with the room, he stepped back towards the door.

One down, three to go.

Walker picked the lock on the back door, a skill he'd learned as a teenager in Toledo, Ohio. He pushed it in, stepped in and closed it. He crouched, like a tiger. His black nylon running suit made no sounds and allowed him to easily creep into the kitchen.

He whistled.

Chambers heard Walker's whistle.

Seeing that the room he was in was clear, he whispered to Grimsley, "I'm downstairs, bedroom one. Walker, you take upstairs."

The dark figure barely heard the whistle. But it was definitely a whistle. He was not sure what to make of it. But he knew it was not good.

Six minutes gone.

He crept from the second bedroom to the third, a much larger room with toys, Xbox controllers and books scattered everywhere. He carefully checked each corner, and avoided stepping on toys that might give away his position.

Walker glided up the stairs. The music was not as loud there, so he had to be even more cautious.

He listened. He slid his hand along the carpet, feeling for foot prints.

His hands moved over a set of footprints that were huge, possibly size thirteen shoes. The indent was deep, fresh, with small grains of gravel. Walker grew tense, sensing the danger. The prints led left.

Walker, instinctively went right. And, still crouching, he crawled to the master bedroom. The door was open. He froze just inside the door and listened.

Where are you, he thought. Come out. Come out. Wherever you are.

"I'm upstairs," he whispered, "master bedroom. Whoever is here is in one of the bedrooms in the east wing. About six foot six, 230 pounds."

"That's Temple," Chambers said, "He'll have a weapon, a Walther PPK with a silencer. Be careful. Don't let that son of a bitch come downstairs."

Walker, suppressing nervous breaths, reached into his pocket and took out the Spyderco knife, unfolded it with his thumb and nestled it in his right hand. He had to force a reaction. First man to fire, he thought, loses.

He peered around the room, trying to make out figures in the dark. Next to the door was a dresser. And next to the dresser was an umbrella.

That would do. He grabbed it, stood up and walked out the door, tapping the umbrella on the opposite wall as he walked.

Chambers was in the hallway again. He crossed the hall in a single step and entered the bathroom. This was easy he thought. Only one hiding place, the shower. He stepped up to the shower, reached up, clinched the first ring and in a single motion pushed the curtain aside.

Nothing. He relaxed.

The bathroom was next to the Den. One room left. Maybe he wasn't there, Chambers thought.

Maybe he gave up, slipped out a window. He stepped into the

room and walked, carefully, cautiously, from corner to corner, pushing aside toys and books and other crap as he went. *Kids, so fuckin' messy*, he thought.

Walker saw the first flash come from the upper corner of the west bedroom. There was no sound. Silencer. Rapid successions of flashes followed.

Walker was already backed up against the north wall and was using the umbrella to scrape the south wall. He recognized the sound of the Walther PPK with a silencer.

He heard bullets whizzing past, crashing into the south wall and the bedroom door. One bullet was so close to his face he could feel the heat as it passed within inches of his nose.

He dropped the umbrella immediately and groaned with pain and stepped backwards into the bathroom behind him. He fell to his knees and groaned louder. The shots continued until Walker heard the sound of the chamber lock.

It was empty.

Chambers did not detect anyone in the family room. It was empty. He checked the window. It was unlocked and partially open. Maybe there was only one assailant. Or maybe the guy changed his mind and slipped out the window.

Feeling more confident, less tense, he said softly, "Grimsley, we're clean down here. I'm heading upstairs."

"You sure," Grimsley asked.

"As sure as I'm sittin' here," Chambers replied.

Chambers did not hear the shots upstairs. He was next to the den and the music was much louder.

"Walker, you there?" Grimsley asked. There was no reply. "Chambers, hurry upstairs. I think Walker's in trouble. Rich, don't come out of there yet."

As Chambers turned and walked towards the stairs he saw the shadow in the corner of his eyes and the dull glint of a blade moving towards his abdomen.

He didn't hesitate. With a single motion, he turned his body, brought his forearm down, and deflected the blade.

With his other hand, he grabbed the muscular arm and twisted it while swinging it back past his face. The dark figure was surprised at Chambers quickness and could not counter quick enough.

Chambers let go with his right hand, gripped the thumb, pulled it back, snapping it instantly.

The figure groaned. The twelve-inch knife fell to the ground.

Chambers jammed his elbow into the head of the dark figure, making a sickening thud. Chambers attacked with his elbow again. Three more times.

He knew this would probably not be enough.

The dark figure, disoriented, struggled. Chambers tied up the figures hands, caught him off guard, partially disabled him, and now he had to finish him off. He leaned the figures body over his left side and kicked him hard in the abdomen. He could hear a rib breaking. He kicked again and again.

The figure groaned.

In a surprise motion, the figure dropped to the ground. Although he was small, his weight was enough to throw Chambers off balance. He kicked at Chamber's knee, landing a hard blow, then wrapped his other leg round Chambers' leg and forced him off balance.

Chambers fell back hard against the wall, his head snapping back and banging against the wall. His grip loosened on the figure; a possibly fatal move.

The figure was not fully recovered enough to attack though. He groaned again and forced his way up to his feet and lunged at Chambers.

Chambers was ready. He turned to his side, chambered his leg and his arm and blocked the kick that rammed into his side. He let lose a kick that landed squarely in the jaw of the figure, then he attacked again. He could not afford to be on the defensive.

He saw the figure reach down to his leg. He was looking for an advantage, another weapon. In those seconds, Chambers moved in close and jammed an open palm under the chin of the figure, followed by another elbow and a rapid succession of knee kicks.

The figure tried to block.

Keep him on the defense, Chambers thought, as his mind churned though what to do next. The figured countered with defensive block. He was good. But not good enough.

Suddenly, Chambers could feel the hand reach for his weapon and yank it from the holster.

The sound of the powerful weapon discharge was deafening. Chambers deflected the weapon only seconds before it went off, or the shot would have hit him square in the heart.

Chambers gripped the hand with the weapon and tried to twist it. But he was hit in the ribs with a hard blow. The pain was intense. He ignored it, gripped the figure by the torso and flipped him to the ground, and dove into the bedroom as another shot rang out and crashed into the door, barely missing Chambers.

Chambers slipped into the darkness, still cautiously stepping around obstacles and froze on his knees under the window. This was not good. The dark figure stepped into the doorway and reached for the light switch.

Walker had to move quickly. It took four point five seconds to reload and chamber a magazine in a Walther PPK if your good. And this guy was good. He could reach Temple in two.

He followed the sound of the cartridge being ejected and falling to the ground. He ran from the bathroom to the open door and leapt at the figure, his body slamming into it as it rammed another cartridge into the weapon.

The impact knocked the weapon out of Temple's hand and the wind out of his gut. Temple was big, but Walker was big, stronger, and quicker.

Walker kicked Temple in the gut and when he doubled over, hit him hard with a knee to the head.

Temple staggered but did not fall.

Walker stepped towards Temple and punched. Temple, gaining composure, blocked and attacked. He dove towards Walker, forcing his 230 pounds on him, using his weight as possibly his only tactical advantage.

Walker could not mount a defense against a freight train, so he had to absorb the attack. When he saw the shadow coming at him, he dug in his left foot, put his bald head down and leaned into Temple as his weight hit him full on.

The crack of their heads butting was sickening. Walker was slightly dazed. Former wide receivers were like that; thick calluses from years of pounding by bigger, stronger and faster guys than temple dulled the impact.

A slight shift in his position after impact deflected Temple's body and he swung off to Walker's right side. Walker jabbed at

Temple's ribs as his weight passed him. Temple grabbed Walker's running suit as he passed and tugged at him, pulling him with his weight and causing Walker to topple to the ground on top of him.

Walker instinctively rolled, did a back flip, leapt to his feet and kicked Temple in the head. His kick was dead on and he could feel temple's jaw shatter on impact.

Temple's body went limp. Walker took out a set of handcuffs from his pocket and locked them around Temple's wrists. The black shadow of the Walther PPK was in the doorway. Walker quickly grabbed it.

He heard the first shot seconds later and immediately ran for the stairs.

"What's happening?" he whispered into the microphone. I hear shots."

"What's happening with you?" Walker, Grimsley asked. *"We thought you were compromised."*

"Sorry, couldn't talk. Temple is secured. I'm going downstairs."

"Chambers has a live one. He's engaged. And he's armed."

"So am I," Walker said, "Walther PPK, like Chambers said."

Walker descended the stairs.

Chambers was listening but could not speak. That would give away his position. He was cornered. This could be it for him. Walker, where the hell are you, he thought.

The blinding light filled the room instantly as the hooded figure, dressed in black, flicked the light switch on. Two shots rang out. One hit the light fixture causing the lights to go back out. And the other hit the dark figure squarely in the shoulder.

The dark figure, stunned, fell back against the wall, and fired repeatedly into the darkness.

Chambers dove to the side as bullets shattered the television set, slammed into furniture and obliterated the window, causing glass to sprinkling down on the carpet and outside of the window.

When Walker reached the last stair, he saw the flashes from the large caliber weapon as it light up the hall, temporarily blinding him.

He aimed and fired. The dark figure turned and ran towards Walker, crouching. He was moving quickly. Walker did not see him until he was on top of him and he slammed into Walker, knocking him back into the kitchen.

The dark figure did not hesitate. Ten minutes. Time was up. Plus, he assumed Chambers would appear seconds later with whatever weapon he had.

He charged for the front door, opened it and darted out, around the corner of the house and ran through the back yard, over the fence and headed for his switch car.

Grimsley's Bronco pulled up in front of the house seconds later along with four squad cars, lights flashing.

Grimsley yelled into his radio, "Chambers, Walker, where are you?"

Chambers answered first, *"We're downstairs, in the kitchen. Walker's a little rattled, but he'll be okay. Temple is secured upstairs and that punk amateur assassin Fitch is on the move. Come on in. I'm going after Fitch."*

"Walker," Chambers said, as he helped him to his feet and turned on the light, "That little toy of yours still working?"

Walker reached into his pocket and brought out the miniature monitor.

"Yep, he's moving."

"That's the LC 2350. I patented the software for that when I was in college. You keep an eye on that. I'll call you in a minute. Get that kid outta that room. He's probably shit his pants by now."

Chambers headed for the door and flicked on the light switch.

Grimsley entered the room, followed by Paulson, Glock drawn.

"Put that thing away kid before you hurt somebody," Chambers said to Paulson, who shot an angry glance at him.

"It's all right," Grimsley followed, "He's one of us. Chambers, PI from Oakland."

Relaxing his grip on the Glock and lowering it. Grimsley noticed the tiny weapon in Chambers' hand.

"That a Darringer?" he asked.

"Yep, saved my neck. Got an ankle holster. Piece of shit thought he had me. One shot took out the light and the other hit him in the shoulder. That's all I had so I had to make it good. Twenty two though. Not good for much more than kangaroo rat hunting."

Paulson said, "I've heard about you, sir. Thanks for all your help."

"Don't mention it pal. But we're not finished yet and I can't stop to chat. Parker Fitch, a penny antsy assassin with some decent skills and a budding career is on the run. He's desperate and clever and will not hesitate to take hostages or kill anyone who gets in his way. Walker's got him on the monitor and I got a few tricks up my sleeve. Keep the cruisers at a distance and we'll keep broadcasting. If he thinks he's clear, he'll slow down and make a mistake."

"Are you going after him on foot?" Grimsley asked.

"Hell no. These are five hundred dollar Bali's my friend. I do not chase scum bags on foot. I'm in that gas guzzling green-land devouring, Oregon tank, the Escalade. Think you can keep up?"

"Sure," Grimsley said. "Simmons can take over here. Paulson, you're with me."

They got in their cars and sped towards forty second street and took a right turn to Alberta Court.

"Walker," Chambers barked into his cell phone headset, "You with me."

"Right here."

"Let's work some magic. I need to know more about where our boy is. I'm going to tap into the Navistar computer. I've got a little subroutine hidden in the software that you'll find interesting. Listen and learn. What are your access codes?"

"Baker, tango, charlie, zebra, password the black knight."

"All right. Hang tight, I'm going to connect with Navistar," Chambers said, as he pressed a button on the dash and the Navistar panel flashed to life. He pressed a button to activate the voice recognition feature.

"Navistar connect," he said.

In seconds an operator's voice sounded on the car speakers, *"This is Jason Pratt, your Navistar onboard navigation system customer service representative, how may I assist you today Mr. Chambers."*

"Listen up and listen good palley. This could be the best day or the worst day of your life and this could be the last day of your career or the first day of your rise to the top of the Navistar organization. I need you to listen and respond to my questions only. If you don't do that, people will die. You understand?"

"Um, I, I, I think so."

"Don't think, Mr. Pratt. Just do. You got me?"

"Yes, sir Mr. Chambers."

"On your little key board are a bunch of keys. I want you to press the following keys exactly as I tell you? With me?"

"Yes, sir, Mr. Chambers."

"Press shift command then type B as in baker, c as in Charlie, A as in alpha, T as in tango, z as in zate, password chamberssubroutinezeta. You follow?"

"Yes, sir Mr. Chambers," Pratt said nervously, "I'm done. Now my screen Is going haywire."

"When it stops, type in the location codes and beacon codes for this tank."

"Done sir," Pratt said. "It seems to be working now. Um, yeah, it's definitely working."

Suddenly, a soft, sultry female voice came over the speakers and said, "Hello Mr. Chambers, welcome to Navistar Subroutine Zeta. I'm Zeta. How may I serve you?"

"What the hell is that?" Pratt asked. "That's not one of our programs."

"Pratt, don't worry about it. Now log off and forget you ever had this conversation. I'm now in command of your workstation. You can take a break, go to lunch. And if you ever mention this to anyone. And I mean anyone, you will regret it for the rest of your life. Now have a nice day. Zeta, disconnect Mr. Pratt."

"With pleasure sir," the voice said. Pratt was gone.

"Chambers, what the hell did you just do?" Walker asked.

"Taped into the subroutines I planted on the Navistar satellite computer. This is Zeta. She's pulled me out of some tough spots before and she's here to help."

"Zeta, input Mr. Walker's satellite access codes. He's using the dormant Enron satellite to map this grid and track signals from a couple of scum bags. One is on the run and I need to track him."

"No problem, Mr. Chambers," Zeta said. "Happy to serve you."

"Jeez, Chambers, you're a real piece of work."

"That's correct Mr. Walker, now give her the codes. Times a wastin'"

Walker gave Zeta the codes and she thanked him. In seconds, a map of the Concordia neighborhood popped up on the Navistar screen and a blinking figure shaped like a man was moving quickly from block to block.

"Mr. Chambers, your scumbag, is running past the Tidy Didy at approximately 2 miles per hour. His pulse rate is 80 over 100 and there appear to be a trail of latent infrared signatures. I believe he's injured, sir, twenty two caliber bullet, specially made for the Derringer two shot."

"Ain't she great, Walker?"

"*Yeah, how do I get me one of those?*"

Ignoring his comment, Chambers said, "I'm turning on to Emerson, past some kind of Hari Krishna center,"

"*He's now heading south on thirty seventh, past the Jones residence. They're having dinner right now. He's entering Fernwood Park.*"

"Thank you Zeta."

"*Your welcome Mr. Chambers.*"

"*This is too much,*" Walker said.

Chapter 111

Jason Pratt had been with Navistar for only two months and was concerned about his career. The economy was not as good as he'd hoped when he graduated from the University of Missouri and moved to St. Louis. To survive, he took a job as a customer service rep for Navistar.

The call had rattled him. His screen went blank and he was locked out, but the disk was still processing at an incredible rate.

Pratt took off his headphones, glanced around at the busy reps in small booths that surrounded him and decided he would report the incidence to his supervisor.

He stood, straightened his thin tie with the piano keys, smoothed back his thin red hair, pushed his thick black glasses up the bridge of his nose and picked a booger he felt hanging from his hawkish snout.

The supervisor's office was in the corner of the room. He could see Mr. Danner beyond the glass, reviewing mountains of paperwork.

He walked to his door, knocked, and was waved in.

"Pratt," He said gruffly. "How can I help you?"

Pratt entered the room shyly, rubbing his hands nervously.

"I, well, I got an unusual call, sir."

"What's unusual about an unusual call? This is Navistar. We deal with customers. Customers can be unusual. They, in fact, can be insane."

"Well, this was different. My computer has been accessed by this customer and it's no longer in my control."

Danner froze and stared at Pratt.

"What was the name of this customer Pratt?"

Danner stood, and brought his round, waddling bulk from behind his desk, past Pratt and closed his door. He then walked over to Pratt and asked again, "What was the name of this customer Pratt?"

Pratt was no dummy. He'd graduated in the top tenth percentile of his class, which was paid for with full chess scholarships. Thinking quickly and remembering Chambers' words, he said, "I, I don't remember, sir."

"Oh, come on Pratt. Surely you remember something. What did he ask you to do?"

"I, um, I don't remember, sir."

"Pratt, let me tell you something."

Danner squinted his eyes and leaning into Pratt.

"Right answer," he said. "Now you can take the rest of the

night off. Go to a movie or something. There's a new super hero flick out. See that. You know what I mean?"

"Yes, sir, um, thank you sir," Pratt said.

"And Pratt, if you ever get a call from this customer or any other's like it, you know what to do."

He winked at Pratt, who's sweat stains were now visible in his arm pits.

"Yes, sir."

Chapter 112

Rich huddled under his desk listening to the chatter in his earphone. When the shots from Chambers weapon crashed through the door, he did something he had not done in years.

He prayed to every God he could think of.

He mouthed the words to himself, "Lord, Jesus, Buddha, Allah, Quetzalcoatl, Zeus, any of you Gods out there, please, please hear this prayer. I just want my family back together again and be with my friends. Don't let it end like this. All my life I try to help people, to do what's right. But I slip sometimes. I fuc—–screw up. I'm human. I'll be better. Can you help a brother out?"

The knock on the door interrupted his prayer.

"RICH, OPEN UP. IT'S OFFICER SIMMONS AND JAMES WALKER! LET US IN!"

Rich was hesitant until he heard Grimsley on the phone line again.

"Rich, it's okay, open the door. We got one bad guy upstairs and the other is on the run. Detective Simmons will take care of you. Walker is still there as well. Rich. You there?"

Rich was in shock and did not answer right away.

"Rich, you all right?"

He finally answered, "Sure, sure. Thank you, sir. I'll let them in. Thank you very much."

"Don't mention it Rich. Give the Journal to Walker and go with him—no one else. Hear me? He'll brief you. And do me a favor. Call me back on speakerphone before you open the door."

"Yes, sir."

The circulation in Rich's legs were cut off. His legs were tingly and numb. As he stretched them out, pain shot up through the nerves and he almost fell as he reached for the phone and dialed Grimsley's number and put him on speaker phone.

He walked to the door. The journal was clamped under his arm. He pushed the heavy bookcase aside, unlocked the door with the skeleton key and opened it slowly.

A tenuous smile crossed his face when he saw the uniformed officer Simmons, and recognized Walker standing behind him in the hallway.

"It's okay, Mr. Franklin," Simmons said, as he pushed the door open. "Are you okay, sir?"

Simmons was tall, muscular and confident. He inspected the room with hawkish blue eyes as he hung one hand on his utility belt and the other on his weapon. He stepped into the room as Rich backed away from the door.

"Rich, you all right?" Walker asked.

"Yeah, yeah, I'm okay, just all that gunfire scared the pants off of me."

"Awful sorry about that Mr. Franklin. We'll get this all logged and cleaned up as quickly as we can. One suspect is incapacitated upstairs and the other is on the run. We'll get him," Simmons said confidently. "I'm going to need to take that journal down to headquarters as evidence."

Simmons reached for the journal and Rich moved away from his hand.

"Sorry, Grimsley asked me to give it to Walker only."

"But that doesn't make sense," Simmons said, confused, "he's not a police officer."

Walker interrupted, "Officer Simmons, let me explain. I work special investigations with Captain Grimsley, so it's okay."

"But who do you work for, Mr. Walker?"

"Well, I can't really tell you that."

"All right then gentlemen, as the presiding officer here for the Portland PD and since I have direct orders from Captain Holister to retrieve this journal and get it to precinct immediately, I'll take possession of it and we can sort this out with Grimsley later."

"Simmons!" Grimsley shouted through the speaker phone, *"Since you and Holister are such good pals, I need you to deliver a message to him. Tell him to kiss my ass. Now, Walker you take that journal and you guard it with your life. Anybody has any problems or questions, they can call me. Simmons, you do have my number don't you?"*

"Yes, sir, I do," Simmons said snapping to attention.

Walker stepped in front of Simmons, said a sarcastic "excuse me," and took the journal from Rich.

Simmons could only look on, embarrassed, humiliated.

"Thank you Rich," Walker said. "I'll make sure nothing happens to this. Come with me, Rich, we're going to go over to my place while they clean up here."

Walker put his hand around Rich's shoulder and escorted him out of the room. The last thing they heard was Grimsley ripping Simmons a new one and hanging up.

"Rich, get your coat, it's sprinkling outside. I figured you could use a walk, too. I'll explain everything to you."

Rich forced a smile and said, "Thanks Mr. Walker."

"Call me James."

Walker escorted Rich out the front door, past the probing eyes of uniformed police officers and plain clothes detectives. Curious neighbors were huddled in small groups on the sidewalks and the block looked like a major drug bust, which most figured it was.

Neighbors he'd known for years strangely regarded him with suspicion but did not inquire, fearing what they might be associated with whatever crime was taking place.

He saw the Peasleys standing, staring blankly at the house, Budweiser's in hand. Still, nothing up there except NASCAR, Budweiser and now another reason to have a beer to celebrate possibly losing a neighbor who had not been taken over by the pods as they had.

The entire block was sealed off as news trucks lined the road on forty seventh street. News helicopters buzzed like giant stalking, mosquitoes in the sky, waiting to come in for the kill.

Walker led Rich through several back yards to avoid the news trucks and paparazzi.

They arrived at Walker's home minutes later.

Chapter 113

"Zeta, tap into the onboard systems of this vehicle, call Captain Bob Grimsley on his cell phone and patch me into 503-234-7677. Transfer encrypted data to Walker's system via wifi. Access codes Tango-Baker-Walker, Password black knight. Make sure all lines are scrambled and make it a three way con call.

"Yes, sir, Mr. Grimsley. Done."

"Grimsley, you there?"

"Right behind you, Chambers."

"Walker, you there?"

"I'm here. Rich is with me. I've got the journal. And I'm seeing what you're seeing. God damn amazing."

"Good," Grimsley said.

"Zeta, where is he?"

"Moving at one point five miles per hour past the monkey bars in Fernwood Park."

"I'm at the entrance. Any access roads? Zeta."

"None, sir. Your vehicle is equipped with posi-track drive train, adjustable hydraulic suspension for additional clearance and adjustable spot lights for visibility and tracking. Shall I adjust the suspension and initiate auto tracking for the spot, sir."

"What the hell is this?" Grimsley asked.

"Just a little trick. I'll explain later. Zeta, make it so."

As Chambers drove, he heard a whirring sound coming from under the vehicle and felt the entire body rising up. Two bright spotlights came on and pointed towards a park that was looming in front of him.

"Systems ready," Zeta said.

"I'm going in. Grimsley, see if you can go around and cut him off on 37th."

"I'll be God damn," Grimsley said, *"Starship Enter God damn prise."*

Chambers idled at the curb. He could only see a small running track and towering trees beyond it. The map showed the park took up seven city blocks. And the blinking figure moved quickly through them.

"Zeta," Show me Grimsley. "Triangulate based on cell signal."

A small red dot appeared on the screen. It showed Grimsley moving fast along Killingsworth and turning onto 37th.

"Grimsley, you're looking good. Our boy is in the middle of the park and heading your way. Set up on Piedmont and wait for my instructions."

Chambers gunned the engine and it jumped the curb, bouncing

and lurching as it navigated the wet uneven ground. The spotlights tracked in the direction of the target even though Chambers had to turn to go around objects.

"*Chambers, does that rig have any weapons?*" Walker asked, half joking.

"Very funny," Walker, "This is a Cadillac, not an urban assault vehicle. You come to Oakland and I'll show you my Ferrari and I'll show you some tactical advantages."

"*You're closing in, Chambers. You ready?*"

"Yep."

"*The suspect is changing direction,*" Zeta reported, "*Now bearing two two, zero, heading southwest.*"

"Shit. Grimsley, you gotta move. Our boy is turning. He's heading back up to Killingsworth. Get moving!"

As Chambers spoke, he suddenly saw why the suspect had turned

"Shit Zeta, what the hell is that!"

He slammed on the brakes, but was too late, the vehicle was sliding down a hill towards a small body of water.

"Where the hell did that come from, Zeta, is it on your map?"

"*There are no obstacles for the next two hundred yards,*" Zeta assured him.

The truck slid and splashed into the duck pond and jolted to a stop.

"Zeta, it's a duck pond. God damn it. I'm in the drink!"

Chambers pressed the accelerator and water shot up from alternating tires. The water was deep enough to cover most of the huge tires. As he gunned the tires, he slid further and further into the pond.

He looked at the map. The suspect had crossed over 37th and was heading west on Ainsworth. A large structure loomed ahead of the image.

"What the hell is that?"

"*Kennedy School, the pride of the McMenamen hotel and restaurant chain. An abandoned school that was built in 1915. In 1998, it was renovated and turned into a historic hotel, with brewpub, restaurant, coffee shop, movie theater and hotel rooms. Occupancy for the restaurant is one hundred and fifty. Hotel occupancy is two hundred and seventy five. And the theater occupancy is two hundred and fifty. Tonight's double feature is Undercover Brother and Triple XXX. Would you like me to make reservations for you sir?*"

"No, Zeta. Thank you," Chambers said, adding, "I'm going to have to find another data source for you other than Zagat and Hotwire. Grimsley, you hear that?"

"I did. I'll call the manager and ask them to seal off the restaurant, and have all hotel guest lock their rooms."

"Ask them to keep their curtains open, too. He's going to get there before you, Grimsley. That's not good. And I'm stuck in the duck pond."

"I'll send a tow."

"Excuse me Mr. Chambers," Zeta cut in, "But we are not stuck. We have not initiated four wheel drive and my calculations show that we should be able to easily navigate this pond."

"Well, come on sister, make it so."

"Engaging four wheel drive now."

Chambers pressed on the gas and all four wheels churned and the vehicle jumped in the mud and moved slowly forward.

"Son of a..." Chambers said, amazed. "Zeta, remind me to give you a kiss the next time I see you."

"That will be quite impossible, Mr. Chambers," Zeta responded, "but I appreciate the sentiment."

"Smartest damn computer I know. We're moving Grimsley. I'll be there in two minutes. Grimsley, you set up on the perimeter in the parking lot. I'll go in after this little prick. I know his MO and I know what he looks like."

"The suspect is inside of the building," Zeta announced.

"Where is he Zeta? I'm not seeing anything."

"The structure is reinforced concrete, built to withstand earthquake, fire and tornado. Early twentieth century school builders wanted schools to be the safest structures around and built them to last. Plus, lead paint was used and was layered and layered over nearly one hundred years. The signal cannot get through. I can, however, still monitor pulse rate and body temperature."

"That will do Zeta. Every thirty seconds. Let me know of any anomalies."

In minutes, Chambers had reached the edge of the park and drove up Killingsworth to the school parking lot. Tiny droplets of rain dotted the windshield and left shinny, glistening marks on the pavement.

The Escalade entered the parking lot with spotlights blazing and underbody LED track lights illuminating the ground as it approached. It screeched to a halt behind Grimsley's Bronco.

Chambers jumped out, checked his shoes, cursed, then straightened his coat, his hat, his tie, buttoned his suit jacket and walked over to Grimsley.

"What are we doing Chambers?" Grimsley asked.

"I'm going in. Turn that light out," he said, pointing to the blinking red and blue light on top of Grimsley's Bronco.

Grimsley reached in and pressed a button.

"I need you to cover me from here and keep an open channel. Zeta still has us all patched in via cell phone. She's my eyes in the sky."

"Is she going to beam you in or are you going to walk?" Grimsley asked.

Chambers stared at Grimsley

"I'm walkin'. You cover me and stay alert."

As they talked, Chambers looked at the building.

"Our boy came in that door. The manager asked the guest to keep their curtains open. If you see any closed ones, call me."

Chambers turned and walked towards the side door of the building.

Grimsley handed Paulson a pair of binoculars and went to the back of the Bronco where he removed a leather pouch and a small tripod.

Paulson scanned the building while Grimsley took out the bolt action pistol and mounted it on the hood with the small tripod. He mounted an infrared scope and pointed it at the building.

Chambers walked cautiously towards the building and opened the front door. He was met by a youngish man with long hair, wire-rimmed glasses and Guatemalan shirt that hung loosely over his faded jeans.

"I'm Sage, the manager here. We did what you asked. We sealed off the theater, restaurant and pubs immediately. But the rooms took a little more time. Some guests were sleeping. But we got all the windows open. We didn't see anyone or anything unusual."

"Thank you young man. He's clever. You would not have noticed anything even if you wanted to. Go back to the office and lock the door. I'll check the rooms."

"Zeta, what's the reading?"

"Heart beat stable. Blood pressure 160 over 140."

"He's resting,"

"That's correct, Mr. Chambers."

"Did he leave the building?"

"Not likely."

"I'm going door to door. You tell me the minute anything

changes. Got it."

"Yes, Mr. Chambers. Always a pleasure to serve you."

Chambers could sense Grimsley and Walker rolling their eyes. But that didn't matter.

He took in his surroundings. In all his days in San Francisco, he had never seen anything like this.

Paintings of every style and type lined the walls of the halls, some depicting scenes from early days of the school. Old photographs of classes and now retired former teachers and principles also lined the wall. Whimsical murals of jesters and maidens decorated whole sections of walls, and the dark woodwork and plaster trim had been meticulously restored.

The lighting was muted to add to the atmosphere, and Persian rugs and huge Indonesian carvings lined the hallways. It all reminded Chambers of some historic cartoon scene with undercurrents of the old-historic men's clubs he'd been to in San Francisco. Only this place was for anybody and everybody. He'd have to bring Sara back here sometime. If he survived.

He focused on the doors, which all had chalk boards covering the upper portions. Each chalk board had the dinner specials and movie schedule scratched on them. And Chambers assumed, each guest room used to be a classroom.

Ingenious, he thought.

He knocked on the first door.

A timid voice asked, "Who is it?"

"Chambers, with the Portland PD, mam. Don't open your door. Everything okay, mam."

"Yes," the voice said.

"Zeta status," Grimsley whispered.

"No change," Zeta said.

"Thank you mam. Keep you door locked until you hear from the manager."

"Okay."

Chambers walked to the next door and knocked. A strong male voice answered.

"Who is it?"

"Chambers, with the Portland PD. Don't open your door, sir. Everything okay?"

"Um, yeah, yeah, sure. Everything is okay."

"Zeta, how we doing?" Chambers asked.

"No change, sir," she said.

"Sir, do not open you door until you hear from the manager.

He'll call with an all clear."

"Does this have to do with what's happening on Wygant street?" the voice asked.

"Don't worry about a thing, sir. We'll fill everyone in when we're all clear."

"Thank you officer."

Chambers went to the next door and knocked.

"Spike, sir, off the charts."

"Thank you sweetheart. Grimsley, call the manager, get the room number."

"Don't need to," Grimsley responded. "A woman just closed the curtain. Room 15."

"Just listen for my queue."

Chambers knocked again, this time a meek female voice answered.

"Um, yes, who is it?"

"Chambers, mam, Portland PD, everything okay?"

"Why, yes officer. Everything is fine."

"Mam, no need to alarm you, but I'm talking to all the guest mam. Could you please open up. I need to ask you some question."

"Well, I'm not decent. I'm, um, getting ready for bed. Can you come back in the morning."

"Pulse rate is increasing," Zeta alerted.

"I understand, mam. This is very important. It will only take a minute."

"Well, okay, but just for a minute."

Chambers could hear the locks being released on the other side of the door and the safety latch being released.

The door opened slowly and Chambers saw the friendly face of an older woman appear through the crack in the door. She opened the door and stepped aside. She wore a two piece night gown with a heavy robe. Her graying white hair was in curlers and she blushed nervously as he entered the room.

"I was just getting ready to go to bed," she said nervously, "I'm very tired."

"I understand, mam, Chambers said, as he scanned the room, "You alone mam?"

"Um, yes I am," she said. "I used to be a teacher here. I come back once a year. I'm retired now. Um, it was a wonderful school."

"Yes, I can see that mam. Has anyone come to your door."

"Pulse is increasing," Zeta warned.

"Um, no."

Outside, Grimsley could see only shadows through the heavy curtains as he listened intensely to Chambers' exchange with the woman and Zeta's regularly timed warnings. He didn't like this.

"Chambers," Grimsley called, "what the hell is going on in there?"

Chambers did not answer Grimsley's question. He couldn't. Instead, he walked to the window and opened the curtain and said, "We asked everyone to keep their curtains open, mam, why did you close yours?"

She was not a good liar, but Chambers appreciated her effort. "Those lights in the parking lot really bother me. I can't sleep with them on."

"Does the sound bother you too, mam?"

"Oh no," she said, excitedly, "I could sleep through a train wreck."

"Well, these walls are about six inches thick, probably fiberboard, lath and plaster, with six inch spaced two by fours. It would take a hell of a loud sound to really penetrate these walls; don't you think so, mam?"

"I guess so," she said, not sure what to make of what he was saying."

"These windows are high, too. Let me see, I'm about six one, so this window is about four feet tall and about three feet from the wall. Man, the architects did a hell of a good job."

"I don't know what you're talking about, Mr. Chambers, but it is a nice hotel."

Outside, Grimsley was leaning nervously against the hood of the Bronco, the Winchester trained on the curtain as Chambers spoke. He dared not take his eyes off the window even though a cigarette right about now would help relieve some of the tension.

Next to him, Paulson scanned the window with the binoculars and listened as well, occasionally using a handkerchief to wipe away tiny droplets of rain that collected on the lenses. The window was open now, and they could see the gray haired woman talking nervously, trying to figure out what Chambers was getting at.

"What's he up to, Paulson?" Grimsley asked, not taking his

eyes away from the scope.

"Don't know sir," Paulson said, "But he's got company in there and I hope he knows what he's doing."

"Body temperature one hundred and one and rising," Zeta announced, seconds later saying, *"Accessing architectural drawing of Kennedy School. Exact distance from the window ledge to the ground is four point three feet. Exact distance from the wall to the window frame is two point three feet. Schematics show that that two point three inches was originally a storage space for school supplies, covered by a sliding chalk board. Permit # 23334567 shows that those storage spaces have been converted to closet spaces for guests."*

Paulson turned to Grimsley immediately and said, "He's in that closet, sir! Chambers is giving us coordinates without tipping him off. Sir, I never thought I'd ask you this, but do you still have that cannon you used at the range?"

"I see where you're going with this. I got better than that. I got a Henry which should do the trick."

"We're going to need that, sir. Chambers wants us to target him through the wall and I think that cannon is the only thing that can penetrate that wall."

"I'll be… Chambers, listen up. I need three minutes to load the Henry. I'll let you know when we're ready."

Grimsley raced to the back of the Bronco and retrieved the long leather case that held the rifle, quickly opened it, removed a single round from a pouch and jammed it into the weapon.

"We're in place Chambers. Only got one round. I'll try to make it count."

Chambers, looked at the woman. Beads of sweat were forming on her forehead. He winked at her and said, "Mam, I admire your taste in hotels."

At the same time, Chambers gave her a quick wink and pointed a thumb in the direction of the open door while simultaneously placing a raised finger over her lips, indicating that she should not speak.

She froze as she was about to respond and hesitantly turned and walked quietly towards the door.

He continued talking, even as she passed through the door.

"I'm a bit of a hotel aficionado myself. San Francisco has some of the best hotels. The Saint Francis. The Huntington. The Fairmont. The Mark Hopkins. Although I prefer the old hotels, I particularly like the new Marriott by the convention center. They call it the jukebox."

As the women stepped into the hallway, Chambers gestured for her to close the door. She did so quietly. Chambers cleared his throat as the latch slipped into socket.

As he turned from the now closed door toward the closet, he heard the rumbling of ninety year old rollers, grinding and squeaking as the Chalk board slowly slide open. The light exposing a disheveled, hunched figure in black, one arm limp at his side, the sleeve of his jacket soaked in dark shiny liquid, and frantic, angry eyes peered out at Chambers.

In one hand, the dark figure gripped the three fifty seven. He raised it and pointed it at Chambers' head. His grip was tenuous as his hand trembled, but still sure enough to not leave Chambers many options.

"You're a loser Fitch," Chambers said, "I knew only a low-life, amateur like you could be behind something like this. Give up now and you may live through this."

Fitch pulled the black stocking cap up to his forehead. His eyes were blazing red as he grimaced with pain. Spit dripped from his mouth and he clenched his teeth as he stood, teetering, attempting to block out the pain from the single bullet wound in his shoulder.

"Chambers," he said, struggling to push the words out. "Way I see it. I've got the upper hand here. Howz about I blow your fuckin' head off right now?"

Chambers, for the first time since he arrived in Oregon, smiled and said, "Hold it pal. You don't mind if I call my sweetheart and tell her goodbye, do you?"

"Are you fucking kidding me, Chambers?" Fitch said. "What do you take me for some kind of idiot."

"That's correct," Chambers replied. "Plus, you only die once. And there's a dame I'm crazy about in San Francisco."

"Don't even fucking think about it Chambers," Fitch screamed.

"Sorry pal," Chambers said. "She means more to me than you do."

Chambers reached into his pocket and gripped his cell phone.

Fitch, seething at his audacity, raised the weapon, cocked the hammer and squeezed the trigger.

The sound the weapon made when it fired was ear-shattering. Grimsley flew backwards against the hood of a car parked. He cried out in pain as his back crashed against the car.

"Jeeeeezus fucking H Christ!"

Smoke shot out in all directions. Paulson winced and, for a moment, thought he felt the earth rumble as the powerful shotgun went off.

The impact of the bullet ruptured the wall and a gaping hole appeared. Paulson, focused on the window now. He could see the silver steel of the handgun pointed at Chambers' head. He mouthed, *fall you bastard, fall.* He hoped the bullet had hit its mark.

Smoke and dust filled the room and obscured Paulson's view. Fitch had fired a round, Paulson thought.

He feared the worst for Chambers.

The explosion of dust and smoke surprised Fitch, who's eyes, still fixed on Chambers, opened wide with shock. Dust from the plaster shot out from the wall and quickly obscured Fitch's view. He pressed the trigger, but nothing happened.

Chambers, continued to remove the phone from his pocket, put Grimsley and Paulson on hold and called Sara.

"Chambers, is that you?" Sara asked.

"Yeah, baby, I'm all right. I miss you."

"I miss you too. I've been watching the news and they're talking about a paperboy in Portland. Are you involved in that?"

"Sure thing kid, but everything is going to be all right. There are a couple of scum bags that won't though. One will be doing some self actualizing in prison and the other is about to meet his maker."

Sara did not respond right away.

Then she said, *"When do you come home?"*

"Two days. Don't worry cupcake. I'll see you soon."

"Okay?"

"By bye baby."

"Chambers," she said, before she hung up, *"hurry home."*

"All right baby."

He hung up, punched the button to connect Grimsley, and Paulson, and said, "Thank you gentlemen."

The plaster dust settled quickly and Chambers saw the pistol drop out of Fitch's hand as he doubled over and fell to the ground. The side of the wall was obliterated where the forty-four cal slug entered and slammed into Fitch's side. His insides were pulverized and entire body went into shock. He was not allowed the luxury of a scream before dying.

Chambers reached into his pant pocket and pulled out a single bullet. Lucky seven he thought. He never kept the eight round in his weapon.

"Walker," Grimsley said, *"We need to move fast. Send a cleanup crew here, pronto. We can't let this one get out of control."*

"They'll be there in a few minutes."

"Pulse 0, temperature 80 degrees and dropping rapidly," Zeta said.

"Grimsley, meet me in the Detention room," Chambers said.

"Detention room?" Grimsley asked as he replaced the Henry in it's case and placed it in the back of the Bronco. Paulson was already on his way into the building.

"Sure," Chambers answered, "It's a broom closet that's been converted into a bar. We need to talk. Walker, you stay on the line, okay?"

"Sure Chambers," Walker responded.

"Paulson's on his way in. He and Walker's crew will work on clean up and containment. And we'll figure out how to spin this one as well."

"What kind of Scotch you drink?"

"Blue," Grimsley answered.

"Expensive."

"Only the best."

"See you in a few."

Grimsley walked around his Bronco and headed for the door. Six cruisers with flashing lights silently entered the lot and stopped near the entrance.

Grimsley walked to the side of one cruiser and spoke to the officer who stepped out. Seconds later an ambulance entered the lot and stopped near the cruisers.

Two paramedics with white coats draped over dark suits, exited the truck, retrieved a gurney from the back and walked towards Grimsley. When they reached him, they stopped and spoke to Grimsley who escorted them into the building and to the room.

Grimsley found Chambers nursing a Scotch at a corner table in the tiny dark bar. He had nearly missed it until he heard Chambers call his name as he walked past the entrance.

The room was no bigger than a large closet. The walls were covered with colorful Indonesian batik fabrics. Small red and orange Tiffany style candles cast dancing shadows on the dark maroon walls. The tables were small and circular and intimate.

In a corner, was a paltry bar next to a pot-bellied wood-burning stove. The vent extended to the ceiling. Red and gold flickers of flame blinked through the silver cast iron grill.

The bar was deserted.

"Close the door, Grimsley," Chambers said, "and help yourself. It's all arranged with the management."

Grimsley looked suspiciously at the bar, then at Chambers, then retrieved a glass, the bottle of Bushmill Blue that was perched on Chambers' table, and poured a drink.

"Sit," Chambers said. "We've got some more detective work to do before we call it a day. And we'll do it right here."

Grimsley sat at the table and held up his drink.

"Here's to more detective work, San Francisco style."

"Cheers my friend."

They both winced as the strong Scotch burned their throats and warmed their guts.

"Let's get started. Zeta, Walker, are we ready?" he said, touching a finger to his earphone and placing his micro computer on the table. He clicked a button for a speaker phone connection and listened for a reply.

"We are ready, Mr. Chambers," Zeta said.

"Ready," Walker said.

"All right, then. As these young people say today, let's rock and roll. I pulled this off of our boy's hand."

Chambers held up a wrist watch with dull silver casing, flat cover with an apple on it and a black leather band.

"It's the latest Apple MP 388 wrist watch."

"What's so special about that?" Grimsley asked.

"This is not available for the public. It never will be. You gotta understand that there's a huge market for underground technology. Apple has as much of a stake in it as Microsoft. Billions is invested in technology that's too expensive for the public but perfect for the Feds, INTERPOL and scum bags like Fitch. The scum bag market is a multi-billion dollar industry, but you won't see it on the NASDAQ. This little baby has a wireless, satellite receiver, has a 200 gig hard drive, 100 gigs of flash ram. There's more horsepower here in this tiny watch than in most laptop computers. It also has wireless remote access so it can tap into a dedicated mainframe anywhere in the world."

"Can you access it?" Grimsley asked.

"As a matter of fact, I can't. All the data is encrypted and it's got duel layers of security."

"So what good is it to us?"

"Well, Zeta can probably get into it. We'll see." Chambers took a plug out of his pocket, plugged it into his computer, then plugged it into a small opening in the watch.

"Zeta, access my computer and tap into this device via wireless remote, access number ocean, parker, tango, bravo, password chamberhomelink."

"Done," Zeta responded immediately.

"Tap into the mainframe. Scan data for names."

"Done."

"Search for Neil,"

"No references."

"Search for Senator."

"No references."

"Search for deposits and accounts."

"Fifty found."

"Search for Insurance."

"One found."

"Bank."

"Numbered account, Switzerland, account number one, one, six, five, four, three, zero, two. Last deposit amount one hundred thousand dollars. Transferred from Trans National Insurance Company."

"Cross reference Debartola."

"Done."

"Correlations?"

"One."

"Who."

"Delbert Debartola, Senior Executive Vice President of Finance, Trans National Insurance Company, Portland, Oregon. Address…"

"Thank you Zeta. Grimsley, shall I continue?"

"Sure," he said, "this is just starting to get interesting."

"That's the guy in Trixie's Journal." They heard Rich say in the background.

"He's all over her journal, Chambers," Walker added, "a real sick puppy. I read some of the entries. He stuck his neck out pretty far on this one. Pedophile, statutory rape, tapping into the corporate till to pay for his perversions and goons. I'd say he's got a lot to lose here."

"Zeta, cross reference Debartola address with Qwest broadband or any other internet service providers."

"Done, DSL account identified."

"Look for an open com line and hack into it."

"Done."

"Access daytimer software and financial software."

"Done."

"Match account numbers and transfers and Fitch."

"Done. Three matches. Account number, transfer date and amount and Fitch on laptop."

"Scan for Trixie."

"Done. Thirty references found in Day-timer and thirty references found in Quicken. Fifty thousand dollars recorded withdrawals correspond with appointments over a three year period."

"Download records to Walker servers."

"Done."

"Modify desktop app to access microphones and digital cameras. Display on Walker's screens."

"Logitec digital video located on office and two bedroom computers. Displaying."

"Walker, you reading these?"

"Got it. I'm seeing the office."

"Switch to the bedroom one, Zeta."

"Done."

"I got him," Walker said. *"He's leaving the master bedroom. In the hall now. Lost him. Looks like the wife sleeping in bed."*

"Display camera in bedroom two."

"Done."

"Bedroom two looks empty," Walker said.

"Display bedroom three," Chambers said.

"I got him. Door is opening. Can't see anyone else. Looks like a girls room though...wait, there she is. Light's on in the closet. She's in there. Looks like she's hiding or something."

"What's going on Walker?" Grimsley asked.

"I can't tell," Light's out now."

"Zeta," download and install infrared webcam app. Enhance.

"Done."

"That's better," Walker said, *"He's going over to the closet. I can hear her crying."*

"Zeta, keep monitoring. And see if you can wake the mother."

"Trying, sir. Will initiate and alarm through Outlook."

"Chambers," Walker reported, *"I* don't think that's going to work. I

saw a bottle of sleeping pills on her table and a half glass of water. I think that's how he does it. Puts the mother out and has his way with his daughter."

"Walker," Grimsley said, "Hang up and get Sam Talbot with Lake Oswego PD. Tell him he needs to get a search warrant and to be at the Debartola residence in ten minutes!"

"Let Zeta handle this," Grimsley, jeez, don't you see what's happening here. Zeta, contact Talbot and explain. Tap into the LOPD computer and initiate a search warrant and friendly judge digital signature. Alert judge, and e-mail the search warrant copy."

"Processing. Done."

"Where's he at, Walker," Grimsley asked.

"He's trying to get the door open. She's screaming for help."

"God damn it. What can we do?"

"Dial the number Zeta," Chambers commanded.

They could hear the phone ring in a downstairs room.

"He's not biting," Walker said.

Grimsley's phone beeped. He quickly reached into his pocket and took it out, pressing the three way button to add Talbot to the line.

"Grimsley, this is Talbot."

"How the hell are you?" Grimsley asked.

"Not so good. Listen, no time to explain, but I got your message and a copy of the search warrant in my hand. I don't know who you know, but we'll be there in two minutes."

"You better hurry. The girl is locked in the closet and he's going after her," Grimsley said.

"Don't worry, friend. We'll get there."

"He's dragging her out of the closet now," Walker announced.

"Good God," Grimsley said, "What can we do?"

"Zeta, tap into the alarm system and trip it," Chambers ordered.

"Done, sir."

In the headphones, Chambers, Walker and Grimsley could hear a faint alarm in the background.

"That's good," Chambers said. Your boys will be there in a minute. Zeta, keep broadcasting. We'll need this tape."

They could here the cries and screams of Debartola's daughter as she struggled to free herself from his grasp.

"The alarm only distracted him for a few seconds. He's tearing her clothes off now and she's begging him to stop."

The small LOPD force enter quickly through the downstairs front door, and neither Debartola nor anyone else heard them over the alarm and the screams. But they heard a crash as the door gave in and several uniformed officers with flashlights charged into the room and pulled Debartola off of his daughter and slammed him to the ground; one officer pressing his knee deep into his back and roughly placing hand cuffs on his hands and escorting him out of the room.

Walker watched as a female officer covered the sobbing, partially naked girl and comforted her.

"Zeta," Chambers ordered," Cameras off. Access laptop hard drive and scan for registered weapons."

"Nine millimeter Baretta, purchased..."

"Thank you, Zeta. Zeta log off, encrypt access logs. Return work station to Navistar control."

"What about that weapon," Grimsley asked.

"Get the weapon. I'll explain later. I'm sure you all understand, gentlemen, that this is not admissible in court. So, Grimsley, you're going to have to get a confession out of him. You can use these tapes to influence, but if you don't get that confession tonight, all bets may be off."

"I see your point," Grimsley said. "Walker, take the account records, journal, DVDs, and audio logs to the Lake Oswego PD now. I'll call Talbot and let him know we're on our way and explain where we're at on this. You can trust him. Best damn interrogator in the business."

"I'll take care of it."

"And keep that paperboy close until we get all this figured out. I'm going to call the mayor and fill her in," Grimsley said, continuing, "Chambers, can you call Paulson and brief him on this Temple character? Help out where you can. We need him to sing as well. I don't want to spend the next thirty years trying to pin something on him. And I don't care so much about Temple as I do about the Senator. Temple's going down either way. But that son of a bitch in Washington who thinks he's got a Teflon cock is who I really want."

"Where will you be Chambers?"

"Right here, my friend. I'm going to finish my Scotch, let my shoes dry on this here stove then head back to San Fran tonight."

Grimsley stood, shook Chamber's hand and said, "Thank you for all your help. One of these days, you'll have to tell me how you did that. You just caught a glimpse of the future."

"Don't mention it pal. Like I said, I owed a friend a favor. Maybe, before I leave town, we can have another Irish coffee at Huber's. Damn fine restaurant; almost as good as San Francisco. I'll let you in on some of my secrets. But, you know, like Criss Angel, I can't tell you everything. That would ruin it for you, now wouldn't it?"

"God damn man of mystery aren't you?"

"That's right palley," Chambers said, tipped his hat and said, "Keep your head down. This ain't over till it's over."

Chambers picked up his phone and dialed Paulson. Grimsley headed for Lake Oswego to rendezvous with Rich and Walker.

Chapter 114

Temple sat in the stark room considering his situation. Needles of pain distracted him and the handcuffs and chains that restrained his hands and feet were a constant irritation.

A single fluorescent light blasted torrents of whitish blue light off the dull gray walls, and the centerpiece of the room—no doubt purchased from interrogation room surplus—was a puke green table with cigarette burns, coffee stains and various death threats carved into the Formica coated top.

Across from temple, a large two way mirror reflected his pathetic image. His hair scattered in every direction and purple bruises blotched the areas of his face not covered by bandages.

He lost. The thought was slow to sink in. Hard time in jail was his next stop. This is a bridge he never thought he'd cross. Thoughts of tough guys flooded his head; Bond, Stallone, Eastwood, all the movies he'd seen thousand of times over.

The good guys never got caught, never had to face hard time. Then, in an instant, Temple considered something he'd never considered before. He was not a good guy. He was one of the bad guys. They would do everything in their power to lock him up for as long as they could. Neil would walk; find somebody to take his place. He thought about how he might end up a statistic in the prison morgue before he ever breathed free air or touched any of the cash that was waiting for him.

Did he want that? No. Was there honor in singing; ratting out his boss? No. Could he handle prison? Maybe.

The door opened and Paulson came into the room, pulled out a chair and sat down. He took out a pack of Marlboros, tapped it lightly on his wrist, pulled one out of the pack, lit it and offered one to Temple, who, with a slight head gesture, refused it. He didn't smoke but he knew how to play the game.

As the white smoke filled the room, Paulson took a small tape recorder and microphone out of his jacket pocket and placed it in front of Temple. He showed no expressions, and Temple regarded him with defiance.

Paulson leaned back and hooked his thumbs on his belt and stared at Temple, finally speaking after an awkward silence.

"Mr. Temple, this recorder is not on. It will not be until I'm finished saying what I have to say."

Paulson then stood up, walked over to the mirror, his back to Temple and winked at the invisible faces on the other side of the mirror.

"You're in a shit load of trouble. And we don't want to spend a lot of time dicking around with you. We've got you on murder of a police officer, attempted murder of a state and federal officer, conspiracy to commit murder of a civilian, firearms violations and based on circumstantial evidence, we can probably pin Trixie's murder on you. You're looking at some hard time Mr. Temple. A lot of hard time. You may be pissin' in your own private bed pan in the senior wing of Sing Sing by the time you're eligible for parole."

Temple was expressionless as Paulson walked back to the table, pulled his chair close to him, leaned into his face and continued.

"You'll rot in prison while your employer plays golf every day at the Washington Heights Golf Club, finds another young girl to fuck over; another chump to be his patsy, and continues to rape the public trust. That's all on your shoulder's my friend."

He paused again to give Temple a chance to consider his situation.

"Meanwhile, you're looking at a hundred years hard time, and we'll make sure you get fucked in the ass every day by some four hundred pound gang banger. And believe me, Mr. Temple, even the toughest guys I've seen sent up, squeal like pigs when they're fucked in the ass without any lubrication and they're left weeping in their own piss and shit. That, Mr. Temple, is your future."

He stood up again, reached over, held his finger over the red button that would start the device recording and said, "You're a smart guy. You know your rights. You don't have to talk to us without a lawyer. But consider this: we can make prison life a little easier for you. That's all we can promise. Or, we can make it harder. What you say next, well decide your fate. Your future, Mr. Temple, is in your hands. We want to know everything. I want you to tell me about Senator Neal. I want to know who your mole is in the department, and I want all the journals back."

Paulson pressed the button and left the room, not bothering to look at Temple again.

Chapter 115

As Paulson opened the door to the adjoining observation room, he was shocked to see Captain Holister standing near the glass, staring at Temple, a smoldering cigar in his mouth and a shifting bulge of chew protruding from his cheek. He did not look at Paulson.

Simmons and one other uniformed officer stood near the back wall of the room, each with one thumb hooked on their utility belts and the other resting confidently on their weapons. Both resembled Aryan Nation storm trooper clones, each with expressionless, clean shaven faces, tightly trimmed brown hair, and both gave Paulson a hateful look, the kind of look he'd seen in the eyes of southern segregationist in old newsreels of the civil rights movement. They had sacrificed their souls for the sake of racial purity.

Paulson was immediately on guard.

The two officers Paulson had selected to observe were in one corner and looked at Paulson, shrugged their shoulders with confused expressions and apologetic looks, not knowing what was happening.

"You didn't think you could carry on an interrogation like this without my involvement, did you Paulson?" Holster asked.

Paulson could feel his pulse rising. His first reaction was fear. He knew Holister. Fear was appropriate for someone like him with guns.

But that reaction was fleeting. Grimsley's instructions were clear. *Don't let Holister bully you.* You're smarter than that and watch your ass. Grimsley did not tell him what to do. That, he had to figure out.

Paulson walked to where Holister stood and planted himself in front of him. Holister was taller and folded his powerful arms across his chest. He continued looking past Paulson at Temple beyond the mirror.

"Captain Holister, I'm going to ask you to leave," Paulson said forcefully, "And take your clones with you."

Holister's nostrils flared as blue rings of cigar smoke came flowing out. He fixed his cold, angry eyes on Paulson, removed the cigar from his mouth, and leaned forward and spit a long dark stream of tobacco onto Paulson's shoes.

Paulson caught a whiff of the acrid, minty tobacco and spit smell that emanated from Holister's mouth. He did not budge.

"Paulson, you're stupider than I thought," said Holister. He leaned into Paulson's face.

"You've been spending too much time with that cock sucker Grimsley. I'll tell you what Paulson. He can't protect you. I'm going to kick your ass so far out of this department they'll have to hire search and rescue to find you. Now you take your little panty waists ass into that room and turn that recorder off and end this interview NOW!"

Even though his heart was beating like a freight train, Paulson kept cool and said, "That's not going to happen, Holister. And if you try to stop this, you'll have to go through me."

As the standoff continued, the overhead speaker crackled as Temple began to speak.

Chapter 116

Temple's first reaction was anger. Thoughts like *fucking nigger cop* automatically jumped into his head. Then his imagination took over and he imagined he was James Bond. He could make some miraculous, impossible escape and shoot Paulson in the head on the way out, and saying something clever as he did so.

His mind was processing faster than he could keep up with. He did not want to go to prison, but he realized that could not be avoided now. As he tugged at the handcuffs and the chains the stark realization sunk in further.

He was captured, jailed, a prisoner. The gig was up. He was one of the bad guys who *always* lost in the end.

He debated the pros and cons of being a rat fink prisoner, singing like a canary, terms he did not want to associate with himself. Would they punish him in prison for this? What would the newspapers write about him? What would Neil think of him? And he could see his wife reading the reports and gloating. That fried him more than anything else. What about the children? Daddy was a coward and cracked under pressure; *sang like fuckin' Celine Dion when the pressure was on,* he imagined them saying.

The more Temple thought about it, the more he thought that if he was going to go down, he did not want go down alone. He hated Neil; hated his arrogance; hated the fact that he had more power and money. He also did not trust him to keep his word; never did. These were the times, he thought, that try men's souls.

Temple knew plenty of ex convicts, enough to know that there were two prison worlds; one of privileged and one of depravity—the protected and the unprotected, controlled by people like Paulson and Grimsley. If they put in the word about a "protected" prisoner, the gang leaders would get points in their parole hearing. It was a nice system for everyone. Temple wanted to be protected.

He leaned into the microphone and, straining to move his jaw, and speaking barely audibly said, "First off, fuck you people."

He struggled to swallow and flinched as the pain consumed him.

He then continued, "I didn't kill the girl or the police officer...Se...sena...Senator Sam Neil is my employer. There's a safe in my house with details..."

He paused again, closed his eyes and continued, "Neil has the journals...and...and paid me to cover up his involvement with Trixie...to...get the missing journals...his...his relationship started with Trixie three years ago when she was fourteen...he knew that…was obsessed with her, with her intelligence, her beauty and he played out secret fantasies with her…"

Once again, he cringed as pain gripped him. He continued.

"You people should watch your backs…you, your own Captain is playing you. He's been feeding me information…"

Chapter 117

When Holister heard his name, he raised his arm, snapped his fingers and the two officers who were standing near the back wall drew their weapons, one pointing his at the two confused officers and the other pointing his weapon at Paulson.

"Secure their weapons and the door," he ordered. Simmons immediately removed the officer's weapons and pushed them to the ground, ordering them to place their hands on their heads and not move.

Holister reached inside Paulson's coat and removed his weapon, ejected the clip and threw them to the ground,

"You're a dumb niggar fuck, Paulson. If it weren't for affirmative action, we would not have to smell the stink of your kind around here, and things would be the way they're supposed to be, with our people running things."

"Don't flatter yourself Holister, you're people did a fine job of fucking up the world. And now you're pissed because now you have to watch the Black, Native Americans, Hispanics and the Jews clean up the mess people like you made. You don't fuckin' scare me Holister. I've got your number. You're days of intimidating and bullying people around here are numbered. I'll make sure to that."

"You're speaking out your ass, Paulson and you can save the history lessons for someone who gives a shit," Holister said. "You know, cops get killed all the time in escape attempts. Right now, I'm going to show you exactly how it works."

Holister withdrew his Glock and chambered a round.

Overhead, Temple continued to describe Holister's involvement in the cover-up. Holister, wanting to end Temple's singing, gestured for Simmons to take care of Temple.

As Simmons reached for the door, it crashed in, knocking him to the ground.

Surprised, Holister turned towards the door and in that instant, Paulson pushed Holister's weapon aside and kneed him in the groin.

As Holister doubled over, cupping his balls, Paulson, landed a solid fist to his throat, grabbed the gun from his hand and landed a hard elbow across his temple. Holister collapsed to the ground unconscious.

Six helmeted offers in SWAT uniforms and wielding M-16s charged into the room, pointing weapons at Simmons and his clone, screaming for him to drop his weapon.

Seeing the futility of a fight, they placed weapons on the ground, and, while begging them not to shoot, put their hands behind their heads.

A woman dressed in a dark suit entered the room behind the SWAT team. She walked with confidence and authority to where Paulson stood, and, expressionless, looked down at Holister, unconscious with one hand on his throat and one covering his crotch and said, "Pathetic. And to think I trusted him."

She looked at Paulson, who was breathing hard, but standing at attention.

"Paulson, good work. Get this garbage out of here and finish your interrogation. We heard what we needed to hear."

"Yes, Madam Mayor."

"You and Grimsley report to my office tomorrow morning at eight o'clock sharp. I want a full briefing."

"Yes mam," Paulson answered.

"And Paulson," she said, "Don't be some God damn uptight around me. You've earned my respect already. You don't need to act like you're in the middle of an enema all the time."

The mayor's stern expression transformed into a smile, and Paulson reciprocated, "Mam, mayor, are you giving me shit like Captain Grimsley never seems to stop doing?"

"God damn, right Paulson. Where do you think he learned it from? Get used to it."

She turned and walked towards the door.

"Eight o'clock sharp. Don't be late." She was gone.

Chapter 118

The Lake Oswego Police department was everything a police department should be, clean, bright and friendly. It was in a new building with high security and surrounded by sculpted grounds with plenty of parking.

Grimsley felt uncomfortable in this station. At any moment, he expected groups of spit shined policemen to walk up to him and start singing old barbershop quartet medleys. *By the Light...Of the Silvery Moon...*

Talbot ran a clean shop, thought Grimsley as he, Walker and Rich entered a small room marked OBSERVATION ROOM B. They were being escorted by an officer Ortega, a friendly Hispanic American with a gait in his gout who greeted them with a smile.

All of this pleasantness threw Grimsley off. He jokingly referred to them as the Stepford police officers.

As Ortega opened the door, he announced, "Grimsley, Walker and Franklin, sir,"

"Thank you Officer Ortega."

Talbot, a handsome man with salt and pepper hair, tailored suit, wire rim glasses and a face so handsome, even men did double takes.

"Thanks for coming down, Grimsley," he said as he sat on the edge of the desk and glanced at the two way glass. "He's been in there like that for an hour. We've read him his rights. His lawyer is on the way. You want to have a go at him?"

Grimsley, looked at Debartola, hair frazzled, breathing heavily, slowly looking around the room, occasionally his stare fixing on the glass. He was expressionless.

"Yes, Talbot, I'll see what I can do."

"Good luck," Talbot said, "I've seen these kinds of circumstances before. I've known Debartola for years and know he's an insider; plays hardball. If you're going to crack this nut, you'll have to have some powerful medicine."

"Just give us ten minutes. If we don't get anywhere in ten minutes, we never will."

"Okay, let's go." He walked towards the door.

"Walker, it's up to you and me. Rich, stay with Talbot. This is the paperboy who helped us crack this case."

Talbot said, "Good work, son. Let's hope we can close the deal on this one."

Rich gave Talbot a tenuous smile and shook his hand. Two stalwart uniformed officers stood near the door, expressionless, politely stepping aside as Talbot and Grimsley walked through the door.

Grimsley and Walker entered the room.

Debartola stared at them with contempt. He did not speak. He looked down to the ground and did not look up.

Walker and Grimsley sat on either side of him. Walker placed a Sony DVD player in front of Debartola, a microcassette recorder and turned it on. He hit a button on the DVD player and sounds of Debartola's daughter screaming could be heard.

Debartola slowly looked up from his lap and stared at the image of him attacking his daughter.

"How did you fucking get that?" he screamed. "How did you fucking get that you mother fuckers!"

"Easy, easy Debartola," Grimsley said. "How we got it is not the issue here. The fact that we got it is the issue. Now, you don't have to talk to us. You've requested a lawyer. You know your rights. But you also have the right to waive those right."

Grimsley, took out a pack of cigarettes and, before lighting it, offered one to Debartola. He nodded, yes, and Grimsley placed the cigarette in his hand and lit it after Debartola placed it in his mouth and sucked in deeply and blew out the white smoke.

"Right now, there are a hundred reporters outside waiting for a story about you. As far as I can see, you're goose is already cooked. How cooked it will be all depends on you. Now, I'm going to tell you something and I want you to listen closely, because I'm only going to say it once. Then, I'm going to need you to make a decision, a decision that determines whether your wife and daughter, friends and other family get dragged through the mud feet first by YOU, Mr. Debartola. Are you with me?"

Debartola, nodded.

"We know everything. Fitch, Trixie, your daughter. We have Trixie's Journal. Let me repeat that, Mr. Debartola. We know everything. Now, I need you to tell us in your own words. If you do, we have some influence to spare your family this humiliation. Not all, but some and we'll do what we can. Do you understand, Mr. Debartola?"

Debartola nodded, yes.

"Do you waive your right to have an attorney present?"

Debartola eyes were panicked. Then tears formed in the corners of his eyes. He knew the noose was tightening and his decision would have far reaching implication. And there would be no turning back.

He nodded.

"I'm sorry Mr. Debartola, I need you to answer into the

microphone," Grimsley requested.

Recognizing that he was beaten, Debartola leaned forward and said, "I waive my right to have an attorney present. What do you want to know Gentlemen?"

"Thank you Mr. Debartola, You are making a wise decision. Tonight, we will call all the editors of the local newspapers and discuss how we spin this. We'll conference with your attorney and you when he arrives. Now, Mr. Debartola, you and I will spend the next few hours discussing in detail a few matters. I want you to start with Trixie's murder. Can you please describe how that happened?"

As Debartola began describing the night Trixie was killed, Walker and Grimsley both looked at each other and winked. Up to that point, they still had no clue who had killed Trixie or how she was killed. What Debartola described was a scenario they never even considered.

Chapter 119

It was well after four a.m. in Washington, when the doorbell of Senator Sam Neil's suburban Virginia home rang. His wife and daughter were sleeping upstairs and would be awakened by the unexpected visitors.

Neil was awake in the den downstairs, unable to sleep. He was aware of what was happening in Portland, three thousand miles away. Such a shit hole of a city, he thought, could have such an influence on his life.

In front of him, a, loaded, polished, silver handled Colt forty-five sat on his desk. He stared at it.

He could end it all right now, spare his family the humiliation. Or he could walk downstairs, answer the door and let the federal agents take him quietly, strike a deal and land in some federal prison somewhere, disgraced, but alive, maybe even make a comeback with a run for the presidency some day.

He picked up the gun, examined it closely, chambered a round and raised the weapon to his temple. Before he pressed the trigger, he thought about Temple and what a coward he was. This could have worked out well for him if Temple hadn't talked. The thought of Temple turned his despair into anger. He considered that if he ended it here, Temple would win. And he was not going to make it that easy for Temple. He still had a few friends and would not rest until he made sure Temple got what he deserved.

Neil was also arrogant enough to think he could bounce back from this humiliation. Great men, he thought, never stop dreaming, never stop facing adversity, never stop manipulating outcomes. This situation was no exception. Arrogance was more powerful than lust, greed and anger. Arrogance was what drove great men. And he had more than enough to weather whatever was coming. So he thought.

Neil placed the weapon back on the desk, stood, walked around the desk into the living room and opened the front door.

"Senator," the stern-faced agent said, "I have a warrant for your arrest. You have the right to remain silent..."

Five other officers rushed past him into the house. He was handcuffed and hustled out the door.

Neil turned and saw his wife and three children huddled by the stairway; his wife pleading with the agent to tell her what was happening.

He made eye contact with his loyal wife of twenty-five years and mouthed, "I'm sorry."

The door closed and he was gone.

Chapter 120

Things had returned to normal at the Kennedy school. The room where Fitch met death was secured, his body removed, the wall patched, and all the guest were given the all clear and a free night's stay.

There was little evidence of police activity, only a few officers stayed behind to keep an eye on things.

Chambers' final call was to Enison, who irritated Chambers by still being sketchy about why Franklin was so important. Chambers was not buying the way Enison dismissed his curiosity only promising to explain more when Chambers returned.

They made an appointment to meet at Tosca's in North Beach and talk.

As Chambers hung up the phone he saw the frail frame of a woman enter the bar.

"They told me you were in here," said the women who had spent the few tense minutes in the room with Chambers and Fitch.

Chambers stood up and tipped his had, "Oh, yes mam, how are you? Listen, I'm sorry about all that back there in the room."

She waved a hand and smiled a warm smile that reminded Chambers of apple pie, golden retrievers chasing linens on the clothes line, and carefree summer days on a country farm.

"Don't mention it. I just wanted to meet you and thank you. I was pretty scared back there."

"I understand, mam. Names Chambers, private di..excuse me mam, private eye from Oakland."

"I'm Irma Shepherd from Bend."

"Pleased to meet you again, under, well, better circumstances, mam. Can I buy you a drink?"

"You certainly can young man. Just don't get fresh."

"Why, thank you mam. I'm honored."

He walked around the small table, and pulled out the chair for her, and scooted it in when she sat.

"And don't worry mam, I'm a gentleman, especially with such a classy dame like you."

He sat and winked at her.

Sage, the bartender, had taken up residence behind the bar and other guest, hoping to grab a stiff one after all the stress of the evening, quietly talked at their tables, the light from the candle dancing on their faces as they sipped their drinks.

"What'll you have mam?"

"A Manhattan."

"Coming up," Chambers said. He waved a hand to get the

bartender's attention.

"Sage! Can you please get this young lady a Manhattan?"

"Right a way Mr. Chambers," Sage answered, smiling.

For nearly two hours, Irma and Chambers reminisced about the "good" old days and mused about their favorite big bands, actors and cities.

Around midnight, Chambers, bid her good night, escorted her to her new room. He returned to his hotel room and packed his things. He wanted to get home. He missed Sara. He missed San Francisco. He also needed to buy some new shoes, and he needed take Sara to Clown Alley for their famous hot dogs Frank Sinatra singing *Witchcraft* on the Juke box.

Chambers called Hertz and said he was keeping the car and driving back to San Francisco that night. He asked them to fax the bill to ACS's office, care of Sam Enison.

Chambers stopped at the Texaco station and mini-mart, filled the gas tanks, grabbed a gallon of coffee and purchased nine CDs, one for each hour of driving.

As he passed the Rose Garden on to I-5 south, he pushed the Escalade up to ninety miles per hour, turned on the built in fuzz buster and slipped Frank Sinatra's greatest hits into the CD Player.

Witchcraft filled the spacious compartment and Chambers thought about Sara and sang, *Those fingers in your hair/ that sly come hither stare/ that strips my conscious bare/ it's witchcraft...*"

Chapter 121

After the interrogation with Debartola ended, Walker invited Rich to spend the night at his house instead of going home. He explained that repairs would be done on his house by noon the following day and any blood stains would be professionally cleaned by that time. He assured Rich there would be little evidence of the night's activities.

As they drove on I-5, back to the city, Rich was mostly silent. He explained that April was at their beach house in Lincoln City but did not elaborate, so, after twenty minutes of punctuated silence, Walker broke the ice.

"Listen, Rich, we know why April is in Lincoln City."

"What?" Rich said. "How do you know that?"

"Rich. I'm surprised you would ask having seen all you've seen today."

"Oh, yeah," Rich said, absorbing the shock of realizing there were no real secrets. "Right. Everybody knows everything. We're all under one big microscope. I get it. I see how it works. But is that going to help me get my family back together?"

Walker did not answer right away.

"No, Rich, maybe not, but it can help you understand just how small the world really is; how connected we all are. You know, Rich, I used to be just like you."

"And what's just like me?"

"I'm black."

"No kidding," Rich replied sarcastically.

"And," Walker continued, "I thought I was smarter than everyone else. It was hard being smarter than everyone else and at the same time thinking the world was against me, even those who were closest to me. You know what I mean, Rich?"

Rich hesitated before answering.

"Yeah, I see. I'm sorry. Didn't mean to be sarcastic. This is a lot of shit to absorb and everything is fucked up. I'm glad all this craziness is turning out OK for you and Grimsley. But at the end of the night, my life is still going to be screwed up."

"I know. I know. Rich. There's no easy answer. Listen, all I can say is, let people help you. Most people are good, Black, White, Hispanic. Not everybody wants to hold you back."

"I know that," Rich said. "Now."

"I know you know it. But, Rich, knowing is not enough."

"I don't know what you mean."

"Simple, Rich. Now, you've got figure out how to live it as well."

They were silent after that.

The light rain wet the highways enough for water to splash up from under tires, wetting the windshield and blurring the vision so the rows of headlights looked like a meandering, blinking snake that went on for miles.

Walker flicked on the windshield wipers.

It was well after midnight and Rich was exhausted and apprehensive about what the next day would bring. He was still processing some of the unanswered questions about Trixie, Walker, and Chambers.

Walker, knowing Rich was a Herbie Hancock fan, placed a CD into the holder. The first song was Herbie Hancock playing *Maiden Voyage*.

The rhythmic thumping of the windshield wipers caused Rich to drifted into deep sleep almost immediately.

Chapter 122

April put the children to bed around nine p.m. She was oblivious of the events that were taking place in Portland.

The ninety-year-old cabin was tiny—all they could afford to buy. It was old and sparse but comfortable. The frame and the furniture were all made from the old growth pine, fur and cedar that was cleared to build it. Even the bowls and wall scones were made from large mushrooms, dried, sanded and finished with a clear polyurethane coat.

It was equipped with a small kitchen, two hand-hewn bunk beds in one tiny bedroom and a small queen bed in the master bedroom.

The fireplace took up most of the living room. It was made from river rocks and included an iron bar to hang kettles on and boil water.

April was exhausted. She fielded the questions from the kids about why they were there and what about school and where's daddy.

They were cute but relentless. After she finally got them to bed, she was glad to have a few minutes to herself to think about her situation.

The blazing fire cast an amber glow into every corner of the main living room. The walls answered the warm light by casting an orange glow back and playing hide and go seek with them in the shadows.

April curled up in a black, comfortable blanket on a aged and worn couch and nursed a glass of white wine while she listened to Luther Vandross singing through the small speakers of a stereo near the fireplace.

She was torn, angry, hurt and frustrated. She did not know what to do and was glad to have this time away from everything; time to think; time to reflect; and time to figure out how to handle this situation.

She thought it might be nice to have someone to talk to, but at the same time, she was independent and believed in her ability to solve her own problems. She and Rich complimented each other that way.

When Luther Vandross began singing *A House is Not a Home* April wept softly. This was *their* song. And without really agreeing to it, they had built a life around the simple lyrics.

A chair is still a chair/Even when there's no one sitting there...

As she cried, April thought of Rich.

They had cried together many times. Each time, Rich described what he did when he was alone, sad and crying. He found the nearest mirror and looked at himself. The sight of his face contorted, mouth twisted up in a knot, reminded him of famous face contortionist like Jerry Lewis and Jim Carrey and it always made him laugh. It turned a sad moment into a funny one, even if for a few minutes.

April stood up and looked into the massive mirror that was mounted over the fireplace.

At first, the sight of her dainty face twisted up into a knot, lower lip sticking out, cheeks puffy and red and snot hanging out of her nose, frightened her.

She did not recognize herself.

All the muscles in her neck contracted when she sniffed and her lower lip was quivering, and her mascara was streaming down her cheeks. She looked like a killer clown from outer space.

Once the shock wore off, she couldn't help bursting into laughter at the sight of herself unrecognizable face. Her spirits immediately lifted. She could still laugh.

All was not completely lost. Laughing was great therapy for her complicated situation.

Chapter 123

Kyle arrived at Portland International Airport around five a.m., rented a car and began the long drive to Lincoln City. He called Lisa on his cell phone to let her know he had arrived. She told him about the news reports she had seen about Rich.

Kyle could only laugh and say, "I warned that boy about leaving Kansas. Once you leave OZ, you got to deal with the real world."

Lisa laughed and told Kyle that Rich was okay and in an undisclosed location and that the reporters were mentioning the release of his book today. The publisher's PR machines were already working and looking to capitalize on the publicity.

Grimsley and Paulson met at Grimsley's house to debrief and plan how to handle the coming media storm. It was well after two a.m. when they both, exhausted, fell asleep on the couches in Grimsley's den.

They discussed Rich's situation and agreed to take the trip to Lincoln City to talk with April in person and fill her in on what happened the night before. They left around five thirty.

Rich called the newspaper delivery station around three o'clock and told Jimmy he would not be in.

"I seent the news fella," Jimmy said. "You all right?"

"I am, thank you Jimmy."

"You know, they ain't saying much 'bout what really happened. I could tell. When Negros involved, they usually go on about race this and race that and try to show pictures of the ghetto. They ain't sayin' nothin'."

"I know Jimmy. The police kind of have a lock on this one. It's really complicated."

"Well, buddy, Brad's going to be pissed, but he understand. You gon' be back tomorrow, be ins as how you a celebrity now n all?"

"Yeah, Jimmy, I'm going to be back. I miss you."

"Go on. Ain't nobody gon' miss a old timer like me. I had my time, now it's time for all you young peoples."

"Jimmy, I never said this before, but you're a good man and I appreciate all the advice you give me. You remind me of my Uncle Pappa Dave back in Kansas. And, yes, Jimmy, I miss you."

Jimmy was quiet.

"Ait, young man, you don't need to get all sensitive. Young Negroes got to stay strong 'cause thays always somebody nipping at yo heels. And Rich, you gon be all right. You smart 'n I see a lot of good things in you. Africa came in this monin' and bowed to me. I don't know what you said to him but he 'ain't the same. Rich, you somethin'. Jus' take care of yo bidniz. You know Negroes got to take care of bidniz."

"All right Jimmy. Thanks. I'll see you tomorrow morning early."

"All right chief."

Rich went back to sleep. He awoke around seven o'clock and called Phil, Scott, and the school principle and was candid about what was happening and where April was. He did not try to hide behind half truths. He was ashamed of what happened and he told himself he would not try to gloss things over.

Phil offered to come over and spend time with him and talk if he wanted.

Brenda arrived back in Portland around 8 a.m. She had enough time to spend a few hours with her parents and jump back on a red-eye to Portland after she saw the news reports and Phil had told her most of what was happening.

When she arrived, she called Phil to let him know he was back and he then filled her in on what had happened with the note she left.

She was devastated by the news. That was not what she wanted to happen.

She tried to call Rich, but he was not answering his cell phone. Probably lots of calls. She wanted to do something. So, she decided to go to Lincoln City to see if she could explain her note to April and maybe help fix things for Rich.

She picked up her car at the airport parking lot and headed directly to Lincoln City.

As Rich watched the news reports, he noticed that his books had been mentioned in several of the reports. Somehow news reporters had gotten his cell phone number and were hounding him for interviews.

Walker advised him against doing any formal interviews until later that day. He was ignoring his cell phone all morning, so, when he finally decided to check his messages, there were 50 to sift through.

It took him almost twenty minutes to listen and delete.

The forty eighth message was from his agent, who left a brief message saying that he was aware of the situation. His novel would be arriving in stores around noon and the publisher had their spin doctors at work taking advantage of the publicity.

Before he hung up, he also said that Rich needed to be in San Francisco that afternoon to meet with the publishers and be available or an impromptu publishing party that evening. The publisher said he could decide where, but he had to be there to meet the publishers in person or they might have to hold off on any additional press runs.

The publisher ended the message by saying, *"Sorry, Rich, I know this is all pretty sudden, but things work fast these days. And so it begins. Call me."*

Rich called and made arrangements.

He talked with Walker then called Grimsley to let them know what was happening.

Grimsley told Rich he was going to Lincoln City and would convey a message to April. Rich told him he would back in the morning.

Chapter 124

Kyle was subconsciously on his guard when he turned on to the long dirt road that led to Rich and April's cabin. At any minute he expected camouflaged militia men to jump out of the woods and surround his rental car.

He had to consciously dismiss those thoughts, which were based on years of misinformation he'd seen about Oregon and Washington being the home breeding ground for the Aryan nation, skinheads and other racist cults.

He acknowledge that Kansas also had its wackos. The only difference being that there were no places to hide on the prairie.

But Oregon, Kyle thought, had all kinds of places for mufukas to ambush you and shit. Kennewick man, he thought, was a brutha who got fucked up by some crazy ass racist Neanderthals and the Natural History Museum was still trying to cover that shit up.

Kyle relaxed more when he saw April's car and the quaint little cabin nestled amongst the lush, green foliage.

When Rich finished his phone calls, he told Walker about the reception and invited him to join him. Walker said he'd love to and told him that he was his responsibility for the next couple days, too, and he had some friends to look up in SF as well.

They left for the airport around 11 a.m. and were in the air by noon. Rich had never flown first class before and was enjoying the attention and a gin and tonic from the bubbly attendant as he and Walker talked about jazz, movies and politics.

Almost as quickly as it seemed they took off, they landed at San Francisco International Airport.

The day was clear, and fog blanketed the hills of the south bay as usual.

As Rich thought about what was happening, he panicked. He had spent years avoiding this, he thought. He did everything in his power to remain anonymous.

Now, he thought, the cat was out of the bag. He would have to perform for the public, like a circus monkey. What if the public didn't like what they saw? What if they were over critical? Could he handle that? He didn't know.

What if he ended up like Ken Kesey, a two hit wonder and eccentric with a hippy school bus. Rich did not want to become a cult classic. He just wanted to tell stories and raise his children.

Walker noticed Rich quietly staring out the window as the jet taxied to a stop. He nudged Rich.

"Listen, Rich. Don't worry about all this. You'll be fine."

Rich turned and looked at Walker.

"I hope so Jimmy. You know, I always tried to imagine how I'd feel if this all became reality. How would I react? Would I feel smug and superior like I'm better than others? Or would I still be just, well, just me. You know?"

"I know. I knew Denzel before he was a big star. Brutha was always smooth and a nice guy. Even after he hit it big, he was still smooth. Still a nice guy but a little wiser. You know, Rich, money and fame doesn't have to change people. People decide to change because of money and fame. They can decide to be better people. Or they can decide to be jerks. I'm not worried about you buddy. You'll be all right."

"Thanks James. I need to hear that right now. You're cool. Even though you won't—or can't—tell me more about what you do, you're still all right."

James laughed and they gathered their bags, got their rental car and headed downtown. Their meeting was in the Transamerica Tower with the Chronicle Books publisher.

When April heard the knock on the door, she couldn't imagine who she would know in Lincoln City. Then she panicked, fearing it might be bad news from Portland.

She ran to the door and yelled, "Who is it?"

"It's me April, Kyle."

"Oh my God!" April yelled, and she pulled the door open quickly. "What are you doing here?"

"Hey, baby," Kyle said.

He stepped in and gave April lengthy hug.

"I was just passing through. You know, I always got bidnez way out here in the middle of fuckin' nowhere."

April Laughed.

"Kyle, you're yanking my chain. Come in."

She took him by the hand and pulled him inside and closed the door.

"Kids, look who's here."

Juan and Antonio were in their room playing with their Gameboys.

"Who is it," Antonio yelled.

"Put the GameBoy away and come out here and see. NOW!"

First Antonio peeked out. His eyes lit up.

"Uncle Kyle. Uncle Kyle!"

He ran out of the room and gave Kyle a big hug. Juan followed, both smothering Kyle with hugs.

"Man, you two done got big. You been eatin' steaks for breakfast?"

"Mom tries to make us eat vegetables. Yeech," Juan said.

"Well, you got to eat those too. Along with them steaks."

"We like ice cream and chocolate," Antonio admitted and giggled.

"Well, the way it worked for me when I was a kid was I had to eat fifty thousand peas and my momma gave me a ten gallon barrel of chocolate ice cream. That's what you got to do."

"Na aaah. Mom, Uncle Kyle's telling stores," Juan teased.

"Yeah, you kids too smart for me. Listen, you like Bionicles?"

"Yeah! Yeah!" They both yelled and started jumping up and down, reaching for a plastic bag Kyle held just out of reach. He lowered it and both Kyle and Juan scrambled to remove the two boxes containing Lego Bionicles.

"Coool," Juan said, I got Megazord.

"Way far cool, I got Spectra," said Antonio.

April stepped in and scooted them towards the bedroom.

"Say thank you and you boys go put your pajamas on. You can work on your Bionacaccles, or whatever they're called together. Uncle Kyle and I got some catching up to do."

Juan and Antonio said thank you in unison and ran to their rooms, giggling all the way.

Chapter 125

Kyle sipped the strong coffee April made and grimaced.

"Damn, baby, yo coffee still kicks my ass."

"Coming from you, Kyle, I know that's a compliment."

She sipped her coffee.

"So it sounds like you and Lisa are doing great. I wish I could say the same about us."

She smiled uncomfortably and looked into her cup of coffee, knowing that she was opening a can of worms that she was not sure she was ready to open.

"April, I know this is hard for you," Kyle said, picking his words carefully. "I didn't come here to lecture you or talk sense to you or stand up for Rich, even though I've known him a lot longer than I've known you."

April looked up at Kyle.

"I love both you and Rich, and I know that you and him are kindred spirits. I also knew that you would never call anyone or go crying on anyone's shoulders because you one tough lady. You'd rather listen to Luther's greatest hits and figure shit out on your own. Ain't nothing wrong with that. All you got to do is listen to Luther and he's got the answer to any relationship situation you can think of. Break ups. Make ups. Love found. Love lost. Love misplaced. Group love. Puppy love. Any kind of love or loss you can think of. Luther be there. But you still need to talk to somebody real, flush shit out. Maybe—and don't take this the wrong way—hear some things you might not want to hear."

April look into her coffee cup again, deep in thought, then said, "You're right, Kyle. I would never talk to anyone else. I'm just too embarrassed. I'm just so terribly hurt I can't talk to anyone.

She began to cry. Kyle moved his chair closer to her and hugged her.

"Baby, you got to cry. This shit ain't easy, especially when you love someone as much as you love Rich."

They were silent.

"Let it all out girl," Kyle said.

"I traveled fifteen hundred miles just to do this. So, I'm hoping you'll hear me out and take what I have to say to heart."

Kyle paused and thought about what he had to say.

"You know, April, I write screenplays. One question was I always have to ask is how close is art tied to reality. And what influence does art have on real people and real situations. To look for script ideas, I spend hours and hours reading court cases. The one thing that

I see all the time is the process of introducing character witnesses."

April wiped her eyes and looked at Kyle, not sure what he was getting at.

"I'll get to the point. When we're in trouble, we have to ask the question of who will stand up for our character and how much weight will that have on the verdict. Right now, Rich is on trial in your heart. And the least I could do was to come here and vouch for his character."

April stood up, took her coffee and stood by the fireplace.

"Now, I know this is not what you want to hear right now, but hear me out. And I'll be brief. Rich is a man. There is no man out there who has not been tempted by the opposite sex. That's a testament to the power of woman. That's how you two got together. And when circumstances are absolutely perfect, any man could step over the line. But that doesn't mean they don't love you more than any one else could. That means they were weak and confused and being a stupid motherfu..um...a dumbass. I told Rich that he got to get his shit together and not screw up the best thing he's got going in his life. I also told him you two could always divorce and start over."

April's turned and looked at Kyle.

"You told him that?"

"Damn straight I did," Kyle said, "But I told him he'd be a fool to not try to make this work out. You two got too much going for each other and you'd be lost without each other. I see that. I think he sees that. And I'm hoping you see that."

Kyle walked over to April and touched her shoulder.

"I wouldn't blame you if you threw up a wall right now and wrote him off. The only thing I would ask is that you explore and understand what happened and why it happened. 'Cause I think what you'll find—what I hope you'll find—is that there's more to the story. Every day I tell Rich he's fucked up. You know, we always jivin' each other. I don't mean it. But, April, I know that all he talks about is you. He loves you more than anything. And I hope you two can figure this thing out and grow old together."

April was silent as she thought about what Kyle said, then she looked at him and said, "Kyle, I suppose right now most people—women—in my position would be feeling sorry for themselves and wondering where they failed."

"That's right April. Is that you?"

"No, that's not me. I may be hurt and embarrassed, but I know I'm not the one who screwed up here. Kyle, you're right. I know Rich. I know he's a sneaky bastard, elusive, kind of a mystery man. But I knew that when I married him. And I love that about him. And Kyle, I'll tell you something that you will never repeat. I knew this day would come. I just didn't know when. I didn't know who. And I didn't know how I would respond. Rich's problem is that although he's a sneaky guy, he's also incredibly compassionate, incredibly kind and incredibly smart. Those were all things I was looking for in a person. Does being incredibly stupid at times cancel out all those other GOOD qualification? Maybe. Maybe not. That's what I'm here to decide. And, Kyle—or should I call you the witness for the defense—I'm glad you came. I'm still not decided yet, but you're little soliloquy may sway the jury."

April smiled along with Kyle and they hugged again. Then there was a knock on the door.

Chapter 126

On the way to Lincoln City, Paulson assumed that Grimsley's mood would be somber. Instead, he was animated, talkative and Grimily engaged him in discussion instead of lecturing him.

It wasn't until they were nearing Lincoln City limits that he mentioned the case. By that point, Paulson was actually enjoying Grimsley's company and was disappointed to have to talk about work.

"Paulson, you did a hell of a job on this case."

Paulson looked at Grimsley and said, "I agree, sir. I had a lot of help too."

Grimsley smiled. He knew he was rubbing off on Paulson and he liked that.

"The scum bags are in jail and you'd think our work would be done."

"Not yet, sir."

"Howz that Paulson?"

"Well, we owe a paperboy a favor. And I don't mind saying, sir, that I hope we can do some good here. Our boy did a good job of screwing things up with his wife, but I like them both and if everyone can walk out of this better off, than I know I'll sleep better at night."

"But don't you secretly hope," Grimsley asked, "that they somehow don't make it. That they divorce. Wouldn't that prove your point of people sticking to their own kind?"

Paulson knew this one was coming. He took a deep breath and answered.

"I've had a change of heart Grimsley. I've been doing some thinking and reading lately. That little speech Rich gave the other night also got me to thinking."

Paulson looked out the window before continuing.

"You knew this before we first talked about this that if we even dig a little into cultural and ethnic evolution and cultural anthropology that all evidence does not support separate races but instead supports ethnic blending. Man could not have evolved with out ethnic and cultural intermixing and migration. Leakey's research supports this. I've made the same mistakes that White people have and all racist have made. I made decisions based on one person's opinion, ignoring all he evidence, ignoring common sense and most of all ignoring my gut."

"Hell, Bob....may I call you Bob?"

Grimsley looked at Paulson, surprised, "Hell yes, young man."

"Well, I saw those two together. There are no two people more in love. And those two kids of theirs are going to make waves in the waters of life. In a way, I'm kind of jealous. My wife is wonderful. We are very much in love, but we've always play it safe; our friends; our family; where we go and what we do. Rich, man. That son of a bitch has got guts."

"Spoken like a true intellectual, Paulson. "Welcome to the club."

They laughed.

They turned onto a small road that was lined with trees. They could barely see the gray clouds hovering above as they neared the small cabin. The trees were tall and thick enough to completely obscure the sky.

Two cars were parked near the front door and blue smoke curled out of the tall stone chimney. The front of the cabin was almost obscured by tall ferns and shrubs and stacks of firewood lined one side of the cabin wall.

"Paulson," Grimsley asked, "are we ready. Nothing more dangerous than a woman pissed off you know."

"At least we have some back-up; a friend from Kansas. Let's do this."

Chapter 127

"Captain Grimsley, Lieutenant Paulson. What are you doing here?"

"Mornin' mam," Grimsley said. "Just needed to talk with you."

Paulson and Grimsley greeted April and she introduced Kyle as they entered the small cabin.

"Is everything all right?" She asked, panicked.

"Yes, mam, everything is okay now. We just need to talk to you about something important."

"Well, come in. Coffee?"

Both Grimsley and Paulson said yes.

"You de cops—uh—you de police officers Rich told me about," Kyle said. "Man, from what he said about you two, you some kind of super cops, heroes and shit."

Grimsley gave Kyle a tenuous smile and said, "Yeah, we're the ones. Heroes? I don't think so. Just doing our jobs."

"And it's so cool to see a brutha kickin' mother fucker's asses."

Kyle extended a fist to Paulson, who first looked at Grimsley, then smiled and extended his fist and tapped Kyle's on top, and then Kyle tapped his fist and shook his hand.

April brought coffee and sat everyone down in front of the fireplace. Kyle placed more logs into the fire.

Grimsley spoke first.

"April, you're pretty isolated out here, so we came here to tell you that there's been an incident at your house."

"Oh my God!" She said, covering her mouth with shock.

"Take it easy, April," Paulson said. "Rich is okay. We have, for the most part, solved Trixie's murder case. And you and Rich are no longer in danger. But things got pretty messy last night."

Paulson and Grimsley explained what happened with Temple and Fitch. April could only sit, in shock, listening.

She finally asked, "Where's Rich at?"

"Rich is with Walker. Stayed at his house a few blocks away from you. Now the unofficial reason for our visit mam is to let you know that Rich is getting ready to go to San Francisco right now. He got a call from the agent we mentioned at dinner Monday night and they wanted him to be there by one o'clock this afternoon to meet the publishers. Because of the media storm this case has generated, they're stepping up the press run dates on his book. Mam, it hits the book stores today."

"No shit," Kyle said. "I'll be God damn."

"You're kidding right?" April asked, suspicious.

"Mam, we're cops," Paulson said. "We don't kid. We fight

crime, remember."

Kyle and April looked at each other, then at Paulson, who said, "Just kidding, mam."

Paulson and Grimsley smiled.

"This is all on the level. We spoke with Rich this morning and he asked us to convey a message to you."

"What message is that?"

April folded her arms across her chest, suddenly defensive.

"He said he loves you very much—and forgive me mam, I'm not saying it with the passion he said it in. He's sorry, and he would drive out here as soon as he returned. And he said he would not leave until you were all a family again."

April didn't know what to say. These circumstances, she thought, seemed like something out of a movie, not her life.

"Mr. Paulson, thank you for conveying the message, albeit lacking the drama that Rich may have interjected, I appreciate it."

"Now, one last thing, before we head back to Portland and catch a flight to San Francisco to go to this reception thing Rich has arranged. He assumed, by the way, that you would not want to go, considering the circumstances, but asked us to mention it anyway. And finally, we have something to show you."

Grimsley gestured to Paulson, who removed a portable DVD player from his bag and set it on the coffee table.

"We're not marriage counselors, you understand," Grimsley said. "But I will say that both Paulson and I have developed a fondness for you and Rich. So, we decided to go out on a limb here and see if we could help, well, you know, help get you to back together."

Grimsley blushed slightly and Paulson was not sure what to do with his hands. They both seemed to stumble over their words and seemed uncomfortable with the situation. April and Kyle looked on with amusement.

"We have something to show you, mam," Paulson said. "And maybe this might help."

"Well," Grimsley groused, "get on with it Paulson. Time's wasting."

"Because of the risk posed by recent circumstances, we had one of our operatives follow Rich to the retreat last weekend. And, mam, this is classified information. In order to assure Rich's safety, we had our man attend the conference and, well, and we bugged the trailer Rich and Brenda stayed in."

"You didn't?" April said, "No, no. You didn't. I don't want to know this.

"No shit," Kyle said. "I knew this kind of thing happened. I'm going to watch my back."

"Anyway, mam, we also placed a concealed camera in the trailer so we could keep a watch in case the trailer was compromised," Paulson said.

"What are you saying Captain? That you have a video tape of what happened this weekend," April Asked.

"Yes mam, that's correct. We have burned a DVD and can show you now."

"Is this something I want to see?"

"Yes, mam," Paulson said.

"Why don't you just tell me."

"Mam, I don't recommend that," Grimsley said.

"Why not?"

"You've seen me try to paraphrase Rich. I suck. Mam, watch the video. You won't be disappointed."

"Mr. Grimsley, I know you enough to know you and Rich are same sons from different mothers even if he is African American. So, I know you're up to something. Mr. Paulson. Mr. Grimsley, roll the tape."

"Thank you mam," Paulson said, and pressed the play button.

An image appeared in the small screen. It was moving back and forth, like an amusement ride.

"Whoa," Kyle said. "What is up with that?"

"Our operative was cop and an aspiring writer. Both practical and creative conflict at times. He placed a small micro camera in one of those seventies cat clocks. You know, the ones where the tail is the pendulum and the eyes move back and forth."

"He didn't?" asked Kyle.

"He did. It was not plugged in at the time. The camera is concealed in one of the eyes. But Rich plugged in the clock, so now the image is moving. It's wide angle, so we'll be able to see what's going on, but we may need some Dramamine when we're done. Oh, here, this is what I want you to see."

The tiny screen showed Rich and Brenda sitting on the couch. "You have to listen carefully." Paulson turned up the volume.

April, Kyle, Paulson and Grimily moved their heads back and forth with the image. They looked like they were watching a tennis match. In the picture, Brenda and Rich were locked in a hug on the couch. Suddenly, Rich stood up and started pacing the living room. In the background they could hear Dick Blake playing *How deep is the Ocean*.

"What's wrong Rich," Brenda asked.

"This is all wrong, Brenda. I'm sorry. I can't do this."

Brenda was silent as tears formed in her eyes.

"Listen to this," Grimsley said, smiling. "This is great."

April shot him a disapproving glance.

"Sorry, mam."

Rich continued.

"I don't know how to say this, Brenda. But I'll first say, you are a lovely, beautiful, wonderful woman. So, please don't take this the wrong way. It's just that…it's just that this is not me. This whole situation is not me. It's all wrong for me. So I can't. I can't do this."

April covered her mouth as she listened. In the screen, she could see Brenda sitting on the couch, hanging her head, listening to Rich.

"I've spent my life manipulating my circumstances so that everyone round me benefited from my actions. I help people. That's what I do. I help them find jobs. I help them find love. I help them understand life. I help them find music. I amuse, challenge, and anticipate. And the reason I write is so I can understand life and all it's crazy possibilities and why I do all the stuff I do."

Rich paused, rubbed his forehead.

"And occasionally I screw up. That's me. But not like this. I…I can't do this. This hurts too much. I'm feeling pain deep inside, like I'm slowly cutting my heart out with a dull serrated edge knife."

"God damn," Kyle said, "I knew that mufuka was bad."

"That's not all. The best is yet to come. Watch this," said Grimsley.

Rich went to the couch and sat down next to Brenda. He reached over to her and lifted her head.

"Brenda, look at me. Think about what you see AND what you feel. What you see is a man who is so in love with his wife that the very thought of betraying that trust is enough to cause me to grieve. And it's not fear, Brenda. It's something more meaningful than that. Brenda, I don't need to betray my wife. I don't need to have an affair. I don't need to be loved more by anybody else. April fulfills all that in me and more."

"God damn," Kyle said, "I need to write this shit down. I could use it in a script."

Grimsley, April and Paulson all looked at Kyle, who immediately recognized his misplaced overzealousness.

He said, "Ait, ait, I'm cool. I'm cool."

Rich continued, "What I need from you Brenda is different. I need you to be whole, for you to find your way. I'm willing to help you help yourself. Listen, Brenda and listen carefully, having an affair with me will NOT help you become a better person. It will not help you find your way. It will not help you confront your demons and it will not help you find love. It will...it will help you find pain and may destroy you. I will not help you do that. That's somebody else. Somebody with no honor. No sense of self, and most of all, that's somebody who cares more about himself than about others; about you. Brenda, I have enough love in me to share with you; with my friend Kyle, with Phil, and probably the next hundred thousand people I may meet in my lifetime. But one thing I will never do is betray that sacred trust; that sacred bond I have with April. And most of the love I have in me will always be reserved for her...and for my children."

"I got to call my agent," Kyle said, "Yo, Paulson, you got to get me a copy of that. That's tight."

"Sorry Kyle. This doesn't exist technically."

They all focused their attention on April, who was sobbing quietly. Not sure what to say next. Paulson turned off the CD.

"Not much more to see from here, mam. She went to bed and he stayed up all night listening to Dick Blake and pounding away at that manuscript. Emailed it to his agent on Sunday. They talked about her journals and participated in the conference. Now, mam, I wanted you to see this part first. This is not everything, but this is the most important part. So, you'll have to draw your own conclusions."

"Thank you Mr. Paulson, Mr. Grimsley."

There was silence in the room.

"Mam, we've got to get back to the City if we're going to catch our flight to San Francisco. Again, mam, a little business and a little pleasure," Grimsley said. "I've got some family there I need to see and we can ask Rich about some final details of the case."

Paulson looked at Grimsley, surprised.

"You never told me you had family there. Who's there?"

"You never asked," Grimsley replied, "and I have a daughter there. In college at San Francisco State, working on her PH.D in mechanical engineering."

"Well, let's not waste any more time," Grimsley said. "Gotta go."

They hugged April, shook hands with Kyle and left. Kyle called Lisa, who filled him in and told him about Rich's invitation.

"Isn't that some shit," Kyle said. "Nigga full of surprises. I'm going to call and make some reservation. I'll go to San Francisco and keep an eye on that nigga for you. Don't you worry. Then I'm going to tell that fool he been watching too many God damn Kevin Kostner movies. He needs to give that shit up."

April laughed for the first time since Kyle arrived.

"Now that's what I like to see. You have one beautiful smile. I'm going to leave you alone. I know you don't need my black ass around here taking up space and getting in the way. Whatever happens, April, you are welcome in our house in Kansas any time. And I expect to see you at least once a year as usual. All right?"

"All right, Kyle." April said, "and thank you."

Kyle gathered his coat and walked to the door.

"Boys, come and say good by to Uncle Kyle."

"God damn. You wouldn't even know they were in there."

"Bionicles. They could build those things all day and you'd never hear a peep."

Juan and Antonio came charging out of the bedroom and hugged Kyle.

"You boys eat mountains of vegetables, breakfast, lunch an dinner, even vegetable ice cream. Hear?"

"Yeeech," Juan said and stuck out his tongue, feigning throwing up.

"Bye Uncle Kyle. Thank you for the Bionicles and tell Kyle Junior we said hello."

"All right sport. Be good."

Chapter 128

Chambers drove through the night at an average of 90 miles per hour. He was pulled over on only one occasion. When the police officer saw who he was, he complimented Chambers on his rig and told him *"that was a hell of a bust up in Portland."* He then told Chambers to be careful. There was fog ahead.

By nine o'clock, Chambers was crossing the Golden Gate Bridge. He phoned Enison.

"Enison, where the hell are you?"

"I'm at the office. Where are you?"

"I'm in Frisco."

"What are you doing there? I thought you flew into Oakland?"

"Drove."

"Drove what?"

"That rig you got me. Nice rig."

"You liked that, huh. That rig has a history you know?"

"Yeah, it does now."

"Even before you."

"What history?"

"I repossessed it from a Seattle drug dealer, real high roller, liked to flaunt his cash. Only one of those were made. And, as you already know, it's stocked. I made a deal with Hertz. They buy it and market it as an exotic rental and I'll rent it whenever I'm in Portland."

"Smart thinkin' pal. Well, I decided to keep the vehicle."

"That's okay, I'll have Hertz deliver it back to Portland. Just put it on your expense account and fax it to me. I'll take care of it."

"I'm way ahead of you. There's probably a fax there for you now."

"Hold on. Amy is bringing it now. Here it....is."

Chambers smiled. He wished he was there to see Enison's face.

"What's the matter Enison. Cat got your tongue?"

"Chambers, what the hell is this?"

"I'm keeping the rig. Like I said."

"But Chambers, this bill is for sixty-five thousand dollars. I think they made some kind of mistake. You are only renting the car for a few extra days?"

"Wrong, pal, I'm keeping the car. It suits me. And I'm coming to see you. We got lots to discuss, including the rest of my bill. See you at Brandy Ho's at noon."

"Chambers, you..."

Chambers hung up before Enison could finish.

Chapter 129

For the first time since Enison put his plan to work, he was panicked. There would be no way in hell to bury or even justify a $60,000 car purchase without having to explain it to Baker.

He threw the fax back onto his desk and it landed on top of the *Oakland Tribune*. Seeing the cover story brightened his mood and lessened the impact of seeing Chambers' bill.

The headline read, PAPERBOY UNCOVERS MURDER CONSPIRACY, SENATOR AND PORTLAND INSURANCE EXEC ARRESTED.

The story covered the details of Trixie's death, the journals. And under the story was a picture of Chambers, and a caption that read, OAKLAND PI PROVIDES KEY INTELLIGENCE.

Enison's phone rang.

"Mr. Enison. This is Rich Franklin. How are you?"

Putting on his official face and voice, Enison answered, "Mr. Franklin, what a surprise. I'm fine. How are you?"

"Not so good Mr. Enison. There's a lot going on right now and I'm not sure how I feel about it. Can I talk to you for a minute?"

"Sure, Mr. Franklin. This is a first. You calling me."

"I know, Mr. Enison. I needed to say something to you and I don't have much time. I have to catch a flight soon."

"Rich, you have my attention. What's on your mind—Oh, and thank you for the check—by the way."

"Sure thing, Mr. Enison. Listen, I, um, I wanted to thank you, Mr. Enison, for your patience and your understanding. I know this may sound a little weird. But you've been the only person I've felt I could be honest with. And I feel as though I've even let you down."

"Mr. Franklin, I'm not running a confession line here. People do what they have to do. I, of all people, understand that."

"I know, Mr. Enison. You've been great. You've given me more opportunities than I deserve. And I appreciate that. I also want to let you know that I'm going to come clean with April on this. We're going to take care of these debts like I should have months ago."

"Listen, Rich, I'm not pressuring you. You don't have—"

"Mr. Enison, listen. This is something I have to do. Dragging this on and on is not a smart thing to do on my part. And, I, um..." Rich paused while trying to decide how to tell Enison about April, *"...well, I really screwed up this last weekend and, well, I have to be honest with April. I have to make things right. Our relationship is dependent on it and I'm tried of sneaking around. It's taking its toll, Mr. Enison. If I conceal stuff from her, I subconsciously conceal stuff from everyone I know and don't even realize it. It becomes habit."*

"Rich, you don't have to…"

"Hear me out, Mr. Enison. I need to do this. I got a book deal last week and a small advance. I sent you most of it. I'm sorry I didn't tell you about it. I was scared to. But I'm not afraid any more."

"Rich, that's great. Congratulations. You're very lucky."

"Maybe Mr. Enison. Maybe. Mr. Enison a lot has happened. I don't know what to make of some of it. But I'm not going to fight this. I was invited to San Francisco to meet the publishers for a day. I'm not sure why they insisted, but I'll be there at one o'clock. Then there arranging some kind of reception this evening. They said I could invite anyone I wanted and have it anywhere I wanted. They'd take care of everything for me. So, I wanted to invite you personally…I…"

"Well, Rich, I don't usually mix business and pleasure."

"Please, Mr. Enison. It would mean a lot to me."

"Well, all right Mr. Franklin. As long as it's someplace exotic with lots of dark wood and it's in the city."

"You'll like this Mr. Enison. It's at the Fairmont Hotel. In the Venetian Room. I saw Ramsey Lewis there years ago and told the publisher's it was there or nowhere."

"All right Mr. Franklin. What time?"

"Seven o'clock. I have to be on a plane back to Portland by ten."

"I'll be there. Mind if I bring a friend."

"Not at all."

"I'll see you then."

Chapter 130

It was only noon and April was exhausted. What was supposed to be a quiet morning turned out to be full of surprise visits and unexpected turns.

The boys were playing in front of the fireplace; content, happy children, wanting for nothing and confident that they had the love of both of their parents. She thought about what a life as a single mother would be like.

It was something she felt she had to consider; shared custody; packing and unpacking for visits to either parents house, the uncertainty it would bring. Their world would be very different from what it is now and there would be changes in their disposition and tantrums and anger. But that was the reality that she faced and she could not gloss that reality over because once she thought about it enough, there would have to be action after that.

There was another knock on the door.

In frustration, she threw up her hands and said out loud, "Oh, for heaven's sake, who could that possibly be?"

She walked to the door, and, without asking who it was, opened it quickly and froze when she saw a familiar face standing there.

"Oh," she said, "I'm sorry. I didn't know who it was."

"Mrs. Franklin, my name is Brenda. I'm Rich's friend and I was hoping I could talk to you for a few minutes."

April could only stand there with her mouth agape. She didn't know what to say.

She finally said, "Brenda, what a surprise. I never expected..."

"I know Mrs. Franklin. I'm sorry. I know this must be very uncomfortable for you. But I felt I needed to come here and explain the note and explain what really happened."

"I know what really happened, Brenda."

"Honestly, Mrs. Franklin, Rich was great—I mean, we started to—well—we could have—but—um, he said he loved you—and I was stupid to think—I—um—"

"Okay, okay, Brenda, I know all about it."

"You mean you know ALL about it."

"Yes. I know exactly what happened Friday night and for the rest of the weekend."

She smiled.

"Now come in here where it's warm. Those fashions you young people wear don't leave much to the imagination...or protect you from the weather."

She glanced at Brenda's exposed midriff as she offered her

hand and led her into the cabin.

"We have a lot to talk about," April said and closed the door.

Chapter 131

The Chronicle Books offices were on the twentieth floor. Rich grew more and more nervous as the elevator groaned to a stop and slid open exposing a plush lobby with black leather couches, large impressionist's paintings and huge glass windows looking out on a bustling North Beach neighborhood. Coit Tower loomed in the background.

Rich and Walker walked to the receptionist who seemed to be submerged behind a too-tall wide oak counter.

"Welcome to Chronicle books. How may I help you?" she asked, with a slight squeak and a forced smile at the end of each sentence.

"I'm Rich Franklin and this is James Walker here to see Mr. Pendergrass."

"Oh, Mr. Franklin. Mr. Pendergrass is expecting you. Right through that door, first office on the left," she said, pointing to a large wood door to the right of them.

"Thank you," Rich said.

They walked through the door into a palatial office. At the far end of the room a large man in a crisp gray suit with an elongated face, overpowering chin, balding hair and friendly face stood up and in a booming baritone voice said, "Mr. Franklin, come in. Come in."

He walked over to Rich

"I'm Tom Pendergrass. Damn glad to meet you. And you are?" he said, turning to Walker.

"James Walker. A friend."

"Yeah, Grimsley told me about you. Pleased to meet you. Come on over here Rich. There's someone I'd like you to meet and someone you've already met."

Rich recognized Sunny Manns, the agent he'd met at the Center for the Performing Arts and perhaps his black guardian angel.

"Sunny. Nice to see you again."

"Nice to see you too, Rich," Manns said, flashing one of his spectacular smiles and winking at Rich.

"This is David Fisher, your agent."

A slight man with thick dark hair arranged in a bouffant with thick Elvis Costello glasses, a vintage suite that may have been from a Beetles garage sale stood up and said, "Mr. Franklin, I'm so pleased to meet you. Thank you for coming to San Francisco on such short notice. What we wanted to discuss couldn't wait."

"Gentlemen, please sit down," Pendergrass said, pointing to the chairs. "And let's get started. I have another appointment in ten minutes."

Rich, Walker, Manns, and Fisher all sat down and there was a brief silence. Pendergrass stared at Rich and said nothing.

"Rich," he finally said, "I didn't get to be publisher here by taking too many unnecessary risks. That's not how I work. But when I see a good thing, I don't hesitate to stake my claim."

Pendergrass stood up and walked around to the front of his desk and sat on the edge for show.

"You're a smart kid. And you're lucky. Things are falling into place for you and I'm not afraid to say that's of great benefit to us. Your book is great. We already knew that or we wouldn't have taken a chance on a small run. This business in Portland is unfortunate but good timing and could be the catalyst to really jump start sales. So we didn't skip a beat in getting the book out there. And now we're prepared to go the distance with you. You know what I'm saying here?"

"Yes, sir, I do," Rich said.

"Let me cut to the chase. All copies from the first run sold out about an hour ago. Can't find it anywhere. So, we're going to increase the press run. It will be in all major book stores nationwide by the end of the day. Second, we want to option a screenplay. Thirdly we want to buy international rights. Fourthly, we are going to reprint your other books, the relationship handbook and the newspaper carrier handbook. Fithly—and I'm not sure that's a word or not—we're going to give you an advance to write a follow up book. And finally, you can do us a favor. And guess what? We'll pay you for that favor."

"What's that Mr. Pendergrass?"

Rich was wondering where the air came from to ask the question since he had been holding his breath while Pendergrass talked.

"We've known Captain Grimsley for along time. He's had a brilliant career and he's got stories to tell that will curl your toes. Know what I mean? But he's also as stubborn as an old Missouri mule. We've offered him unmentionable sums of money for rights to his manuscripts. I have a very rough one in a safety deposit book at Wells Fargo just down the street because I know one day he's gonna sign and it's going to be published. You get my meaning here? Well, he's a good writer but he needs somebody to work with; somebody to ghost write with him because he hates spending too much *"God damn time behind a God damn computer"* as he puts it. Now here's where you come in. He says he'll sign a contract today for all twenty of his manuscripts, including editing Trixie's journals for publication if you'll work with him as a ghost writer."

"Are you serious Mr. Pendergrass?" was all Rich could ask.

"Sure I am kid. He loved your book. And he thinks your a swell kid. So, congratulations, you've got a fan. But I have a feeling he won't be the only one. Now, let's get to what we're offering for all this. Mr. Fisher here and Mr. Manns have ironed out the details, so I'll just give you the numbers and ask you to sign when I'm done. You've already given Mr. Fisher the power to determine your future and I've been very impressed with his thoroughness. Now, if you trust your agent, as they say, the rest is icing."

"I've only known him for a week, but I trust Mr. Fisher. He's done everything he's said he would so far. So please, Mr. Pendergrass, tell me what you have in mind."

"I'll skip the details, Mr. Franklin. I have an advance here for one point five to get us started. There will be two more installments along with royalties and further negotiations for film rights to future works in the next 30 days. How does that sound?"

"Well, Mr. Pendergrass, fifteen hundred bucks sounds a little low."

"Mr. Franklin, you misunderstand," Pendergrass said, laughing, "that's one point five million."

Rich looked at Walker, then at Fisher, then at Manns and was embarrassed at his verbal faux pax in the middle of the most important day of his life.

"One point five million dollars?" Rich asked, to make sure he heard what he thought he heard.

"Absolutely Mr. Franklin. Listen, it sounds like a lot but believe me, it goes fast. And don't be so surprised Mr. Franklin. To make money in this business, we have to spend a lot more than that. You remember Rodney King? Offered him two million for his story. Dumb shit never delivered. Kato Kaelin. Four million. Did okay on that one. Heidi Fleiss, ten million. The public appetite for books is voracious. Mr. Franklin, here's the contract. And truth is, even as many writers as there are, we have a hard time finding new, fresh ideas. That's where you hit the jackpot my friend."

Pendergrass handed Rich a two inch thick stack of papers. "Two copies there. One for you and one for me. You can take it and read it. Or you can sign it. If you sign it now, you can pick up your check on the way out. Either way, welcome to the Chronicle books family."

Rich glanced over the contract, still in shock.

He looked at Fisher and asked, "Mr. Fisher, should I take this home or sign it now."

"I reviewed it thoroughly, Mr. Franklin, I have no issues with this agreement and there are appropriate out clauses and adequate compensation."

"Well, then, Mr. Pendergrass, it's a done deal."

Rich placed the contract on the desk, took a pen out of his planner and signed. As he signed, tears formed in his eyes and he paused to wipe them from his face, trying as much as possible to mask his feelings.

"Don't worry, Mr. Franklin," Pendergrass said, "I cried when I made my first million too. All that hard work has paid off for you; sleepless nights, sweating over words, and of course the best one, your wife and kids accusing you of playing on the computer all day. That one used to really fry me."

Rich smiled. He was happy and sad. Happy his dream was coming true and sad April couldn't be there to share it with him.

"And, Mr. Franklin, I know about your wife, and that's nothing to be embarrassed about. Things will work out. I sincerely believe that."

Rich stared at Pendergrass. The room was silent enough for him to hear his own heartbeat. The tears continued to stream down his cheeks, landing on the contract. Rich leaned on the desk, took one last look at Walker and Fisher, then signed the agreement.

"Great. I'll have a copy mailed to you. Mr. Fisher has arranged everything for the reception tonight. You'll get to meet all of our editors, some of our local writers and you get to have all your friends there. We're setting it up just as you discussed with Mr. Fisher this morning. You have very particular taste Mr. Franklin—exquisite, I must admit. But it's all on our dime and I don't mind footing the bill. I'm sorry I won't be able to be there tonight, but I know you'll have fun."

"Thank you Mr. Pendergrass," was all Rich could say.

"Don't mention it," Pendergrass replied. Just keep your pencil sharpened. There's a lot of work to do.

"I will, sir."

"Well then, Gentlemen, I have another appointment. Enjoy your stay in the city. Mr. Fisher. Rich. We'll be in touch. Mr. Walker. Pleasure."

He hustled them out of the office and Rich picked up the envelope on the way out.

"I'd say it was time to have some lunch and a drink, gentlemen. Can I interest you in lunch and a drink at Alioto's?" Manns suggested?

Chapter 132

After lunch, Fisher dropped Rich off at the Fairmont and told him he had a suite reserved for the day; for the night if he wanted. Rich thanked him for everything and told him he'd see him in the evening. Fisher also told him to arrange any additional clothing, food and a tux for the evening with the concierge and not to worry about the tab.

His room was a spacious two bedroom suite with a bar, antiques in every corner, Persian rugs, ornate crystal chandeliers and a big screen television in every room. He walked to the window and looked out. He could see Chinatown immediately below and Alcatraz in the distance. The sky was clear and sunny.

The first thing, he thought, Juan and Antonio would do is run from room to room, turn on all the lights, then end up in the bedroom pretending the bed was a trampoline. There would be the laughter and giggles and thrill of a new place to explore. April would smile and say "This is nice."

Instead, there was only the hum of the small refrigerator under the bar and the sound of the Cable car as it rolled down California Street. Rich was exhausted, but he could not sleep. There was too much to think about and his brain would not allow him to rest. It was on auto pilot and would not stop processing until he either collapsed or he resolved all the issues swirling in his head.

So, Rich decided to do the only thing he could do—what he used to do when he lived in the city; to go for a long walk, peripatetic, like the Greek philosophers used to do. Walk and think, pick up a few supplies, then stop at the Pier One Café and read the *Examiner*. Just like old times, he thought.

Chapter 133

Baker was distraught. He hadn't heard from Chambers. He tried to follow Enison again but lost him on the Embarcadero when his car ran out of gas. Anxiety and frustration were consuming him. He needed to know what was happening.

As he sat at a MUNI bus stop near Pier three waiting to catch the bus to the BART then back to Oakland, his cell phone rang.

Before he could say hello, a stern voice said, "Baker that you?"

"Yes, yes, Mr. Chambers. Where have you been?"

"That's for me to know, Baker. Now shut up and listen up. Meet me tonight at the Fairmont Hotel. Eight o'clock sharp, in the lobby. Got it."

"Yes, Mr. Chambers. What's happening? Did you find out more?"

The phone clicked. Baker was starting to resent Chamber's attitude. Mental note to self, he thought, have Chambers fired when this was all over. Baker felt he didn't get the respect he deserved. He was a scholar, an intellectual giant and he held the key to the company's future and success.

Get what he needed and discard him when it's done, he thought.

As the bus approached the stop, Baker waved it off. The thick cloud of fumes burned his nose and the wind wake of the bus caused his baggy suit to flap indiscriminately.

How could he kill time until tonight? He would go to Ray's bar on Pine and Hyde. Ray's was a dark, seedy, dive with no windows where Baker sometimes spent hours brooding after his ventures into the porn dens of the Tenderloin.

There he could throw down a few whiskey's and build his courage. After his night out with Chambers, he swore off Daiquiris and Tequila Sunrises and froofie mixed drinks. He could drink less and achieve the same results with straight, hard liquor. Why not?

Chapter 134

It was a quarter to seven and Rich stood in front of the six foot tall mirror and examined his attire. He was dressed in a black tuxedo and a bow tie. He had special ordered a brim from the Mad Hatters on Montgomery Street. And the crowning touches were the spats, like Cagney used to wear in those gangster movies he liked to watch.

Rich didn't know who would show up, but he assumed if Fisher said it would all be arrange, he didn't need to worry about it. He learned a long time ago from a friend, a restaurant owner he'd spend a lot of time with named Kito, that if even one friend showed up that he could spend time with, he was rich and the party was a success.

He looked in the mirror, adjusted the red kerchief sticking out of his breast pocket, smiled and said, "Showtime."

The Venetian Room at the Fairmont was a lavish room with grand crystal chandeliers that cast diamonds of light in every corner of the room. Ten foot tall murals and paintings covered the walls and intimate Victorian tables filled the center of the room surrounded by high-back, plush booths.

When Rich entered the room, to his surprise, it was filled with people and he could hear familiar music coming from the intimate stage at the front of the room. In one corner of the room, Rich spotted Dick Blake, eyes closed, head down playing *Sophisticated Lady* as Tipsie, Fingers, Highnote, Sweet Cheeks, Smiles and Forbes played in perfect time.

Forbes spotted Rich and smiled, holding up a drumstick and calling to the other band members, who looked up and smiled. Rich waved and gave them a thumbs up.

Fisher was waiting for Rich and walked over to him.

"Rich, I think we got most everything you asked for. The band was the hardest, I'll admit. One of the older band members, at first, refused to fly, said planes fall out of the sky too much. But the train would have taken too long. So we had to sweeten the offer. Said he wanted to meet Sade. Said she had the most beautiful voice, like the songbirds of olden days. Mr. Franklin, I happen to have a few connections and told him I'd arrange it. Feisty old badger."

"I know. Thank you Mr. Fisher," Rich said. "I'll let you in on a little secret."

He glanced at Fingers, eyes closed, smiling, completely at home.

"That band member played here with Ellington in forty nine. All he ever talked about was coming back here sometime. This, Mr. Fisher, is a dream come true for him. You do know he is over eighty years old. He probably would have done it any. But a meeting with Sade is icing on the cake."

"I assumed so. Changing the subject," Fisher said, "we'll be putting everyone up at the hotel tonight."

"Perfect."

"Now, there are a few people from Chronicle books I want you to meet, plus, you have a few old friends who are anxious to chat with you."

Chambers, always a showman, drove up to the entrance of the Fairmont and parked the Escalade at front of the door. The Escalade's built-in police-style emergency lights were flashing. The spot lights blinded the valet and the blue neon running lights under the vehicle reflected off of the pavement, making the SUV looked like a space ship from *Close Encounters*.

Everyone stopped to stare.

Chambers pressed a button and the air shocks released, slowly lowering the car to within inches of the ground.

Chambers stepped out after the valet opened the door. Chambers walked around to the other side and took Sara by the hand and helped her out.

Sara was wearing a thirties-style evening gown. Her hair was curled and bounced easily as she stepped out and smiled.

All the valets froze in their tracks, staring. Chambers was in a midnight blue tuxedo with a wool herringbone overcoat and a matching brim. They looked like movie stars.

Chambers snapped his finger and pointed at a young pimple-faced valet who was standing at the entrance gawking.

He rushed over.

Sara extended her elbow to him.

"Hey, sonny, hold the girl for a second will ya?"

It was more of an order than a question. The Valet nervously complied.

He looked at another valet and snapped his fingers at him. He ran to Chambers and said, "Yes, sir, how can I help you?"

Chambers took him by the arms and walked him around to the driver's side of the Cadillac.

"Listen sunny. What's your name?"

"Eddie," the kid said, nervously.

"Eddie. Good. Listen, you look like a bright kid."

"Thank you, sir."

"Here are my keys," he said, handing them to the kid while pulling something out of his pocket. He reached over and put the object in the Vale's shirt pocket.

"Here's five hundred bucks."

The kids eyes lit up and he said, "Thank YOU, sir."

"Not so fast kid. I used to be a valet. And I know what goes on. You take that five hundred bucks and the keys, and you get in this jalopy and you take it to a safe place and you don't leave I for nothing. Then you deliver it back here in four hours. You understand?"

"Yes, sir, but what about my job, sir."

"This is your job for tonight. Any problems, you tell them to talk to Chambers. Understand."

"Yes, sir."

"And listen up kid. This rig has some extras, including a fart detector. You fart in there and I'll know it. Understand me?"

"Yes, sir," the kid said, scrunching up his face in confusion.

"Just kidding kid. Just take care of it, okay."

Chambers patted the kid on the face, walked around to the other side and recovered Sara from a kid who looked like he had wet his pants.

"Thank you, son," Chambers said and handed him a hundred dollar bill.

"Don't mention it sir, the kid said and ran to show the other valets his spoils and to brag about Sara. Chambers and Sara entered the hotel.

Chapter 135

Rich was on cloud nine and enjoyed all the attention and the smiling faces. Things were close to being perfect and couldn't get much better. Some people he hoped would be there didn't show up, but he could understand that, considering the short notice. But the fact that Fingers made it, made him very happy.

Then he saw the afro towering over everyone and the smiling goatee'd face he'd seen so many thousands of times; a face he recognized from many years ago and his heart leaped.

He yelled, "Kyle!"

And Kyle looked at him and smiled a smile that could stop a ship. He ran to Kyle and hugged him longer than he normally would, not caring if it was too long. Not caring if he seemed overzealous. Kyle reciprocated.

"I didn't think you would make it. God damn it's great to see you."

Kyle leaned into Rich's ear and said, "Nigga, don't fawn over me, just point me to the mufukin food, the bar and the White women."

They both laughed so hard, most everyone near them stopped to look.

"It's great to see you buddy," Kyle said. "You doin' all right?"

"Yeah, I'm doin' all right. Considering. Let me get you something to drink. I'm so glad you came. It wouldn't be the same without you."

Grimsley arrived at the hotel in a standard issue rental car. He was dressed in a sports jacket, jeans, plaid shirt and cowboy boots. He ditched Paulson after they arrived at the airport so he could meet his daughter and bring her to the party.

The valet opened the door for her and she stepped out. She was tall, and beautiful and Grimsley always wondered how she came to be. Her hair was jet black and her eyes were hazel and intelligent, and she wore an elegant evening gown.

"Daddy," she said, "this is great. Who is this guy again?"

"The kid from the stories, the paperboy."

"Oh, him. I tried to get his book. But they were sold out. Will I get to meet him."

"Yes, sugar. You will. Now, don't be nervous."

"I'm not the nervous one, daddy. I know how you hate these kinds of events. But I'll keep you company."

She hugged Grimsley and kissed him on the cheek.

"All, right sweetheart. Enough of that affection stuff. I'm only your father, not some kind of deity. I don't want you to worship me, just keep me company and have fun."

"All right daddy."

Paulson had never been to San Francisco, so he spent a few hours on Fisherman's Wharf, buying souvenirs from Pier 39. He took a cab to the hotel and arrived minutes after Grimsley and Chambers in the orange Dodge rental.

He was slightly embarrassed to be stepping out of the simple rental car amid such opulence, but he straightened his suit and held his head up and tipped the valet two dollars as he entered the hotel with the plastic bags from the pier.

Rich and Kyle reminisced and caught up on current events. He introduced him to Walker, Fisher and the band members. Kyle did not mention his trip to Portland. But Rich did mention what he planned to do when he got back to Portland.

"You go bro. That's what I always write into my scripts. The man got to go after the girl. Don't work the other way. If she does, she looks weak and desperate. The American public does not want to root for a weak and desperate woman."

Rich could only smile and say, "I know what you saying bro. Every day we write the scripts of our lives. And the same themes lay themselves out over and over and over. But each is unique. And if the guy can get the girl in the end, everybody's okay with that."

"Thas right."

"Well, Kyle, I'm afraid my script may be a sad one 'cause I don't think I'm going to get the girl."

"Rich, don't be so sure. Give April some credit. Ait?"

Rich sipped his drink and said softly, "maybe."

"Now, keep on enjoying yourself. As long as theys another day and you have air passing through your lungs, there's hope. Stan what I mean?"

"Show you right bro."

"I'm proud of you for not sittin' around feeling sorry for yourself. I know April ain't doin' that. She's just thinking about how to handle all this. But life goes on, you know?"

"Yep," Rich said, then he raised his glass and said, "here's to my oldest and dearest friend."

As they toasted, Rich spotted Grimsley walking towards him with the tall, stunningly beautiful woman at his side. Paulson walked over to them at the same time with his Pier 39 bags. Grimsley seemed uncomfortable as he introduced his companion to everyone.

"Gentlemen," he said, clearing his throat, "this is my daughter Crystal Annette Grimsley. She's in the doctorate program at SF State."

Rich noticed Paulson's face first, a noticeable look of shock washed over his face like a tsunami hitting a sandy beach.

"I, I, I'm pleased to meet you," he said.

Rich was not surprised. He knew to expect the unexpected from Grimsley.

"Pleased to meet you Crystal. That's a lovely name," he said.

"Was her mother's name," Grimsley added. "She died from complications when she was born."

"Sorry to hear that," Fisher chimed in.

"She must have been beautiful, 'cause yo looks couldn't have come from pops here," Kyle said, causing a wave of laughter from the group.

Even Paulson laughed. He finally settled on the fact that Annette looked like Naomi Campbell and Vanessa Williams rolled into one. She was part African American. And he now put the pieces together about Grimsley, but dared not ask. No matter how you slice it, the obvious is still the obvious.

Chapter 136

Chambers lit up the room when he walked in, glancing around for Enison. When he spotted him, he walked over to him and introduced Sara.

"Say," he said, this is some kind of classy doins."

"It is. Both of you look fantastic tonight."

"Thank you my friend. Is everything set?"

"Absolutely. But we have to be downstairs at eight sharp. We don't want him to make it to the party or there'll be a scene."

"Okay. Where's the kid, the paperboy?"

Enison pointed to him.

"That's him there. I'll introduce you."

Enison escorted Chambers to the group where Grimsley, Chambers, Walker, Rich, Kyle and others stood talking.

"Everyone," Enison said, "This is our very own international man of mystery, Mr. Chambers."

Rich was the first to step forward and shake Chamber's hand rigorously.

"Mr. Chambers, it's a pleasure to meet you. And thank you, by the way, for all that you did. That was pretty amazing."

"Mr. Franklin," Chambers said, "first of all, shake it don't break it. And second, I'm sure you would have done the same for me."

His comment drawing smiles as Sara complimented them on a fine party and the music. While everyone talked, Enison slipped away from the group first. Then Chambers followed minutes later, leaving Sara with the group and headed for the lobby.

Baker walked up the hill to the Fairmont from Ray's bar. It was only four blocks down the hill, but it was a steep incline most of the way. When he reached the entrance to the hotel, he was drenched with sweat and breathing heavily, and weaving from too much Scotch.

The concierge intercepted him, threatening to keep him from entering the hotel. When Baker said he was there to meet Mr. Chambers, he was allowed to pass reluctantly.

Enison walked around the corner as Baker stepped into the lobby.

When Baker spotted him he yelled, "Enison, what the fuck are you doing here?"

"I'm here to see you, Baker," Enison said, as he walked up to Baker.

"What?"

"Oh, yeah, I'm here to see you squirm."

"What the fuck are you talking about?" he said defiantly, drawing stares.

"Mr. Baker, we know all about it."

"About what you fucking piece of shit?"

At the moment, Chambers walked around the corner and over to where Enison and Baker stood.

Baker, weaving and wiping sweat from his brow, said "Chambers. I'm so glad to see you."

He gave him a nervous smile and put his hands on his shoulder, breathing heavily into Chamber's face, causing him to wince. He slurred his words when he said, "Come on, tell Enison what you know. Tell him he's fucked."

"I'm afraid I can't do that, Baker," Chambers responded. "If anyone's fucked here, it's you."

A police car drove to the front door with lights flashing and two officers stepped out. Behind them, a black jaguar pulled up as well and Jeremy Goldberg, president of ACI stepped out with Amy, the receptionist, both dressed in black, stylish formalwear. They all entered the hotel.

"Gentlemen," Goldberg said, "is everything okay, here?"

"Mr. Goldberg," Baker said, "glad you're here. Enison is screwed. He's been screwing the company for years and Chambers knows all about it. Don't you Chambers?"

"On the contrary, Mr. Baker," Chambers said. "Baker, your paranoia got the best of you. I been in this business long enough to know that people who try to destroy other people usually have something to hide. Oh, I thought you have some legitimate gripes at first, but you were just too fuckin' desperate. So I did a little diggin' in to your accounts, Mr. Baker."

Panicked, Baker looked around like a trapped raccoon and said, "I don't know what you're talking about! Enison is the one who's screwing the company, fucking you in the ass Mr. Goldberg while you sit around a let him do it. He's a fucking crook, insolent, disrespectful—"

"Save it for the jury, Mr. Baker," Chambers said coolly. We have records from all the phony accounts you set up. This charade you set up was good. Nerdy CFO driving the piece of shit car, big suit.

You're good. We would have never known if you hadn't gone after Enison. You tied your own noose, my friend."

"No! No!" Baker screamed. "You've got it all wrong! It's Enison. He's the one you want!"

The two officers grabbed Baker by the arms and handcuffed him and dragged him towards the squad car while reading him his rights.

"Enison, you cock sucker!" he screamed. "You'll never make this stick. I have a PH. fucking D. I'm smarter than all of you mother fuckers put together. I'll beat this! I'll beat this! I'll come back and fucking get you!"

In seconds, the squad car sped away and Goldberg, Chambers and Enison smiled at each other and said, "well done, gentlemen. Seems there's a party about to start. Shall we?"

Chapter 137

It was around eight thirty when Dick Blake stopped playing and received a rousing round of applause. Darryl Grant then took his place. He was dressed in a natty gray and black tux. He launched into a series of Jimmy rushing songs as Rich had requested, then he would introduce songs from his new album, *New Bop*.

Enison was scheduled to leave on a flight that night, so he walked over to Rich and asked him if he could speak to him in private. He and Rich went to the Tonga room on the other side of the Hotel.

The Tonga Room was an exotic tropical bar at the opposite end of the hotel. It was quiet. A few patrons were sipping fruity, umbrella-bedecked, multicolored drinks.

Rich and Enison entered and found a seat at the bar. There was a crash of thunder and flashes of lightening as the simulated tropical storm started up as if on queue. Then a steady crescendo of rain fell from the ceiling into the massive pool that occupied the center of the bar and was surrounded by dimly lit booths. It was a marvelously staged storm that automatically started every half hour.

"Rich, let me buy you a good Scotch," Enison offered, 'Cause I think you're going to need it."

"Sure, thing, Mr. Manns."

"First of all, My name is not Manns."

"What? Rich said, confused.

"Hold on Rich. Bartender, two Bushmill blues here, straight up."

"No, Rich, I'm Sam Enison."

Rich shook his head and turned up his mouth.

"No, Mr. Manns. I don't think so. I don't. I don't understand."

"Rich, I'm not Sunny Manns. I'm Sam Enison."

He repeated the news and did not elaborate. He simply stared at Rich through thoughtful, intense, intelligent eyes, a slight smile extending across his face.

All Rich could do was process. He didn't know what to say. And when it finally hit him, all he could say was, "you're Sam Enison?"

"That's right Rich. I'm going to give you a few minutes and we're going to drink a couple shots, then I'll fill you in."

"Fuck me blue, this has been a day of surprises, hasn't it?"

They drank the Scotches in single gulps and Enison proceeded to tell him the truth.

"Rich, I've taken an interest in your career ever since we first spoke. I learned everything I could about you. That's how I work anyway. And when I saw an opportunity for me to do something to benefit us both, I took advantage of it."

"So, that chance meeting at the Dalai Lama's lecture was not a chance meeting at all."

"Not at all. In fact, I just wanted to meet you in person. Rich, to be successful in my line of work, you have to be smarter and better than the competition. I do this sort of thing all the time."

"Again, Mr. Manns, er, Enison, I'm speechless. This is not happening."

"Yes it is, Mr. Franklin, and I can't think of a better person for this to happen to."

"I assume there's some connection between you and everyone else. Must be."

"Must be. Chambers works for me. I sent him to Portland to save your ass."

"Why would you do that?"

"Because Mr. Fisher, and Mr. Pendergrass are both personal friends of mine. Mr. Fisher is also a, well, an account."

"You mean, he owes you money?"

"Owed, Mr. Franklin. I put you and him and Pendergrass together because Mr. Fisher needed a hit to pull himself out of debt. He'd been doing well for a long time before a couple of misfires with losers put him in a financial dog house. Mr. Franklin, I like him too. It just so happened that you had mutual needs. You had a product in need of an agent and Pendergrass was sniffing around for something new. Something big."

"So why the charade?"

"Why not, Mr. Franklin. You've spent the last year living out a charade with your wife. What makes you so unique that you're the only one who can do that sort of thing?"

Rich had set himself up with that question. He didn't answer. There was no answer.

"So, Mr. Enison, what do you get out of this?"

"Simple, Mr. Franklin," Enison said. He reached into his breast pocket and pulling out folded documents. He proceeded to tear them up.

"This is your file and the file of Mr. Fisher. They are now closed."

"And I assume there's some kind of finder's fee."

"Smart boy," Enison said, "and that is privileged information. But you can rest assured that starting tomorrow, my roll with ACS will change. I will, be, as you say, self sufficient."

Rich thought for a moment.

"If I understand things correctly, your livelihood will be dependent on how well I perform."

"On the contrary, Mr. Franklin. My fee was a lump sum. That was good enough for me. I'm afraid, Mr. Franklin, that you're on your own now. But you're in good hands. Mr. Fisher is one of the best God damn agents in the business. He'll take good care of you. I had faith in him. And I have faith in you."

"I only have one more question."

"Fire away."

"How come you never told me you was a brutha all this time?"

Enison laughed.

"Because, Rich, that's the beauty of it all. Nobody expects me to be an African American. I can walk into people's lives and they never know it. You'll be surprised to know that in one particularly tough account in New York, an investment banker who thought he was clever, I actually became his best friend who visited him once a month on business. You can imagine the look on his face when I collared him, uncovered all his phony corporations and recovered nearly five hundred thousand dollars from him.

"You know, Mr. Enison, now that I think about it, it all makes sense. You're one smooth operator. Well, maybe this isn't the appropriate thing to say, but I hope we can work together again some day. Here's to the original under cover bruther."

"And that's another reason not to let my accounts know I'm Black. 'Cause once they know, they start talkin' all ethnic jive shit; brutha this, nigga that; tryin to get an edge. And the folks who are White racist will come at me with coon, nigger, spear chucker, every conceivable racist epitaphs. Crazy mother fuckers."

"I see. Show you right blood."

"Listen, Rich, I gotta go. Heading to Omaha, Nebraska, to check on a pig farmer who thinks he's pretty slick. Maybe we will meet again. I would like that. I like you Rich and I'm glad everything is working out for you. Stay black. And stay strong. It's a cruel God damn world, but always remember that there are good guys too."

He winked at Rich, shook his hand and walked out of the bar.

There was a loud boom from the fake lightening and thunder storm. Rain poured from the ceiling. A small calypso band started playing *Jamaican Farewell* on a bandstand island in the middle of the swimming pool, connected by a thin access bridge.

Chapter 138

When Rich walked back into the Venetian room, the party was in full swing. Sara and Chambers were cutting the rug on the dance floor as Grant bopped in the band, and heads bobbed up and down. The huge murals of San Francisco scenes on the walls added another dimension to the scene and Rich could feel his heart flutter, partly from the whiskey and partly from the joy he felt.

Phil and Rock arrived later in the evening, greeting Rich with his usual bear hug. When it was Rock's turn for hugs, he defied Black convention and the hug lingered for almost fifteen seconds.'

"Rich, you all right," Rock asked.

"What do you mean?" Rich asked.

"You…the hug. That was almost fifteen seconds. You know. We bruthas and everything."

Rich leaned into Rock and said, "it's okay Rock. I'm just glad to see you."

Rock nodded his head and said, "show you right. Show you right."

"Hear the pilot is great."

"It's more than great, Rich," Phil said. "It's solid gold."

Rock smiled. "Better than that."

"So, where do we go from here?"

"Well, Rich," Phil said, we got an air date.

"No!"

"Yep. OPB. Two weeks."

Rock continued smiling and nodding his head, then said, "you one bad brutha. One bad brutha."

"Now, that's enough shop talk. Rich, I want to meet some of your 'other' friends. Rumor has it that you know *other* people. And I need to verify that to see what my competition is like."

They laughed. Rich walked over to them and stood between them, took them by the arms and escorted them around the room, one by one, introducing them to Chambers, Grimsley, Sara, Kyle, James, everyone he could think of, each time, describing them differently, but each time beaming with affection and pride for all his friends.

Rich stood marveling the entire scene, thinking it was more like something out of a dream, when a familiar voice interrupted his thoughts.

"Hey chief. Where's the party at?"

Rich turned around and saw Jimmy, limping towards him, smiling. He wore a dark polyester leisure suit and a straw fishing hat.

"Jimmy," Rich said, hugging him. "How are you?"

"Well, my bunions still acting up, but I made it. You know, wouldn't miss this chief."

"I'm glad," Rich said, smiling. "The party is in full swing. Come on. I'll introduce you around."

"Thank you, son. And, by the way, congratulations on getting that book done."

"Thanks Jimmy."

"You plannin' to keep slingin' papers?"

"Only if it means I can spend more time with you, Jimmy," Rich said.

Jimmy was silent.

"Well, buddy, I only got a few more months to go."

"You'll get some well-deserved rest when you retire."

"I don't know. I don't know nothing else. Been working fo' what seems like a fo' ever."

"Jimmy," Rich said, concerned. "This is an opportunity for you. Now, you'll have time to learn some new things, explore, maybe go back to school and get that degree."

"What degree you talking about? I ain't much for schoolin'."

"Jimmy, you don't realize it, but it takes a certain kind of man to work 30 years at something, put his kids and grand kids through school and still get up in the morning optimistic. You got a lot of living to live. And, all due respect, if I hear that you've given up and are sittin' around feeling sorry for yourself, eating TV dinners with some scrappy old dog in a flea bag of a residential hotel, I'm going to find you and personally kick your butt."

Jimmy snickered.

"You right. You right. Maybe I do something like get my GED and some kind of degree. But I don't know what in."

"Jimmy, it's obvious what degree you been preparing for all your life."

"What buddy?"

"A degree in Negro studies. That way, you can lecture to all them 'young peoples' about the Negro. Not only will they have to listen to you, but you get paid as well."

"Get out of here!"

"That's right. You can get paid to talk about the Negro situation all day."

"I like that. Where do I sign?"

Rich and Jimmy laughed.

"When I get back, I'll take you down to Portland Community College and help you get enrolled. Dr. Parker is head of the Negro studies department and he owes me a favor."

Jimmy smiled and said, "you all right, buddy. You all right."

Rich introduced Jimmy to everyone and focused his attentions on a stately looking woman standing near the band with an envelope in her hand. He walked over to her.

"Enjoying the music Mrs. Westfield?."

She turned to Rich and smiled.

"Yes, Mr. Franklin. You might be surprised to know that some of these gentlemen's children and grandchildren have come through my classrooms over the years."

"Knowing you, Mrs. Westfield, I would not be surprised. Thank you for coming. It's great to see you."

"Likewise, Mr. Franklin," she said. She gave him a warm, smile and a hug that caught him off guard.

"Mr. Franklin, I speak for myself and all the families at Baldwin Elementary when I say we are very proud of your recent publishing accomplishments."

She took Rich by the hand and rubbed it gently.

"We are also sorry to hear about the recent circumstances you and April find yourselves in. We had an assembly this afternoon and you would be amazed at the tremendous outpouring of love that was in that room for you and April. We are all hoping that you and April can see your way through these difficult times."

She handed Rich the oversized envelope.

"This card is signed by every parent in our school. Rich, we are all behind you."

Rich was speechless.

"Thank you Mrs. Westfield. This means a lot to me, especially considering my bad attitude."

"Rich, no bad attitude. You're just another confused artist trying to be a normal person. Believe it or not. So am I. Now, Rich, this is your night. I'm just here for the band. Go and enjoy yourself."

"Thank you mam."

She turned towards the band and tapped her toes and snapped her fingers to the beat.

Chapter 139

Around nine thirty, as Grimsley entertained an attentive group with stories about one of his cases. Rich whispered into Kyle's ear that he was going to go out for a few minutes. He needed some air and would be back at ten.

Kyle said he'd make sure everything was okay and would call him if there was any problem. Let everyone know that at ten o'clock I have a special guest.

Rich went downstairs and hailed a taxi. He asked him to drive to Aquatic Park Pier near Ghirardelli square.

The taxi dropped him off on the corner of Bay and Van Ness. Rich stepped out of the cab. A cold blast of air shot though his tuxedo, instantly giving him the chills.

One block away, the blinking lights of Ghirardelli Square created a carnival-like atmosphere, but where Rich stood it was dark, quiet, and only a few brave souls ventured down the hill to the mostly deserted pier at the base.

Rich stood and looked around, reflecting on the many times he visited the pier, alone, and then with April after they met. This was his sacred place. This was where he came to think and to reflect.

He waved the cab driver off and began walking down the hill. Next to the street that led to the pier was a high, dark, ominous wall with a single set of decaying and moss-filled stairs that led up to the abandoned batteries of Fort Mason.

He walked past them. The bay wind becoming more prominent as he walked past the wall and stepped on the first wooden planks of the Pier.

On either side, waist high thick metal posts were tipped with a fluorescent yellow light encased in a glass dome. They ware spaced every twenty feet. The smell of decaying fish was strong, filtered only by the salty ocean air that bit at his face.

Rich turned up his collars, shoved his hands in his pocket and walked slowly towards the tip of the pier, some two hundred feet out.

As he walked, he passed whispering lovers stealing kisses on wooden benches and a diehard Asian fishermen, fussing with a bucket of crabs and fish, while his four poles bobbed and weaved in the wind.

He looked at Rich suspiciously and turned away, picking up a pole and methodically reeling in a small bit of line and tugging on it intermittently to see if anything had bitten.

Rich suddenly realized that he was becoming more and more sober as he neared the pier point which curled round and ended in a circular observation area.

Rich and April would walk to the end of the pier, laughing and cuddling all the way, musing and reflecting on their future plans, their hopes and their dreams. On one of their visits, Rich proposed marriage and presented her with a silver ring he'd picked up in Tijuana.

Rich's face was getting numb.

He looked into the black mysterious waters and listened to the waves lapping on the wooden supports.

He glanced round to see if anyone was watching. Noone.

Rich looked again into the mesmerizing darkness below him and said out loud, "This is as good a time as any. If I'm going to do this, I'm going to do it now. Get it over with."

He unbuttoned his coat. The cold snaked through his shirt causing him to shiver.

He reached into his breast pocket and took out a small CD player and placed it on the railing. From the hip pocket he took out a mirror. From his jacket pocket he took out a CD and a pair of head phones.

He placed the CD into the player and turned it on. He placed the headphones in his ears and turned the volume up.

Rich looked at the moon hovering over Coit Tower and observed the blinking lights of the last tour boats of the Blue and White fleet returning to Pier 39. Then glanced out at Alcatraz and listened to Luther Vandrose singing *A chair is still a chair...even then there's noone sitting there...*

The tears flowed instantly as Luther sang and streamed down Rich's cheeks. Each breath became more difficult as the pressure built up in his lungs. The torrent of emotions conflicted with the natural need to breathe regular, steady breaths.

Noises he didn't recognize came out of his mouth; noises that could only be interpreted as pain pushing it's voice to the surface, the heart wailing because it is injured.

He could not hold back. He felt his face turn and twist into shapes he never imagined, like silly putty formed by the raw emotions that were now surfacing.

Streams of snot followed as he struggled to contain the torrent with his red silk handkerchief. But it was too delicate to absorb the flow. *Who cared?*

He was alone.

It was just him, facing the city, confessing his pain, expressing his agony and the only one who cared was the wind and the stars.

The final act, he thought, in this painful ceremony was next. It was time to end it and be absolved but not forgiven for his emotional transgressions.

A room is still a room...even if it's filled with gloom...

He reached into another pocket and took out small compact, flipped it open, removed a flash light from another pocket, shined it on his face and looked in the mirror.

His face was a sight to behold, wet, contorted, forehead furrowed well beyond its limits; eyes red from tears and Scotch and something else; something else caused him to stop and stare in shock.

Now and then...I close my eyes...and suddenly your face appears...

At first he thought it was his imagination.

He ignored the image and laughed out loud.

As Luther sang the last words of the song and Rich's laughing wore down, he saw Aprils face in the reflection of the mirror again.

He shook it off. It was an illusion.

Then he felt a delicate hand touch him gently on the shoulder. He turned around. He wiped the tears from his eyes, caught the scent of China Rain, and saw April standing there, tears flowing down her cheeks too.

She hugged him and he felt the warmth of her body against his. He melted into her arms and wept more.

"You know, Rich," she said softly, between breaths, "you're a pretty pathetic sight out here weeping and laughing and carrying on."

"He looked into her eyes and said, "I know. I'm trying to spare the world the sight. I don't want to traumatize small children and send people scrambling for psychotherapists."

"Oh, God, Rich, I missed you."

"But, but, I don't understand. What are you doing here? I thought. I thought you—"

April's arms relaxed and she stepped towards the rail. Rich noticed she was dressed in a tight black sequined evening gown with heels; not her everyday dress. There was more here, he assumed, than meets the eye.

"Rich," she said, hesitating, "I'm not sure where to begin. You've made a real mess of things."

Rich looked down, embarrassed. He was sure she was there to tell him it was all over.

"But in spite of your attempts to screw things up with your crazy schemes, gratuitous and spontaneous helping of people and obsession with writing some book they tell me shot to the *New York Times* best seller list in a day, I fell in love with you years a go for one simple reason."

She looked at the moon, wiped the tears from her eyes and glanced at Rich.

"I knew you were my soul mate. And as long as I love you that will never change."

She was silent again, listening to the wave crashing against the jagged rocks near the fort.

"April, let me explain. I can explain. There's been a terrible—"

"Rich," she interrupted, "I know what happened at the retreat."

"But, how could you—"

"Trust me, Rich, I know EVERY thing that happened. Brenda and I spent a couple of hours together this afternoon, and, no, we did not spend the whole time talking about you. She's a lovely girl. Young. Impressionable, vulnerable. And, Rich, you *did* and you didn't do the right thing."

"I know, honey, I can explain, I—"

"Rich," she said sternly. "Let me finish. As I was saying, you found your way back without going TOO far. And I emphasize TOO far."

"Um, April, I also have to get something else out in the open. Because if I don't, we won't be able to go on. I won't be able to face you another day knowing I have kept things from you."

"Rich, it's you and me. You can tell me anything, and you should always trust that. I may hate you for a few minutes but those feelings will always be fleeting; always be beaten down for the love I have for you."

"I made some bad business decisions with this last publishing venture. I got into debt and didn't know how to deal with it. I was too afraid to tell you and convinced myself I could handle this alone. There's a collection agent I've been working with, he—"

"You mean Sam Enison?"

Shocked, Rich looked at April with his mouth open. He didn't know what to say.

"Rich, I'm not stupid you know. A woman knows things. She knows when her husband changes moods and behaviors that indicate something's up. And, fortunately for you, Mr. Enison is a perfectly respectable, smart man. He called me months ago and told me what was happening. At first I was so pissed I was ready to shoot you. But he talked me down. He talked to me about men's egos and how a single word or confrontation on this type of issue could destroy our relationship forever. He told me you had to bring this issue to me and that I couldn't confront you unless there was some clear and present threat to our livelihood. Rich, Enison and I both worked out how this would be handled if and when we got to that point."

"April, I, I—"

"Rich, you sound surprised," she interrupted. "You think you're the only one who can be a sneak? Not hardly."

All Rich could do was look into April's eyes and wonder if he was a lucky man or in a lot of trouble. April was not giving him any signals either way.

"Rich, I'm sure that right now you're probably thinking that you've been one-upped. But, trust me, that's not what's happening here. Listen, you're a creative guy, mysterious, benevolent, multi-dimensional and, well, ubiquitous."

She touched his face and said, "I'm okay with that. That's what makes you who you are. And you wouldn't be the man I fell in love with if you weren't that way. I know you'd be that way with or without me."

She paused, looked down and said, "Just don't cut me out anymore."

"April," Rich said, "I promise, I will do my best. I love you too and want us to grow closer together not further apart. And we have two little rapscallions who are depending on us to do that too."

"They certainly are. So, Mr. Franklin, should we rejoin the party?"

"Yes, Mrs. Franklin, we should. But only after I steal a kiss."

"Why, Mr. Franklin, you are fresh," she said.

She pulled him close. Their kiss was long and slow and time seemed to stand still. Both Rich and April enjoyed the moment. In a distance a fog horn from Fort Point could be heard through the thick wall of fog that began moving past the Golden Gate Bridge.

Rich and April quickly walked back up the hill to Van Ness Street, then hailed a cab and were back at the hotel in minutes.

When they walked into the room, they heard someone across the room start clapping, then others joined in. Soon the entire room was clapping and looking at Rich and April. They stood, both embarrassed, waving, gesturing for them to stop.

"Rich," Forbes said through the live microphone, "we've been waiting for you two love birds. Congratulations, man. Come on up here and say something, man. We been waiting for hours. You know we all love you two. Come on up man and say something."

Both Rich and April walked to where the band was playing.

Brenda appeared from the crowd with Juan and Antonio at her side, grinning. She walked them to Rich and hugged him.

"Thank you Rich."

Then she hugged April and walked over to Forbes to watch.

Rich took the microphone and looked at the admiring faces. Most he knew and some he didn't recognize. He cleared his throat.

"Um, thank you, everyone, for being here. This really means a lot to me. And I know some of you have traveled a long way on short notice. But the fact that you did that makes this extra special for me."

Rich had to catch his breath. His heart was racing with excitement and nervousness.

He looked at April, who winked at him.

"I'm so happy to have my family here with me. Um, I know that some of the events that led up to today are coincidence. Some are perhaps because of divine intervention. And some are due merely to that thing called destiny. Whatever the case, I want to take a few minutes to recognize someone who is a no longer here with us but is someone who is a part of this all. Not be cause she was a celebrity or because she was anybody you'd pass on he street and recognize. She was prostitute, a lady of the evening, considered by some to be a persona non grata. But she was much more than that. She was a little girl who grew up in a screwed up home, endured unimaginable emotional and sexual abuses. Her name was Patricia Sophia Derby. But she went by the name of Trixie. Trixie was finally removed from her family and they ended up in jail when she was in her early teens. After that she was bounced from foster home to foster home before finally running away to live on the streets and fend for herself. But Trixie was smart. She tested out at a genius level when she was very young. She was determined she would try to help everyone and every living thing she crossed paths with."

Rich paused and scanned the group.

"A week ago Trixie was murdered by a sick, perverted insurance executive who was seeing her regularly. He was afraid Trixie would expose him as a pedophile. After he left her van one early morning full of hate and anger, he parked a block away, took a thirty eight special out of his trunk, walked back around the block, crept up in the bushes and, seeing an opportunity he blew her brains out and hoped someone else would get the blame. She died quickly and didn't suffer much pain, at least not as much as she endured in life. You see, Trixie fancied herself a Buddhist and somewhat of a spirit guide for some of the lost souls in her life, Chico, the Mexican American of, well, very little brain, a senator, and even a few others."

"Trixie made a lot of money using her body AND her brains. She donated up to fifty thousand dollars to the SPCA, allowing them to build a new 100,000 square foot facility to shelter and care for the cats she so loved."

"She donated to the Oregon Food bank. She helped finance a new wing of Outside In, a nonprofit that serves homeless youth. All of this done through small corporations and fictitious names. And, ladies and gentleman, she even did her own taxes and actually received refunds."

"It took some digging, and the help of two detectives, a special investigator, a private eye, and a collection agent, if you can believe that, to unraveled the mystery that was Trixie and put the bastards responsible for her death behind bars."

"I have developed a deep respect and admiration for Trixie. I've read some of her journals. She was bright, articulate and troubled. But most importantly, she was a beautiful human being down to her core, who just wanted to figure out why she existed; figure out the meaning of life; and she wanted to know how she fit into the general scheme of things."

"Sound familiar?"

"I want us to remember and think about Trixie tonight. She inspired me. She is a part of all our lives."

"And one thing Trixie and I shared was our taste in music. In her journal she wrote a lot about a singer who seemed to capture the essence of the searching spirit. So I invited her here to sing one of Trixie's favorite songs and help us celebrate our lives, our friendships, Trixie's life, her struggles and to entertain us with her limitless talent."

"In memory of Trixie, please welcome Jill Cohn."

Applause filled the room as a petite, almost frail dark-haired woman walked to the band area and hugged Rich. She looked at the crowd.

"I'm flattered, ladies and gentlemen, to be here. Wasn't sure I could make it 'cause I was working at a deli in Eugene when I got the call. When they told me *why,* I HAD to be here, I caught the first plane I could. And they said they'd cover my wages for the day, too. Which ain't much, but every little bit helps."

She sat on a stool and tuned her guitar as she spoke.

"I can relate to Trixie as I'm sure she could relate to me. Many of my songs derive from loneliness and questioning and longing, especially these days."

Her smile charmed the audience.

"This song is dedicated to Trixie and to all of you."

Cohn closed her eyes and started to play her guitar and sing. Her voice was strong and sultry.

My bus broke down in Kayenta but I was born again…

When she finished, there was only silence in the room. Many in the crowd were crying, including April.

The applause started slowly and built up to a feverish pitch. Cohn bowed, took her guitar off and walked into the crowd.

"Thank you Jill. Thank you. I want to let everyone know that we have the room until midnight. April and Juan and Antonio will be staying tonight at the hotel. A special round of applause to the greatest band in the world, the Scott Forbes trio, featuring three hundred years of jazz experience.

Whistles, claps and cat calls filled the room and as Rich looked at James Clarance Walker, who was beaming, smiling from ear to ear, he mouthed thank you to him.

"You guys are heroes," Rich added. "They'll be playing for another half hour, then we have a D.J., Mix Master Fresh Juice or something like that, joining me in the Tonga Room for a disco dance party; music from the seventies and eighties. Everyone who traveled gets a complimentary nights stay here, thanks to my agent, Mr. David Fisher over there."

He pointed out Fisher who smiled and waved.

"I love you all. Thank you for being, well, for being who you are. You are all an important part of me and my family. And I love you."

Rich handed the microphone back to Scott, hugged him and the other band members, then walked over to April, Juan and Antonio, took them by the hand and melted into the chattering crowd.

Epilogue

Rich logged on and clicked the button to connect instant video messaging.

Kyle's face appeared in the screen instantly. He was in pajamas, rubbing his eyes and scratching his arm pits. His afro was flat on one side and he yawned as the images appeared, froze, then refreshing every thirty seconds.

"What you want nigga? Don't you ever sleep mother fucker."

"Can't sleep,," Rich answered, typing furiously, "Got to warn the world about you mother fucker. THE WAKING NEGRO! DUH DUH DUH DUHHHHHH. SAVE YOUR CHILDREN! HE'S BLACK! HE'S HALF AWAKE! HE'LL SCRATCH HIS ASS!!! RUN WHILE YOU CAN! RUNNNNNNNN!

"Nigga, shut the fuck up. Tell me what you want. I got impotent mother fuckers just sitting out there waiting for me to contact them, mufuckas been up for days hoping to get five minutes of my time. Nigga I got shit to do!!!"

"Ait. Just wanted to talk about Negroes and trash."

"What!"

"Yeah. I been noticing shit."

"No shit mother fucker. What you been noticing."

"Niggas won't pick up shit in they neighborhoods. The throw shit down and spect other mother fuckers to pick that shit up."

"Nigga you can't say that kinda racist shit. Theys trash everywhere you go. In every neighborhood."

"Not like this. Check this. I go down to the Kentucky Fried Chicken. Did an impromptu survey and shit."

"Here we go. Nigga ain't you got shit to do other than that?"

"Anyway. As I was saying before some mother fucker interrupted. Mind?"

"Nigga, please. Talk yo shit."

"Ait, so I'm sittin in my seventy two Cutless. You know, the one with the fucked up bumper, dice and leaport skin upholstery. You know, a mother fucker got to blend in when doing these surveys."

"Hurry the fuck up mother fucker."

"Well, one out of every ten Negroes threw their shit out the window when they was done. I seent mother fuckers walking down the street and throw shit right on the ground. Didn't look back. FIVE days later that shit was still there; all kinds of mother fuckers walkin' by it. Nobody bothering to pick it up."

"Your point?"

"Okay, went to Lake Oswego Kentucky Fried Chicken. No Negroes. Only White folks. Little girl threw some shit out the window.

Seconds later, SWAT team surrounded the car, dragged those mother fuckers out, threw them to the ground. Then the head dude, big ugly mother fucker, walks up to the little girl and said, 'This your straw little girl." She be cryin' and parents be screamin' 'leave her alone. leave her along.' Mean ugly mother fucker say 'mam we don't put up with this kind of behavior out here. I need you and your family out of Lake Oswego by midnight. Sergeant, escort these people to the Black neighborhood in Northeast Portland.' Bad ass mother fucker. They was cryin' and shit, pleading for him to let them stay. 'Please officer, there's Negroes up there. PLEASE!!' He not budgin'.

"Nigga, thas bullshit."

"Aiit nigga. This is true shit. Then, this big ugly scary mufuka sees me parked on the kona in my seventy two Cutless Supreme, you know, the one with the fucked up bumper, fluffy dice an leopert skin dashboard, and he sick his boys on me. I got the fuck out of there so fast, looked like the black streak.

"Now, you see what I'm sayin' don't you?"

"Nigga, how is anybody supposed to see what you sayin' God damn, you so fucked up it's pitiful."

"Well, you check it out next time you at the Kentucky Fried Chicken."

"Well, fuck that. How are you?"

"Doin all right, but Pittsburgh is fucked up. It's hotter than hell here and there's a bunch of backwoods, steel-town, gravy sucking, cheese steak eatin' mother fuckers here. Onleaist good thing is Grimsley got me a day gig with the Pittsburgh Post Gazette writing features. I'm digging that."

"You sure you doing the right thing?"

"Yeah I'm sure. You know when Grimsley asked me to help him on this case, I had to say yes. Nobody can pitch papers like me. And he needed an insider operator. Plus, he figured we could have writing sessions once a week."

"Well, from what you said, that mother fucker who been killin' paperboys and customers sounds like a fucked up cat. You bed be careful."

"I will. Walker, Chambers, Paulson and Grimsley all got my back. Plus, I got a new rig that Chambers fitted with some high tech shit. Believe me, I'm good."

"Well, just be careful. I'll give April and the kids a hug for you," Kyle said. "Man, what the fuck was that. What the.... Man, Rich, I got so many God damn kids around here I don't know what to do. Open a mufukin closit. They one. Open the hood of the got damn car. They go one. Some of these yos nigga. You owe me. Good thing I love 'em like my own."

"I know. I know. They been wanting to spend some time with you for a long time. And I left specific instructions for them to be a pain in the ass. And guess what? I'll join all of you as soon as this case is over."

"*You bed do dat. I'll be lookin for your black ass. Just make sure you use the back door. This is a respectable neighborhood. If my neighbors knew you was here we'd have to move.*"

"Fuck you too nigga. I'm out."

When Rich looked up at the screen, he saw something he never thought he'd see in his life. Kyle had stood up, bent over and pressed his ass up against the camera. Seconds later the sound of a tremendous fart blasted through the speaker.

Rich yelled, "No you didn't! No you didn't!"

He laughed until his side ached!

After the shock of what Kyle did wore off, he dressed in his uniform, black sweats, cotton, loose fitting turtleneck, black stocking cap with the X on it. Even though it was June, it was still cold at two a.m. He slipped on his new Vans ATS shoes, grabbed his pitcher's tracks CD and headed for the front door of the house he rented in the working class neighborhood.

Showtime, he thought. Showtime.

End

Made in the USA
Middletown, DE
20 July 2023